What readers are saying about Zero Point

"A rollicking and engaging adventure to prevent a shocking cataclysm from the far reaches of the Atlantic Ocean."

—*Dirk Cussler, New York Times Bestselling Author of Poseidon's Arrow*

***

"An evil mastermind... A terrifying new weapon of mass destruction... A clever young archeologist with a streak of reluctant heroism... An ancient secret that could change everything...
Tim Fairchild's breakout novel, ZERO POINT is pure white-knuckle adventure at its very best."

—*Jeff Edwards, award-winning author of Sea of Shadows, and The Seventh Angel*

***

"Spine-chilling action, and hold-your-breath thrills places this fresh and engaging adventure yarn at the top this year's thriller list."

—*Kerry Frey, Director of the Adventure Writer's Competition & author of Buried Lie: A Young Ace Roberts Adventure*

ZERO POINT

ZERO POINT

TIM FAIRCHILD

STONEWALL PRESS

Acknowledgments

The science and theory surrounding Zero Point Energy is a topic highly debated within the scientific community. This story is based on that science, and the works of many scientists postulating the theory of free energy from the vacuum of space-time, and the potential threat of Electromagnetic Scalar Weapons. One particular book that was a helpful source of data in the writing of this novel was *"Oblivion--America On The Brink"* by Dr. Thomas Bearden.

The science and data surrounding the mega-thrust tsunami comes from the BBC Horizon documentary *"Mega-Tsunami: Wave of Destruction."*

Special thanks to Bob Minichino for his naval technical advice. To Kimberly Sain for her proof and edit work. Her tireless efforts are very much appreciated by this author.

Finally, I want to thank my family and friends for their support, encouragement, and advice during the writing of this novel.

For my wife, Beverley

"Others [terrorists] are engaging even in an Eco-type of terrorism whereby they can alter the climate, set off earthquakes, volcanoes remotely through the use of electromagnetic waves... So there are plenty of ingenious minds out there that are at work finding ways in which they can wreak terror upon other nations...It's real, and that's the reason why we have to intensify [counter terrorism] efforts." — Defense Secretary William Cohen, 1997

1

2008, Bismarck Sea, New Guinea

J osh Turner stood on the foredeck gazing upon the calm evening sea as the vintage cargo freighter Southern Star made her way along the rugged New Guinea coastline. The evening air was still thick with humidity from the day's torturous heat. Longing for the cool of the coming evening, he watched the sun descending behind the deep green canopy of the receding mainland.

One of the few World War II Victory ships still in service, the four hundred fifty-five foot *Southern Star* had picked up Turner after off-loading supplies at the Port of Aitape earlier that afternoon. She was outward bound now, and after her next port of call, Turner would then return to Port Adelaide in Australia. There he would catch a puddle jumper flight to Sidney and then, at long last, home.

A mere mile away, Turner regarded the flickering lights from the small island of Tumleo, giving him the only hint of inhabitants along the sparsely populated northern coast of Papua.

He was exhausted from the arduous three-month archeology excursion with his young interns deep in the mountainous interior of Papua. His two 'cub' interns, as he dubbed them, Susan Hendrich and James Pond, were graduate students from the University of Melbourne.

The two students dove into the project with all the vigor of what Turner had termed a couple of bears merrily rummaging through a trash dumpster. Turner, on the other hand, had shown little interest from day one in excavating and cataloging the remains of a two hundred year old native village. Teetering on the verge of heat stroke during the day, then being devoured alive by insects at night was not on his bucket list. He had only done so at the insistence of his father, Eli Turner. It was just another favor to one of his father's many fellow archaeologists worldwide.

Turner longed to be back on Tenerife in the Canary Islands with its dry, temperate days, cool nights, and many colorful festivals, all of which he enjoyed. He had just begun working on an ancient site once occupied by the island's original inhabitants, the Guanche, before giving in to his father's wishes and coming to Papua.

I'm so glad this trip is over, he thought, tasting the thick salt air and feeling the warm, gentle sea breeze blowing through his coarse, slightly graying hair. He closed his deep, piercing blue eyes for a moment, relishing the completion of this mission as he felt the ship's engines vibrating the gray, steel decking beneath his feet. He missed his longtime friend Samuel, and had discovered during this trip how much he really missed Maria.

Turner looked up at the bridge wheelhouse located amidships. In the fading light, he could make out the silhouette of the ship's captain, Alfred Cleary, guiding his vessel through the narrow straights toward deeper waters.

Alfred Cleary had spent twenty-five years sailing these waters, and Turner felt a bit saddened at the prospect of the gruff captain's ship being sent to the scrap yards at the completion of this voyage, and that Cleary would probably be forced into retirement.

He recalled listening to Cleary boast to the harbor master while unloading cargo at the pier in Aitape, saying, "The *Southern Star* is a fine ship and has never failed me through the long years. She's sturdy and agile with her sixty-two foot beam and twenty-eight foot draft, making her ideal for these waters where many larger and newer vessels wouldn't dare navigate."

Turner made his way up the ladder to the bridge and entered the darkened wheelhouse, thick with the smell of cigarette smoke and sweat. He stood by the doorway receiving no sign acknowledgment from the captain focused on his task of piloting his vessel through the dangerous Tumleo Straight.

"What is our current depth, Mr. Harkness?" Cleary asked his first officer.

"Seven point six fathoms, Captain, and falling away," the younger officer replied. "We're clear to navigate."

"Thank you, Mr. Harkness; you have the bridge," Cleary said, jotting down a few notes in his log. "Set a course for Wuvulu Island. That'll be our final stop. We'll take on a few passengers, then set course for home."

"Aye, Captain," the younger man replied, taking the wheel of the ship. Cleary simply grunted, causing Turner to smile. He turned, gave Turner a toothless grin, and then gestured with his hand toward the hatchway leading out to the deck.

Stepping out of the wheelhouse, the pair climbed down a flight of steps and began walking toward the bow of the ship. The gruff, unshaven captain lit a cigarette as they strolled. Reaching the bow, they looked landward to see the dim lights of Tumleo Island flickering in the darkness as the last vestiges of day faded into night. They felt the gentle, rumbling vibration of the six thousand horse power Allis Chalmers marine steam turbines turning the vessel's eighteen-foot diameter propeller.

"Josh," he asked after a long silence, "at my age, how the hell will I ever find another ship to master? I'm almost fifty-seven years old."

"Maybe it's time you start that charter fishing business in Adelaide. You once mentioned it to my father," Turner responded, still eyeing the island lights in the distance. "I think you'd make a fortune from the tourists who vacation there. Some of the best sport fishing in the world, I've been told."

"To tell you the truth, the more I think about it, the more I realize I couldn't deal with those assholes, Josh. I know for damned sure I'd wind up in prison for tossing one of the sons-of-bitches overboard for telling me how to do my job," he said, causing Turner to laugh. "But considering I still have to earn a living in order to keep beer in the fridge, I'll keep your suggestion in mind, young Mr. Turner." He then tossed his cigarette butt over the side, turned, and headed back toward the wheelhouse.

His eyes now adjusted to the evening, Turner noticed the form of Susan Hendrich, his intern, approaching him bathed in the soft glow of the ship's port running lights.

"Good evening, Dr. Turner," she said, coming up to the rail beside him.

"Please don't call me that, Susan. That's my father's title, not mine."

"But you *do* have your doctorate in archeology, Josh. You should be proud of that."

"I not impressed by titles. That's my father's gig. His view on archeology is cocktails with diplomats, or dinner with prospective sources of funding. Ever since he got the United Nations involved with his International Consortium for Artifact Preservation project, I've been stuck doing most of the field work while he attends dinner functions with diplomats."

"Josh, you should be proud of your father's concept of ICAP. Involving so many nations with preservation, has helped to curtail the black marketing of many artifacts that would have otherwise been lost to some rich collector and—"

"Whoa! What the hell is that?" Turner interrupted his young intern, pointing toward the eastern sky.

The two viewed a glowing object on the horizon that shimmered with an orange-yellow tint as it arced across the night sky trailed by flames. It rushed toward the west, and, as it approached, they could clearly make out a distinct roar; like that of a locomotive.

They watched the object in stunned fascination until suddenly, it slowed, then spiraled downward plummeting into the sea some twenty miles distant. After a moment came a flash of light as bright as the sun followed by a thunderous boom. The two stared in silence as the night once again regained its normality.

Captain Cleary rushed out of the wheelhouse and onto the catwalk.

"Did you see that, Josh? It looked like a meteor, and a damned big one, too!" He yelled.

"I never saw a meteor slow down and turn on its own, skipper," Turner replied.

Suddenly, they heard and felt a rumbling followed by the sight of a fiery blast in the distance where the object had fallen just minutes before. The intense shock wave that followed the blast hit the ship before the two could react, knocking both Turner and Susan off their feet and onto the hard steel decking.

"Go to the staterooms, Susan, and get Pond up here with your life jackets," Turner said as he got up. "If I'm right, we may have a big problem coming our way."

As Susan ran off, Turner raced back up the gangway to the bridge to find Cleary staring out at the darkened sea. His first officer, Harkness, was issuing an order to the engine room to slow to quarter speed.

"Was there any damage to the ship, Captain?

"I sent a man below to check, Josh." Turner could sense the nervousness in the elder man's voice.

"I have a bad feeling about this, Captain," Turner said, staring out the window into the darkness.

"I'm way ahead of you, Josh. I've already directed her bow toward whatever it was."

Cleary picked up the bridge intercom microphone and shouted to the engine room. "Mr. Mallory, I want all you can give me—full ahead."

"Full ahead—aye, skipper," the ship's chief engineer

responded from below.

"Did you get a fix on the flash point?" Cleary asked his first officer.

"Aye, sir, twenty degrees off our starboard bow."

"Make for that heading, Mr. Harkness," Cleary ordered, his eyes straining in the darkness.

"Aye, sir."

As Turner stood in the wheelhouse, he felt the steel plating begin to rumble under his feet as the forty-four hundred ton vessel shot forward like a thoroughbred bolting from its starting gate.

"What's our present depth?" Turner asked, hoping that his fears were wrong as he watched the crescent moon rising on the horizon ahead of them.

"Six point zero fathoms and the bottom is rising, Josh," the Captain replied, sweat now forming on his brow as he gazed at the depth finder.

"Damn it!" Cleary yelled. "We should be in deeper water by now."

"Four point nine fathoms now, sir!" First Officer Harkness yelled with rising panic in his voice.

"We should be over twenty-five fathoms at this point. Get to your people, Josh. You know what's coming…hurry!"

Turner raced out of the wheelhouse and descended the gangway. Not sure what to do, he ran down the walkway toward one of the many small, inflatable Zodiacs located on the *Southern Star* and began frantically looking fore and aft for his two missing interns.

"Damn it!" He yelled, knowing time was short. "Where the hell are they?" His frustration cut short by the sickening sound of the ship's hull scraping sea bottom. His fear rising, he heard the tormented shriek of tons of steel as the *Southern Star* began to spin on its axis. It finally came to a jarring halt, throwing Turner hard against the bulkhead.

Getting up, he began to untie the ropes to the davits that held the small Zodiac against the ship's side rail. When Susan Hendrich came bounding out the door from the staterooms below deck, Turner could see the sheer terror in her eyes.

"Where's Pond?" Turner asked angrily as he untied the last of the davits then lowered the inflatable to the deck.

"He went down to the hold to get the artifacts we brought with us, Josh. He thought it would be—"

"Damned fool," He said, slamming his fist against the bulkhead in frustration.

The *Southern Star* then began to roll precariously to starboard, coming to rest at a fifteen-degree angle. Turner, managing to keep his footing, moved to grab the outboard motor end of the Zodiac. He looked over the side, and, in the ship's lights, he saw to his horror the sea below churning with foam as a raging torrent of water rushed passed the stranded ship headed away from land. For what seemed an eternity to Turner, the tortured metal of the aging ship groaned in protest as tons of pressure assailed the ship's superstructure firmly wedged in the muddy sea bottom.

"What's happening, Josh?" Susan cried out in wide-eyed fear. "There's a tsunami coming, Susan," he yelled back at her above the roar of the water below them. "The sea's running outward, so it won't be long before it hits. We're sitting high and dry and the bow of this ship is no longer facing into the wave. If it hits us broadside, we're done for!"

The torrent of rushing water beneath the *Southern Star* diminished. Turner could see from the glow of ship's emergency lights they were now sitting on muddy sea bottom that was once a deep channel.

"Quickly, Susan, grab onto the front of the inflatable. We need to get it to the bow."

"What about Pond?" The young intern asked tearfully.

"There's no time left to go down and look for him, Susan.

I hope he'll find us in time."

The two managed to get the small craft to the bow of the ship where they met First Officer Harkness coming down the companionway from the bridge.

"The captain's ordered all hands to lifeboats. Sweet Jesus, how the hell can we abandon ship with no water beneath us?" He said in near hysteria. "Cleary's also refusing to abandon the wheelhouse. I can't get him to leave."

Turner looked up to the darkened wheelhouse and could see the soft reddish glow of a cigarette through the port window.

Knowing there wasn't much time left, Turner then focused on removing the 9.9 horse Yamaha outboard from the transom of the Zodiac.

"What are you doing?" Harkness asked.

"This motor will be torn off its mount the instant the tsunami hits. We need buoyancy, not power," Turner replied, tossing the motor over the side. "I'm going to leave the water proof cover on and leave just enough opening for us to get in. I know it's a long shot, but I don't see any other option. There's room for four. Are you coming?"

"No, Mr. Turner. I'm going below to make sure all the crew is topside." He then ran off into the darkness toward the aft end of the ship.

"Get in the Zodiac, Susan, and tie one of the raft cleat lines around you. I'll keep an eye out for Pond."

Turner helped the intern into the dinghy then looked toward the stern of the ship, now eerily back dropped by the crescent moon. While focusing on the doorway that Pond should emerge from, he glanced to the lower edge of the crescent moon on the horizon. The moon's bottom edge began disappearing into the darkness.

As if being devoured by a mythical beast, the rising blackness soon engulfed the entire moon then began swallowing the evening stars along the horizon. Turner realized to his horror that this was the crest of a huge wave bearing down on them.

"Cleary!" Turner yelled to his friend in the wheelhouse. "Don't be a fool. You don't stand a chance up there."

"Someone's got to issue the Mayday, Josh," Cleary yelled back from the doorway to the wheelhouse. "I'll keep at it as long as I can. Give my best to your father, Josh."

"Good luck, my friend," Josh said, sadly aware the old captain had sealed his fate. He then climbed into the Zodiac where Susan lay trembling in fear.

"Is Pond coming?"

"I'm sorry, Susan. Something must have happened to him below. Otherwise he'd be here by now"

Turner refastened the last of the snaps to the canvas top of the inflatable, and then wrapped the stern cleat line around his waist.

"Josh, I don't want to die," Susan cried, now bordering

on hysteria.

"We're going to get through this, so listen to me carefully. I want you to grab hold of the side cleats, and, no matter what happens, don't let go, okay?"

In the darkness of their makeshift pod, the pair heard an ominous roar similar to the winds of a typhoon. Turner raised his head and peered out the small slit in the canvas. To his horror, he saw a huge blackness rising out of the darkness blotting out the night sky as it unfurled over them.

"God help us," Turner whispered as he closed his eyes in a futile effort to escape the nightmarish scene.

The massive ninety-foot wave slammed into the ship broadside, sending the old relic rolling on the seafloor like a toy. The ship's first roll sheared off the bridge superstructure killing Captain Alfred Cleary instantly and trapping intern James Pond, Harkness, and many of the hapless crew below. They drowned in total darkness as the maelstrom flooded the ship in seconds.

***

One week later in the Ginza district of Tokyo, Japan, the phone rang in a dimly lit, plush office and was answered by its lone occupant.

"Yes, what is it?" The voice said in a soft, but icy tone.

"It is Fuyuki. I have the full results that you requested," the man on the other end stated.

"I trust you have good news for me, Fuyuki."

"Yes, Oyabun. The results were successful. Using the region's tectonic plates as the principal target worked better than expected."

"Excellent. Have there been any suspicions raised by the authorities?"

"None that I am aware of, sir. The tsunami has been attributed to an undersea earth slide caused by seismic activity common to the region, and has received little attention in the media. The loss of life was minimal and no report of a fireball has been made to the authorities. There were a few witnesses, but they have been all but ignored."

"Then it seems that our little demonstration was successful. Our benefactor wants assurance the plan will be feasible since he is investing heavily into the project."

"Yes, sir. I'm confident that with his financial backing, we will be more than able to meet his needs, and ours."

"Then I will tell our new friend that Operation Bishamon can begin whenever he is ready to proceed. You have done well, Fuyuki. Goodbye."

Hanging up the phone, he glanced at a map on his desk of the Canary Islands. *La Palma is such an insignificant little island*, he mused as he gently rolled up the map. *But when we're finished, the world will know the name very well; very well indeed.*

2

The Canary Islands, present day

The 1992 Land Rover made its way up the winding and dangerous road leading south from Santa Cruz, the capitol of the island of Tenerife. Josh Turner never tired of this view as he gazed up at the majestic, volcanic peak of Mount Teide, rising twelve thousand feet above him with its snow-capped peaks. It offered a view not seen by many.

Turner found the Canary Islands to be one of the most beautiful places he had ever worked. Looking out the window, his mind drifted as the old, rusty vehicle traveled onward. He found himself thinking of the tragic event in 2008.

His nightmares of the tsunami in the Bismarck Sea were getting worse. It had been a miracle that he and Susan Hendrich survived the ordeal.

The huge wave had slammed into the *Southern Star*. By some divine providence, or through sheer luck alone, their

Zodiac was flung off the bow by the force of the maelstrom as the ship began to roll. Miraculously, it landed face up into the crest of the churning wave. Susan screamed in abject fear for what seemed an eternity as the inflatable rode the head of the foaming torrent. In total darkness, the two were carried by the fearsome wave all the way to the mainland of Papua.

Within minutes, Turner felt the Zodiac's bottom being buffeted by solid objects as it passed over trees far beyond the beach. He had unsnapped the cover and could make out in the moonlit night they had managed to be carried far inland. The nightmare ended when the small raft came to rest atop a high rocky outcrop.

It had taken two days of relying on his jungle survival skills before the pair was discovered by a rescue boat from the Papua Maritime Defense Force.

The tragic loss of his intern, James Pond, weighed heavy on him, as did the psychological damage done to Susan Hendrich from the ordeal. She had never been the same since that night and had given up a promising career in the field of archeology. Turner had tried to encourage her for some time, hoping that she would reconsider, but she soon lost touch with him and faded into obscurity.

A jarring bump in the rocky road brought him back to the present.

"So much for getting over my jet lag after a long working trip in the states," Turner said to Paulo, his driver from San Fernando University. They made their way toward the first of many switchbacks that would lead them to the higher plateau where the team was working. The team, headed by his father, Eli Turner, was currently working on a new pyramid discovery near Guimar, a town on the eastern flank of Tenerife, about twenty-four miles from Santa Cruz.

This was the seventh and newest pyramid discovered. The other six had been discovered by archaeologists in 1998, Turner thought as the vehicle continued up a steep, rock-strewn road toward the site.

Turner and his father had been working together on this new pyramid at the request of San Fernando University Director of Archeology, Carlos Santiago. Eli Turner and Carlos had become fast friends since their work together on the Cueva de Belmaco project years ago. The caves, discovered on the island of La Palma, were a dwelling place for the ancient Guanches, the original inhabitants of the Canary Islands.

"Why was Maria so insistent that I come today? Couldn't it have waited for a few days?" He asked Paulo, pulling his ball cap brim down to shield his eyes from the sun that was now making its descent behind Mt. Teide.

"I don't know what is going on, Josh. Maria was insistent that you come as soon as possible. She said it was important," Paulo replied, then spat his wad of chewing tobacco out his open window.

"Seems odd that she wouldn't tell me over the phone," Turner said, trying to imagine what could be important enough to get him out here on the dig team's day off.

His mind drifted back to all the digs he had been part of during his father's long tenure as an archaeologist. *I've spent so many years with Dad, digging in the dirt in places such as Mexico, Peru, Belize, the Dead Sea region, and countless other locations. Had it been that long?*

He pulled his father's gift, a new Jansen pipe, from his

vest-pocket and placed it in a bag with a pouch of fresh Virginia Cavendish tobacco. He knew it was his father's favorite, so Turner had picked up some for him a few day ago before flying back to Tenerife. As the Land Rover started up the series of steep switchbacks, Turner reminisced how much his life had changed over the years.

After losing his mother in a car accident when he was only five, Turner had traveled the world with his father, constantly moving from one archeology site to another. Never having any semblance of a normal home, he had lived and been tutored throughout his adolescent years in some of the harshest regions of the world.

He learned the skills of an archaeologist from his renowned father, and, over the years living abroad, had mastered the languages of Spanish, Hebrew, and Aramaic.

At the age of eighteen, Turner had left his father and entered college, graduating from Texas A&M with degrees in both archeology and anthropology. He had then moved to Gettysburg, Pennsylvania, after receiving a job offer as director of field research with the National Parks Service, much to his father's disapproval.

"Son, you're wasting your talent there and you know it," a disgruntled Dr. Elias Turner said to him at the time.

Turner remembered the sarcastic response he had made to his father that day. "Dad, they might dig up an old Aramaic papyrus where they fought the battle of the Wheat Field, and I may come in handy being able to translate it for them."

He remembered how his father had just shaken his head and said, "Whatever makes you happy, Josh. That's all I care about, but with your training—"

"Dad," Turner had interrupted in anger, "just because you don't feel that it's valid work, doesn't mean that it's not to me. Why can't you let me make my own life? I'm not you!" Turner had regretted the remark, remembering the hurt he saw in his father's eyes.

Now at the age of twenty-eight, Josh Turner found himself one of the three field archeology directors of the International Consortium for Artifact Preservation.

ICAP began as the brainchild of his father and longtime collaborator, Professor Carlos Santiago, who at the time was director of antiquities at the University of Tenerife in the Canary Islands. The two esteemed archaeologists conceived the idea of an independent, internationally funded organization. ICAP would help countries discover their ancient artifacts, and help fight the growing loss of national treasures to the antiquities black market.

He recalled how after only two years with the National Parks Service, major funding cuts had led to him being let go. Not long after, his father offered the position of ICAP field director to him without comment or judgment, which had angered him. Turner begrudgingly said yes to the offer, knowing he had little choice at the time. In his mind he knew his father was thinking, *I told you so. You should have listened to me.*

Josh promised himself that he would commit to this position temporarily until he found something else. Swallowing his pride, he set out to prove that he was as good as his father; always pushing himself to the limits on each assignment. But now, he was tired; tired of trying to meet his father's high standards.

He admitted to himself it was not all a bad experience.

Through ICAP, he'd made some good friendships. Notably, his two field director counterparts, Dr. Hiram Rabib, director of antiquities at the University of Jerusalem, and Dr. Kim Liao, director of research of the Yangtze River project in Hubei Province, China. Both countries became charter members when ICAP was formally announced to the world five years ago.

Reaching the summit of the last rocky switchback, the dust covered Land Rover followed a small dirt road to the top of the plateau where Turner saw the weathered pyramids come into view. He marveled at the ancient structures and wondered who the builders were, and what had become of their culture.

Turner learned during his time spent on Tenerife the pyramids had been ignored by the local inhabitants. Long thought to be piles of earthen rubble, the ancient structures finally came to light when Norwegian explorer, Thor Heyerdahl, did a study on the ruins. Heyerdahl found them similar in design to the pyramids he had been researching halfway across the world in Tucume, Peru.

The Tenerife structures were step pyramids with facings of black volcanic stone rising to a height of about thirty-nine feet. They were all astronomically aligned with the sunset of the summer solstice. Not exactly the Great Pyramids of Egypt, but enough to convince Thor Heyerdahl to have the area purchased by a Norwegian businessman and researched at length.

The new dig site had been a beehive of activity by many archeology students and workers. Today, however, Turner could see it was strangely quiet. Everyone had gone back to Santa Cruz to prepare for the Dia de Santiago Apostol, the annual festival and carnival.

The Land Rover headed over to the small wood-framed hut located at the far end of the site. Built to act as the command center, it was dubbed 'the dust bowl' by the American students working the dig. It housed the portable generators, food, and water plus served as the dining hall, meeting room, and communications shack for the teams.

Turner smiled when he saw Maria waving at him from the steps of the makeshift office as the Land Rover pulled across the compound, stopping beside the generator shed.

Maria Santiago, daughter of Professor Carlos Santiago of the university, was a stunningly beautiful woman. Of Spanish descent, she was tall and slender with long, flowing black hair and bright blue eyes, which she attributed to a recessive gene indicative of her Guanche descent. That knowledge had given her the desire early on in life to learn all she could about the Guanche people. Over the past few years, Turner came to regard her passion as an obsession; Maria made little room in her life for other things, including him.

"Hello, Josh," she yelled, running over to greet him as Turner stepped out of the Rover. He was surprised by her sudden warm embrace.

"Hey, uh, Maria," was all he could muster as he felt her body against his. He wanted to be with her; be a part of her life, but sadly, he had learned long ago that her work was her only love. "Good to see you again," he managed, regaining his composure.

"How was your trip to the United States?" She asked as the two began walking toward the doors to the operations building.

"It was boring as usual, Maria. Meeting with representatives of countries interested in joining ICAP is not what I would call interesting, but you know my dad. He wants things done his way, with personal visits and such. Why are you still here with the festival gearing up in Santa Cruz?" he asked, changing the subject.

"You know me, Josh. All work and no play," she said as they entered the building. "Now that you're back, I wanted to show you something before I approached your father about it at our weekly meeting tonight in Santa Cruz. You know how ole' Dr. Grant gets when he's not the one making the discovery," she said with a laugh. "Okay, here we go again. Maria, you and the others have to stop calling my father that," Turner said in mock contempt. "It's really starting to bug him."

Ever since Josh and Eli Turner had met Maria, she'd teased the elder Turner about his uncanny likeness to the actor, Sam Neill, who portrayed Dr. Alan Grant in the movie Jurassic Park. Before long, the other students picked up on it and the nickname stuck.

"We would stop calling him that if he didn't wear that damned Australian outback hat all the time," she replied, with a laugh that warmed Turner's heart. "He told me just last week he was wearing that hat long before that movie came out, and that they stole the idea from the photo of him in Archeology Magazine."

"So, Maria, what's so darned important that it couldn't wait a few more days until the festival was over? My aching back was just beginning to straighten out from the long flight."

"I'm really sorry to interrupt your time off, Josh, but I

didn't want word to get out. I figured with everyone away for the festival, you might be able to shed some light on a little mystery without an audience."

"The new pyramid is no real mystery, Maria. They—"

"It's not the pyramid," she interrupted, "but something Samuel and I discovered while hiking on the western slopes of Blanca Mountain, up near the northern ridge of the Teide volcano. We were off the main trail, and made it up the western edge of Blanca when we found a recent rockslide that exposed an ancient lava tube. You know Samuel," she added, rolling her eyes. "He couldn't pass up the opportunity to explore, so we decided to check it out. We found undisturbed Guanche dwellings, artifacts, and burial caves."

"What's the mystery of that, Maria? They're common to these islands and discovered all the time. I'm sure *you* were like a kid in a candy store though," Turner said with a chuckle.

"I know, Josh. It's not a unique discovery, but what we found deep inside the cave is. We took some photos of all we found on the digital camera and left it as is. We told no one so it wouldn't be disturbed until we did a proper field study. Come over here and take a look." Turner followed her past two long tables used for eating, and a corner area set up for the laptop computers.

The small corner table was a myriad of wires, extension cords, and surge suppressors, which were lying about in a haphazard fashion. Outside, the portable generator purred softly, supplying the light and power needed for the small refrigerator, lights, and computer power strips.

"I know the pixel quality isn't very good, but take a look

at these, Josh." Maria said, clicking on the laptop's picture viewer program.

Turner saw on the screen the ancient cave, formed from a volcanic lava tube, its black basalt walls glimmering in the sunlight near the entrance, and then fading into the darker recesses of the cave. Maria continued advancing the pictures, showing items such as two well preserved tamarcos, coats of goat skin that protected the ancient Gaunches from the cold of the mountains. He also recognized a huirmas, a piece of leather worn like sleeves to protect the arms.

"Look at the guaycas," Turner said, marveling at the crude leather legging used to cover the area between the ankle and the knee. "They're remarkably well preserved."

"Yes, they are, but bear with me. That's not what I brought you here for," she said, quickly advancing the picture viewer. "When we approached the darker recesses of the cave, we had to pull out the flash light Samuel keeps in his back pack in order to continue. We saw several bucios, the large conch shells they used as trumpets and a pile of banot, wooden spears plus many other pristine artifacts."

"Okay, Maria, that is all well and good. These are remarkable finds, but what's the great puzzle here?" Turner asked, becoming a little annoyed.

"Here!" she exclaimed as the next slide showed what looked like small carved out fissures with basalt rocks stacked in front of them. "Guanche burial caves similar to what we have seen many times before, but take a look at the one at the far right. It's much different from the others and the cover stone has something etched into it. It was way too faded to make out with one small light, so we'll have to clean up the image to distinguish what the symbol is."

"Interesting that it's different from the others," Turner said, leaning closer to get a better look. "So, is that it?"

"No, we were preparing to leave when I saw something lying on the ground, partially buried in front of the tomb. We took a closer look and discovered a piece of parchment with writing on it. Oddly enough, it's not ancient Guanche, or Spanish," she said as the final slide appeared on the screen showing a close up of a piece of papyrus.

"Is this a joke?" Turner asked, staring at the photo with amazement.

"No joke, Josh," she replied as they stared at the writing on the ancient parchment.

"It's written in ancient Aramaic!" Turner said in astonishment. "What the hell would this be doing in a Guanche tomb on one of the Canary Islands?"

"That's why I called you first. I figured this may be an important find, or a complete waste of our time," Maria said hesitantly as she poured herself a cup of coffee that was at least six hours old. "You understand Aramaic. Can you make it out?"

"It's pretty faded on this picture, Maria. I'd need to see it blown up in order to translate it," Turner replied, still focusing on the strange document. "Do you think that your father at the university can get the approvals for us to begin a proper excavation without the usual red tape?"

"I'm sure when he sees this, Josh, and, if it turns out to be the real deal, he'll find a way. Father has many friends in the Policia Nacional, and in the island administration."

"Has Samuel said anything about this to anyone?"

Turner asked.

"We made a deal not to tell anyone until we could talk to you, your father, and to my father. We didn't want to risk the chance of relic hunters gutting the place before we could survey and document everything."

"Nicely done, Maria; your father will be proud of you. Why don't you take what you have back to San Fernando University and get a translation on this before we announce anything," Turner said as he closed the laptop lid and handed it to Maria.

"I'm way ahead of you, Josh. We burnt the parchment and cover stone pictures to a CD then I sent Samuel back to Santa Cruz University. I'll send them to my father when I meet with Samuel at the university. We're all meeting tonight at the Cofradia de Pescadores restaurant for our monthly meeting. Hopefully, we can discuss whatever we find out from the antiquities department," she said, as the two turned and started walking out of the office.

Locking the door behind them, Turner said, "I'm heading back to the hotel to get cleaned up, so I'll meet you later."

"Okay, Josh, I'll see you there," Maria yelled as she sprinted toward her Jeep. Turner watched her, wondering what it would take to breach that wall of dedication to her work.

Early evening had come to the city of Santa Cruz along with the festive atmosphere, which now enveloped the city streets as Paulo pulled the Land Rover in front of the entrance to the El Dorado hotel.

The El Dorado was one of the few hotels that were affordable to the university since they were footing the bill for Turner's stay. The hotel was clean, and attractive with comfortable accommodations.

"I'll pick you up at seven o'clock, Josh," Paulo yelled as he pulled away from the entrance.

"Oh, that's just lovely," Turner grumbled, looking at his watch and seeing it was already close to six o'clock. "That gives me just one hour to rest and shower."

He passed through the colorful glass doors that led into the hotel's lobby. In the courtyard he saw the now familiar circular bar. The piano player was already into his first set for the evening. The small lounge was a favorite for Turner and Samuel after a long day on the dig site. He then walked over to the front desk where the night clerk was just beginning his shift.

"Good evening, Juan. Are there any messages for me?" Turner asked the slightly balding clerk, who had worked at the El Dorado for fifteen years.

"No messages for you this evening, Señor Josh," he replied looking in the slot for room number 12. "Would you like me to have your drink ready for you in the bar after you've had a chance to freshen up?"

"Not tonight, Juan. It's tempting, but I'll be dining out with Professor Santiago, my father, and the team at the Cofradia de Pescadores and probably won't be returning until late."

"Ah, the meals there are delicious, Señor Josh," he said with a wide grin.

"Thanks, Juan. I've learned to trust your taste in restaurants since I've been on Tenerife," he said as he made his way down the lavishly carpeted hallway leading to the guest rooms.

Turner fumbled in his pocket for his room key. He then opened the door to be greeted by the scent of fresh cut Canary samphire, a wild plant with bright green leaves and golden flowers found on the island's coastal basalt rocks.

Shutting the door behind him, he tossed his coat onto the bed and stripped off his dust laden clothes. This had become a daily routine from the arid conditions on the eastern side of Tenerife with the constant dry winds blowing westward off the Saharan Desert on the African continent.

Showering and then toweling off, he quickly dressed and walked back into the bedroom. He saw the post-it he'd stuck on the closet door yesterday reminding him to call Abby in Washington tomorrow and thank her for setting up his accommodations while he was in the states.

Abby, the first woman Dad has tried to have a relationship with since losing Mom, Turner thought. *God knows, he needs someone in his life.*

Turner had been there when Professor Eli Turner had met Abigail Conger at a dinner function for the preservation of ancient artifacts last year in Washington, D.C. They were immediately attracted to each other, which surprised Josh, seeing his father left little room in his life for anything, or anyone.

Abby was assistant to the Under Secretary of State for Arms Control and International Security at the State Department. *Another one married to their work, never finding time to settle down with anyone,* Turner mused as he grabbed his keys and headed out the door.

Paulo arrived on time as usual, and the two headed off to the restaurant located in the old town near the harbor district. They passed scores of colorful shops and storefronts decorated to celebrate Dia de Santiago Apostol, the annual festival honoring their patron saint, and the town's defeat of the English.

Paulo and Turner made their way through the busy streets of Santa Cruz, bypassing one of the many festival parades marching down toward the Plaza de Espana. The participants of the parade were dressed in flamboyant costumes, the custom for the island's many festivals held throughout the year. There was dancing to the festive rhythms of music provided by live bands along the *Plaza*.

They turned onto Calle de la Marini Street and drove for another five minutes along the harbor before turning into the parking lot of the Cofradia de Pescadores restaurant.

The restaurant was one of the few out-of-the-way establishments visited by locals more often than the many tourists, who came to enjoy the mild, summer climate of the Canaries.

They made their way through the modest entrance of the restaurant and found the interior filled with the sounds of joviality. The intoxicating aroma of fine food drifted through the room, mingled with the soft clinking sound of silverware and muffled discussions in Spanish and English.

The smartly dressed waiters hurried about, serving their sizzling hot entrees to the delight of their patrons seated at spacious round custom-made tables. Each specially designed with its own distinct colorful pattern tablecloth, and accented with large high- backed cushioned chairs.

A young host approached Turner and asked if they wanted a table.

"We are here to dine with Professors Turner and

Santiago.

Have they arrived yet?" He asked the host in fluent Spanish.

"Si', Señor. They are seated and awaiting your arrival," the host replied as he motioned them toward a table in the upper level of the restaurant in the rear of the establishment.

"Hello, Josh, my old friend!" a voice boomed from the end table.

Professor Carlos Santiago was a commanding figure of a man, standing at six feet tall with a broad smile hidden behind a thick goatee. He was wearing his traditional white cotton suit and checkered bow tie, which had become his trademark at the university.

Santiago was something of a legend at San Fernando University. He possessed a jovial spirit, and kindness to his staff and students. However, when he wanted something done, he exhibited all the tenacity and gracefulness of a rogue elephant on a rampage.

"Good evening, Carlos," Turner said as he and Paulo sat down at the table. "Hello, Dad," he added to his father, who was seated next to Carlos.

"Hello, Son. Was your trip to the states successful?" Eli Turner said, cutting right to business.

"It was, Dad," Turner replied, a bit annoyed by the question. "I sent you an email with all the details. Here," he said, handing the bag with the pipe and tobacco to his father. "I picked this up for you in Washington, D.C. Abby told me where to find it."

"Thanks, Son," the elder Turner said, lifting out his new pipe. "I broke the stem on the old one."

"I hope you don't mind that we mix business with pleasure this evening," Carlos said as he signaled the waiter. "We need to discuss this find my daughter and Samuel made up on the slopes of Mt. Teide. She called me from the university an hour ago and gave me a brief overview. If it's valid, I must make the proper arrangements for permits as expediently as possible."

"I couldn't agree more, Carlos," Eli Turner said as the waiter approached the table with pad and pencil in hand. "This could be quite a unique discovery."

"Where are Samuel and Maria?" Turner asked Carlos.

"Samuel and Maria will be along shortly, Josh. They went to meet with the linguistics head at the university before coming here. Hopefully they will have more information for us."

"While we wait, I'll have a Ron Miel," Eli said to the waiter, having grown fond of the local mead rum made with palm honey. "Josh, would you like your usual?"

"I'll have Jose Cuervo Black, on the rocks. Thanks, Dad."

"I'll have another Malvasia; it's one of our finest island wines. Oh, and a soft drink for Paulo because he is driving tonight," Carlos said as the waiter then hurried off to get their drinks.

"What do you two make of Maria and Samuel's discovery?" Turner asked curiously, getting right to the topic at hand.

"I'm a bit intrigued, but just a bit more skeptical, Josh. Finding a parchment written in ancient Aramaic within a Guanche tomb? It's a bit of a stretch," Carlos said, finishing off the last of his Malvasia.

"I'm curious about what is in the tomb, which Maria said was sealed with a flat cover stone. All the other tomb entrances within the lava tube were made with traditional piles of basalt rock," Eli said as their waiter set their drinks down in front of them.

"I'm even more curious as to *who* is in that tomb." Carlos added with a puzzled look. "I had Maria email the enlarged and enhanced photo of the cover stone to me before I came here. I want you to tell me what you see, Josh," he said as he reached beside his chair, pulled out a photo from his brief case, and handed it to Turner.

Eli and Carlos remained silent as Turner studied the photo of the cover stone that had been light-enhanced by brightening the natural rock, which left the etching in a dark shaded pattern. His sharp, blue eyes widened at the image he saw on the stone.

"The Ichthus," Turner said in an astonished voice. "What would the symbol of the early Christian church be doing in an ancient Guanche tomb on the Canary Islands?"

"That's what I would like to know as well," Carlos replied. "We know from our studies the Romans were exploring the Canary archipelago as early as the fourth century. Pliny the Elder, a Roman soldier and administrator did extensive research and documentation of the Islands. We also know that trade had been established by the Romans with the discovery of ancient potsherds dug up on the island of Lanzarote in the 1960's." He paused to take a sip of his wine, and then continued his discourse. "Most of the potsherds were pieces of large amphorae used to carry such commodities as wine, salt fish, and olive oil. Analysis of their clay showed the amphorae originally came from

Campania in Italy, Baetica in Spain, and Tunisia."

"That may explain the symbol on the cover stone," Turner said.

"I'm not so sure, Josh," Eli said. "At that time, the early Christian church was struggling under heavy persecution from the Romans, so I don't believe the early church ever had a presence here. The Guanche worshiped their own Gods, and, it would have been almost impossible to communicate with them, seeing they had their own unique language."

"Do you think the tomb might have been used at a later date?" Turner asked.

"Who's to say?" Carlos said, taking another sip of his wine. "We won't know until we perform a carbon dating on the contents. That will verify the time period, but the real substance will hopefully come from the parchment translation, which I hope Maria will have with her."

At that moment, Maria Santiago strolled up to the upper level followed by Samuel Caberra, Peruvian native and longtime friend of Turner.

Turner knew Maria Santiago's striking beauty and elegance never failed to turn heads wherever she went, and this evening would be no exception. Turner watched her graceful approach with her long, dark flowing hair pulled back in a bun. She wore a bright flowered sundress with spaghetti straps that dramatically accented her dark skin and slim, athletic figure. She slowly made her way toward them carrying her laptop computer under her arm, which amused Turner.

"Hello, Father," she said to Carlos as the four men rose from their chairs. As she approached, she winked at Turner, sending his heart racing.

"Good evening, my dear," Carlos said giving his daughter a hug. "Hello, Maria," Eli added.

"Good evening, Dr. Turner. You're looking especially handsome tonight. It's so nice to be able to see your hair without that hat on," she said with a laugh.

"What's left of my hair anyway," Eli joked.

"Samuel, you're looking as fit as ever," Turner said to his long- time friend, who simply smiled then proceeded to give Turner one of his trademark bear hugs. His ribs aching, Turner pleaded, "Okay, okay. I give up!"

Josh Turner had felt like a brother to Samuel Caberra since their meeting at a pyramid excavation in Lima Peru back in the late 90's.

Samuel Caberra was a Huarochiri Quechua native He was raised in the village of Tupicocha, high in the Andes Mountains of Peru. As a Quechuan, he was a descendant of the Inca, the indigenous peoples of South America who were conquered by the Spanish.

Turner learned from Samuel that much of their heritage and culture had been stifled by the Spanish. Even their native tongue was considered by their conquerors to be 'animal talk'. Only in recent years had their culture been re-established by legislation in an effort to recognize the Quechua as an indigenous people.

Samuel had grown up the eldest son in a poor family of six and worked with his father on the terrace fields raising crops to provide a meager existence for his family. The many years of hunting and working in the high altitudes of the Andes made him the perfect athlete.

He'd be more at home on a rocky slope than in this restaurant,

Turner mused, noting the Peruvian's obvious discomfort at being there.

"Hello, Eli, how goes it?" Samuel said, giving his second father a powerful hug that caused Eli's back to crack.

"Good God, I won't need a chiropractor for a while after that," Eli said rubbing his lower back.

Samuel had first met Eli and his son, Josh Turner in Lima, the Capitol city of Peru. After making the decision to make a better life for himself and his family he left for the coastal city in search of work. At the time, the research team working on the pyramid in the center of Lima made the discovery of a tomb deep within the structure. Eli Turner was invited to aide in the identification and preservation of the many Incan artifacts found within.

Samuel got word on the street that he could find work as a laborer. So, one evening, he went to the site to speak to anyone he could find about gaining employment. but the site was closed down. Before turning to leave, Samuel heard sounds coming from the site entrance and went to see if he could find someone.

Rounding the corner and going down a long ramp out of view of the street, he saw a young man carrying a metal box being shoved about by two rather large men. It didn't take long for Samuel to realize that this was a robbery in progress and immediately, he went to his aid. The two men quickly turned on Samuel, which turned out to be a mistake on their part, as the native Quechuan made quick work of the thieves. The initial punch thrown by Samuel knocked the first man off his feet, dropping him to the ground with a bone-jarring thud. The other hoodlum, seeing he was outmatched, helped his partner up and then fled up the ramp, disappearing into the dusk of the early evening.

A grateful Josh Turner thanked Samuel, and explained that he was carrying Incan relics from the site to the local museum to secure them. On the way, he was ambushed by the two looters, who would have stolen and sold the artifacts on the antiquities black market. Turner asked Samuel to go with him to secure the items, and afterward invited him to come to the facility provided by the University of Lima where he and his father were staying.

Samuel spoke no English, but both Josh and Eli were fluent in Spanish. They broke any language barriers and the three soon became friends. Eli eventually hired Samuel as his project director for the site, acting as a liaison to the workers. He soon became a trusted friend to the Turners. The elder Turner made it possible for Samuel to get the schooling he needed to learn English, and had taught him the basics of archeology with on-site training. Samuel worked hard, and sent most of his earnings home to his family in Tupicocha. Josh and Samuel became inseparable, and spent many years after that working together on many excavation sites around the world.

After all introductions were made, the new arrivals ordered their drinks and made their dinner selections. Turner ordered the Sama frita con mojo Verde, a local fresh, fried fish served in a light sauce consisting of oil, coriander and garlic. It was topped with papas' arrugades, small tender cooked potatoes. The rest of the party ordered the house special that evening: carne de cabra en salsa, a dish of seared goat's meat swimming in wine-based gravy with seasonings.

After enjoying a wonderful meal, they all decided on

gofio de almendras, a rich dessert made with almonds, and then finished off with a round of espresso. It was at that point the conversation went from pleasantries to the business at hand.

"So, Maria, did you have any success with Professor Aguirre from the university in deciphering the parchment you and Samuel discovered?" Eli asked, sipping his espresso.

"Yes, Dr. Turner, he was still working on it after we left for our meeting here, and promised to email the results to me when he was finished. That's why I brought the laptop. They have Wi-Fi at this restaurant."

"Well, if anything, I feel we should commence work on protecting the Guanche artifacts right away. We need to keep the site safe from looters, no matter what the results are from the translation," Carlos said stroking his goatee. "The equipment, tents, and manpower can easily be transferred from the pyramid site within a day."

"What about the permits, Carlos?" Turner asked, knowing the excessive waiting periods for archeology permits.

"That won't be a problem, Josh. I have already received a verbal from the assistant to Tenerife Administrator Fuentes to commence work. He was hesitant when I told him the location of the find, and he kept repeating something about staying clear of the Japanese research facility nearby."

"So, the neighbors aren't friendly I take it?" Turner asked. "Not friendly at all, Josh," Carlos said flatly.

"This will be much more interesting than our current project," Maria said as she opened her laptop.

As the waiter cleared away the last vestiges of dinnerware from the table, she started the computer and opened her email program.

"Great! It looks like Professor Aguirre came through with something," Maria said with excitement as the download began. On completing the download, she opened the document, and proceeded to read with all eyes at the table fixed on her. After a minute, they saw her eyes widen in surprise.

"Oh my God," she whispered, and then turned the laptop to face Turner, who read aloud the two emails sent by Professor Aguirre.

"'Maria, Attached below is the best translation I could procure for you in such a short period of time. This comes from Dr. Rabib of the Hebrew University of Jerusalem to whom I sent an enhanced facsimile of the parchment. Had I known the subject matter of what this document consisted of, I would have been more prudent and not have sent it at all.

If this discovery is valid, it could be a major find, but I fear word will get out quickly due to my carelessness in letting others read the translation. For that, I deeply apologize. Do not delay in getting the site secure as soon as possible, for I fear looting will be imminent. Contact me if I can be of any further help. Good luck, and give my regards to your father.

Alberto Aguirre.'"

Turner looked up at Maria with a quizzical look, and then continued reading.

"'Dr. Hiram Rabib To: Professor Aguirre My Dear Dr.

Aguirre,

Please find below the best translation I could make of your facsimile with my staff. Many parts of the document are missing, or illegible, but if this is not a hoax, it is an astounding find. Translation as follows:

Peace be unto you my Brethren in Thera.
...send to you my brother Simon, a disciple of our Lord.
...Safeguard the Cup of the slain Lamb, and His testament.
...Aide him in protecting the Master's.... Safe passage to....

Joseph of Ramleh.'"

"Interesting stuff," said Samuel, fighting a yawn, "but who in the world is Joseph of Ramleh?"

"If I recall, Ramleh was a town in ancient Judea. Studies now show the ancient maps of the first century don't show what it is called today," Maria stated, turning the laptop back to face her.

"It's called...Arimathea." Turner whispered staring at the candle left burning on the table, "Joseph of Arimathea."

The table fell silent for what seemed like minutes until Maria broke the spell.

"We must start work right away. The word will be out quickly, and I dare not think what would happen if looters get there before we do," she said shutting down the computer and closing the lid.

"Do you think it's possible after centuries of wondering and speculation that we may have stumbled on, by accident, a clue to the whereabouts of the Holy Grail?" Eli asked.

"Many hypotheses have been put out about its whereabouts or who had possession of it, or even if it existed at all. But if the carbon dating comes back close to the first century, we may have finally come close to finding an important clue," Maria said. "Imagine, even the remote possibility of verifying the existence of the cup the historical Jesus Christ reportedly shared with his disciples during the last supper. What a historical discovery that would be!"

"Even if it did exist, Maria, which I doubt, what a firestorm it would create," Turner said. "Could you imagine the debate about its authenticity? A theological war of words would rage for years between believers and non-believers."

"That is not up to us to decide, Josh," Carlos said rising from his chair. "It's our duty to bring artifacts to light, no matter what the controversy. I'll make a few calls and start the transfer of manpower and equipment to the site right away, then see about arranging for some security. I would suggest all of you begin packing your field gear, and start as soon as possible."

"Maria and I can be ready to head up tomorrow," Eli said. "Same here," Turner added.

"Sorry, Josh," his father said. "I would like you to take the permit applications to the Canary Islands Administrator's Office in Las Palmas on Grand Canaria Island right away, if you wouldn't mind."

"Great, Dad. I'm starting to feel more like an errand boy than an archaeologist," Turner replied in protest. "Alright, I'll leave first thing in the morning and with any luck, be back in a few days. That's if I don't get hung up with the red tape. Last time it took me almost five days to get the permits in order. I'll take Samuel with me. That way he won't break anything when you start on the new site."

"I guess that means my days off are canceled," Samuel moaned in mock protest. "The things I do for you guys; I'm so unappreciated."

"One more thing, Eli," Carlos said in a serious tone to the elder Turner as they proceeded out of the restaurant and into the cool night air. "Do me a favor and stay clear of the Japanese satellite facility that Fuentes' assistant spoke of. There are rumors going around that some of the island people who have gone there have disappeared."

"Do you actually believe that, Carlos?" Eli asked, as Paulo headed off to get the Land Rover.

"I don't know, Eli, but you never know about rumors. And one can't be too careful," the professor responded. "Just be vigilant, okay?"

"You worry too much, Carlos," Turner said as he, Maria and Samuel followed the two professors toward their vehicles. "What could someone want to hide on an old, dried up volcano?"

3

Tokyo, Japan

Four days after the discovery on Tenerife, a lone American strolled down Tokyo's bustling Ginza entertainment district. The streets were ablaze with the city's bright neon lights, and throngs of people out enjoying the Tokyo nightlife. They paid little attention to the pale, slightly balding, five foot seven inch American as he made his way through the crowds, holding on to his briefcase with a vise-like grip.

If these people only knew what was in my possession, Robert Pencor thought with arrogant amusement as he rounded the corner, then walked up Yomati Street toward the Masari Club.

The Masari was a two-story private club catering to the more affluent residents of Japan. It offered food, drinks, card playing, and the latest national craze, Pachinko.

Robert Pencor was what one could easily and quickly label as brilliant, yet disturbing. A graduate of Harvard

Business School, he had a knack for profit. He quickly climbed to the pinnacle of success, leaving a trail of broken lives and shattered competitors along his path. His 'take no prisoners' business ethics made him feared by most competitors. Pencor's drive left his personal life devoid of relationships other than the few escorts he paid for when the physical need arose. Some of these women, hardened by a life of prostitution, had left him at the end of an evening utterly shaken and afraid. Adding to these qualities the merciless drive he possessed to achieve power, he had become what colleagues and enemies alike had termed, a textbook sociopath.

Pencor had achieved his wealth through shady business dealings and cut-throat tactics early in his career. He had discovered early on that his future lay in the oil business and with vicious tenacity, worked his way to the top. During his rapid ascent in the business world he managed to secure many domestic and foreign oil companies. These were accomplished by way of hostile takeovers, or strong-arm tactics of which he was not above doing in order to achieve his goals.

By the year 2000, he had risen to CEO of his newly formed Pencor Oil Corporation, which employed thousands of people. He reaped vast profits amounting to millions in assets with worldwide holdings of production and refinement facilities.

None of this was enough for Pencor. He soon began channeling funds from research and development and employee pension funds to his private accounts overseas. He had become accustomed to the many bribes and kickbacks gained from corrupt foreign business executives and leaders, who continued to line his pockets for exclusive refinery and drilling contracts.

His desire for money, and the power it wielded, became an all-consuming obsession. Pencor would not settle for just *enough*.

He wanted *it all*; at any cost, even if it meant eliminating anyone who got in his way. His cut-throat tactics would gain him many enemies along the way, and those enemies played a major role in his personal and financial undoing in 2005.

The high oil prices of the mid-decade had produced an outcry from the public. Fueled by the media, politicians tried to appease their base and divert attention from the crisis. They skirted the truth by holding what Pencor considered 'useless' Congressional hearings on Capitol Hill, hoping to inflame the public with the tried-and-true strategy of crying corporate greed.

Given the recent memory of events in 2002 that led to the downfall of the leadership of Enron, it had garnered good press and a guarantee of votes from a public easily misled. Pencor blamed the public, whom he felt was too quick to believe anything they heard from the media.

Those especially motivated in this witch-hunt were the career politicians, Republican and Democrat, who were more concerned about their political tenure than America as a whole. Pencor had been furious knowing that many of these politicians were the same ones taking his contributions.

He knew the real truth the media had failed to report, and what politicians didn't want America to know. The worldwide demand for oil was far out stripping the supply. As he had also predicted, China now surpassed the U.S. in oil consumption. The world would never know low oil prices again as they continued to sky-rocket to their current level of one hundred fifty-five dollars per barrel.

He also knew career politicians had to appease their base and environmental lobbyists by voting against any new drilling or refineries in the continental United States. This self-imposed ban had been going on in Washington for the last thirty-eight years, which resulted in United States' domestic oil production becoming almost non-existent.

To complicate matters, politicians over the years continued to side-step oil exploration or production in Alaska and the lower forty-eight states. Proponents argued that these regions held more than a thirty-year supply of crude, plus the added benefit of adding thousands of jobs to a weak economy.

Pencor knew it was a no-win situation for the American people and utter hypocrisy, as both Republicans and Democrats feared rocking the boat because hefty donations continued to flow into their war chests. *Those fools deserve what they get by continually re-electing bigger fools,* he thought as he continued up the narrow sidewalk.

It was during a series of Congressional hearings in 2005 that Robert Pencor found himself subpoenaed to testify. That was when the opportunity to exact vengeance upon him by the victims of his ruthless past came into play.

A plant in his organization by a competitor had been able to procure documents linking Pencor to kick-backs and pension grabbing. Add to that a few forged documents, they now had a treasure trove of trumped-up evidence to hand over to friendly politicians and a salivating media. The vultures circled, waiting for the kill.

Pencor had been blindsided by the testimony and revelations directed against him, but knew right away that he was being set up as the scapegoat for the public and for the media to crucify. The tactics used against him were well-planned and flawless. Thus, Robert Pencor and Pencor Oil made the Enron scandal look like a Girl Scout cookie sale.

To save face with the stockholders, the board of directors of Pencor Oil had him stripped of all duties and froze all of his assets, with the help of the Justice Department.

Robert Pencor had become a pariah: a man hated by America and a victim of his own ruthless greed. Finally, in 2005, he fled the country to Morocco to avoid prosecution, taking advantage of its no extradition agreement with the United States. It was there he had invested in secret much of his ill-begotten treasure over the years. In his rage and growing madness, he vowed that one day he would seek retribution on those who had ruined him; an obsession he still held to this day.

As it was with most Americans, he knew their memory would be short-lived and the media would find something else to focus on, thus diverting attention from the Pencor Oil scandal. Life went on, with Pencor slipping beneath the radar. He slowly drew his plans of revenge against the people and nation that tried to destroy him.

Yes, it will be soon, he thought, smiling a grin that usually frightened anyone who gazed upon it. "The fools will pay dearly for their stupidity and short-sightedness," he said, laughing aloud as he came to the entrance of the brightly lit Masari Club.

Once inside, Pencor was greeted by the constant

whirring sounds and clanging of the first floor's Pachinko parlor with its endless rows of machines. He walked through the annoying sound to the back, and then to the flight of stairs leading to the second floor. He noted, with amusement, the groups of businessmen sitting at tables talking quietly while the comfort women, as they were labeled, stood about waiting for a signal to attend their respective table.

Pencor walked briskly up the flight of stairs to the upper level, leaving the smoke filled parlor behind. He entered the swinging doors into the second floor containing a small bar and restaurant. As he walked across the floor, he could hear the soft, melodic sounds of traditional Japanese music played on the Koto; a banjo like instrument, and a wooden flute.

Pencor sat down at an empty table and noticed a group of Japanese men wearing dark suits sitting in the back of the room, who regarded him with suspicious eyes. He also noted the surveillance camera in the corner ceiling. One of the men stood and proceeded to walk over to the door labeled 'office' in Japanese, then knocked on the door. Pencor watched the man give him a quick glance as he entered the room. A waiter came over to him and took his order of deep fried prawns and gyoza, little dumplings of deep-fried octopus, with a glass of sake.

His meal was delivered to him soon afterwards and as he ate, he warily kept his eyes on the men seated at the table. He trusted no one and it was obvious to him the men were armed, judging from the bulges in the sides of their dark suits.

As he sipped the last of his sake, the man who had

retreated into the rear office appeared once again from the room and approached his table. Pencor could not help but notice the missing pinky finger on the man's left hand, and wondered what the poor fellow had done to deserve his ritual penitence.

"Good evening, Pencor-san," the man said with a polite bow. It never ceased to amuse Pencor how formal protocol and honor ruled the lives of the Japanese. Even the most blood-thirsty criminal held to this code and time-honored tradition.

"Mr. Osama is ready to see you now. I do hope your meal was satisfactory," he said politely as Pencor rose to follow him across the room to the door. As they passed the other three men, their steady gaze continued.

"Yes, yes, thank you, the meal was fine," Pencor replied flatly as the man knocked on the door to the office.

"Enter," a voice from within boomed. The large man opened the door and motioned Pencor inside.

"Mr. Pencor is here to see you, Oyabun." Pencor knew the term Oyabun meant father, the formal title given to leaders of the Japanese Yakuza clan. The man then closed the door behind Pencor, and went back to his friends seated at the table.

"Hello, Robert," said a voice from a large high-backed swivel chair.

With the Yakuza leader's back still facing him, Pencor gazed about the room, taking in the elegance of the lavish office. It was impeccably furnished, adorned with bright flowers, native plants, and a myriad of paintings hanging with tasteful elegance on the wall.

The swivel chair slowly turned around to face him,

revealing a well-dressed middle-aged Japanese man. He had short black hair and wore a black patch over his left eye, a commemorative injury from his violent early years.

Yagato Osama was the Tokyo leader of the Yakuza, the Japanese version of the Sicilian Mafia. It was a structured organization with strong clan ties, having a presence in Japan dating from the 1600s. If persons with a grievance could not gain satisfaction from the local authorities, they could most likely find it by going to the Oyabun in their region to have it solved for them. The Yakuza had their own form of justice, which was often swift, brutal, and final.

Pencor knew Osama was the Tokyo regional leader with the honored title Oyabun. His next in command was his adviser called Saiko-komon, and then down to its many members called Wakashu, or children. He knew the Oyabun was to be obeyed by all, even if it meant risking life or limb to do so. He was absolute lord and ruler over his kingdom.

"Good morning, Yagato. I hope you are well," Pencor said, offering the empty platitude as he walked over to the plush high- backed chairs in front of the desk.

"Please sit down, Robert. May I offer you a cup of tea?" Yagato Osama asked, gesturing to the priceless Sucki tea set dating back to the Sui and Tang dynasty of 5th century China.

"No, thank you, Yagato," Pencor replied sitting down and putting his briefcase down beside him. Watching Osama pour a cup for himself, he noticed the tip of the pinky finger on his left hand was also missing.

Pencor knew this was from the practice of Yubitsume. The ritual of cutting off your own fingertip with a knife or sharp item, then wrapping it in paper and sending it to the

Oyabun as an apology for disobedience, accompanied by a note begging for forgiveness. The more transgressions, the more fingertips you would lose. If the transgression was too great, no penitence could be accepted and your execution was assured.

"I've come to check on the progress of our plans," Pencor said, getting right to the point. "What's the status of our project in the Canary Islands?"

"Operation Bishamon is going as planned, Robert, so you need not concern yourself. Our facility on Tenerife is safe and above suspicion. As far as anyone is concerned, it's just another one of the many research observatories located on Mount Blanca's plateau. To the casual observer, it is nothing more than a satellite relay station, and my security keeps a watchful eye out for intruders."

"What about the progress of your Scalar weapon? Is it going as planned?" Pencor asked.

"The weapon has been in operation for months now, and has been exponentially increasing at the rate provided by our lead scientist on site. You must have patience, my dear friend. Your retribution will come soon enough," Osama stated with a malevolent grin.

"Are the seismic sensors on the island of La Palma still functioning properly? It's vital that no one notice any seismic activity prior to the final phase."

"They are working fine, Robert. I must admit, it was a sound idea to have the hundreds of geological seismic sensors located on La Palma replaced by our technicians. How did your fictitious company win the maintenance contract with La Palma?" Osama asked, reaching for his teacup.

"A little matter made simple with a generous contribution to a few well-placed island administrators and officials," Pencor replied with a smirk as Osama sipped his tea. "It's amazing what people will do when the price is right. Greed can be most rewarding sometimes."

"It took our people almost a year to complete the switching of the sensors," Osama said, setting his cup back on its tray. "Now all the geological stations on La Palma will never see any reports of unusual seismic activity until it is far too late. Our men programmed the sensors to give a false tremor indication from time to time, which is a normal occurrence on the island. If they showed no activity, geologists would assume the sensors were not functioning properly and investigate. I must admit, it was brilliant plan, Robert," Osama said, nodding with approval. "As for the Scalar weapons, my organization has been working on the Longitudinal Wave Interferometers weaponry for the last fifteen years with a varied success rate. The world would be shocked to know that we have been wreaking havoc in many regions, focusing mainly on locales that would not suspect anything, such as Australia and Indonesia. The Americans are aware of the technology, but have stifled it for decades save a few scientists who have tried to make their government aware of the threat. They are also aware of the possible economic gains of finding an alternative fuel source, such as the one you have successfully developed in Morocco."

"I've read the reports of your organization's handy work with the Scalar weapons," Pencor said. "You've caused much of the earthquake, volcano, and tsunami activity in this region of the world for quite some time with tremendous and catastrophic results with no one the wiser. I was convinced by your little demonstration in New Guinea in 2008 that your weapons would suffice my needs."

"It is still not an exact science, Robert. The Longitudinal Wave Interferometers do work, but they sometimes produce unexpected results, especially when dealing with existing earth fault lines. Our early experiments using the Electromagnetic Pulse Cannon had to be discontinued. The resulting energy bursts were not controllable, which often roused the suspicions of too many people," Osama said, pausing long enough to take a sip of tea then continuing. "Our first testing was almost a catastrophe with a plasma fireball exploding over the city of Perth, Australia in 1995. Luckily the Perth Astronomical Observatory concluded the anomaly had been the explosion of a celestial fireball from space and, fortunately, no investigations were ever launched. Regrettably, with the fall of the Soviet Union at the time, our funding by the KGB had all but dried up. We were lacking the major funding needed for our experiments, until you so graciously enabled us to continue and refine the technology."

"So I can expect little trouble with your new weapon's results?" Pencor asked.

"La Palma is a more precise and manageable target grid. We know exactly where to direct the electromagnetic waves using the existing geo-survey data as a marker beacon. We're not causing the event, but hastening something that will eventually occur sometime in the future," Osama said smiling, as he poured himself another cup of tea.

"A naturally occurring catastrophe from an unnatural weapon…how fitting," Pencor said with a smile.

"And what's the progress of your plans for the worldwide deployment of your Zero Point Generators, or ZPGs as you call them?" Osama asked, tapping the stub of his missing fingertip on the polished desktop.

"Production is continuing, and, the first two shipments from my production facility in Safi, Morocco, can set sail at a moment's notice. You may not realize it, but the facility on Tenerife is powered by a smaller version of my industrial ZPG that I plan to deploy worldwide," Pencor said proudly. "The unrealized quest of a few scientists in America was ultimately silenced by the oil industry's strangle hold on energy, along with the power of their money to buy out greedy politicians. Their dream of free power from the vacuum went unrealized, much to my benefit," Pencor said as he picked up his briefcase and set it on Osama's desk. "The prototype powering my production facility in Morocco has been on line and producing energy for the last two years with flawless results. Imagine, my friend, virtually free energy from a process that has been known to be feasible since its discovery by Tesla in the early 1900s; the Zero Point field theory. Energy from the vacuum of space and time that is going to change the course of history, and *we* will have complete control of it," Pencor exclaimed with excitement in his voice. "The world will see us as the saviors of mankind with the result being a clean environment and an unlimited source of energy. The theory can even be applied to vehicles in the near future and *we* will be in control of it all."

"For a price, of course," Osama added.

"Of course, Yagato," he replied with a grin. "My planned assault on an unsuspecting United States will no doubt result in its economic and infrastructural collapse, the likes the world has never seen. Confusion and chaos will reign supreme. Then, after a short period, we will roll out our ZPGs for global distribution. The oil cartels of the world will eventually collapse. Fossil fuels, as we know them, will eventually go the way of the dinosaur," Pencor said, chuckling at the irony as he opened his briefcase. "The Middle East sheiks and South American despots can all choke on their oil. Before too long, they won't be able to give it away. Take a look, Yagato," he said proudly as he slid the briefcase to face him. "Here are all my final design plans and patents. They will be revealed to the world after our little surprise. No one will ever see the connection, and we will be long gone soon after the weapon has successfully achieved its goal. Until then, Yagato, I want you to safeguard my documents. You have the manpower for it."

"It will be my pleasure, Robert. What about the money?" Osama asked politely as he noted at the stacks of money in the briefcase.

"It's all here, as promised; ten million dollars American currency, plus a contractual 30 percent of all future profits from the ZPGs as they come on-line worldwide. I've waited years for this moment, and can now see success within my grasp. I will not allow anything to interfere with our plans. Speaking of which, I have heard the report of a group of archaeologists beginning work near our facility on Tenerife."

"Yes, Robert. We are aware of their project, and I have made my displeasure known to the fool who approved their permits to excavate the site. They are close to our facility; too close for my liking. When the news of their discovery leaked, the media was everywhere and asking for access to our plant for interviews. They even want camera access over-looking the site they are working on," Osama said.

"We cannot afford prying eyes this close to the success of our plans, Yagato. I trust you will rectify the matter at once," Pencor said, his voice rising in anger.

"I am leaving for Tenerife tomorrow to handle the situation myself, Robert. The island official's assistant who approved the project met with an unfortunately fatal car accident this morning. It was taken care of by my security head at the facility. He knows I do not tolerate failure and took care of the matter personally. I am also concerned that we may have a few scientists at our facility who are having second thoughts about following through with the plan. I will deal with them and the archeology team, who will sadly meet with an unfortunate, fatal mishap," Osama said flatly.

"Very well then. I'll be arriving at your facility in a few days for the final phase and pick up my patents, but first I must finish inspecting the plant in Morocco. I want no loose ends, Yagato. Do you understand? I also want no suspicions aroused when the archaeologists are eliminated. It *must* look like an accident."

"Accidents happen all the time, my dear friend," Osama replied as the powerful Oyabun bowed politely and began to laugh.

4

Bishamon Facility, Tenerife

Two days later, a nervous Yashiro Fuiruchirudo sat at his computer terminal staring at the screen in front of him. His job was to monitor the Longitudinal Wave Interferometer levels, but his mind was elsewhere. The very essence of his soul screamed to him that taking this assignment was the greatest mistake of his life.

They are going to kill me, he thought as he glanced around the Bishamon Facility Command Center. Its sterile environment of metal desks was set in an arc around the wall of a circular room. A large monitor hung from the ceiling at the head of the semi-circle making it look like a cheap Hollywood version of the bridge of a Star Ship. The rear of the room was occupied by banks of electrical circuit panels with large throw switches, and manned by ominous looking men carrying weapons.

Yashiro made his hourly log entry that listed the power output level. He once again sadly noticed the empty chair next to his formerly occupied by his friend and confidant Wari.

Wari had disappeared the night after they discussed their plans to escape the facility of which they were now prisoners, forced to work on Yagato Osama's sick plan of destruction.

Could it be they overheard our talk over dinner the other night? And now that monster Osama is here, he thought, noting his arrival to the complex center this morning. *They must have used the Mind Snapper on Wari.*

Yashiro had seen the Mind Snapper, or psycho-energetic longitudinal electromagnetic gun, a weapon that Osama and his minions used freely and often. Yashiro had seen the results of this terrible gun. It had been used on more than one of the islanders who were caught trying to break into the equipment facility building on the other side of the compound over the past year. Osama always ordered the scientists and technicians to witness the executions as a way to convey what fate would befall anyone who betrayed or failed him.

Yashiro knew the electromagnetic wave gun, set at a low power, could cause all those in its interference zone to fall unconscious. At high levels of output, death would be instant by destroying the entire human nervous system. Every living cell in the body was effectively killed at once, including bacteria. A body hit by this weapon was reduced to the likeness of irradiated meat and horrifically preserved up to thirty days without decay.

In a single flash of immense pain you no longer existed, Yashiro thought, imagining the terrible way his friend must have died.

Yashiro Fuiruchirudo was a brilliant geo-physicist. Graduated from Kobe University at top of his class, he held high hopes for a promising career. That is until he was approached by representatives of the Bishamon Corporation to work on a proposed new energy concept. He was told at the time that it would be a two-year project and it was to be kept confidential. This meant no contact with outsiders, including family, for the entire period.

At first Yashiro was hesitant. However, they offered a small fortune, which would be of benefit to his wife and young son, whom he now missed, and most likely would never see again.

He had figured out the planned assault on America in just the last two months. He overheard a conversation in the control center between Osama and Robert Pencor on Pencor's arrival to inspect the facility. They abruptly halted their conversation when they suspected Yashiro was listening. The stare Pencor gave him had frightened him, but nothing was ever said. Eventually, all the scientists conscripted were made privy to the plan, which troubled him.

At first, Bishamon Corporation successfully kept the different aspects of the project isolated by segmenting the jobs and keeping the workers apart. However, it didn't take long for him and the others to come to the obvious conclusion that this was not an energy project, but rather a pre-empted strike with a frightening weapon.

"What kind of monster would mercilessly kill millions of innocent people?" Yashiro had asked Wari that last night over dinner while they discussed the fearsome plan. "I have a brother who lives in Miami," he said to Wari as they ate.

56

"I know, Yashiro, I also have family in New York," Wari told him. "We will be responsible for their deaths as well."

"Not if we can stop it before it happens," Yashiro said. "We must escape this facility and warn the authorities of the weapon."

"How can we?" Wari said in frustration. "The guards are everywhere and watch every entrance by closed circuit monitor."

"We can escape through the lava tubes beneath the complex that are used to take in supplies from the helicopter pad built on the eastern side of the mountain. It was there where they first excavated for access to the facility when it was constructed. I helped in the design early on and know the cave is not monitored," Yashiro said sipping his coffee. "Every Friday they bring in supplies and take out refuse. That is when we will hide in one of the containers being taken out, which is done a few hours prior to the arrival of the helicopter. After they have sealed the entrance to the facility above us, we'll leave through the tunnel, climb to the caldera's rim, and make our way to the access road."

"What if we are caught, Yashiro? They will kill us for sure!"

"I fear they are going to kill all of us anyway, Wari. They are not going to allow any witnesses to their plans the luxury of leaving this place alive. Especially now they have told us of their plans," Yashiro said in despair.

"Then we'll do it," Wari said with determination. "We'll have to wait a few more days, but in the meantime, we can't act suspiciously. Agreed?"

"Agreed!" Yashiro told his friend, noticing that a guard

had been watching them with interest.

"We'll complete our plan tomorrow. Be quiet Wari, the guard is approaching us," he whispered, and then broke into a loud laughter as the burly guard came to their table.

"What are you two doing?" The guard had asked, pointing his AK-47 at them.

"Wari was just telling me a funny story from his childhood," Yashiro said in Japanese, mustering up the most disarming smile he could produce. He noticed the fingertip of the guard's left hand missing. "Would you like to hear it?"

"No!" The guard blurted out. "You have been here long enough. Return to your quarters at once."

That was the last time Yashiro had seen Wari, and he now assumed that he was either dead or under interrogation. *If they torture him, they will learn of our plan and I'm a dead man for sure*, Yashiro thought now as he stared vacantly at the computer screen in front of him. *I must hold it together for two more days before I try to escape.*

He continued working as he listened to the steady hum of the Longitudinal Wave Interferometer generators located one floor below him. It slowly, but surely, proceeded in its uninterrupted task, which he knew would result in the destruction of the east coast of the United States.

"I must remain focused," he whispered softly. "I must."

5

Grand Canaria Island

After four mind-numbing days in and out of the Commissioner of Cultural Affairs Office in Las Palmas, Turner finally sat in his room at the Hotel Lattagia with the preliminary legal permits for research excavation in his hands. He hated the dance, as he called it, with the local bureaucrats. *They always find a way to delay the process in an attempt to appear relevant in their impious, little world,* Turner thought, tossing the hard fought papers onto the dresser. Adding to the difficulty was the little joke Samuel had played on the commissioner when they applied for permits to excavate the pyramid.

Turner laughed aloud thinking how Samuel, annoyed by the six day wait, had sent the commissioner a nicely wrapped box containing one thousand year old fossilized goat feces as a thank you. *Evidently, the man has a good memory.*

Turner then made a phone call booking the ferry passage back to Tenerife tomorrow for him and Samuel.

Although they could have flown, it was only a four-hour cruise between the two islands. Turner enjoyed the passage, even though being on the open water still brought back frightful memories of that fateful night in New Guinea.

He had seen the message light blinking on the hotel phone when he returned from the commissioner's office but avoided checking it.

It can wait, Turner thought as he grabbed the remote for the room's old TV set. I'm sure Dad is driving everyone nuts with his unyielding protocol when it comes to new digs. I'd just be in the way.

Turner had last spoken to his father two days ago. His father had reported that with the help of Carlos Santiago, the teams and equipment had been successfully transferred from the Pyramid site and the work on the new site had finally begun. He told Turner the students were assigned to documenting and recovering the Guanche artifacts, while he and Maria were keeping the mysterious tomb sealed.

Now waiting for Samuel's return with something to eat, Turner vacantly surfed through the channels on the television. He came to an abrupt halt on the Grand Canaria Channel 3 News where a story in progress made him stare at the TV in disbelief. Standing in front of a nine-by-six foot white canvas tent on the familiar slopes of Tenerife, were his father and Maria. Both looked a bit overwhelmed by all the lights and cameras pointed at them. In Spanish, the news anchor was just finishing his narration of the news segment.

"—that being said, media crews, treasure hunters, and the religious faithful have been arriving here to be a part of this amazing find. This discovery, if true, may turn out to be one of the most significant finds since the discovery and excavation of King Tutankhamun's tomb by Howard Carter in 1922. Stay tuned for weather and sports, coming up next—"

Turner quickly fumbled with the remote and scrolled through the channels. He stopped on another news broadcast where he saw a photo of his father in the upper corner of the screen as the news anchor reported.

"—It came from an anonymous source at the University of Jerusalem, just two days ago, the news that a team of archaeologists may have found a clue to the location of the mystical Holy Grail in a tomb below the summit of the island's extinct volcano, El Teide. Centuries of search and speculation have always failed to prove the existence of this early Christian symbol, but now Dr. Eli Turner and his team may have discovered evidence to its whereabouts on the island of Tenerife in the Canary Islands. The reference to the Grail, the cup supposedly use by Christ during the Last Supper, was found written on an ancient parchment discovered in an old Guanche tomb.

Critics of the discovery, such as Alton Burr, question the validity of such a find. Burr, founder of the Secular America Movement, said in a statement that he would stop at nothing to prove this to be just another fraud perpetrated by the religious community in their continued attempt to control the minds of free thinking people worldwide. Burr, a former ACLU lawyer has rumored that he is considering running for Senate in next year's race in New York. When questioned about Burr's statement, Dr. Eli Turner merely laughed and walked away from our reporters. In other news tonight—"

Turner clicked the television off and stared at the darkened screen in stunned silence. He rose from his chair and walked over to the phone where he dialed the hotel message system. After the pause, he heard his father's voice.

"Josh, it's Dad. Maria and I are up to our ears in news reporters and others here at the site. Things are getting a bit crazy, so if you can get back as soon as you can, it'd be a big help. I'm losing the phone signal, Josh…I'll get back to you as soon as I can when we get the satellite phone from Paulo. I love you, Son. Bye."

With a click, the line went dead. Turner knew in his heart that something was wrong and his father needed him. It had been years since he'd said he loved him. Turner heard him say it at the funeral for his mother after she had been killed in an auto accident when he was five years old. From that point on, his father had buried his feelings; never really talking to him. Every time he tried to get close to him, his father would effectively shut him out. Finally, after years of trying, Turner had given up.

He quickly started packing his duffel bag when the phone rang and startled him. Turner sprang to the phone and lifted the receiver.

"Dad!" He shouted into the phone, hoping it was his father.

"Hi, Son," came his father's voice. "I'm calling from the satellite phone at the site. Did you get my message?"

"Yes, Dad, at noon tomorrow, Samuel and I are leaving on the next ferry back to Tenerife. We should be back at the site by nightfall."

"That's good news, Josh. We could use the help. Besides, Middle Eastern antiquities have always been your forte. I just hope you still want to work with me. With all that has been going on, Josh, I've been doing a lot of soul searching and I owe you an apology. I know I haven't been much of a father to you," Eli said, his voice cracking a little.

"No, Dad. You don't need to explain…."

"I loved your mom with all my heart, Son. And when she died, something inside me died as well. I realize now that I've been trying to push you away; trying to avoid ever being hurt like that again. It's as if…."

"You know I love you, Dad, and I want to be there working with you."

"Thanks, Son. I love you, too. I'm getting too old to be doing this work, Josh. When ICAP is securely established, I plan on retiring and I want you to take over."

"Are you sure about that, Dad?" Josh said, fighting back his emotions. "I think Kim Liao would be a better choice."

"He couldn't hold a candle to your skills, Son. And I wouldn't trust anyone else in keeping the organization going."

After a moment of awkward silence Turner said, "Thanks, Dad.

I promise to make you proud."

"You already have, Son," the elder Turner replied softly, then quickly cleared his throat and continued. "We've had the camp set up and going for a few days now, and have completed much of the excavation in the Guanche tomb. Maria and a few of the students from the University plotted and photographed the entire tomb before removing the contents. We must be sure we do this right.

Many people are watching this one, Josh. Imagine…the possibility of discovering a true reference to the cup of the

Last Supper."

"I just saw the news reports. It's all over the media," Turner said. "How did word leak out, Dad?"

"Unfortunately, it was leaked by one of the students assigned to Hiram Rabib, in Jerusalem. Hiram apologized soon afterward and promised that any further discoveries requiring translation would be done by him personally, and with the highest discretion. All hell was breaking loose here for the first few days, Son. Fortune hunters, religious zealots, and the media were circling around here like vultures," Eli said with frustration in his voice. "Carlos was finally able to send some men from the Tenerife National Guard to protect our discoveries, and our assess. I don't mind saying I'm still a bit nervous. Fortunately, things seem to be calming down."

"Are you sure that you and Maria are safe, Dad? I'm worried about the possibility of crazies coming out of the woodwork."

"Yeah, we've already had a few of them, but Captain Saune and his men are doing a fine job discouraging folks from getting too close. Thankfully, the crowds are starting to thin out by the hour because we haven't reported any findings other than Guanche artifacts."

"Dad, are you sure this discovery could be the real deal? I mean, parchments have been forged in the past by antiquities bootleggers with great accuracy. These so called Holy Grail stories have been popping up for as long as there have been people around to listen."

"We received the carbon dating reports from samples of the parchment we sent to the university this morning, Josh. They've been dated to the first century A.D. The extreme dry climate and w its being sealed for so long in the lava tube preserved it nicely and with little contamination. I hope that we'll find more inside the sealed tomb when we enter it tomorrow."

"Dad, I know you are the best in your field," Turner said with concern in his voice, "but I want you to be careful, okay? We may have opened a hornet's nest. I saw on the news that this guy named Burr was—"

"Yeah, I know all about Mr. Alton Burr," Eli interrupted. "That clown had the nerve to telegraph me demanding he be present during our work. Of course, I told him to go to hell," Eli said with a chuckle. "Alright Son, I have to go. I have a ton of work to do. I'll look for you and Samuel tomorrow after sunset."

"Okay, Dad. Be careful. Bye."

He hung up the phone just as Samuel entered the room. He was balancing two sealed containers in one hand.

"Your favorite, amigo," he said, setting the plastic containers down on the table, "stewed goat meat."

Turner just looked at him and said, "Samuel, I just got off the phone with my dad. We've got to get back to Tenerife. Something isn't right."

***

Late afternoon on the following day, the sun, now descending behind the towering heights of Mt. Teide, cast finger-like shadows on the archeology camp situated on the lower plateau below. The site was set up directly in front the newly exposed opening to the ancient volcanic lava tube containing the Guanche tomb found by Maria and Samuel.

The cool afternoon breeze was a welcome relief to Eli Turner. He watched as the last bus made its way down the hastily constructed access road toward Guimar, connecting to Rt. 82 and the main highway toward Santa Cruz.

"I'm glad that is over with," Eli said as he tugged the brim of his outback hat. He began making his way back up the loose, rock- laden path toward a large twelve-by-nine foot A-framed canvas tent.

The tent, fifteen feet from the tunnel entrance served as a holding station for artifacts before being shipped off to the university. A smattering of smaller A-frame tents were erected about the perimeter, serving as sleeping quarters for workers and students assigned to the team.

One khaki tent Eli Turner was relieved to see stood off near the edge of the path leading down the slope. It served as the quarters for a team of four men from the *Guardia Civil*, or the National Guard of Tenerife. They were assigned to the team at the request of Carlos Santiago to protect the site and keep the throng of spectators, including the media, at bay. Eli saw two of the guardsmen, wearing their faded, green battle dress uniforms sitting in front of their tent smoking as they tended to their campfire.

As he had planned, the bus now left with the remnants of workers and archeology students from San Fernando University back to Santa Cruz, with the final cache of Guanche artifacts. It was there they would catalog and secured them at the anthropology lab.

In the past four days, the crowds of curious onlookers and scores of media crews had slowly dwindled as Eli hoped for. Now, with the site free of the media and observers, the work on the sealed tomb where the parchment was discovered could begin. His purposefully concocted, boring sci-tech babble had driven off most of the television crews by the third day. With the forecast of light rain imminent tonight, he knew it was the perfect time for them to begin work on the sealed burial tomb.

Couldn't have planned it any better, Eli thought smugly as he tapped his extinguished pipe onto his boot heel and emptied its contents before entering the tent.

Opening the canvas tent flap, he saw Maria sitting at a metal table preoccupied with her computer. She was unaware of his arrival amid the drone of the portable generator providing power to the camp.

"Why don't you take a break, Maria?" Eli said as she quickly turned, startled by his sudden appearance.

"Oh, Dr. Turner, I didn't notice you come in. I'm just finishing uploading the digital photos to the computer," she said with a smile that revealed to Eli a distinct weariness in her eyes after the many long days working on this project.

"The last bus just left for the university," Eli said, pulling up a chair and sitting down next to her. "This has been quite an extraordinary find, wouldn't you say, Maria?"

"This has to be the best quality Guanche artifacts and remains found to date, Dr. Turner. I'd go as far as saying this was the burial site for an important Guanche Chieftain, most likely a tribal leader and his family. The anthropology department is going to have a field day with the nearly perfect mummified remains we have found," Maria said as she saved the last file. "Even the cloth remnants are in pristine condition, which must be because of the tomb being sealed off from the climate for so many centuries. Absolutely, a marvelous find," she repeated softly as she slipped the backup CD into a sleeve and shut down her laptop.

"Tonight looks like a go for us to begin work on the remaining sealed tomb where you found the parchment," Eli said with a mischievous smile. "I had a feeling the crowds would become bored after a few days of nothing spectacular to report, and, with rain in the forecast tonight, we won't be bothered with people looking over our shoulders. That way we can take our time doing a thorough study and documentation."

"It will be good to see Josh again, Dr. Turner. I'm glad he and Samuel are finished on Grand Canaria. When will they be here?" Maria asked, carefully placing her laptop into its shock-proof metal case.

"They should get here later this evening. I sent Paulo to the ferry landing in Santa Cruz to pick them up."

"Sure, he gets here after all the grunt work is finished," Maria said with mock indignation.

"I'll be glad to see him," Eli said. "I look forward to working with him on this phase of the project."

They rose from their seats and were walking to the entrance of the tent, when they met one of the National Guardsmen coming in.

Captain Rafael Saune was a hulking figure of a man possessing a no-nonsense persona. Normally stationed at the *Guardia Civil* barracks located near Santa Cruz, he and his three men had been assigned to the dig to maintain security at the site. His gruff attitude the past days failed to mask his pleasure at getting such a light duty assignment for a week or two. This saved him from the daily grind of inspections and the constant reports he had to file. As a twenty year veteran, he had risen up among the ranks and become a trusted adviser to the Island administration. He also served now and then as helicopter pilot, providing tours to the many dignitaries that came to Tenerife.

"Dr. Turner, there's a man here to see you," the Captain reported. "I told him to wait in the parking area below. He demands to speak with you. Shall I send him away?"

"Demands to see me, huh? No, Captain, I'll see him now. Probably a reporter," Eli said exhaling wearily. "I'll bore him to death with more monotonous details. I'm sure he'll soon find an excuse to leave."

The three exited the tent and started down the dry and dusty path of crumbling basalt rock, ever mindful of their steps. At the base of the path in the hastily constructed parking area, a man paced back and forth beside an old Jeep CJ-5. Eli chuckled at the sight of the short, well-groomed man wearing blue jeans, a khaki safari shirt, and new white sneakers; making him look quite out of place in this rugged setting. Eli could faintly hear him talking to himself as he frantically paced back and forth, holding a piece of paper in his hand.

Alton Burr was a man not accustomed to waiting for anything, or anyone. His years as a lawyer with the ACLU had hardened and fine-tuned him into a calculated master of intimidation. Now, with his newly established influence in many Washington political circles, and, the growing popularity of his Secular America Movement, he now garnered an arrogance unsurpassed by even the most pompous of Washington's career politicians.

Burr was on a mission. His strong belief in the separation of church and state had been twisted into a vendetta to persecute all organized religions wherever, and whenever, he could. Fueled by the fires of anger, he and his legal teams left a trail of disillusioned and broken communities in their wake. Many state and local governments they litigated were forced to adhere to judge-mandated policies, limiting a community's right to exercise all religious acts or display religious art in public places. Be they Christian, Muslim, Hindu, or Buddhist, they were *all* in his cross-hairs.

Alton Burr's anger-driven persecution of organized religion had not always been the case. As a young man, newly graduated from Harvard Law School, he looked to the future with a bright optimism and open mind. However, September 11, 2001 changed all that forever. His parents had been in the second of the Twin Towers in New York City. In stunned horror, he watched it collapse before his eyes on television, which also effectively collapsed a part of his mind and soul. When he attended their funeral service, something inside him snapped when the priest mentioned something about it "all being God's will."

"A god's will?" He had cried in a rage at their grave side. "What kind of a god would let my parents die that way?" From that moment on, his anguish manifested into fiery hatred of theism, and of those promoting any religious or spiritual reasoning. Oh yes, he acknowledged God, but only in the sense of blaming Him for his parents unwarranted death. Thus, he'd set out on his personal crusade of purging gods and organized religion wherever he could find it.

After a successful stint with the ACLU, Burr founded the Secular America Movement with support amassed through major donations from ultra-left groups and secular organizations. He quickly became popular within its ranks through his fiery zeal and relentless tenacity. With vast support from his many friends, he now began focusing his aspirations on political office, where he could affect legislation to their benefit.

He came to Tenerife to make sure that any possible pro-religious agenda, brought about by the discovery of any artifacts, would be discredited. If some margin of authenticity to this archeology find became a reality, Burr felt that it could be a major setback in his goal and a hindrance to his political ambitions.

No, he thought on the ride to the dig site, *I won't allow that to happen.*

Eli and Maria reached the parking lot and walked over to the man, who now stopped his pacing and now stood next to his vehicle, glaring at them as they approached.

The captain stood close behind, watching the man intently while the other three guardsmen watched in curiosity from the higher ground at their tent. "Are you Turner?" Burr asked, waving the piece of paper in his hand.

"Last time I checked," Eli replied, annoyed by the little man's attitude. "This is my protégé Maria Santiago. What is it you wish to see me about?"

"You have a lot of nerve sending me a telegram with your smart-assed reply to my request to observe the work here," Burr said as he waved the telegram in Eli's face.

"So, you are Mr. Alton Burr," Eli said smiling, his deep blue eyes focused in an unwavering gaze. This unsettled Burr even more. "I meant what I said, Burr. You, your high priced lawyers, and your group of misguided minions can all go to hell. If you need directions, Captain Saune here will be glad to give them to you," Eli retorted in a menacing tone that surprised even Maria.

"I demand that you grant access to this project," Burr shrieked, his voice rising in crescendo as his anger boiled over. "People have the right to know that you and your team are not trying to deceive them."

"How dare you question Dr. Turner's integrity?" Maria yelled in anger. "His work has always been—"

"Don't let him get to you Maria," Eli said, calmly interrupting her. "He's not worth it."

"I'm sorry, Dr. Turner, but I can't allow someone to criticize your work with no justification."

"Mr. Burr, my decision still stands," Eli said. "I am director of this project, and I'm not going to risk its contamination by you or any other unauthorized personnel. Everything here is being done in a precise scientific manner and unlike you, Burr; we cherish the ideology of integrity in our work. When the time comes, whatever we discover *will* be presented in a professional and truthful manner to the scientific community. Until that time, you have no jurisdiction here, so I suggest you kindly take your concerns to the Tenerife Island Administration."

"You won't get away with this, Turner!" Burr hissed as he approached within inches of the elder man's face and stared into his bright blue eyes. "I'll make sure of it."

"Captain Saune," Turner said, holding his steady gaze into Burr's eyes, "will you show our guest the way out?"

"With pleasure, Dr. Turner," the Captain said, smiling as his bulking figure started toward the lawyer.

"You haven't seen the last of me!" Burr shouted as he turned and stormed back to his jeep, his fists clenched in rage. The three watched the CJ-5 speed back down the access road, throwing debris behind it as its wheels spun wildly in the loose gravel.

"That guy is a nut case," Eli said as they turned and headed back up the path toward the camp.

"Do you think he means it, Dr. Turner?" Maria asked hesitantly, a bit unnerved by the encounter. "Will he cause us any trouble?"

"I'm not sure, Maria, but we should keep an eye open for trouble. Captain Saune, you and your men might want to be extra vigilant from this moment on," Eli said.

"We're on it, Dr. Turner," the captain said. He added, "I see our audience is back." Saune pointed to a black vehicle high above them on the caldera's rim access road.

"Yes, I saw them, too," Eli said as he peered up toward the ridge. "They've been sitting there for about an hour."

"Who are they?" Maria asked, looking up at the dark vehicle shaded by the late afternoon shadows.

"My guess is they are from that Bishamon Research facility just beyond the rim on one of the caldera's plateaus," the captain replied. "They seem to have taken quite an interest in what you have been doing here."

"They make me nervous," Maria said, her voice just above a whisper. "My father warned us about staying clear of that place. He did say something about people disappearing."

"I can understand them wanting their security, but why would a Japanese research facility be so interested in us?" Eli asked as they reached the plateau of their camp.

"I don't know, Dr. Turner, but I'm not comfortable with it," the captain replied as he split away from the two. He was heading back to the Guard tent where the other three guardsmen were tending their camp fire for the coming evening. "You also might be interested in knowing that Bishamon is the Japanese God of War," Captain Saune yelled as he walked away from the two archaeologists.

"Hmm…strange name for a scientific facility," Eli said. "Oh well, let's get a fire going and have supper, Maria. It's going to be a busy night."

As the two walked slowly into the tent, the dark sinister vehicle high above them silently rode out of view, its occupants already planning the coming night's work.

The Lava Tube was eerily dark and quiet now that everyone had departed for Santa Cruz with the artifacts. The kerosene lanterns carried by Eli Turner and Maria projected ghostly silhouettes against the smooth, black basalt walls as they walked onward, deeper into the recesses of the lava tube.

Following closely behind them with flashlights in hand were Captain Saune, armed with his 45-caliber sidearm, and one of his privates, his M-16 loosely slung over his shoulder.

Eli knew that Maria was not happy about the men carrying their weapons, but the captain had insisted considering the events that transpired earlier that day. Eli told Saune that he had an uneasy feeling, so Saune left the other two guardsmen on post outside at the guard tent. They were to keep an eye on the camp, while he and the private would keep watch over the two archaeologists working inside the cave.

Eli led the small group carrying a backpack with his usual fare: pointing trowels, a tape measure, a horsehair brush, a small hammer, and a chisel for chipping away at the harder sediment. He also threw in a few sandwiches for later. Maria carried her backpack bearing a notepad, a digital camera, and water canteens, plus two night-vision goggles in the unlikely event the lanterns would fail.

They slowly walked past the recently excavated tombs located on various levels of the cave which was honey combed with carved-out chambers.

Turner marveled at how the chambers held the mummified Guanche remains for almost two thousand years. According to the ancient tribal hierarchy of the Guanche culture: the higher the chamber in the catacomb, the more important its occupant's status. The four made their way to the location of the last sealed chamber. Beyond it, the lava tube continued upward into the darkness of the dormant volcano through a narrow opening.

"This is it," Eli exclaimed, setting his lantern down close to the sealed chamber entrance and dropping his backpack.

The entrance to the ancient crypt was about three feet in diameter. Sealed for the centuries by a flat chiseled piece of limestone, the Ichthus symbol on the cover stone was now clearly visible since Eli had treated it earlier that day with a mild acid solution.

"It looks like the centuries of natural settlement have fashioned a tight seal around the cover stone. We'll have to chisel it out carefully," Maria said.

"We'll take turns chipping away at the natural rock that surrounds the cover stone so we don't damage it," Eli said to Maria as he pulled the tools from his pack.

"Fine by me, Dr. Turner," Maria replied, digging out the digital camera from her pack. "I'll start taking some photos."

"You gentlemen might as well get comfortable," Eli said to Captain Saune and the private, who looked and felt out of place inside this volcanic lava chamber.

"We'll stand watch over there," the captain said, pointing to a recently abandoned burial chamber because it commanded a view of the pathway leading back to the entrance.

Leaving the two archaeologists, the soldiers walked to the empty chamber. Climbing in, they slumped down against a wall and switched off their lights.

"Okay, Maria, let's get started," Eli said as he started to chip away at the basalt rock. "It's going to be a long night."

After fifteen minutes, Maria took over the task. This routine continued for more than two hours before the last of the basalt rock surrounding the cover stone was finally removed, freeing it from its earthen lock. By then, both Maria and Eli were coated in perspiration from the work, causing them to feel a slight chill from the cave's cool interior. Putting the tools away, Eli stared for a long moment at the freed stone, his mind wondering what could lay beyond the seal in front of them.

He glanced over to where Captain Saune and his subordinate sat silently in the darkness of their chamber, their presence made known only by the glowing embers of their cigarettes in the surrounding blackness.

Outside the cave, the two guardsmen chatted silently about their upcoming leave after this assignment, unaware their lives were about to end. As they quietly conversed, silent forms stealthily approached them in the blackness. A light falling rain hissed as tiny droplets hit the red-hot embers of their campfire.

6

Yashiro Fuiruchirudo slowly inched his way through the Bishamon facility's main utility shaft. The narrow, steel corridor ran the entire length of the complex. It carried the complex's power, communication cables, and, the building's fresh water supply, which was fed from a gravity tank located outside of the building. Though cramped and covered with dust, it was large enough for a man to traverse safely.

Yashiro ceased his crawling every ten feet or so to catch his breath or to wait in stark terror as people passed directly below him in the corridor that ran parallel to the shaft. His heart pounding in his chest, he moved closer to the end of the darkened passageway that ended abruptly over the supply and refuse storage room at the far end of the facility. The room contained the refuse bins that would be lowered down to the excavated lava tube below the complex.

A helipad was constructed on a level surface just below the outer entrance to the lava tube. Yashiro knew the Sikorsky CH- 53K heavy-lift helicopter was due in the morning to re-supply the facility and take out refuse.

If all goes well, I'll be long gone by then, he thought as he reached one of the ventilator grates that offered a view of the corridor below.

Yashiro held no doubt that his plan was a long shot at best, but fear had overcome reason at this point. He knew in his heart that if he remained, he would surely die.

Seeing no one below, he inched carefully toward the final grate that would ultimately lead to his freedom. As he crawled onward, he vividly recounted in his mind the encounter he had with Yagato Osama earlier that day. There was no doubt now in his mind about the plans he and Robert Pencor had in store for millions of unsuspecting people in the United States.

Yashiro had been at his workstation monitoring EM levels as usual that morning when one of the guards came to his desk and ordered him to follow. The two went down the corridor to the stairway that led to the complex's second level, which housed the suites, security, and conference rooms. Walking up the stairway, they approached the door of the suite belonging to Yagato Osama.

This is it, I'm a dead man, Yashiro thought in terror as they entered the room. He saw Osama sitting at his desk, sipping a cup of tea. He then smiled an evil, knowing grin that caused Yashiro's stomach to convulse.

"Good morning, Yashiro," Osama said in an animated voice. "I'm so glad you could join me."

"Good morning, Mr. Osama," Yashiro replied as he nervously looked around the room.

"Leave us," he barked to the guard, "and wait outside the door."

After the guard obediently left the room and closed the

door behind him, Osama gestured for Yashiro to sit in one of the three chairs that was conspicuously placed in the center of the room. "Yashiro, you have been part of our project since its inception and have done great service to our planned success. That is why it pains me to discover that you want to leave our little project before its completion," Osama said. "I want to know if anyone else in the facility shares your sentiment."

"No one that I am aware of, Mr. Osama," Yashiro said as Osama stared coldly at him.

"As one of our more astute scientists, I'm sure you are aware of our plan and know that we are close to its final stages."

"Yes, I know of your plan, but I don't understand. Why would you want to kill millions of innocent people?" Yashiro asked bravely, knowing it mattered little since he had been found out.

"It's not your business to understand why our benefactor, Mr. Pencor, wants to use our expensive toys," Osama hissed. "The Scalar Interferometer wave is on schedule thanks to your diligent work and we can go to optimum EM levels in two days. I am willing to forgive your poor lapse in judgment, but you must realize that you cannot remain here. With Pencor arriving here today, the final plans will proceed and I want no mistakes. "

"Pencor is coming here?" Yashiro asked in surprise.

"Yes, that's why I have a special assignment for you. I am sending you on tomorrow morning's helicopter supply flight to Pencor's plant in Morocco. You'll be overseeing the production of the Zero Point Generators that he has been manufacturing for shipment. You *are* versed in the technology of Zero Point energy, are you not?"

"I have studied the research of nuclear scientists working on the process in the United States and the use of Scalar weapons,"

Yashiro said. "They have had minor success in developing a test device in a laboratory setting only. I know the device produces an output that exceeds the level of its energy input, thus, creating a self-sustaining supply of energy." Yashiro remembered how amazed he had been after discovering the fully operational Zero Point Generator located in the lower level of the facility. "Basically," Yashiro continued, "it's free magnetic energy, which can be replenished indefinitely from the vacuum of everything around us. If Pencor has succeeded in this quest to mass produce the ZPGs, why wouldn't he want to share it with the world instead of devastating the entire eastern seaboard of the United States?"

"The opportunity for unbounded wealth and absolute power," Osama replied. "In the wake of a massive natural catastrophe, can you think of a better way to control a country than by having a strangle-hold on its power needs? With the money Pencor paid us for the development of our Scalar weapon technology, we provided Pencor the means to consummate his mad quest for vengeance while reaping vast profits as well. From our share of the profits in the Zero Point Generator deployment worldwide, the Yakuza will posture itself in not only becoming a dominant political force in Japan, but also a major player in the geopolitical arena. What that madman Pencor does is of no concern to me as long as the Yakuza reap the benefits. So, it is settled; you will leave in the morning," Osama said flatly.

"You're letting me leave?" Yashiro asked, knowing the truth. He knew Osama would never let him leave the complex alive knowing so much of their plans.

"Yes, Yashiro," Osama said with annoyance in his voice. "You will be paid for your work here. Once in Morocco, I expect you to oversee the technical development at the factory and report directly to me."

Yashiro knew at that moment he was marked for death and he would never see the morning. Osama was toying with him, hoping he would lead him to any other scientists that shared his reservations.

His mind raced with thoughts of his wife and son, and of Wari. "Where is my friend Wari?" He asked with false bravado.

"Your friend suddenly took ill and taken to the hospital in Santa Cruz," Osama responded quickly. "You need not worry about him."

Yashiro knew at that point his friend was most likely dead.

"No more questions. Go back to work and, at the end of your shift, pack your belongings. One of my men will pick them up this evening and take them to the supply room to be loaded on your flight out tomorrow," Osama said in finality.

"Thank you, Yagato-san," Yashiro said politely as he stood on wobbly legs, bowed, and left the office. His mind reeling, he went back to work knowing that he had to try to make his desperate escape attempt before Osama's man came looking for him that evening. He felt the cold stare of the guards watching his every move, knowing it would be a death sentence for anyone he talked to. He had waited until his shift was over to make his move.

Now crawling and sweating profusely, Yashiro finally reached the last ventilator grate and looked down over the supply room beneath him. To his horror, he saw a guard below him with an AK-

47 slung over his shoulder, reading the supply manifest on a clipboard. He remained motionless, fearful that the sound of his heart pounding in his chest would cause the guard to look up. After five agonizing minutes, the guard finally left, closing and locking the door behind him.

It's now or never, Yashiro thought as he lifted the hinged grate open enough for him to get through. Holding on to the water supply pipe running in the middle of the shaft, he lowered his legs through the opening. Letting go of the pipe, he dropped to the floor beneath him with a loud thud. Looking back up, he thankfully saw the grate had fallen back in its proper position, leaving no trace of being disturbed.

Yashiro took note of the four refuse bins on the opposite side of the room next to a hinged metal hatch on the floor. The hatch covered a man-made shaft leading to the lava tube below the complex. As he started to make his way silently toward the refuse bins, he heard the sound of voices coming from the corridor outside the locked door.

In a panic, he leaped over to the closest bin. Lifting its lid, he threw himself inside and landed on a soft mound covered by a canvas tarp. With fear racing through his mind, he squirmed sideways and pulled the canvas tarp free from the mound. He covered himself just as the door to the supply room opened.

Yashiro, with his eyes closed tight in terror, heard the

sound of two men talking as they approached the refuse bins. He felt his bin starting to roll on its metal wheel casters. When Yashiro finally found the courage to open his eyes, he discovered the glazed, dead eyes of his friend Wari staring back at him. Yashiro fought the urge scream as the bile rose from his stomach and caused him to gag.

Even after days, Wari's body was perfectly preserved with no sign of decomposition because of the Psycho-Energetic Mind Snap gun. Only his slightly glazed eyes showed any hint of death.

The anger of the senseless murder of his friend now overcame his fear. He knew this was the fate planned for him if he remained. Yashiro steadied himself to the task at hand, as he heard the sound of the motor that opened the large metal hatchway leading to the tunnel below. He felt his bin starting to swing freely as it was lifted by a pulley that attached to four corner hooks of the refuse bin. Yashiro held his breath, hearing the sound of the electric motor to the lift diminish in volume as the bin was lowered down onto the tunnel floor below.

Almost there, he thought, feeling the cool air of the lava tube wash into the bin. After a few moments, he felt the soft thud as the bin touched down on the rock floor of the lava tube. He heard one of the men climb down the steel ladder that was attached to the basalt walls and undo the hooks on the refuse bin. The man then pushed Yashiro's escape bin to the side so that he could lower the remaining three.

After what seemed an eternity, Yashiro heard the muffled thud of the metal door above him closing, thrusting him suddenly into an eerie silence. Taking a deep breath, he threw off the canvas that was covering him and climbed out of what was to be Wari's coffin. He knew they would probably dump his body into the sea long before heading to the airport in Santa Cruz.

The small-framed scientist kept still for a moment, allowing his eyes to grow accustomed to the low lights of the lava tube. His eyes adjusting, he noted the tube ascended upward about one hundred eighty feet to the cave entrance and then down to the helipad outside. In the opposite direction, the tunnel made a gradual decent into the deep, dark recesses of the volcano.

Making his way slowly toward the exit of the lava tube, Yashiro saw the first of many overhead lights. They were suspended from an electrical conduit and spaced about thirty feet apart.

He saw one of the emergency kits mounted on the cave wall and opened it to retrieve its halogen light. Yashiro knew they were stored there in the event the complex ZPG power supply ever failed. Being that it was still night time, he knew he would need the light to traverse the rocky terrain of the caldera outside. Yashiro checked his light as he continued walking upward toward the entrance and began to think that, just maybe, his desperate plan would succeed.

Just then, he heard the sound of footfalls coming from ahead of him and his hopes of success were dashed. With no time to get back into the bin, he panicked, turned, and started running for his very life. Headed down the lava tube in the opposite direction, he ran past the ladder as the hatch above was being raised. He then heard the shouts of the men chasing him from behind. Seconds later, the excited shouts in the lava tube were drowned out by the deafening echo of gunfire. Yashiro felt a hot stinging pain in his left arm. Feeling the warm trickle of blood flowing down his forearm, he continued to run and ignore the blinding pain. The light from his halogen lamp flashed wildly on the black basalt walls casting bizarre shadows as he descended into the blackness of the lava tube.

7

Around the same time Yashiro had been crawling through the ventilator shaft in his attempt at freedom, Eli Turner and Maria Santiago were painstakingly sliding the circular stone slab from the entrance of the tomb sealed for almost two thousand years.

Out of breath and exhausted from their endeavor, they laid the cover stone gently on the floor of the cave. The two silently looked into the darkened tomb, both lost in thought as to what they might find in its interior. Even the staunch Captain Saune's interest was piqued as he and the private climbed out of their darkened crypt and joined the two archaeologists.

Holding the lantern out in front of him, Eli strained to peer inside as the flickering light reflected the swirling dust surrounding the entrance, disturbed by their recent digging.

"Here, Dr. Turner, use my flashlight," the captain said as he offered his light to Eli. "It has a lot more power to it."

"Thank you, Captain," he said, taking the light and pointing it at the opening. "Let's see what we have inside." He smiled at Maria, then launched out on all fours and crawled head first through the tiny orifice.

Making his way through the entrance, he was immediately struck by the peculiar, muffled silence of the tomb's interior. His eyes now adjusting to the darkness, he focused the beam of light starting from his left, and then slowly scanned along the perimeter of the tomb. The light's beam danced off the glittering crystals embedded in the black basalt rock, then came to rest on a mummified corpse near the rear of the burial chamber.

"Come on in, Maria. We have human remains in here," Eli yelled as he continued his visual sweep of the crypt's interior.

On the far right, he focused the light's beam on an ancient amphora still intact. It was standing upright, surrounded by the scattered potsherds of other broken amphorae that littered the tomb's sandy floor. "Be careful of your hand and foot placements, Maria. There may be other fragments of papyrus lying about."

Maria slowly came up behind him carrying the lantern, which bathed the once darkened room with a soft, yellow ambiance.

"There's not much in here, Dr. Turner," Maria noted, coming to his side.

"I'd never grow tired of this, Maria. Even if the tomb was empty," he said in an awed whisper. "Knowing this crypt was last visited almost twenty centuries ago is quite a humbling experience." "These mummified remains are well preserved," Maria said as the two made their way over to the ancient, dust-covered corpse. She began taking photographs of the remains lying in the thickened dust of what was once bedding. "I'd say this was an adult male, but definitely not a Guanche based on his short stature."

"Maybe this was our friend Simon, whose name was found written on the parchment," Eli offered. "I guess there's no way we'll ever know for sure."

"Look at the condition of that amphora," she said excitedly as she carefully crawled over to the earthen vessel on the other side of the crypt. It was surrounded by the bones of an animal. "Early Mediterranean, and, based on the design, I'd date it around 30 to 60 A.D. Most likely Roman from the design of the two handles at the top and its broad middle. We found others similar to this off the coast of Lanzarote. The animal remains look to be that of a goat."

"Maybe that was this guy's last meal," Eli said with a laugh, pointing back at the human remains.

"Always the pure scientist," she said to him with mock disapproval.

Eli noted the amphora was slightly faded from its centuries of entombment, but its artwork was clearly visible through the film of dust on its exterior. The six-inch opening at the apex was covered by a material that folded down about five inches from the opening, and was wrapped by some cord that effectively sealed its contents.

After she finished taking photos, Maria put the camera in her vest pocket and carefully placed her hand on the amphora's cover, gently feeling the material.

"This is most likely goat skin," she noted, lightly brushing the centuries of dust from the cover.

"It probably belonged to that poor fellow over there," Eli said, pointing to the animal remains lying about. "Let's see if we can get this out to the brighter lights of the cave where we can study it better." Moving around to the back of the amphora, he said, "You take the top end and I'll support the base."

"Okay, Dr. Turner," Maria said as she gently pulled the top toward her. Eli grabbed the base with both hands and gently lifted it. With their prize in tow, the two slowly backed their way out of the crypt and into the main tunnel.

After setting the amphora down on one of the backpacks, Eli gazed at the ancient relic that once used to hold items such as wine, salt fish, and olive oil. In the brighter light of the cave, he could see the intricate dark red pattern painted around the amphora at its center, with smaller curved pattern lines painted toward the opening.

"Hand me my tool kit, Maria. I want to remove the cover skin and see what we have inside before we crate it up and send it to the university," Eli said, kneeling down beside the ancient artifact.

Maria dug out the small tool kit from Eli's backpack and handed it to him as the two soldiers, now intrigued by the find, silently moved closer to get a better view.

"Okay, here goes," he announced as he grabbed the long nose pliers from his kit, then gently started to untwist the ancient twine from the amphora that kept its contents secure for centuries.

"Are you sure you want to do this here, Dr. Turner?" Maria asked, questioning Eli's decision as he continued working on the vessel.

"It's not holding up too well," Eli said. He ignored her question as the two thousand year old twine, mummified by centuries of arid conditions, fell apart in small pieces. "Here we go," he whispered, gently grasping the petrified goatskin covering and lifting upward. It came off in one piece as Maria took some more photographs. "So far so good," he said, setting the skin on the ground, then taking a deep breath. He took the light, leaned over the amphora, and directed its beam into the interior.

"What do you see, Dr. Turner?" Maria whispered in an anxious voice.

"It looks like a small papyrus, Maria."

"There's nothing else?" Maria asked expectantly.

"If you mean, is there a grail in there? No," Eli said flatly. "Such is the way of our profession…one mystery reveals another. We still may have an important find here. It looks well preserved and—" his observations were cut short by the startling sound of gunfire reverberating from outside the cave.

Eli watched as Captain Saune sprang instinctively into defense mode. He motioned Eli and Maria to get down as he drew his side arm. Using the wireless transmitter, he tried to contact his men outside.

"They're not responding. You two stay here, out of sight," he said as he and the private sprinted off toward the entrance and faded away into the darkness.

"Do you think we're being raided by looters?" Maria asked nervously as she knelt down beside the amphora.

"Either that, or our new friend Alton Burr," Eli replied as he stared off into the darkness where Captain Saune and his man had been a moment before. "I have a bad feeling about that guy."

"I'm sure the guards outside will take care of the situation," Maria said hopefully.

"The papyrus!" Eli exclaimed as he stood up and

reached his hand into the amphora. Ever so gently, he grasped the ancient parchment by its end. When he slowly slid the papyrus out of its ancient sanctuary and into the light of the cave, a lightly rolled parchment was revealed.

"Dr. Turner, what are you doing?" Maria gasped, startled by his actions. "That should be done at the university."

"No time for that now, Maria. If the worst should happen, I don't want this to fall into the hands of looters or the likes of Burr," Eli said as he deftly opened the flap on his backpack and carefully slid the document into the pack between two peanut butter sandwiches. Setting the backpack down, Eli knelt, scooped up some dry sediment of the cave floor, and proceeded to pour handfuls into the amphora.

"If they are looters, all they'll find is an amphora and what looks to be a document crumbled to dust after many centuries."

Hearing the sound of footsteps echoing in the cave and heading their way, he looked up to see Captain Saune and his private slowly appearing in the low lantern light of the lava tube. They were walking toward them with their hands behind their heads. The shadowy images of three men dressed entirely in black appeared behind them pointing AK-47s at their two captives.

Eli could tell by the Captain's eyes that he was mad as hell at being captured without a fight.

They must have been waiting at the cave entrance and easily surprised the two soldiers, he thought. He also noted the terrified look on the private's face.

The group slowly approached the two archaeologists as

they stood up, startled by the scene playing out before them.

"Good evening, Dr. Turner," said one of the black clad figures as he pulled the ski mask from his head. "I trust my men and I haven't disturbed your work here?" he said with a grin and then shouted an order to his men in Japanese. The other men in black removed their masks and motioned by gunpoint for Saune and the frightened private to join Eli and Maria.

"Who in the hell are you, and what right do you have coming in here holding us at gunpoint?" Eli yelled, glaring at the obvious leader of the three assailants. The man smiled at him in return.

"You are in no position to ask questions here, Turner." The man sneered as he swiftly swung the butt of his weapon upward to strike Eli. A glancing blow to the side of his head sent him sprawling backward and hitting the ground.

Eli felt the blinding pain as he hit the ground, but somehow managed to remain conscious.

He heard Maria scream, "Stop it! Don't hurt him."

Maria knelt down beside the elder man and cradled his head, wiping the blood that started to flow from the open gash to his temple.

"Bind them," the leader barked to his subordinates as he took off the satchel he had over his shoulder and laid it down. "I'm afraid you're little expedition has made my employer nervous. We cannot have the prying eyes of the scientific community or the media at our back door right now, so we must end your little archeology project. Unfortunately, we didn't expect resistance from the two soldiers stationed out front, but that evidence can be cleaned up quickly enough before the accident is discovered in the morning."

"What accident?" Maria said glaring at their antagonist.

"No more questions," the man barked as he set about his task.

The other two mercenaries bound Eli and Maria's hands and feet with plastic tie wraps, and then unceremoniously threw them down at the tomb opening. Captain Saune saw the look of confusion on Maria's face at the leader's comments, but he knew exactly what was going to happen.

They have no plan to let us leave the cave alive, he thought as he desperately looked for a way to manage a counteroffensive against his captors. Saune eyed the men carefully, and saw to his horror the leader removing packs of C-4 from the satchel he had carried. He now understood what was to happen. They planned to seal them inside the cave with explosives.

"How is Dr. Turner?" He asked Maria, trying to distract her from her shock as he closely watched the men in black setting the C-4 packs along the walls of the cave toward the entrance.

"Uh…I think he's okay," Maria answered tearfully.

"I have one hell of a headache," Eli said, his eyes still closed, "but I'll be fine."

"I'm afraid none of us will be fine for long," the captain said tersely. "They're placing explosives on the cave walls, and I don't think they have plans of letting us out before they seal this lava tube. If I'm right, it's our friends from the Bishamon facility on the ridge above that have been watching us."

As he spoke, he heard a crackling noise on his wireless transmitter's earpiece, which was still in his ear, then the sound of a voice.

"Hello…anybody home?"

Outside the lava tube in the camp, Josh Turner and Samuel Caberra knelt silently on either side of the cave's entrance as the light misty rain slowly tapered off. Both of their minds were focused and their bodies steeled for action.

After their arrival on Tenerife, Josh and Samuel, along with their driver Paulo, had made their way up the access road toward the archeology camp. They were less than a quarter mile distant when Paulo had suddenly pulled over to the side of the road and shut off the engine.

"What's the matter, Paulo?" Turner asked, looking at the driver staring off into the misty darkness.

"I thought I saw a muzzle flash, Josh," Paulo said as he continued staring ahead into the gloom. "It looks like it came from the site."

"Are you sure it wasn't lightning?" Turner asked, peering into the darkness ahead.

"I'm positive," he replied.

"It might be looters raiding the camp," Samuel said from the backseat. "Your dad was concerned that it might happen."

"Dad and Maria are still there," Turner said in a worried voice. He turned to look at his friend in the back, and saw the concerned look on his face. "We have to get up there now, Samuel."

"We should go from here on foot, just in case something is wrong, Josh. If there's trouble, they'll for sure hear us coming in the rover. It's not that far from here."

"Paulo, I want you to head back and get help," Turner said as the two men opened their doors and got out of the vehicle. "Keep your lights off until you make the far bend in the road up ahead. From there, you'll be okay."

"Hold on, amigo," Samuel said, reaching into the glove compartment and pulling out his eight-inch hunting knife. He slid the sheathed knife into his belt. "I never leave home without it."

"One knife against guns?" Turner asked.

"Hey, we have to give them some sort of fair chance now, eh amigo?" Samuel replied with his usual dark humor. The two then started jogging up the road towards the camp.

Paulo had started back down the access road when Turner and Samuel finally reached the parking area below the camp.

"Over there, Josh, is the guards' tent," Samuel said, pointing to the slightly glowing embers of the campfire that was almost completely extinguished by the misty rain.

"That's as good a place to start as any," Josh replied as the two men swiftly and silently sprinted up the slope toward the dying fire. They found two forms slumped over each other as they arrived at the tent.

"This one is dead," Josh said as he checked the one man for vitals, "it looks like his throat was cut."

"This one's dead, too," Samuel replied, looking at the grizzly scene before him. "He must have been able to get a couple of rounds off before they got to him. The poor guy is still holding his side arm. It's a good thing he managed a few shots or we would have walked right into this."

"Dad and Maria must be inside the cave. There's no one else out here," Josh said, with fear rising at the possibility of his father and Maria meeting the same fate.

"I don't see any other bodies lying about. That could

mean Captain Saune is in there with them."

"I have an idea," Turner announced, reaching over the bloody corpse of the soldier. He removed the wireless transmitter designed like a hands-free cell phone attachment along with the ear piece that had popped out of the dead man's ear. "If our captain friend is still alive, hopefully he still has his receiver on."

"I see where you're going, amigo," Samuel replied, quickly retrieving the other unit from the second fallen soldier. "Better grab their side arms as well, Josh." The two then retrieved the army-issued 45-automatics from their former owners and stuffed them in the back of their pants.

"Let's get to the entrance and out of this light," Turner said as the two men set off up the remainder of the path to the lava tube's entrance. Then, flanking each side of the cave, they pulled their weapons and knelt down in the misty, darkened silence.

Back inside the cave, a startled Captain Saune regained his composure after hearing the unfamiliar voice in his earpiece. Inconspicuously, he switched on the wireless transmitter located in the breast pocket of his fatigue coat then lowered his head and spoke softly.

"Who is this?"

"Josh Turner," he replied. "Is this Captain Saune?"

"Affirmative...being watched...must keep my talk brief."

"What is the situation, Captain?" Turner asked, afraid to ask about the condition of his father and Maria.

After what seemed an eternity, Saune replied. "Four of us...your father injured, but okay...three targets that are well- armed, placing C-4 to blow up cave, and us along with it."

"Roger that, Captain," Turner said, his anger growing at the news of his father being injured. "Samuel and I are just outside the entrance and armed. We'll signal you before we take action."

"Roger," Saune whispered as one of the assailants came past him.

"Did you get that, Samuel?" Turner whispered to his friend on the other side of the entrance after switching off his microphone.

"Yeah, Josh, I got it, but what action are you talking about? If we go busting in there like Butch Cassidy and the Sundance Kid, a lot of people are gonna get hurt," Samuel said.

Turner managed a smile. He knew, with the trust built over their years of friendship, that Samuel would follow him into any situation without hesitation.

"I'm making this up as I go, Samuel. Don't rush me."

"Oh swell, I feel much better now," Samuel said as he chambered a round into the Army 45. "Whatever your plan is, we better move soon before the bad guys get antsy."

"Okay, here's Plan A...." Turner then began to inform Samuel of his idea.

Since his initial communication with the younger Turner, Captain Saune had made a mental note of all the locations of the C-4 packs on the basalt walls as far as the light in the cave allowed him to see.

They were spaced about thirty feet apart; with the closest just a stone's throw from him. He had watched as the killers pushed small detonator plugs into the C-4 packs, which told him there must be a wireless detonator switch probably in the hands of their leader.

He once again heard the voice of Josh Turner in his receiver.

"Captain, what's the situation with the explosives?" Turner asked.

"The C-4 packs are mounted at eye level on the cave walls about thirty feet apart. Each is armed with remote detonator plug that is activated by a hand-held detonator. You must pull the detonator plugs to render them inert," he said as the Yakuza leader barked an order to one of the mercenaries who then proceeded to walk toward the cave exit. "Stand by…one target is heading your way, Josh."

"Got that, Captain," Turner replied. "It looks like we go to Plan B, Samuel."

"Plan B?" Samuel whispered incredulously. "I wasn't that hot about Plan A."

Turner was hoping for an opportunity to gain access to the cave without notice, and now that opportunity was walking right out toward them as the two men heard the footsteps getting closer.

The pair stood and pressed their backs to the basalt walls as the mercenary approached. The young assailant had been ordered by his leader to stand guard outside the entrance, while the remaining two finished their work inside. Pulling the black ski mask over his face, he forgot one basic rule of his trade; always be aware of your surroundings.

The young mercenary exited the cave carrying his flashlight and never noticed the two men, nor did he see the arc of the pistol butt of the 45-caliber as it hit him in the head from behind. The Yakuza soldier was unconscious before he even hit the ground.

"Nice work, amigo," Samuel said as he dragged the man off to the side. "One down, two to go."

"I hope this guy is a close fit," Turner said, as he started to remove the black outfit from the unconscious man.

"You've got to be kidding me, Josh." Samuel said wide-eyed. "You're just gonna go waltzing in there like one of the boys?"

"I told you I was making this up as I go," Turner replied. He quickly took off the transmitter and proceeded to put on the unconscious assailant's black jump suit. "Hey, this should give us a few more precious seconds, which is more than we had two minutes ago." He pulled on the ski mask, and then tucked the mercenary's knife and the 45-automatic into his waistband.

"Alright, I'm going in. Tell Captain Saune to cause a distraction when he sees me come into view. When the fun starts, have him head for the nearest detonator plug and start yanking them out. Give me a minute's head start, and then you follow me in and pull the detonator plugs on this end of the cave. We'll wing it from there."

"Gee, that puts me much more at ease. Can we go back to Plan A?" Samuel quipped, knowing that this was their only option.

Turner picked up the mercenary's flashlight and quickly started into the cave, knowing his friend would not fail him or those inside.

Samuel relayed the message to Captain Saune, who quietly whispered to Maria to get ready to hit the floor. He saw the puzzled look in her eyes, but there was no time to explain as he spotted Turner in the black outfit coming into view in the dimness of the cavern.

As Turner made his way through the tunnel towards the light of the lanterns, he thought of all that had transpired in the last day. He wondered if he would even live to be reunited with his father in their new found relationship. He thought of Maria and now longed to tell her how he felt about her, but he pushed those thoughts from his mind as the light of the cave revealed the situation.

His reflexes and senses tuned and ready, he had only seconds to survey the situation and to act. His eyes took in the field of action. When he saw his father lying on the floor of the cave with dried blood on his head, anger welled deep within him. He knew that he was not a violent man. However, the sight of his fallen father and Maria with dried tears on her face unleashed his need to stop these men at any cost, even if it meant risking his own life.

As Turner entered the perimeter of the group, Captain Saune recognized his cue. Surprising everyone in the chamber, he started yelling wildly as he fell prone to the floor and began rolling towards the first C-4 pack on the wall nearest him. Those precious few seconds were enough for Josh to spring into action as he quickly launched himself upon Saune and proceeded to grab him around the neck with his back to the mercenaries.

In one fluid motion, he pulled his knife from his waistband and deftly cut the tie wraps binding Captain Saune, who in a flash was on his feet sprinting towards the first detonator.

After their initial hesitation, the Yakuza leader and his remaining subordinate realized what was happening, but by then, it was too late. The leader of the trio knew their plan to murder the archeology team was now in dire jeopardy, so he instantly sprang for the satchel containing the remote detonator.

I will not fail my Oyabun, he thought as he fumbled through the satchel retrieving the remote detonator switch in his hand, *even if it means my own death.*

The remaining Yakuza mercenary, who had frozen in the first few moments that transpired from Turner's appearance, raised his AK-47 and aimed it at Saune, who was now running for the first C- 4 pack. At that same instant, Turner whirled around and fell on his back to face his adversary. He drew his weapon and quickly fired off three rounds in succession before the hapless mercenary had a chance to pull the trigger. The first bullet missed and ricocheted off the cavern wall; the second found its mark, shattering his right shoulder and rendering his gun hand useless. Before he could react to the pain in his shoulder, the third bullet entered his forehead, killing him instantly.

During the melee, Captain Saune focused single-mindedly on getting to the detonator plug and removing it from the C-4 pack before it could kill them all. He had just pulled the plug successfully when he heard the sound of gunfire. He spun around to see the one Yakuza soldier fall to the ground. He then eyed the leader of the group scrambling for the satchel containing the C-4 and, most likely, the remote detonator switch.

Being too far from the man to be of any use, he yelled, "Stop him, he's going for the detonator switch!"

"Put the gun down or I'll blow us all into oblivion," the Yakuza leader hissed, now holding the detonator in his hand and backing away from the group towards the narrow entrance of the cave. "You," he said, pointing to Saune, "get back over there with the rest of them."

Turner could see Saune giving him a look that said *take the shot* as he slowly made his way over beside Maria, Eli and the private, who were all still bound hand and foot.

Saune glared helplessly at the Japanese man holding the remote switch in his right hand. He desperately looked for a way to reach him, but knew he would never get to him in time.

Turner, still wearing the ski mask, stood there with his 45 raised and leveled at the antagonist, hoping to stall him long enough to allow Samuel the needed time to make it through.

"What do you expect to accomplish by this?" Turner asked the mercenary, hoping for a few precious moments.

"I'll give you five seconds to drop the gun," the man snarled, obviously rattled by the recent turn of events.

"Are you looking for these?" a voice asked from the shadows behind him as a shower of detonator plugs came raining down around the startled assailant.

Samuel walked into the light of the cave with his hunting knife in hand just as Turner ripped off his ski mask, grinning like the Cheshire cat while giving his friend a thumbs-up sign.

"Josh, thank God you and Samuel are here," Maria said as tears of relief rolled down her cheeks.

"Hello, Son," Eli said weakly. "I was hoping for a nicer reception for you."

The reunion was short-lived, however. The Yakuza soldier pressed the detonator switch in his hand, causing the small plugs scattered about to pop like a string of fire crackers. Luckily, there was no explosion.

"You know, pal, you shouldn't play with fireworks. You could get hurt," Samuel said, scoring a verbal direct hit on the mercenary, who was now infuriated by his ill fortune.

"I think you owe us an explanation as to who you are, and why you want to kill us," Turner said, lowering his gun as Samuel walked past him to cut the ties off the three remaining captives.

"I will tell you nothing," he said, throwing down the detonator switch and knowing he had only one option left to him. "You might as well kill me."

The mercenary realized now that he might still complete his assignment. He raised his hands in mock surrender with the satchel still in his left hand. He then slowly bent over and lowered the satchel to the ground.

What Turner couldn't see was the military M-67 fragmentation grenade in the satchel. Though not as powerful as the C-4, it was effective up to forty-five feet. The mercenary's moment to act came in a split-second when he saw Turner looking toward his father and Samuel preoccupied with cutting the rest of the captives loose. With quick reflexes, he deftly reached into the satchel and pulled out the grenade. Pulling the pin, he launched himself towards the narrow chamber leading out.

Captain Saune, being the only one to see the action, raised the alarm. "Josh, he has a grenade!"

"Everyone get down!" Turner yelled as he swiftly swung around and wildly fired off three rounds at the shadowy figure. With all three missing their mark, he watched as the figure disappeared into the darkness of the tunnel. Seeing the grenade pin lying on the cave floor, he instinctively threw himself over his father as Maria, Samuel, and the rest hit the ground covering their heads.

The ear-splitting explosion that ripped through the cavern preceded another deafening sound as tons of rock and basalt came crashing down into the tunnel. Amidst a cloud of dust and debris, they were effectively sealed inside the ancient tomb.

A strange, muted silence pervaded the ancient lava tube as dust and debris began settling to the floor of the cave. Only the dancing shadow of a lantern light that flickered in the gloom gave hint to any sign of life.

***

After leaving Turner and Samuel to trek to the site, Paulo managed to turn the Land Rover about and was heading back down the gravel access road towards the main highway to obtain help. He never noticed the black SUV that pulled out behind him with its lights out when he passed the access road leading to the summit where the Bishamon facility was located.

I'll go to the police outpost in Guimar, he thought as the ominous SUV moved closer and closer behind his vehicle. He sped around the many treacherous curves leading down from the summit with no clue as to the unexpected visitors that were approaching him from behind. Paulo cursed himself for leaving the satellite phone at the camp when he set off earlier to retrieve Turner and Samuel at the ferry landing.

As he rounded one of the sharp curves, he felt a sudden jarring thud in the back of the rover as the lights of the SUV suddenly illuminated. With his vehicle immediately accelerating out of control, he found himself careening helplessly toward an embankment overlooking a four hundred foot drop to its rock- strewn bottom.

Paulo screamed in terror as the Land Rover was forcibly pushed over the precipice. The vehicle plummeted end-over-end down the rocky cliff face, exploding in a fireball when it hit the bottom of the ravine.

Still conscious in the flaming wreckage, Paulo felt the heat increasing around him. He tried to move in a desperate attempt to escape the conflagration, but found he was pinned within the vehicle. He shrieked in unimaginable pain as uncaring ears listened and watched from high above. The two men, satisfied with their gruesome handy work, headed back to the black SUV.

"We're lucky to have seen this vehicle leaving the site," the one man said, lighting a cigarette as the two went back to their vehicle. "Osama would have been extremely angry if anyone would have escaped before we had the opportunity to remove the bodies from outside of the cave."

"Osama will never know, will he?" The other man said casually as the ominous black SUV headed back to the dig site to clean up the gruesome remains of the soldiers killed during the assault, and to extricate the assault team.

***

Back in the dim light of the lava tube, a stunned Josh Turner raised his head and looked about as the dust and debris finally began settle. His ears still rang loudly from the grenade explosion.

"Is everyone alright?" He asked, brushing the dust from his hair. "We're okay, Josh," Samuel answered as he and Maria rose off the floor of the cave.

"Fine here as well," Captain Saune said as he and his man rose quickly and headed over to what had moments ago been their only way out.

"Are you okay, Dad?" He asked, rising on his knee and helping his father.

"Other than being a bit woozy from that madman whacking me on the noggin, I'm alright," Eli replied as he picked up his hat. "Good to see you and Samuel again, Son. Your timing is impeccable."

"I'm so glad to see you, Josh," Maria said as she ran over and threw her arms around him. "I don't know what would have happened if you and Samuel hadn't shown up when you did," she said, tightening her embrace around him.

"I really missed you," Turner whispered. He returned her warm embrace, succumbing to the fragrance of her sweat mixed with the scent of her perfume. Feeling her body against his, he looked deep into her fiery blue eyes and saw the longing look that he had so naively failed to recognize for so many months.

"Alright you lovebirds, get a room," Samuel said sarcastically, walking past them in the direction Saune and his man had gone moments earlier. He stopped when he saw them returning.

"Well, the good news is that lunatic is dead," Saune reported. "The bad news is he succeeded in sealing us in here. Most of the access tunnel has collapsed, and what's left doesn't look too healthy. We're lucky he didn't set that off in here or we'd all be dead."

"This keeps getting better and better," Samuel brooded as he took one of the flashlights and began walking towards the access tunnel. Turner, brought back to reality, reluctantly released Maria's embrace and walked over to his father.

"I take it these guys weren't just your run-of-the-mill looters," he said to his father, who was gently feeling the gash in his temple with his fingers. "They were definitely pros."

"We're pretty sure they were from the satellite relay facility found on the ridge above this site. It's owned by Bishamon Corporation, a Japanese business," Eli responded. "Carlos warned us about them, but I didn't think they were cold-blooded murderers."

"Why in the hell would a scientific research facility want to kill all of you?" Turner asked, brushing the dust off his arms. "Unless…maybe the complex is not exactly legitimate?"

"Drugs maybe?" Samuel offered, returning from his inspection of the cave-in.

"Seems like an elaborate cover just for drugs, Samuel," Eli countered.

"Well, whatever the reason," Turner said flatly, "you must have gotten too close to something they didn't want you, or anyone else, to see."

"That would explain why they went to so much trouble making this look like an accident," Saune said, kneeling next to the dead Japanese man that Turner had eliminated. "They could have easily shot us all at any time. Did you manage to neutralize the guy that left the cave before you came in?"

The Captain asked as he pulled the AK-47 from the man's death grip.

"Just knocked him out, I'm afraid," Turner replied, looking at his friend Samuel. "But, when he wakes up, he'll most likely believe they have succeeded in their plans."

"Believe they succeeded!" Samuel stated incredulously. "From the looks of things, I'd say they hit a home run, amigo. There's no way were going to be able to dig our way out of here. It'll take days for rescue crews to get to us and there's no guarantee the rest of our little casa here won't collapse on our noggins in the process."

"We don't have too many other choices open to us," Eli offered flatly as he walked over to the backpack containing the papyrus next to the amphora. "We might as well get comfortable."

Eli opened the pack and carefully lifted out the ancient parchment. He held it up to the lantern for a better look.

"What's that, Dad?" Turner asked as he and Maria move closer to inspect the item in Eli's hand.

"We found this in that amphora in the crypt, just before those cretins interrupted us," Eli replied. "Thinking it was just looters, I stuffed it in my pack for safe keeping. Care to have a look?"

"Not exactly good, sound archeology," Maria said, chastising the elder Turner.

"That's my Dad," Turner offered with a grin to his father.

"We might as well take a look. We certainly have plenty of time on our hands." He knelt down closer to the parchment and then carefully, began unrolling the ancient document.

"Would *you* have a look at this?" Eli exclaimed. "The text is in Aramaic just like the one Maria and Samuel found. How's your memory in ancient Aramaic, Son?"

"A little rusty, but I'll give it a shot," He grabbed the lantern and set it down next to the ancient parchment. Lost for almost two thousand years, he could see the ancient papyrus was well-preserved and missing only a few fragments. Turner began a slow translation of the text as the rest of the group listened intently from the gloom of their rock prison.

"'I, Simon, a Disciple and follower of our risen Master, Jesus of Nazareth, write this as a last testament to my fate, and to tell all, the privilege bestowed upon me by my mentor, Joseph of Ramleh, so many years ago.

The precious gifts of our Lord entrusted to my care are now safe from the hands of the unbelievers, who seek their destruction. I pray that to whom may find this that your heart would be of one with mine.

Death draws close to me now. I know I will die here, far from home and the loved ones I once knew, but I pass on from this life secure in the knowledge that I go to paradise with my work here in this world complete.

I and my travel companions, and fellow believers, Titus and Philemon, fled our homeland long ago as word of the treasures in my possession reached those in Rome, who seek us, and persecute other believers even unto the pain of death for our faith.

After many years in relative safety in Thera, we were betrayed by one of our own to the Romans and narrowly escaped with our treasured possessions. We traveled far and eventually found refuge in Mauretania under the rule of

Ptolemy, king of Mauretania, and vassal of Rome. They welcomed us, and even under the constraints of Roman jurisdiction, let us share the Gospel to many. We repaid their kindness applying our trade as merchants. We were then commissioned to lead an expedition to the Isles of Bliss to the west off the coast of Mauretania to establish trade with its people.

Knowing my death comes soon from illness, and that my journey is soon finished, Titus discovered a resting place for the Master's earthly vestiges, and there they now lie in the hopes that one day, men will come to cherish them.

The Teme of this Island of Ninguaria, whom we attribute as being their king, has allowed my friends to intern my body in his family catacomb when my passing comes. These people have offered so much kindness towards us; though they are a strange and heathen culture, we are much in their debt.

Titus and Philemon have sworn before God to guard the secret of the resting place, which holds our Lord's gifts to the world, until the time is once again favorable.

To you that find this and seek the truth, know that you will find the Master's cup; his last meal with his Disciples, the symbol of his Divinity. The crown of thorns, that adorned the Master's brow, which was the symbol of his humbling before God, and the last written word of our Lord, the symbol of his humanity and ministry to us on earth, on Junonia beneath the Hands of God.

May you who find them use them to his honor and glory, Amen.'"

The group stared at one another in stunned silence for what seemed like minutes after Turner finished translating the papyrus. Eli broke the silence.

"This is incredible; a document penned by Jesus. Just think of the implications to the historical community."

"Or the consequences of what it might say," Samuel interjected. "Why would he go to so much trouble to hide that, with the cup and crown of thorns from the world?"

"Simon states that he was protecting them from nonbelievers that would destroy them, along with a fledgling Christianity," Maria added, watching Turner stare intently at the lantern flame flickering in the cave's dim light. "At the time of Ptolemy's rule of Mauretania, or what is now Morocco, Caligula was Emperor of Rome and thought of himself a God. He wouldn't have thought twice about eliminating any competition then. What better way to crush a threat than to destroy its symbols?"

"Well, it seems like he went to an awful lot of trouble to hide them all the way here in the Canaries," Samuel said, now also curious about Turner's pensive look.

"I think I might know where they are!" Maria exclaimed excitedly after a few moments of reflection. "Our Simon wrote the artifacts rest on Junonia. We know the ancients called these islands the Isles of Bliss, or the Fortunate Islands, because of their favorable climate, and they named La Palma Junonia." She kneeled down and drew a crude map of La Palma on the dirt with her finger.

"Located here," she said as she poked a dot with her index finger on the crude map. "On the western flank of La Palma is a rock formation that was once in the shape of hands clasped together. Today it is called the rock of the Blessed Virgin, which was partially destroyed in the volcanic eruption occurring in 1949. A fault as wide as twelve feet was created by a landslide along that ridge because of the volcanic activity close to the rock, but it's still recognizable today."

"A lot of good that does us trapped in here," Samuel said morosely, reminding them of their current predicament. "There's no way out of here."

"Maybe there is, Samuel," Turner offered quietly, still staring at the flame of the lantern. "We're going to walk out of here," he announced to the startled look of the others in their basalt-rock jail. "I don't see where you're going, amigo," Samuel said. "Look at the lantern's flame," Turner said, pointing at the burning wick. "Only moving air could make the flame dance like that in here.

We start walking that way," he announced, pointing toward the back of the cave. He was pointing to the small entrance to the darkened, foreboding lava tube that led upward into the depths of the long-silent Volcano

8

At the Bishamon facility, Robert Pencor paced back and forth in the office of Yagato Osama like a caged lion. Expecting things done in a timely and orderly fashion, Pencor was furious the lone physicist, Yashiro, somehow managed to escape. To add to his growing anger, there was no word from the assault team sent hours ago to eliminate the archeology team.

"Relax, Robert," Osama said from his chair as he nervously eyed the phone on his desk. "You can rest assured that my men will not fail in their task."

"Have they caught the scientist who escaped yet?" Pencor asked, still pacing.

"Not yet, but he has nowhere to go and will most likely be lost in that lava tube and never found, or...."

"Or, he could find a way out and reveal our plans," Pencor shot back, halting in his tracks and staring menacingly at Osama. "That cannot be allowed to happen because according to *your* scientists, only one more day is needed to release the fault successfully."

"Yes, Robert, that was unexpected. The ground sensors

we placed on La Palma indicate the core temperature is rising at a much more rapid rate than anticipated. Using the magma chamber deep beneath the island like a gigantic pressure cooker is a far more controllable means of executing our plans than just having it totally erupt without control. It is—"

The buzzing of the phone interrupted his thought and he quickly picked up the receiver.

"Yes?" He said, staring intently at Pencor as he listened. "Bring him in," he said, and then hung up the phone.

A few moments later the door to his office opened and two armed guards entered, followed by the young assault team member that had been knocked unconscious by Josh Turner outside the lava tube.

He regained consciousness moments after the explosion sealed the cave and was confused as to what had transpired. He assumed all the others died in the cave-in, and the one who hit him over the head died inside as well.

I dare not tell Osama that I was rendered unconscious, he thought as he entered the room, politely bowing to his superior.

"What is your report?" Osama barked at the man, now wearing a tan jump suit supplied to him by the men in the SUV that killed Paulo.

"We were successful, Oyabun. The archaeologists and their guards have been eliminated as you ordered," he said stiffly. "I was ordered to stand sentry near the tunnel entrance when I heard the sound of gun fire from within. Before I could return inside, an explosion occurred and knocked me backward," he lied. "The flames from the C-4 set my clothes on fire as I proceeded in to help, but the ceiling of the cave started to collapse so I ran out and threw myself on the ground to extinguish my clothes." Growing more confident in his fabricated story, he continued. "After removing my smoldering clothes, I checked all the tents for anyone hiding. I found no one other than the two guards we eliminated outside, so I waited for the support vehicle to arrive. I helped them remove the dead guards and clean up the blood, so that no evidence of anything unusual would remain, other than the cave in."

Finishing his report, he looked downward to avoid the probing eyes of Yagato Osama. He nervously awaited a response from the Yakuza leader.

"Are you certain they are all dead?" Pencor asked, staring coldly at the anxious soldier.

"Yes, sir, I guarantee they are all buried under tons of rock. None of them could have survived. My comrades, unfortunately, were killed in the process."

"You have done well," Osama said to the young Yakuza soldier, relieved the mission had been completed. "Take him back to his quarters so he can get cleaned up." The two guards politely bowed, then escorted the man out of the room and shut the door behind them. The two men were left alone once more.

"You see, Robert? I told you not to worry. My men have sworn to succeed, or die in their duties."

"But what of your men who were buried in the cave along with the archaeologists? Won't that raise questions when they are found?" Pencor asked.

"It will take weeks to dig the bodies out, if ever. By the time they do, which I doubt will happen, we will be long gone. Add to the events that will transpire in one more day and little attention will be paid to a few unfortunate archeologists buried in a cave-in," Osama replied with a sense of self-confidence as he poured a cup of tea. "The dead National Guardsmen brought back by our support team will be dumped in the ocean on the supply flight leaving in the morning. They will never be discovered. All traces of our activity will be eliminated."

"That only leaves the matter of the scientist that escaped earlier," Pencor countered. "I'll relax when he is dead as well. We can't afford any more of these mistakes, Yagato."

"You underestimate our organization's resiliency, Robert. Our Yakuza organization is much more thorough than our predecessors," Osama said. "For years, the AUM Shinrikyo Religious Sect in Japan secretly worked with the Russians developing the Scalar weapons that we have now perfected. Their work was sloppy and careless, risking everything in the name of their ideology. Their leader was a mad man, bent on destroying himself and the organization's long hard work with their foolish gas attack on the subways in Tokyo back in 1995. If it were not for our operatives implanted in the AUM sect at that time, the Scalar weapon data would have been seized by the authorities and all would have been exposed.

"The EM plasma guns they used then were inefficient as well, and could be traced due to their use of what the Russians called the 'Woodpecker Grid'. It was their crude way of targeting the weapon. They also lacked the funds to enhance the technology after the fall of the Soviet Union. After 1995, we took over the development of the Scalar weapon research. Thanks to your funding, Robert, we have perfected the weapon so that its signature is only measurable with an EM detector," Osama said, bowing politely to Pencor with a false flattery that usually worked on the man's enormous ego.

Somewhat relieved for the moment, Pencor said, "Once we have incapacitated the economy and infrastructure of the United States, we'll introduce to the world our means of eliminating its dependence on oil. We will be rich beyond our wildest dreams. No doubt, your organization will rise to power in Japan with you as its leader."

"No doubt at all," Osama replied with little emotion.

"The industrial Zero Point Generators I am developing will forever change the strategic and economic face of the world. We will totally control the world's power needs," Pencor gloated with a smug smile, vainly staring at his reflection in the mirror on the wall. "Oil will no longer be a viable market. It will become more uneconomical to produce or refine once we start supplying countries with the ZPGs. Those who oppose will sing a different tune when the oil starts drying up and their lights start going out. America will no doubt resist, as I expect, and I will take great pleasure in bringing them to their knees," he concluded as he began to laugh maniacally.

Osama smiled politely, knowing that he had made a deal with a deranged and dangerous man, but the ends would justify their current unholy alliance.

I won't need this lunatic much longer, Osama thought as Pencor continued to laugh, *not much longer at all*.

"One smaller item, Yagato," Pencor said, brought back to reality. "Once the final phase is in motion for the weapon, I want the rest of the scientists disposed of. Do you understand?"

"The remaining scientists on site will get a first-hand demonstration of the Mind Snap gun, my friend," Osama said with a grin. "As you so eloquently stated, there will be no loose ends."

9

During the assault on the archaeological site by the Bishamon hit squad, the rented CJ-5 sat in the dark on a small rise overlooking the access road. Alton Burr had been there since sunset, brooding and pondering his next move. He had seen the Land Rover pass earlier, headed for the site, and watched in morbid fascination as on its return, it was forced over the high embankment by the dark SUV.

Believing it prudent to remain hidden for the time being, he heard the muffled explosion coming from the location of the dig site.

Now, sitting in his Jeep, he thought of his earlier confrontation with Eli Turner; how it infuriated him to the point of taking drastic measures. He ran his fingers over the stock of the 9mm Glock on the seat adjacent to him. He thought with zealous righteousness that he was destined to protect the world from the lies that would come once Turner's discovery became public.

Alone in the dark, his tormented mind went on a tirade. The world is stagnating under the yoke of organized religion. The Christians try to deny us the free pursuit of science, of free thought, and of self-gratification by trying to forcing its legalistic antiquated, moral edicts on society. Radical Islamic extremists are killing innocent people all over the world in the name of their god.

"It's madness!" He shouted aloud in the darkness of his vehicle. He longed for the day when religion would be replaced by a new order. *An order founded on the principals of science, acquired reason, and free thought and I intend to be a catalyst in its creation.* "I *will* succeed," he said arrogantly as he gazed out the windshield into the overcast night.

His grandiose thoughts were halted by the sight of the dark SUV returning from the direction of the archeology site. Burr sat upright, watching the vehicle as it slowed and made a turn off the main access road. It then started up a narrow road in the direction of the caldera's summit and, moments later, disappeared over a ridge.

The answer must lie with those people, he thought. *They might be able to solve my problem for me, but what were they doing at the dig site? Did they find anything?*

As he sat there in the darkness, he knew he would have to follow the SUV and see where they were going. First, he decided to make a quick visit to Turner at the archeology site.

"Time to go to work, Alton," he said chuckling in twisted amusement, gently stroked the gun barrel. "Time to go to work."

***

In the dim light of the collapsed lava tube, all eyes were

fixed on the flickering flame of the lantern as it danced about, fueled by a gentle breeze cascading through the chamber.

"Josh is right," Captain Saune said, walking over to the gear pack he and Private Gonzales brought in earlier that evening. "The lava tube must connect to other branches farther inside the volcano."

"Shouldn't we wait and see if help comes first?" Samuel asked. "I don't intend to just wait here and have this place fall in on us," Turner stated, picking up the dead Yakuza's AK-47 and tossing it to Private Gonzales.

"That goes for me, too," Eli said, rising up from the floor and getting his backpack. "We have to do something other than just sit here and wait."

"I've been hiking the lava tubes on Tenerife for years," Maria said. "They could meander for miles, leading to dead ends, but there also may be a skylight: an opening to the surface formed when a portion of a lava tube's ceiling collapses. If we can find one, there might be a breakdown pile caused by the collapse of magma that we can use to climb out."

"What do we have in the way of supplies?" Turner asked as he emptied the contents of the dead Yakuza leader's satchel, containing only duct tape, wire, and a blood-stained knife used on the unsuspecting guards outside the cave.

"Two D-112MG night vision goggles with head gear, two full canteens, and one old AK-47. Unfortunately, we were relieved of our weapons when captured earlier outside the cave," Saune said.

"I have two old AN/PVS night vision scopes with head

gear," Maria responded, "plus canteens and the flashlights we came in with. We can use the lanterns to make the hike. We'll need as much light as possible to avoid the deep drop offs where lava has up- welled from lower levels."

"I have two peanut butter sandwiches," Eli said as he gently rolled up the parchments, and then placed them back in his backpack.

"Hey, I'm hungry!" Samuel said from across the chamber. "At least Eli packed sensibly," he added, throwing Maria a wink when he saw her looking at him incredulously.

"Only you would think of food at a time like this," Eli said jokingly, as he tossed one of the sandwiches to Samuel. The rest of the group began gathering their gear.

Saune and Gonzales strapped on their night vision gear and flipped the scopes up to their resting position on top of the headgear. They checked their flashlights as Maria put on her night vision gear and handed the other to Josh.

"I didn't know that you were an experienced cave hiker," Turner said, standing close to her. He stared longingly into her warm blue eyes, which now showed the strain of the night's deadly encounter.

"There's a lot you don't know about me, Mr. Turner," she replied with a coy smile. "I'm full of surprises."

Turner paused, frozen in the moment. He inhaled her perfumed scent as she lingered close to him, not wanting the moment to end. He vowed to himself that he would stop at nothing to get her and the others to safety.

"When we get out of here," he said softly, taking her hand, "I know a nice little restaurant in Santa Cruz where the view of the bay is quite romantic and they have a great soloist. What do you say?"

"It's a date," she said, smiling a smile that would steal the heart of any man. She then quickly leaned forward and kissed him lightly on the lips. Turning, she confidently adjusted her backpack and started climbing through the small opening to the lava tube as Turner watched her shapely figure vanish into the gloom. He glanced at the others around him, smiled at their quizzical looks, then he and the rest of the unlikely entourage followed her into the darkness.

They walked through the ancient lava tube at a good pace, ever mindful of their footing, with Maria leading the way. Even after their harrowing experience and brush with death earlier, they all marveled at the awesome display of nature before them.

The channel they traversed was a myriad of twisting turns and inclines leading upward to the heart of the dormant volcano. The tube was a naturally occurring conduit; once a pathway for the flow of two thousand degree magma that hardened as it traveled beneath the cooler surface. They were in one of the main tubes that branched into the many smaller vents as the ancient lava slowed and drained out away from the erupting volcano.

As they walked onward in the dancing yellow glow of the lantern, Maria explained the lava marks on the cave wall that showed the height of the once rushing molten river of rock.

"Look at that," Eli marveled from behind, as he pointed to the sharp-edged columns suspended like ghostly fingers from the cave ceiling.

"They're basalt stalactites, Dr. Turner," Maria said. "They formed because the lava dripped from the ceiling as the vent slowly cooled. Some even bear a close resemblance to sharks' teeth."

"What is that reflecting off the stalactite? Did we hit the mother lode of gold?" Samuel asked with a chuckle as he walked up beside her.

"I'm sorry to burst your bubble, Samuel," Maria replied. "It's only the reflection of a deposit of calcite crystals. These caves are loaded with calcite and gypsum. Some lava tubes at other places in the world are known to go as far as twenty miles."

"I hope that's not the case here," Turner said.

"I knew you were getting soft, Josh," Samuel said in mock contempt. "Too many burgers when you were in the states, huh?"

"We have to watch for break-outs in the floor that lead to lower chambers," Maria interrupted. "If one of us were to fall in, there would be no way to get out without the proper climbing gear."

"How are you doing, Dad?" Turner asked his father, worried about the effects of the blow to the head he received earlier.

"Ah, I'm okay, Son. I'm a tough old bird, but I promise you that when we get out of here, I'm gonna pay a visit to those bastards that tried to kill us," he said in an angry tone.

"Not so fast, Dr. Turner," Captain Saune said from behind the two men. "We don't know who we're dealing with, and I would strongly suggest that we get the manpower to launch a proper raid on that Bishamon complex."

"I agree with the captain, Dad. We need to go to the authorities first. Do you have any idea why they attacked you?" He asked, as the group continued going around a gaping chasm in the floor that dropped into the deep recesses beneath them.

"My guess is a drug smuggling operation," Samuel said, jumping into the conversation, "but it just doesn't make any sense as to why they would risk exposing their operation like this."

"Hey, we all know that crooks aren't the brightest people in the gene pool," Turner offered. "And hopefully, as far as they suspect, we're all dead. I'm hoping the guy we sent nighty-night outside of the cave woke up and reported the cave-in to his superiors."

"I can have a tactical unit ready in a moment's notice," Captain Saune said. "The warrants though, could become a diplomatic problem since this is a foreign interest. We—"

"Shush," Maria said from the lead position. "Everyone stop.

Put out the lantern Private Gonzales."

Gonzales quickly put out the lantern, thrusting the group into total blackness. Samuel switched on the flashlight, keeping the beam aimed at the floor, which cast a dull light sufficient to see within a few yards.

Turner, Maria, Captain Saune and the private quickly flipped down and powered up their night vision goggles, casting their world into an eerie green glow.

"What's the matter, Maria?" Turner whispered. He walked up to her in the lead as she crouched, her eyes and ears intent on something ahead of them in the darkness.

"I could have sworn I heard footsteps coming from that way, Josh," she said, pointing to a branch in the lava tube ahead of them that split into two directions. "It sounded like it came from the left branch."

"Are you sure it wasn't the echo of our footsteps?" Turner asked.

His question was answered by the sound of gunfire up ahead, echoing throughout the cavern as he, and the rest of the group, instinctively crouched low against the lava tube's wall.

"That definitely came from the left branch," Turner said in a whisper to Maria, who had taken his arm and now held it tightly. "Quick, Maria, head back to Samuel and give him your night vision gear," he whispered.

"Hey," she retorted defensively. "I can take care of myself."

"I know you can, Maria, but Samuel is armed and we'll need him to have the night vision gear," he responded, gently brushing her cheek with his fingers. "I don't want you to get hurt. I couldn't live with that, alright?"

"Okay," she replied in agreement, "but only because I'm not that good with guns anyway."

She turned to go back as Saune and Gonzales reached the lead where Turner, now crouched low, was looking ahead.

"Captain, please have Private Gonzales take Maria and my father into the right branch of the tunnel divide and find them some cover."

"Do it," Captain Saune ordered to his man, sending him back as Samuel appeared out of the darkness wearing the night vision gear given to him by Maria.

"What's the story, guys?" Samuel asked, adjusting the headgear on his goggles and then pulling the 45 from his waistband.

"Sounds like more of our friends from Bishamon are headed this way," Turner answered.

"Do you think they heard us coming?" Samuel asked.

"I don't think they were close enough," Captain Saune replied and then added, "but from the original report of gun fire, I'd say they were a good distance away. Don't ask me what they were shooting at."

"See that lava pool off to the left?" Turner said, pointing to an almost perfectly rounded three-foot depression in the ground that he had seen before they first heard the shots. "We can use that for cover. Let's go," The three men sprinted across the thirty-meter wide cavern. One by one, they dropped into the lava pool using the high side of the ancient depression as cover. Saune swung the AK-47 to the ready as Turner and Samuel brought their 45-automatics to bear on the darkened tunnel ahead. Turner could see Gonzales in his night vision goggles leading Maria and Eli into the right branch of the lava tube and, thankfully, out of danger.

After a few minutes, they all heard the distinct sound of footsteps growing ominously louder and coming directly towards them. Then, just as quickly, they saw a dim beam of light as it came around a bend no more than fifteen feet from the three men in the cover of the lava pool.

To Turner, the figure coming at them wearing a lab coat hardly looked like a mercenary. He could see that he was unarmed and saw the blood stain on his jacket. He could see the halogen light he held was dying as the man slowed his approach.

Breathing heavy from fatigue after his long flight down the lava tube, Yashiro Fuiruchirudo failed to notice the three figures watching him from the recess of the lava pool. Exhausted beyond all reason, he slowed, turned around, and began walking backward.

He listened for the sound of his pursuers, who had relentlessly followed him from the access tunnel at the base of the facility.

He could still hear the men coming for him, their footfalls echoing in the cavern as they drew ever closer. His fatigue now outweighed his fear, as he had been on the run for over two hours. He stopped now and then only to catch his breath and to listen for his pursuers. He knew they were toying with him, like a cat toying with a mouse; playing with it until it was time for the lethal bite. He could hear their laughter as they relentlessly followed him down through the lava tube.

Yashiro agonizingly realized that his time was almost up. He was exhausted and his halogen light was now going dead. In complete despair he would now wait here in the darkness; wait for the final shot that would put him out of his misery.

Yashiro missed his wife and child, and longed to be able to say good-bye.

He let out a muffled scream as a hand suddenly cupped his mouth and he found himself being brutally dragged into a pit. As Yashiro fell, he let go of his light. It hit the floor and shattered its lens, turning his world into one of total darkness. Yashiro felt the cold steel of a gun barrel being pressed against his head. A voice said, "Give me a real good reason as to why I shouldn't blow your head off, amigo."

"Please!" Yashiro pleaded in a hoarse voice. "Please help me.

They are going to kill me."

"Who's going to kill you?" Turner asked in a whisper.

"The guards from Bishamon," Yashiro said weakly. "They're trying to keep me from escaping and warning the authorities," he said in near panic.

"Here they come," Captain Saune said in a whisper as he brought his AK-47 to bear over the lip of the ledge. "Get ready."

"If you want to live, keep your head down and don't try anything cute. Understand?" Turner said to Yashiro, who for the first time tonight felt a glimmer of hope as he scrambled behind the men in the darkness. He laid flat on the ground with his hands over his head.

The four Bishamon guards rounded the turn in the lava tube, knowing they were near their prey and closing in for the kill. The leader told the others that he wanted the first shot to wound him, but afterward, they could indulge themselves. The four wore night vision goggles and carried a light as they walked through the tunnel nonchalantly, like hikers on a holiday. They never expected to encounter a trio of armed men, and were caught off guard when they heard a loud voice.

"Drop the weapons now!" Turner yelled, pointing his 45 at the man on the far right.

The lead guard spotted the three in their protected position in the lava pool, but made the fatal mistake of raising his AK-47. He was instantly cut down by a blazing onslaught from Captain Saune's weapon. The other guards foolishly followed his lead and met the same fate in a hail of bullets from the trio in their ancient bunker. The Yakuza soldiers fell dead on the floor in a spreading pool of blood.

"That's for my men you butchered," Saune hissed, as the haze and burning odor of spent weapons permeated the cavern.

"Is everyone okay?" Samuel asked, rising from the floor and cautiously walking over to the Bishamon guards.

"We're fine, Samuel," Turner responded. He then yelled, "Alright Dad, the coast is clear. You're safe to come out."

"Those guys are all dead, Josh," said Samuel, returning from the scene of the carnage just played out.

"They would gladly die before ever giving up," said a relieved Yashiro, who now slowly stood up off the ground.

"Who were they, and why were they after you?" Turner asked, retrieving the lantern and lighting the wick with a match. Once again the chamber was cast in a ghostly yellow light. Switching off the night vision, he flipped up the unit into the stow position and looked at the young, disheveled Japanese man sitting in front of him. Private Gonzales and his charges walked over to the group and knelt down in the soft yellow light as Yashiro started to speak.

"They were Yakuza soldiers; members of the Yagato Osama clan, and are sworn to do his bidding even unto their own death."

"Isn't the Yakuza the Japanese equivalent of our Mafia?" Eli asked the fatigued scientist.

"Yes, but our version have been around since the seventeenth century in Japan. It was originally known as the Hatamoto-yakko, *or* Machi-yokko, which means servants of the town. Those men you killed are part of Osama's Gurentai; his gang," Yashiro replied, flinching as Maria touched his wounded arm.

"You're wounded!" She said reaching for the canteen in the backpack.

"Just a slight graze from a bullet. It's not serious."

"Let's clean it up to be sure," she said, helping the shaken scientist remove his lab coat. Maria began cleaning the wound as Yashiro took a grateful drink of water from the canteen.

"Alright, friend, who are you and what were you talking about when you said you had to warn the authorities?" Turner asked as he squatted down next to him on the cold rock floor of the cave.

"My name is Yashiro Fuiruchirudo," he said in broken English, "and I am a geo-physicist from Kobe, Japan. I was hired originally to work on a new energy source by Bishamon Corporation, a Japanese company set up and funded by an American named Robert Pencor."

"Pencor? I remember him," Eli said. "Wasn't he under indictment by a Federal Grand Jury back in the middle of the last decade? Not a very nice man from what I've read. I heard that he fled the country."

"Yashiro, I'm Josh Turner and this is my father Eli. Over here are Maria Santiago and Samuel Caberra," he said pointing to the pair seated next to them. "Those two fellows over there are Captain Saune and Private Gonzales from the Tenerife Guardia Civil. Some thugs from Bishamon tried to kill them earlier and make it look like an accident. I think you owe us an explanation," he stated emphatically.

"Have you ever heard of Scalar weaponry?" Yashiro asked, rubbing his sore leg from the fall he incurred when he was pulled into the lava pool.

"Can't say I have," Turner replied, taking a drink of

water from the canteen.

"It is a weapon that comes from the study of Zero Point energy and—"

"Zero Point what?" Samuel interrupted with a confused look. "Let me put it to you in simpler terms," Yashiro said, seeing he had to keep it understandable for his listeners. "In the world of quantum mechanics, it was discovered many years ago an energy source exists all around us. All matter at the atomic level is surrounded by a vacuum in space-time, which is filled with particles of negative energy. It was discovered that this energy could be tapped and utilized as a free, never-ending supply of energy."

"Free energy?" Turner asked, still somewhat confused. "There's no such thing!"

"Yes there is, Josh," Yashiro continued. "Free electromagnetic energy that can be harnessed for many uses. A man named E.T. Whittaker, back as early as 1903, introduced the theory of what we now call Scalar Interferometry. Not many people know this, but after World War II, the Russians used this theory to develop and actually test weapons of great power they referred to as the science of energetics. They later found an unholy alliance with the AUM religious sect and the Yakuza organization of Japan. They proceeded to test these terrible weapons on a worldwide scale. After the collapse of the Soviet Union, the Yakuza took the technology back to Japan and continued for many years in an effort to refine the process and conduct testing."

"You mean to say the Japanese government was involved in this?" Maria asked in surprise.

"No, the government of Japan had no knowledge.

However, the Yakuza organization is deeply entrenched in the government and in large business corporations such as Bishamon, headed by Pencor and Osama. They work around the system to develop weapons of mass destruction so terrible that no one on the planet is safe. Funding is of no concern. Signs of testing have been evident for years on a worldwide scale without notice. The documented plasma fireballs over Australia and mysterious flashes of energy that appeared similar to nuclear detonations off the coast of Africa. You may recall reading of the unexplained sonic booms off the east coast of the United States back in the 1980s. They were the result of early testing by the Russians. In recent testing, they actually succeeded in creating earthquakes and tsunamis off the coast of the Philippines and New Guinea," he said, stunning his silent audience.

"New Guinea?" Turner said in numb shock. "You mean to say a freak tsunami, which killed an associate of mine and damned near killed me in 2008 could have been caused by these people?"

"If you saw an anomaly in the sky prior to the event, then yes.

It was most likely them, Josh."

"But what does all this have to do with Bishamon being here on Tenerife?" Maria asked, seeing the stunned and angry look on Turner's face. "The Canary Islands are not a very strategic target for anyone."

"I hate to interrupt," Captain Saune said, picking up the lantern. "But I think we need to get moving before some of their friends come looking for them." He motioned to the dead Yakuza soldiers lying across the chamber.

"I agree, Captain," Turner said as he stood up, still

stunned by the revelation of what could be the truth behind his nightmares. "If you are well enough to walk, Yashiro, you can fill us in with more details as we go."

"I'm well enough to make it." Yashiro then added, "But if we go back the way I came, it will only lead us to the access tunnel beneath the Bishamon complex. There are no other exits to this lava tube along that route. Can we make it out in the direction you came from?" He asked.

"No way, amigo-san. Your friends sealed the only other way out I'm afraid," Samuel replied. He stood up and brushed the dirt from his pants and then added, "This explains why those guys tried to do us in. We were just a little bit too close to their operation for comfort."

"They must be testing or developing weapons up there," Eli added as the group began walking again on the route that led towards the Bishamon facility.

"It's worse than that," Yashiro said in response to Eli's observation. "The Interferometer weapon is now in use and, if not stopped, will result in the complete devastation of the entire east coast of the United States in less than a day. We may be too late already."

"What? How can that happen from Tenerife?" Turner asked, once again shocked by Yashiro's revelation.

"Not from Tenerife, but rather from the island of La Palma," Yashiro pointed out. "More precisely, it is the Cumbre Vieja's volcanic ridge on La Palma. Scientists have proven the volcano fractured across most of the ridge on its western flank in the 1949 eruption. It left a rock almost twenty kilometers long in a precarious position that *will* slide into the seas eventually. It's not a matter of if, but when," he said as the group rounded a sharp turn in the passageway and started on an upward track. "When the fault does finally release its hold and slide into the sea, a massive tsunami will form and strike the east coast six hours later.

"My God," Eli said in a hushed voice, "the entire eastern seaboard?"

"Yes," Yashiro replied. "It will strike Boston, New York, and as far south as Miami, leaving a wake of destruction as far inland as twelve miles or more. Even South America and the Caribbean will not escape the wave, though it will be less destructive. The resulting flood and devastation will be massive, wreaking havoc on the western hemisphere's economy and killing millions of people, who will fail to evacuate because there will be no warning."

"How are they doing it?" Turner asked, now understanding the graveness of the situation as they walked on.

"The Bishamon complex has been exposing Cumbre Vieja's magma chamber to the Scalar Interferometry weapon gradually, over a period of time, using exothermic electromagnetic waves. The weapon is designed to super heat the magma chamber, causing internal pressure to build up on the western fault of the volcano."

"But how can they be sure it will happen as planned?" Turner asked.

"In simple terms, the Cumbre Vieja is like a layer cake on its side, with layers of solid basalt and sediment built up over millions of years. Between those layers, centuries of groundwater have been filling up between them with no way of dissipating, basically becoming a gigantic reservoir. Normally, without internal pressure, the fault holds by its sheer friction-force weight. However, by raising the water pressure on these huge reservoirs through massive heat generated in the magma chamber, it will lose its hold and simply slide off, similar to that of a snow avalanche. Swiss scientists have done many models and have come to the same conclusion," he stated.

"Why haven't geologists noticed anything on their sensors?" Eli asked. "I know they monitor these islands."

"Geologists in the region, who monitor the seismic activity, won't see any changes until it's too late. Pencor's people altered the ground sensors on La Palma."

"How big would the tsunami be?" Samuel asked, as they passed a deep breakout fissure that dropped into the darkness below.

"The models done by scientists were based on a half-trillion ton of rock hitting the ocean in one massive slide," Yashiro explained. "The initial wave height projected to leave the island would be massive; as high as a thousand feet or more. It would travel at the speed of about six hundred miles per hour, spreading its mass throughout the Atlantic basin. Best estimates have put the wave height at one hundred fifty feet or higher when it reaches the Americas. It has happened before; the massive wave at Lituya Bay in Alaska in 1936, and actually witnessed in 1958. In both occurrences, the wave height washed out trees as high as four hundred fifty feet. Both waves were generated by huge landslides."

"How does the Scalar weapon work and why hasn't anyone detected the EM waves you mentioned?" Turner asked.

"It's difficult to explain. Simply put, a Scalar Potential Interferometry Weapon utilizes the space-time medium to emit longitudinal EM waves. They are purposely transmitted out of phase, and received at the target point by means of a computer- generated marker beacon. In this case, the marker beacon's target is the Cumbre Vieja's magma core. Since the EM waves travel in quantum space-time, there is no visible ray or detectable path source. The EM waves are transmitted and received instantaneously at its focal point. These zero vector EM waves, as they are also called, can literally pass through oceans and even the earth's core, with no interference or conventional means to detect it."

"And Pencor is behind this plot?" Eli asked incredulously.

"Yes, he and Yagato Osama are responsible for this mad scheme," Yashiro said, anger rising in his voice. "They're completely mad. Pencor plans to cripple the economy of the United States with the tsunami and then flood the world's market with his Zero Point Generators."

"Another Scalar weapon?" Turner inquired.

"No, they are a positive creation from the field of quantum energy," he replied. "These devices could supply the world's energy needs based on the free Zero Point energy from the vacuum theory. The ZPG, as it is called by some, is a transformer with a core of nano-crystalline material. This material interacts with a standard input field from a conventional permanent magnetic source, forming a flux field of output energy. This energy can be redirected back to power the unit itself, thus becoming a self-sustaining and free energy power source."

"Why haven't these ZPGs, as you call them, been developed by the industrial nations of the world before now, especially when oil production has been historically so costly to produce and such an unstable factor in world events?" Maria asked.

"There have been a few bold scientists in America that have taken the lead for years in the research and development of the ZPGs. All research was paid for out of their pockets, and their frequent request for research funding fell on the deaf ears of your nation's politicians," Yashiro replied to Maria. "I have no doubt the oil companies, with their lobbyists and deep pockets, have a strangle hold on the politicians in Washington

D.C. With so much to lose, they are willing to do anything to protect their profits and control of the world's oil-based energy needs for as long as they can."

"That sounds like our esteemed elected officials," Eli said sarcastically. "They're always willing to sell out their constituents for a buck, or a vote."

"Pencor has managed to mass-produce the ZPGs from his port facility in Morocco, and stands ready to ship them at a moment's notice. He has the means of totally realigning the face of the global powers and reaping vast profits. Oil becomes an irrelevant commodity if he is supplying the ZPGs," Yashiro said.

"What about this Osama character? How does he fit in to Pencor's plan?" Turner asked as they continued upward, entering a wide chamber filled with glistening stalactites.

"Yagato Osama, with his weapons and new found riches from his partnership with Pencor and the Zero Point Generators, will no doubt rise to power in Japan. His tentacles now reach into every corner of the government, and many who have opposed him have simply disappeared. With unlimited access and control of the ZPGs and the threat of the Scalar weapons, the two have the means to control the world's power consumption. They'll also possess the weapons at their disposal to eliminate any who stand in their way." Yashiro stumbled on a rock and nearly fell down.

"Wow!" Samuel said in disbelief. "No wonder they wanted us dead."

"That is why we must escape," Yashiro responded to Samuel. "We must stop them."

"You said this was going to happen soon?" Turner asked. "How much time do you think we have before he unleashes the mega-slide?"

"A day, at the very most, but I fear we may be down to hours," Yashiro said pessimistically.

Captain Saune came up to the group from behind and asked, "What kind of resistance, in the way of guards or surveillance, can we expect when we get to the complex? We're getting low on ammo."

"They won't be expecting us, especially if they think you are all dead. They most likely sent the tunnel guards after me and, hopefully, it will be empty when we get there," Yashiro said with optimism in his voice. "There are no surveillance cameras in the tunnel itself, but there is one in proximity of the helicopter pad. My plan was to exit the tunnel, then scale the rock face up to the caldera's rim using an old path. After that, I planned to flee down the parking lot access road in the cover of darkness. Unfortunately, returning guards from the pad spotted me so I had to come this way instead. That's when I ran into you."

"We'd be sitting ducks until we made the tree line," Samuel said. "There's not much in the way of cover and it's going be light in a few hours."

"We'll have to worry about that when the time comes, Samuel," Turner responded. He then asked, "How much ammunition do you have left, Captain Saune?"

"What's left in the gun and a spare clip," he replied.

"Not too many rounds left in mine either, amigo," Samuel added sourly.

"I'm down to my last few as well, so we'd better use them sparingly," Turner said.

"How far is it to the access beneath the Bishamon complex from here?" Maria asked Yashiro as she guided the group around a cluster of shimmering stalagmites that protruded from the tunnel floor.

"It shouldn't be too far ahead," Yashiro responded. "We'll see the lights in the tunnel well before reaching it."

"I take it you have another plan, amigo?" Samuel asked Turner, with light sarcasm in his voice.

"Piece of cake," he responded, slapping his friend on the back. "Piece of cake."

"Why doesn't that make me feel all warm and fuzzy?" Samuel said warily as the assemblage pressed on to what lay ahead.

10

The control room of the Bishamon complex was a beehive of activity as the six remaining scientists hurried about, pulling printouts and entering data into the complex's vast computer database. The armed guards posted about the complex control room made them all uneasy, but they continued their work, fearful of what would happen if they didn't comply.

At a door on the far end of the control room, Robert Pencor and Yagato Osama entered, preceded by two burly looking guards. Lead scientist and associate to Osama, Fuyuki Seijun saw the pair enter the brightly lit control room and quickly walked over to greet them.

"Good evening, Oyabun," Fuyuki said to Osama in Japanese, bowing politely.

"Please speak in English for the benefit of our guest," Osama said to the scientist, bowing slightly in return.

"My apologies, sir. Good evening, Mr. Pencor. I trust you are well," Fuyuki said in broken English as one of the other scientists approached holding a clipboard in his hand.

"Here are the latest data and seismic reports, Dr.

Seijun," the stocky scientist said as he handed the clipboard to his superior.

"What is your current progress on the Scalar weapon?" Pencor asked curtly, cutting through the pleasantries and irritating Fuyuki.

"We are mere hours from completion, Mr. Pencor," the scientist said, failing to hide his contempt for the American. "Our sensors on La Palma show that ground temperatures have increased exponentially for the last five days, increasing the static pressure on Cumbre Vieja's fault line. With the slow build-up in pressure, seismic activity has been minimal, and reports of unusual activity by the locals living on the island have been few," he stated proudly. "Our spotters on La Palma are reporting the appearance of new steam vents on the ridge line, which could be a problem if looked into, but the geological survey team is not expected to do their annual survey for another month."

"And what about the report of a film crew that showed up last week?" Osama asked as the three men strolled over to the nearest computer console.

"A slight annoyance," Fuyuki said, waving his hand in dismissal. "Just a National Geographic film crew doing a television documentary on the slight possibility of a landslide causing a tsunami," he replied with a grin. "We're keeping an eye on their activity."

"They are going to have quite a documentary to televise when we are finished," Osama said, breaking into laughter at the irony.

"Are you confident in your projections, Seijun?" Pencor asked, not amused at the display of joviality.

"Robert," Osama said, "I trust Fuyuki's work

emphatically. He has been working on our Scalar projects since the days we were associated with our Russian friends in the KGB. He was instrumental in the first plasma ball testing that exploded over Perth, Australia, and many other events that have ensued through the years."

"Thank you, Oyabun," Fuyuki said proudly. He coldly eyed Pencor, who had the audacity to question his work. "I have complete faith in my projection. After the Scalar Interferometer adjustments are made within the hour, the final phase will be totally automated. In approximately twelve hours, one last EM oscillation burst will force the rupture in the fault."

"Can it be done sooner?" Pencor asked, purposely avoiding looking at the scientist as he stared at the computer screen that showed the oscillating EM waves and their current power levels.

"No, it must be done in conjunction with the ambient temperature levels in the magma core reaching the desired zenith. If we were to initiate the final EM wave burst prematurely, we could cause an explosive eruption within the magma chamber whereby the fault line could feasibly collapse. Basically, an implosion would occur and the weak western flank on Cumbre Vieja would collapse in on itself rather than slide towards the sea. This is a precise science, Mr. Pencor, and, as I'm sure you are aware, an unstable one at that," he said, with the slight barb directed at the American.

"Keep Yagato advised to your progress. I have a meeting today with my friends in the Canarian Parliament at a University luncheon," Pencor said curtly as he turned and walked away from the two men.

"Patience, Fuyuki," Osama said in Japanese, seeing the hatred in Fuyuki's eyes as Pencor strolled away. "Soon we will no longer need our American benefactor. Once the slide and tsunami have occurred, our obnoxious friend will meet an unfortunate end. Our team in Morocco is awaiting my word to seize the shipment of ZPGs at the port of Safi and transport them to Japan. With Pencor out of the way and our having the patents and designs, we will control the world's power supply. I have arranged for documents to be uncovered that will link Pencor directly to the tsunami with assistance from the AUM sect in Japan. Pencor is expendable, my friend."

"It is a brilliant plan, sir," Fuyuki said, bowing politely to his Oyabun.

"Once the final countdown begins, you know what must be done to the remaining scientists," Osama said to Fuyuki in a hushed tone.

"When the computer takes over the final phase, it will be totally out of human hands. There can be no witnesses left to tie us to the landslide," he said with no sign of emotion in his one cold black eye.

"Pencor has his karma, and we have ours," Osama said nonchalantly, laughing as he turned and headed out of the control room.

11

Safi Seaport, Morocco

It was well past midnight and the old Assif Hotel's restaurant was still a beehive of activity. Throngs of people ended their busy day by drinking and enjoying fine Arab-Berber cuisine. The rustic establishment was the nightly haunt of many of the city's commercial fishermen, and tonight was no exception. The old bar, beneath its spinning cane ceiling fans, was two-deep with drunken fishing captains that were boasting of how they could fill their holds with fish faster than anyone else in the fishing fleet.

The Assif was an older establishment, one of many near the seaport of Safi, a city of eight hundred thousand residents located on the northwest coast of Africa. The recently enacted Arab Free- Trade Agreement had been an asset to its floundering economy, bringing much-welcomed business investors and trade agreements from the outside world. Most importantly, it supplied much needed jobs to the mainly

Arab-Berber peoples.

It was just another lazy night at the Assif on the Avenue de la Liberte, a mere two blocks from the busy loading docks and piers that had grown exponentially as business boomed. The restaurant's interior was quaint in design. Many of its tables tonight were occupied by executives staying at the hotel, along with a smattering of European tourists. The strong aroma of spices tickled the senses as its patrons enjoyed their meals, the sound of local music permeating the premises.

In the far back corner, a lone figure sat unaccompanied at his table, nursing a scotch and water as a waiter came over and poured him a cup of coffee.

It had been a busy night, Kasim Buruk thought as he lit a cigarette and took a sip of coffee. He was almost discovered after his break in at the Safi Bishamon production plant, and the near failure unnerved him.

Earlier that evening, Kasim and his three associates cut the chain link fence in the rear of the brightly-lit plant. Under the cover of the many argan trees that thrived in the dry, arid conditions of Morocco, they swiftly made their way to the back of the factory where a lone, unattended door led to the assembly area within. Quickly cutting the pad lock with bolt cutters, they stealthily entered the plant and stayed in the shadows as they went about their work.

Kasim noted the massive crates that were placed near the large, metal sliding doors that led to the loading area out front. He wondered what they contained that was so important. Inconsequential to him, he put the thought out of his mind as he and his associates went about their task. He found over the years that his success was mainly because he never asked questions of his employers.

Within minutes, as they observed many armed Japanese guards patrolling the interior of the facility, it became clear to the intruders that this was not just any plant. With extreme effort and practiced stealth, they managed to complete their work and leave the building, unobserved by the many guards.

Upon reaching the safety of the outside of the fence, they noticed a pair of armed men coming around the building's front. It was dumb luck they hadn't encountered them coming into the fenced-in perimeter.

Why hadn't they forewarned him of the heavy security at the factory? He thought now as he sipped his coffee in the restaurant. *It had made it almost impossible for us to complete our task. The fools should have given us more data.*

The ringing of his cell phone interrupted his thoughts. He pulled the phone from his coat pocket and answered.

"Yes," he said firmly.

"Were you successful?" The voice on the line said with an accent that betrayed his true nationality.

"The parcels have been delivered, per your instructions, to the predetermined locations within the facility," Kasim answered, still annoyed at the lack of information regarding the production factory. "Why wasn't I briefed on the high security at the Bishamon warehouse?"

"You are compensated quite handsomely by my associates for your work, Kasim," the man on the phone said irritably. "The particulars you encounter are of no concern to us. All we expect are results. Is that clear?"

"Yes," Kasim said sourly, "quite clear."

"Have you proceeded with the second phase?" The caller asked. "As we speak, the packages are being delivered to their recipients," Kasim replied. "Our work here will be complete by dawn."

"Excellent, Kasim. We will contact you at dawn for confirmation, and then we will assume control of the parcels from here," the stranger said. "Once the objective is met, one million dollars will be transferred to your account in Saudi Arabia, per our agreement."

"Very good, it's always a pleasure doing business with you and your associates," Kasim said flatly.

"Y'all have a good night, son," the animated voice said. With that, the line went dead. Kasim sipped his scotch and water and thought about this current operation, but quickly dismissed it.

"I just do my job," he said aloud as he snuffed out his cigarette.

While Kasim was finishing his drink, two container ships sat quietly at their berths at the Safi port loading area. Since being partially loaded the preceding day, they both sat in relatively low water. A stiff eastern breeze off the Atlantic snapped at the stern pennants, revealing the name Bishamon.

Two guards stood at each of the vessel's gangways, keeping a watchful eye on the occasional fishermen that passed by on their way to the vessels that were farther down the pier. The guards stood at their post, smoking cigarettes and chatting occasionally to relieve their boredom. Though vigilant in their duty, the guards were oblivious to the air bubbles rising to the surface from beneath the water, as men in scuba gear moved freely from ship to ship doing their callous and premeditated work.

12

They walked in silence through the ghostly light of the lava tube, each lost in their own thoughts about the night's bizarre occurrences: the attempt on their lives, the cave in, and the gunfight in the tunnel. And now, the startling revelation made to them by Yashiro of the mad plot to devastate the United States, made by men blinded by ambition and wealth.

Turner walked silently, thinking of how crazy things had been since his arrival in Tenerife.

These men are merciless killers, like something out of a twisted movie script, he thought as they continued on, only their footsteps softly echoing in the silence. He watched Maria walking ahead of him and a rising dread began to build. He knew that Osama's men would not think twice about ending her life or his father's, with no pity or remorse. "Not on my watch," he said angrily to himself.

"Say again, Josh?" Replied his Quechuan friend, who walked by his side.

"Nothing, Samuel, I'm just thinking aloud." He looked at his father and asked, "Dad, are you still friendly with that woman from the State Department?"

"Who? Abby? I call her maybe once a week, but I'm afraid the relationship is going nowhere. She's just too wrapped up in her work."

"And you're not?" Maria said with a soft chuckle, the sound of her gentle laughter sweet music to Turner's ears.

"What's that supposed to mean?" Eli retorted sourly.

"I was thinking, Dad. When we get out of here, we could use her connections at the State Department to get a warning out about Pencor's plans. We could—"

"They'd never be able to launch an assault in time, nor could the Parliament of Tenerife," Yashiro interrupted. "First, they would hardly take seriously a wild scheme to attack the United States from a group of archaeologists. Even if they did, it would take days to implement a plan and then carry it out," he stated grimly.

"I will go to the Parliamentary Council myself," Captain Saune said defensively. "They will listen to me."

"They will do nothing until it is too late," Yashiro argued. "You don't understand. Osama and Pencor's money and influence have far-reaching tentacles. You can rest assured they have bought and paid for key government officials here on Tenerife. How do you think they got the contract to replace the seismic sensors on La Palma? They have men everywhere and...."

"Quiet," Turner said as they approached a huge lava boulder ahead of them. "I hear machinery up ahead. Wait here and I'll check."

He headed off in a light sprint in the direction of the sound of the machinery, becoming louder as he advanced. Coming to the side of the huge slab of basalt, he peered around its cold black surface to see lights on the walls about forty-five feet distant. As the whirring sound suddenly ceased, Turner watched as bodies were unceremoniously dropped from the opening at the top of the ladder, each of them hitting the floor with a sickening thud.

Wonder who those poor bastards were, Turner thought, tightly gripping the side arm in his hand. Just then, the sound of the mechanism started again and he could see the light from the opening in the ceiling fade as the steel door closed with a muffled boom. "All clear," he said to the group as the cave was thrust into silence once again.

"Looks like they don't appreciate the help around here," Samuel said, reaching his side and seeing the bodies up ahead.

"Can you see any guards further ahead?" Saune asked, arriving next.

"None that I can see, Captain," Turner replied. "Someone was dumping bodies down from the ceiling hatchway," he stated coldly. "More of Pencor and Osama's dirty work, I assume," Samuel said, clicking off the safety of his weapon.

"Let's get moving before some of their goons decide to come back," Turner said.

Rising up, they walked into the open tunnel that led to the ladder beneath the facility. Turner then gestured to Yashiro to join him at the lead. "Yashiro, I want you to lead us out of here once we check the entrance to make sure that it's clear. Are you up to it?"

"I can do it," the Japanese scientist said with new found optimism and courage at the sudden turn of events that had snatched him from the jaws of certain death.

The group came up to the ladder beneath the trap door

and Turner's earlier observations were confirmed as Yashiro looked in horror at the macabre scene before him.

"They have killed the remaining scientists. No witnesses," he said, his voice shaking a little as he stared at the mound of bodies stacked atop each other like a grotesque pile of firewood. "That tells me they are very close to triggering the landslide. The entire process is now automated."

The group passed the final storage bin at a quicker pace now, and towards the lava tube opening just ahead of them. "Once we clear the tunnel," Yashiro said, "there is an old path to the right of the entrance that leads to a worn switchback pathway. It will lead to the complex's main gate above."

"Let's go to night vision," Turner said to Captain Saune and Samuel as they approached within fifteen feet of the tunnel's exit. The three men flipped down their goggles and powered them up. Upon reaching the lava tube's end, the three crouched down and surveyed the perimeter for any sign of activity.

Scanning the area with the night vision goggles, the men were relieved to see no movement and continued to scrutinize their surroundings. Just to their left was a conveyor belt that descended down ninety feet to what appeared to be a loading platform on a natural plateau. Turner made a mental note of the conveyor belt's control levers located next to them. He continued his scan of the loading area far below and saw the plateau was studded with landing lights. Sitting there were two helicopters.

"Do you see what I see, Captain?" Turner said, pointing to the sleek aircrafts as he signaled for the rest of the group to join them.

"I know where you are headed, Josh. Those are R-44 Ravens and, even though I can fly them, the Robinson only carries one pilot and two passengers. There's no way we could get everyone out," he said.

"I guess that will have to be Plan B," Turner replied as he stood and directed Yashiro to lead the group towards the path up to the complex's main gate.

"Here we go with the Plan B crap again," Samuel groaned as he and the weary group followed Turner up the pathway.

"Captain," Turner said straightforwardly, moving ahead of the others. "If things go badly, I want you to get my father and Maria out of here in one of those helicopters. Promise me you will try."

"I don't think it will come to that, but I promise I will do my best." Saune said, knowing he had come to trust and respect this man and he would do his utmost to honor his request if the need arose.

Led by Yashiro, the group started out along the narrow ledge that ran parallel to a steep, vertical drop off that descended to the bottom of the ancient caldera. Each was mindful of their steps and avoided the occasional glance into the blackness below them. They followed in single file until Yashiro, leading with a flashlight, stopped and directed them to the first switchback leading up to the Bishamon facility's main gate.

The group began their assent upward, not knowing what awaited them at the top of the rise. The eastern sky above them hinted at its first sign of the coming dawn.

13

Tenerife, Southern Airport

Hiroshi Tanaka yawned sleepily as he rose from the comfortable lounge chair in the commercial airways facility at Tenerife Sur Reina Sofia, the Island's southern airport. This airport, larger than its counterpart Aeropuerto de Tenerife Norte in the north of the island, was a commercial hub for the Canaries, leading to the surrounding islands, as well as out-bound to Africa, Europe, and beyond.

Hiroshi strolled over to the old white Mr. Coffee and grabbed an old, stained cup. He proceeded to pour the ancient brew, hoping it would jar him awake. Taking a sip of the foul hot liquid, he grimaced, put the cup down, and lifted the cargo manifest for this morning's run.

Hiroshi had been flying the latest string of supply runs to the Bishamon complex on the old volcano for the last three months. He was glad that he would be relieved by a new pilot after today's run, affording him a few weeks off for a much needed rest.

An experienced chopper pilot, Hiroshi had been flying the *Big Iron,* or more precisely the Sikorsky CH-53 Heavy Lift, for many years. He had amassed hundreds of flight hours during the Iraq war with the Japanese Defense Force, and now for the Bishamon Corporation.

It will be dawn in an hour and I want to be loaded and airborne, he thought as he began to peruse the manifest. His plan was to arrive at the mountain facility at first light, unload the supplies, and get back to the airport quickly. He had already booked the next flight back to Japan for a hunting trip on the northern island of Hokkaido.

Walking out of the hanger, he felt the cool Tenerife breeze blowing gently off the Atlantic Ocean as he quickly rechecked the cargo manifest. Finishing his inventory, he kept a watchful eye on the ground crews as they moved about completing their pre-flight procedures on his heavy lift chopper.

Stopping halfway to the craft, he admired the refurbished CH- 53K with its gross weight of eighty-four thousand pounds and lifting capacity of another twenty-seven thousand pounds.

I'll never get tired of flying this old workhorse, he thought, looking at the craft with true admiration.

The *Big Iron*, that he was so fond of, was leased to Bishamon for the duration of the business venture on Tenerife. Though ungainly in appearance, it was state-of-the-art with its three new General Electric six thousand shaft horsepower engines and composite airframe.

Hiroshi loved the new drive system; its split torque main gearbox and advanced digital fly-by-wire system made it an agile but tough flying machine. He now recalled how Osama reinstalled the ramp mounted Herstal GAU-21, 50-caliber 12.7mm gun in the rear of the craft on a swing-out mount.

Why he added that killing machine is beyond me. The only things to shoot at on this rock are the seagulls, he mused, laughing aloud and lighting a cigarette.

Hiroshi saw his copilot approaching from the hanger with an object under his arm.

"You almost forgot your new toy," his copilot, Kentaro Udo, yelled to him over the din of a fuel truck that went clambering by.

"Ah, thank you, Kentaro," he responded in a cheerful voice, as the copilot handed him his new Mathews Switchback hunting bow and carbon-tipped arrows. "I plan to use this on my hunting trip next week. I hear the hunting season has been exceptional in Hokkaido this year."

"You're in a good mood today," his copilot said with a grin.

"I should be. It'll be good to get away from here for a few weeks of long deserved rest," he replied happily to his copilot. The two men headed out on the tarmac towards the CH-53K.

Things had not always been lucrative for Hiroshi since the Iraq war. He was laid off from Japan Airlines after one year of piloting corporate executives. Nothing came his way in terms of a steady paycheck for a long time. Then a friend told him that a position as a chopper pilot was available in Yagato Osama's organization, working in the Canary Islands. Hiroshi knew going into the venture the reputation of Osama and the risks involved, but the generous salary offered to him for his loyalty made it impossible to refuse.

It was not all bad, ferrying supplies to the Bishamon complex on the old volcano. It disturbed him knowing that occasionally he was ordered to hover over the Atlantic Ocean as Osama's men would dump something out of the loading ramp into the sea. He looked back that first time and saw two men tossing a body from the rear of the craft.

The two men had then given him a look that said, *do your job and mind your business, or else.* The event unnerved him at the time, and for many days he tried to put the grizzly scene out of his mind. *Just fly,* he told himself, *just fly.*

The last of the supply crates was being secured in the cargo hold of the Sikorsky by the loading crew as the two men reached the rear of the craft. They walked up the steel drop downloading ramp to prepare for takeoff. Hiroshi strapped himself in his seat and powered up the craft's six thousand SHP engines. His co-pilot went back to ensure that all the crates were secure.

"We're secure in the loading bay," Kentaro said as he returned and hit the lever that closed and secured the loading ramp.

After getting clearance from the airport tower, the deafening roar of the Sikorsky filled the pre-dawn stillness as the lumbering behemoth lifted off its landing pad and headed towards the southwest.

"One more trip," Hiroshi whispered, smiling as he took a quick glance at the new hunting bow that was sitting on the flight deck beside him. Turning to his copilot, he spoke through the ANR flight headset. "Let's take the coastal route, Kentaro. We're twenty minutes early, and it's going to be a beautiful sunrise. *Nothing* is going to spoil this day."

The lumbering seven-blade helicopter flew over the sleeping town of San Miguel and then banked to the southwest, heading for the western coast of Tenerife.

14

As night began to shed its veil of darkness, cautious eyes watched two lone guards that were stationed inside the Bishamon compound's main gate. From their concealed position on the edge of the caldera's rim, Turner and the others sat single file on a rocky ledge just below the compound access road. They surveyed the nine-foot chain-link fence topped with razor wire. It surrounded the entire complex and ended at a menacing looking guard shack adjacent to a rolling gate. Inside the gate sat four black SUVs, parked side by side along the building in close proximity to the main door.

The building itself was a two-story steel pre-fabricated modular structure. Its width was a mere forty-five feet, but the length was unusually long at about two hundred feet. Seeing the ominous, windowless building again made Yashiro uneasy as he whispered to Turner in the growing pre-dawn light.

"If you decide to just open fire on the guards, you will alert the whole compound," he warned.

"We may not have much choice," Turner replied. He

was focusing on the pair of armed guards who now faced each other, preoccupied in conversation. "We're losing the darkness fast, and we have to get moving."

At that moment, Turner and the others heard the distinct sound of a vehicle approaching the compound from the access road. The two guards, upon hearing it as well, hit a switch on the guard shack. The area surrounding the gate was bathed in a bright light, and the mechanized rolling gate opened as they brought their rifles to bear on the approaching vehicle. Turner and the others quickly ducked below the rise as the two guards came out of the gate to intercept the vehicle.

Not expecting an armed welcome, Alton Burr quickly slid the 9mm under his seat as the two guards approaching him waved their hands for him to come to a halt.

Alton Burr had waited quite some time from his earlier vantage point before finally deciding to go to the archeology site, after the dark SUV returned from its gruesome clean up at the camp. Arriving at the dig site, Burr found it empty and the entrance to the lava tube buried under tons of rock.

He was hoping that his efforts to stifle Turner's discovery had been accomplished for him. *Who were they?* He pondered this on the drive back from the archeology site. *What was their interest in this, and did they take anything the old man may have found?* Driven by his demons and arrogance, he opted to follow the SUV to get some answers.

As fortune would have it, Burr's CJ-5 came to a halt just feet away from Turner and Samuel as they discretely peered over the edge of the dirt barrier. One of the guards came around to the passenger side, too intent on its occupant to notice the eyes watching him from the ledge. The other guard went to Burrs' side with his rifle raised and in a menacing tone said, "Step out of the vehicle."

Turner's plan materialized in an instant. He gestured to Captain Saune, who was positioned adjacent to the rear of the Jeep, to go around the back of the vehicle. Turner then signaled that he would take out the guard closest to him. Saune gave Turner an approving nod, but hesitated for a moment when he heard the distinct whomp-whomp sound of a helicopter approaching from behind them.

As the roar of the chopper increased, Captain Saune sprang into action, going behind the Jeep, while Turner and Samuel set upon the unsuspecting guard who turned to see the supply helicopter coming into view. The guard saw his assailants a split-second too late as Turner reached him and threw a wicked right cross to the man's jaw. The blow knocked him back against the CJ-5 with a loud thud. The dazed guard started to raise his AK-47. In a flash, the steel grip of the Peruvian native grabbed the man by the coat and easily tossed him over the edge of the steep precipice of the caldera's rim. The terror-stricken scream, unheard over the roar of the arriving helicopter, was cut short by the guard's neck snapping like a twig as he cartwheeled like a rag doll down to the bottom of the ancient crater.

Saune rounded the rear of the Jeep with his AK-47 leveled at the guard just as Alton Burr opened his door to get out, blocking the guard's line of fire. The Yakuza guard, distracted by the commotion on the far side of the Jeep, failed to see Saune rushing him and was shocked to feel a rifle barrel pointed at his head.

"Drop the weapon now," Saune hissed. He suddenly recognized the guard as the one that came out of the lava tube earlier that night and was knocked unconscious by Turner. "This just isn't your night, friend," Saune said coldly as the startled guard dropped his weapon to the ground and raised his hands.

Alton Burr, stunned by what had transpired so quickly, sat back down in the seat of his Jeep as the passenger door was thrown open. He turned to stare headlong at two 45-caliber weapons pointed at him.

"Don't shoot!" Burr yelled in a panic. "I just came from the Turner archeology site. I saw the lava tube had caved in and I came up here to get help," he lied.

"Well, if it isn't our old friend, Alton Burr," Eli said sarcastically as he, Maria, and Gonzales approached the vehicle. The thunderous roar of the CH-53K Sikorsky passed overhead, making its way over the caldera ridge and slowly descending to its landing zone.

"No time for us to talk now, Dad," Turner said. "Mr. Burr, would you be so kind as to take my father, Maria, and Yashiro out of here and get them back to Santa Cruz?"

"That's not a request, amigo," Samuel stated grimly, waving the handgun at Burr.

"I'm not leaving you here, Josh," Maria said in a pleading voice as she ran up to him.

"Nor am I, Son," Eli protested.

"Listen, both of you, we can't all fit in this Jeep. Someone has to get back to Santa Cruz and get out a warning about the tsunami," Turner said, knowing that time was running out. "Please don't argue with me and get going," he said, pulling the passenger seat forward as Yashiro climbed into the rear seat.

"Don't worry about us. We have a way out of here,"

Turner said in a desperate attempt to quell their fears and quickly get them out of danger.

Maria threw her arms around him, and whispered ever so gently, "I'm tired of saying good-bye to you, Josh. Please be careful." Turner held her tightly, wishing the moment would never end, but knowing that it must as he pushed her into the Jeep.

"Go to your father's place at the university. We'll meet you there later," Turner said

"Be careful, Son," Eli said, holding back his emotion as he hugged Turner. He then got in the front passenger side of the CJ-5 with the backpack carrying the parchments.

"Let's get out of here before more guards show up," Burr said, knowing it was too dangerous a situation to remain here any longer. He would be able to deal with Eli Turner once they got safely back to Santa Cruz.

Burr started the engine and quickly spun around the soft gravel lot, then proceeded to speed back down the rocky access road.

"What do we do with this guy?" Saune asked, still pointing his gun menacingly at the guard. The big Sikorsky slowed its decent to the landing site, now brightly lit with landing lights.

"He goes with us for now," Turner replied. Then he added as he pointed at the big chopper, "Captain, can you fly that rig?"

"I'm checked out on the heavy lifts, but it may be tough getting to it," he said, looking at the landing pad far below.

"How about commandeering one of those SUVs?" Samuel asked as he pointed to the black vehicles parked within the compound.

"Let just see what our friend here says." Pointing his 45 at the nervous guard, Turner spoke. "So we meet again, eh? Listen pal, I'm tired, pissed off, and in no mood for games, so I'll only ask you once. Are the keys in those vehicles?" he hissed, pulling back the hammer on the big gun and placing the barrel against the man's forehead.

"No," he pleaded nervously in broken English. "They remain locked, with their keys up in the security office on the second floor. I swear to you, that is the truth."

"It may be quicker to go back down the way we came and make a run for the helicopter," Samuel said. "It's getting light, and the visibility will be far better than it was coming up."

"Let's do it now," Turner said, starting back down the path leading to the tunnel's entrance. "Bring him with us, Captain," he added, motioning to the hapless guard.

"You heard the man, get moving. Gonzales, get his weapon," Saune ordered. The private picked up the AK-47 and followed the group back down the switchback towards the descending Sikorsky.

The morning sun was now breaking over the eastern horizon as Turner and the others quickly descended the rocky, slippery path. They reached the bottom in no time, as the big Sikorsky lightly touched down on its landing site on the lower plateau.

The group moved briskly now, retracing their path back to the lava tube's entrance, mindful of their steps. They quickly made their way along the narrow path, while the rear-loading ramp of the heavy lift chopper began to lower.

As they left the path and moved in front of the tunnel's entrance, Turner saw four workers and two armed guards approaching them from the cave's interior to off-load the newly delivered supplies. Without warning, chaos erupted in the entrance way as the two guards began to open fire on the group.

"Get down!" Turner yelled. He pushed his friend Samuel forward, sending him spiraling into the conveyor belt's control box. Turner quickly returned fire with his 45, sending the unlucky workers scrambling for cover within the cave.

During those first seconds, Turner saw Private Gonzales take the brunt of the opening blaze of gunfire, killing him instantly. Captain Saune was spared the same fate only because the captive guard to his left was struck in the leg and fell to the ground wincing in pain.

Saune's instincts took over as he immediately leveled his AK-47 at the assailants. He then unleashed gunfire into the cave and sent the two guards diving for cover behind the storage bins. In that brief pause, Saune was able to scramble over to Turner and Samuel on the right side of the cave's entrance.

"Now what, boss?" Samuel asked as he fired a few more deterrent rounds into the cave. "I'll even settle for a Plan C at this point."

"It's time to take a little ride, Samuel," Turner replied, hitting the power button on the conveyor control box. The rolling conveyor was brought to life as the reinforced rubber belt started noisily tracking downward.

"You've got to be kidding me?" Samuel said incredulously as he watched Turner jump onto the belt. Lying prone on the conveyer belt as it started tracking toward the landing pad, Turner waved for the rest to follow.

"Remind me never to go with you anywhere again!" Samuel yelled as he followed Turner's lead and jumped with Saune onto the moving belt. Making their way on the rattling belt to the loading platform below, Turner saw one of the Yakuza soldiers cautiously exiting the cave high above just as he spotted them on the conveyor belt.

"Don't let him kill the power switch," Turner yelled. He let lose a barrage of bullets as the other two joined in, forcing the unfortunate guard to retreat back into the cave.

"That's it for me as far as ammo," Samuel yelled, throwing the empty pistol away.

"Me, too," Turner said, looking down to see they were only a few yards from the base platform.

"Let's go," he yelled, rising up and running the remainder of the distance down the belt and then jumping off at the base. He was quickly followed by the other two men. The trio ran wildly across the plateau toward the now open loading bay of the Sikorsky.

Because of the engine noise, Hiroshi and his copilot inside the craft were oblivious to the battle raging outside. The two decided to go back and find out why the loading crew had not yet arrived to unload the supplies.

Turner, Samuel, and Saune were running up the ramp as bullets from the guards above whizzed around them and hit the steel bulkhead. Reaching the safety of the interior of the craft, the three ran into Hiroshi and Kentaro as they leisurely strolled toward the rear.

Leveling his empty 45 at the flight crew, Turner yelled, "Both of you get off the helicopter now!"

"Don't shoot," Hiroshi said, throwing his hands up in surrender as he ran off the aircraft with his copilot in tow.

"It's your show, Captain," Turner said, pointing toward the flight deck. "We'll cover the loading bay from here. Leave us your weapon, and hurry. We don't have much time."

The burly captain tossed Turner the AK-47, then turned and ran for the flight deck. He quickly took the pilot's seat, throttling up the big General Electric engines. In a few moments, the heavy lift chopper rose off the landing pad and threw a huge cloud of dust onto the plateau. Bullets ricocheted off the loading ramp as the chopper cleared the pad and started up towards the caldera's rim and out of the line of fire.

Looking out of the yawning opening in the rear of the aircraft, Samuel yelled to Turner above the roar of the rotors and wind as the lumbering chopper rose higher above the complex.

"Do you see what I see?" He yelled, pointing down to the building below. Turner's heart sank as he saw one of the black SUVs speeding out the main gate, pursuing the Jeep that only moments ago had whisked Maria, Yashiro, and his father to safety.

"Damn it!" He yelled, then turned and ran up to the cockpit followed by Samuel.

Seeing the two men, Saune signaled for Turner to put on the copilot's ANR flight intercom headset so they could converse above the sound of the engine noise. Putting the headset on, he saw Saune pointing to the lever on the upper right of the flight console.

"Activate that ramp lever; it will close the loading bay," Saune said.

"Got it," Turner said as he flicked the lever into the

stow position. After moving Hiroshi's Switchback hunting bow out of his way, Samuel put on the spare ANR and sat in the crew seat behind them.

Turner spoke as the ramp began to close. "We've got more problems, Captain. We saw one of the Bishamon SUVs leaving the compound. They must be going after my father and Maria. We have to help them."

"I'm on it," Saune said, quickly banking the huge chopper to the right and bringing it down toward the access road.

The sudden turn saved them all from instant death as a shell from a RBR-64 mm hand-held rocket launcher exploded just behind the right engine cowling. The explosion shook the big aircraft violently. Captain Saune quickly shut down the starboard engine and fought to control the heavy lift chopper as it began to lose altitude, veering downward towards the barren mountainside below.

"What the hell was that?" Samuel yelled through the intercom as Saune finally managed to level out the helicopter a mere one hundred fifty feet from the ground.

"We've got company," Turner said, pointing out of the right cockpit window at the small Robinson R-44 helicopter above and to the right of them.

"I've shut down the starboard engine," Saune reported, pointing outside to the black plumes of smoke belching sickeningly out the cowling of the damaged engine.

"Can we out run them?" Turner asked, seeing the R-44 coming about for the final kill.

"Normally, yes, but with an engine down, no way. We've got to put down and extinguish the fire before the whole thing blows," he responded as the billowing smoke trail became thicker.

"Put her down, Captain," Turner said, grabbing the AK-47 and hitting the lower switch on the loading ramp. "I'll try to keep them at bay while you tend to the fire." Ripping off the headset, Turner scrambled to the rear of the helicopter as the access ramp lowered. Seconds later, the heavy lift touched down and Turner sprinted down the loading ramp. Surveying his surroundings as he ran, he saw a cluster of huge boulders to his left, which he decided to use as cover. *This should draw them away from the Sikorsky,* he thought as he ran head-long toward the boulders.

The Raven continued coming closer but, just as suddenly, stopped its descent. Hiroshi, who had been unceremoniously conscripted to chase the trio in the small R-44, nervously decided to halt his descent when he saw the armed man running towards the rocks.

"What are you doing, you idiot?" The Yakuza guard yelled to him from the seat behind him as he set down the rocket launcher and picked up his AK-47. "Go after him," he yelled, glaring menacingly and pointing his weapon out the open door behind Hiroshi.

"But what about the Sikorsky?"

"The Sikorsky is crippled and is not going anywhere. Once we eliminate him," he said, gesturing to Turner, "we'll deal with the others. Now get this craft in position for a clear shot."

Hiroshi cursed his luck, knowing that he should have been on his way back to the airport by now. However, he obediently swung the small craft to the right and continued its descent as the soldier took aim out the door.

Turner heard the report of gunfire from above him, and

dove headlong into a small opening between a few boulders just as a spray of bullets hit the rocks above his head sending shards of rocks and dirt flying about. Taking a deep breath, he sprung up and unleashed a barrage from his weapon at the helicopter. Unfortunately, he managed only to splinter the landing strut underneath. As the chopper reacted defensively by rising upward, Turner anticipated the move. He aimed and squeezed the trigger, hearing only the clicking sound of an empty ammo clip.

Damn! How could I have been so stupid? He thought, angry at himself for leaving the last clip in the Sikorsky. He saw the Raven hovering lower and could see the soldier within smiling widely as he brought the rocket launcher out the door of the craft.

Turner knew at that moment he was a dead man. With no place to run and no one to help him, he simply stared at the man aiming the rocket launcher. Watching and waiting for the final sting of death, he suddenly saw the flash of an arrow from the Mathews hunting bow. It struck the neck of the Yakuza guard, piercing it completely. Turner saw the soldier's eyes widen in pain and shock as he collapsed forward onto the pilot, jamming the flight stick in the same direction. The Raven yawed wildly and began spiraling toward the ground. Hiroshi's final thoughts were that of his hunting trip as the small helicopter hit the ground and exploded into a fireball.

Turner stood and gazed over to the Sikorsky. He saw his friend Samuel standing at the base of the loading ramp, smiling and slinging the hunting bow over his shoulder. Captain Saune, who rushed over and opened the engine cowling, was busy emptying two fire extinguishers onto the heavily smoking engine.

Snatched from the jaws of death, a relieved Turner ran over to join his friend at the ramp.

"I owe you one, Samuel," Turner said gratefully. "I thought I was a goner."

"Hey, what are friends for? Besides, I can't let you have all the fun," Samuel replied, smiling and slapping Turner on the back.

"It's a good thing you're a good shot," Turner said, amazed by the precision of his friend's archery skills.

"Remind me to take you hunting back home in the Amazon rainforest someday. I'll teach you how to use a *real* long bow. This stuff is for weekend amateurs," he said in disdain, tossing the bow back up the loading ramp. "I tried at first to set this damn thing up," he explained, pointing to the Herstal 50-caliber gun, "but the angle was too steep."

Captain Saune walked over to the two men and tossed the last empty fire extinguisher on the ground. "We were lucky," he said, wiping his blackened hands on his BDUs. "The electrical system took the brunt of the damage on the starboard engine. If it had hit us a little more forward, we wouldn't be talking right now."

"Can we still fly with one engine out?" Turner asked the fatigued soldier. "Maria and my father are still in danger."

"We can, but I can assure you we won't have a lot of speed or maneuverability," he answered wearily as the trio headed up the loading ramp. "I'll get us airborne and see if I can find them."

He started walking back to the flight deck, while Turner and Samuel remained at the rear, looking out at the still smoking, twisted remains of the Raven helicopter.

The two remaining GE engines whined loudly as the big seven- prop Sikorsky roared to life. They started to slowly lift- off as Turner pulled back the bolt on the Herstal 50-caliber machine gun.

"We won't need the bow and arrows now," Turner declared, feeling the anger well inside of him as he thought of all the death and destruction that had occurred since the previous evening.

Weary from the long night, the young archaeologist ached all over and longed to close his eyes. However, the adrenaline now coursing through his body kept him going as they passed over the ridge and headed east; following the route their friends had taken.

"They'll be okay, Josh," Samuel said, seeing the trepidation in his friend's eyes. "Your father will look out for them."

"God help them if they hurt my father and Maria," Turner said in an acerbic tone, looking his friend in the eye. "God help them all."

15

The morning sun wove a tapestry of bright orange and yellow hues across the eastern sky, as seen from the ancient volcanic ridge. The ridge spanned the entire length of the island, from north to south, like the backbone of some primordial beast. Only the sound of Alton Burr's CJ-5 disturbed the morning calm as it wove its way down the gravel access road.

Burr managed to retrace his route from the Bishamon compound. He now headed towards Guimar and Highway One, which would be the quickest route back to Santa Cruz. The loose and narrow gravel road had many dangerous turns with steep drop- offs that slowed their escape from the island's high ridge of Mt. Blanco.

Eli saw that Maria was exhausted from the long dreadful night. She had drifted off into a restless sleep in the back seat, while Yashiro, lost in his thoughts, stared out the window.

As they rode, Eli conveyed to Burr what had transpired the night before. He spoke of Pencor's plans to cause the landslide and unleash the tsunami on the United States.

"You can't be serious," Burr said incredulously at hearing

the ominous plot recounted by Eli.

"I'm dead serious, Burr, and that fellow in the back seat will confirm it. Hopefully, we will be able to stop this wild scheme. Pencor and Osama were more than willing to kill us all to protect his plans and you can bet he won't give up easily."

"I want to apologize to you for my boorish behavior yesterday when we met, Dr. Turner," Burr lied, switching gears in hopes of getting Eli to disclose information about what he discovered in the tomb. "It's a shame they destroyed any chance of you discovering relevant artifacts. I'm sure you know of my beliefs and that my zealousness sometimes gets in the way of my desire to find the truth. I hope you understand."

"Forget about it, Mr. Burr," Eli countered. "I didn't exactly help matters much myself. The good news is that we were able to recover another important document from the tomb before Osama's men showed up. Once we get this mess taken care of, we're going to search La Palma for the discovery of a lifetime."

"If I can be of any assistance to you, Dr. Turner, I'd be more than happy to help you in your quest," Burr continued in his deception. "My private helicopter is at your disposal."

"I just might take you up on—" his answer was cut short by the explosive shattering of the rear window in the Jeep by a barrage of bullets.

"It's Osama's men," Yashiro yelled, looking out the gaping hole that used to be a window and seeing a black SUV closing in on them.

"Get down!" Maria yelled, snapped awake by the assault and pushing Yashiro to the side. "Those guys just won't give up."

"They will not stop until we are all dead," the tiny Japanese man replied in frustration as he hunkered down in his seat.

"Under my seat, there's a gun," Burr yelled at Eli as he sped up in an effort to put more distance between them and their pursuers. Eli fished under his seat and came up with Burr's Glock 9mm pistol.

"Give it to me, Dr. Turner. I have a clear view from the back," Maria said.

Eli pulled back the chamber of the Glock, loading the weapon, and handed it to her. Burr slowed the vehicle to negotiate a sharp curve to the right. This allowed the SUV to gain ground on them while Maria sprang up and fired two shots at the menacing vehicle. One bullet harmlessly ricocheted off its bumper, while the other put a hole in the upper left corner of the front windshield. The SUV backed off momentarily, and then began to close the gap once again. Maria took aim and started firing. She emptied the clip as the SUV swerved back and forth in a defensive mode, receiving little damage.

"God, I hate guns!" She yelled in frustration, handing the gun to Eli in the front seat. "Is there any more ammo?"

"That's all, miss. I don't usually get into running gun fights," Burr yelled above the noise. He took the next curve a bit too fast and fish-tailed the rear of the Jeep, almost spinning the vehicle out of control.

"That was close, Burr," Eli said looking behind and seeing the ominous vehicle still on their tail. "They can take these curves better than us with the weight of their vehicle. It's only a matter of time before they catch us."

"We have to lose them somehow," Burr responded, regaining control of the Jeep and speeding down a straightaway towards the next turn.

"It's only another seven miles to Guimar and the main highway," Maria said from the back seat.

"We'll never make it before they catch us," Burr said as he came around the next sharp turn in the road. Coming out of the turn, Burr spotted a road leading off the access road to the right. He quickly applied the brakes and spun onto the smaller road in an effort to lose the oncoming assailants.

"No!" Maria yelled in anguish. "This road leads to a stone quarry. There's no way out."

"Damn it!" Burr yelled in anger as he headed up the small road to the quarry, which sat upon a hill overlooking the eastern slope of Tenerife. "Maybe we can get help there," he said fearfully. Eli looked behind them. The big SUV that originally passed the turn was now backing up and following them onto the road to the stone quarry.

Two quarry night shift workers noticed the Jeep coming up the steep gravel road. Thinking that it was part of the day shift reporting for work, they went back to their duties monitoring the portable cone crusher, protected from its deafening noise by the ear protection they wore.

Burr finally reached the old facility at the top of the rise and drove up to the main entrance next to the cone crusher building. He slammed on the brakes and slid the vehicle to a halt just as the black SUV reached the summit. It stopped one hundred fifty feet away from them.

"Get out of the Jeep, now!" Eli yelled, throwing the door open and jumping out. He ran to the facility's main door only to find it locked. He pounded on the door as the others finally reached him. Unfortunately, the deafening sound of the CAT diesel engines that ran the plant drowned out any hope of anyone hearing him beat on the rusty, steel door.

"They can't hear with all this noise," Eli yelled as he turned to see the two men climbing out of the back of the SUV, while two remained in the front. Eli and the others froze in their tracks as the men slowly approached and leveled their weapons at them.

Eli tugged on the rim of his hat defiantly and said, "Maria, I'm going to make a run for it. I want you and the others to make a dash for the Jeep and try to get around them."

"Run to where? This whole place is surrounded by chain-link fence," Burr yelled in panic as the two Yakuza mercenaries closed in for the kill, taking aim at the helpless group.

Their deadly intent was suddenly interrupted by a noise that overwhelmed the loud quarry diesels. They quickly turned; surprised to see the *Big Iron* Sikorsky rising up from the ridge beside them. The two guards calmly waved to the chopper thinking they were sent help from the Bishamon facility. The hovering craft spun on its axis, revealing to them the open loading bay and a man aiming a monstrous 50-caliber machine gun at them.

As the Sikorsky swung around to face the SUV, Josh Turner saw the two men raise their weapons at him. Pulling the trigger, he quickly unleashed the deadly firepower of the Herstal 50-caliber machine gun. Splintering bone and flesh, the two men were instantly torn apart by the two hundred rounds-per-minute discharge of the frightening weapon. Turner, furious at seeing his father and Maria so helpless against these murderers, then turned the weapon on the big SUV and unleashed its steel-jacketed fury. The vehicle was shredded inside and out by the Herstal's horrific firepower; pieces of metal and blood stained glass flew everywhere from the lethal onslaught.

Turner, shaken by what just transpired, stared at the shattered remains of the vehicle and what was left of the two mercenaries lying at its side.

"For what?" He whispered silently as Captain Saune swung the helicopter around for a quick landing on the quarry compound. "You died for what?" He let go of the gun, weary of this nightmare, and wishing it would end.

As the big chopper set down, Turner ran down the loading ramp to greet his father, who was running over to join him.

"Are you all okay?" Turner asked in a weary voice as Maria, Yashiro, and Burr followed the elder Turner.

"We're fine, Son," he replied, seeing the distressed, weary look on his son's face. "Another minute, Josh, and those goons would have done us in for sure. Those guys definitely weren't here just to talk."

Maria reached for the younger Turner and hugged him tightly as she cried tears of relief.

"It's alright, Maria. No one is going to hurt you. We're going to get out of here now," he said softly as she trembled in his arms. "Go into the chopper," he said to the rest of the group, motioning them to the loading ramp.

"You had to do it, Josh," the elder Turner said gently to his son. He put his arm around his shoulder as they walked towards the waiting aircraft. "They didn't leave you any other choice, Son. It was either them, or all of us."

"I'm just tired of the killing, Dad. When is it all going to end?" Turner replied as they reached the safety of the helicopter's cargo bay. Samuel, in the flight deck, activated the stow switch on the loading ramp, removing from view, the grizzly scene outside.

"You saved us all, Son. I'm proud of you," Eli said in an effort to comfort his son. "When we get back to Santa Cruz, we'll get help to expose Pencor and Osama's dirty plans, and we'll be done with all of this."

"Hey, amigo," Samuel yelled, coming to the rear from the flight deck of the helicopter. "The Captain says he's going to take us to his Guardia Civil base in La Laguna where we can get a hold of the authorities." He then plopped down in one of the many crew seats in the rear of the craft.

"I'm afraid this isn't over; not by a long shot, Dad," Turner said. "I'm sure they will have men scouring the island looking for us after they realize we've escaped. We have to find a safe place to regroup. Professor Santiago's house at the university is our best bet. We will go there and then decide what our next move is going to be."

"But, Son, the authorities can—"

"Dad, from what Yashiro has told us, they will never react in time to stop the landslide on La Palma," he said, interrupting his father.

A weary Josh Turner sat down next to Samuel and closed his eyes, endeavoring to wipe out the images of death engrained in his mind. All sat in silence as the noise of the huge Sikorsky filled the void of the large cargo bay, each of them wondering what the next few hours would bring.

16

Puerto Naos, La Palma Island

It was another tranquil island morning on the western beachfront of La Palma, with scores of tourists enjoying their breakfast at the Los Tilos restaurant located in the Sol La Palma Hotel. The four-star establishment, built in 1999, was renowned for its luxurious amenities, beautifully decorated suites, and world class dining.

Located in the midst of a banana plantation, just off the Calle Del Remo highway, the luxury hotel offered its guests a lavish view of its black volcanic sand beaches along with panoramic excursions to the natural parks on the island for the more adventurous.

The tourist and locals went about their daily lives, while waiters of the Los Tilos hustled back and forth serving a variety of breakfast dishes to its many guests. A slender, dark-haired woman, fit from years of rugged work, sat alone looking out the restaurant window to the blackened beaches below.

Wearing her trademark Timberland hiking boots, Massachusetts Institute of Technology jersey, and jeans, Rosalie Harris sipped her herbal tea as she pressed the cell phone to her ear.

The Sol La Palma had been her home for the last two weeks, while she and the film crew for the National Geographic Channel filmed their documentary. She was pleased with all the amenities the TV channel had lavished on her as a perk for acquiring her particular talent, but felt a bit uncomfortable in these luxurious surroundings.

'Rugged Rosalie', as she was known to her co-workers and friends, was a seasoned field scientist with the U.S. Geological Survey. With over twenty years of experience, her job sent her all over the world, climbing in and out of dormant and active volcanoes. Rosalie's current assignment, not by her own choice, was acting as scientific consultant for the documentary, providing filmed interviews and on-the-scene accounts, which she felt rather uncomfortable doing.

Rosalie now tapped her fingers impatiently as the hold signal on the phone clicked relentlessly, just as it had for the last five minutes. She took another sip of tea, recounting the unsettling occurrences that had transpired over the last few days while filming on the Cumbre Vieja fault line on the western flank of the island.

The filming had gone fairly well thus far, with the crew setting up each shot from different vantage points on the volcanic ridge. Based on her expertise, she explained the theory of the remote possibility that an eruption of Cumbre Vieja could cause a major mega-thrust tsunami.

The volcanic eruption would cause the fault line to collapse into the sea and a massive tsunami would occur devastating the western hemisphere. The BBC had done a special on the theory years before, but the National Geographic Channel wanted to do a follow-up program, which to them meant good ratings.

Just two days ago, she and the crew were taping at the twelve foot fault running down the spine of the southwestern slope of the island, a result of the 1949 eruption. She had noticed the unmistakable signs of active volcanism that only she could interpret with her years of hands-on experience. Rosalie knew the multiple active steam vents and abnormally high ground temperatures indicated an active magma chamber. Seeing these ominous clues set off an alarm in her head because she had witnessed them so many times before in the past. The only thing missing were the seismic tremors, and this perplexed her.

On yesterday's film shoot, they had suddenly encountered four Asian men on the ridge. The men told the crew they were on private property and, for their own safety, they should leave. She found it quite disconcerting that two of the men were armed under their jackets.

She and the film crew left at Rosalie's insistence, and immediately traveled to the park office for clarification. They were assured there was no restriction about going up to the fault ridge, and the men they encountered were in error. Much to Rosalie's growing trepidation, the film crew decided to try again in the morning.

Rosalie sent the film crew ahead of her this morning, explaining to them that she had to contact her main office in Washington

D.C. to report her observations. She would hire a ride to the fault line located high above the tranquil beaches later on. The crew teased her, saying she was becoming a regular Chicken Little worried about the sky falling. Reveling in their joke, they left her ninety minutes earlier to set up the equipment for the day's film shoot.

The phone in her ear finally clicked. It was followed by a man's voice that said, "USGS Data Center: Peter Markson speaking."

"Hi, Pete. It's Rosalie," she said, relieved to no longer be on hold.

"Hey, Rugged Rosalie, how goes your new reality TV show?" Markson said, teasing his co-worker about her latest assignment.

"Very funny, Pete," she replied, annoyed at being the brunt of jokes with her peers. "You know I was right in the middle of my field work on Mt. Etna in Sicily. The main office could have sent anyone here if they wanted."

"Calm down, Rosalie. I was just kidding. Besides, could you imagine seeing our director of operations doing a TV documentary?" Markson said, laughing aloud. "You were a much better choice. So, what's up?"

"Pete, I'm calling for a favor. I need you to pull up the sensor and seismic data on La Palma in the Canary Islands. I just got off the phone with the local research center and their sensors show a normal status for the Cumbre Vieja," she said to her friend in Washington.

"I'm at my computer now, Rosalie. I'll retrieve it for you. Why do you need it?" he said with concern in his voice.

"Pete, I'm seeing all the distinct signs of active volcanism on the Cumbre Vieja. I've got numerous steam vents and elevated ground temperatures, but nothing is registering on the sensors here," she reported.

"Do you have any seismic activity?" Markson asked, knowing his friend was a seasoned professional and not prone to making idle warnings without good cause.

"That's the part I don't get. I am seeing all the signs, except for that," she said in a puzzled tone. "We're right on top of it, yet we haven't experienced any seismic events at all."

"Hang on, here comes the data," Markson said as he perused the data screen in front of him. "Ground temps are within normal parameters, according to this data. Seismic activity," he paused, scanning the month long report. "I show nothing that's out of the ordinary, according to our historical data. A few tremors here and there, but that is to be expected. Without active micro-gravity monitoring on-site to identify activity in the magma feeder tube conduit, it's a wild guess."

"Damn!" She said in frustration. "When was the last satellite photo taken of any uplift zone indications in the caldera? Any pressure in the magma chamber would cause uplift on—"

"I know, Rosalie. I'm looking at it right now," Markson interrupted, already ahead of her train of thought. "Okay, here it is. It was taken over two years ago. I can schedule a pass over today if you really think it's necessary. GEOS is over the eastern Atlantic now," he said as he began the programming for the satellite.

"That would be great, Pete. You're the best. If you do

see any uplifting in the dome, call me on my cell right away, alright?"

"Will do, Rosalie. You take care of yourself," he said to his longtime friend.

"I will, Pete. Bye," she said as she flipped the cell phone off. She finished her tea, stood up, and started heading for the door to the parking lot. It was then that she saw the film crew's local contact, Andreas Conti, coming in the door with a police officer.

"Miss Rosalie," he said in a relieved voice. "I'm so glad to see that you are alright."

"What's the problem, Andreas?" Rosalie asked, suddenly concerned.

"There has been a terrible accident on the slope of Cumbre Vieja, Miss Rosalie," he said tersely. "The film crew's van went off the cliff going up to the ridge fault. We thought you were with them, but we couldn't find you in the wreckage."

"What wreckage? Where is the film crew?" she asked, totally shocked by the news.

"I…uh…I'm sorry Miss Rosalie, but there were no survivors," he answered. "It's lucky that you were not with them."

Rosalie sat back down, stunned by the news of the film crew's deaths. *Could it have something to do with those men on the ridge yesterday? Was it really an accident?* She wondered how fate had somehow spared her from the same demise. *Get a hold of yourself, girl. You're getting paranoid in your old age. It was just an accident, and nothing more.* Reaching for her phone, she began to call the States with the terrible news.

***

As the island's inhabitants went about their daily routine, primordial forces were at work in the volcanic magma chamber four kilometers beneath La Palma.

Normally, magma rising from fractures deep within the earth's crust is far less dense than its surrounding rock. As it ceases to rise, it forms a chamber, or pool, of magma deep beneath the surface.

As more magma wells up into this pool, the pressure on the magma chamber increases. This increased pressure causes it to expand upward, resulting in a volcanic eruption.

The immense, glowing plasma field generated by the Scalar Interferometer weapon was being directed from the island of Tenerife. It had been increasing exponentially in size over the prior months, super-heating the center of the La Palma magma chamber and expanding outward.

Without the natural forces deep within the earth that would normally up-well the molten rock, the super-heated liquid rock frothed within its chamber. This sent unimaginable temperatures cascading up towards the surface. The ancient Cumbre Vieja volcanic ridge, kilometers above the molten boiling tempest, was able to release some of the gigantic pressure from deep within the bowels of the earth through its many surface vents.

On the western flank of the island's ridge, high above the black sandy shoreline, millions of liters of water trapped between layers of soft sediment and basalt rock boiled under the vast heat of the super-heated core with no means of release.

Minute by minute, almost a trillion tons of softer surface rock above the natural aquifer began to loosen its grip. Now, near the point of no return, it struggled to free itself from its ancient confines and slide into the sea far below.

Nature's awesome fury had been set in motion and the stage was set for its final act.

17

Robert Pencor was furious as he slammed his fists on Osama's desk. "All of this manpower, yet you let them slip between your fingers!" He continued raving as the Japanese Oyabun patiently tapped his fingers on his desk, his tolerance for this man's insulting behavior reaching its limits.

As Pencor's diatribe became more menacing, the burly Yakuza guard standing at the doorway slightly raised his AK-47 in an automatic defense of his Oyabun. Osama quickly shot him a look, which he readily recognized and lowered his weapon immediately.

"All of our efforts may be in vain because of your inefficiency," he yelled as the calm pretense of Yagato Osama wavered ever so slightly. "Your scientist insists that we need at least eight more hours to ensure a proper build-up of the Interferometer weapon. By that time, the authorities will be on top of us if Turner and his people sound the alarm." His face began turning scarlet red from the rage he now leveled at Osama, with eyes that betrayed any sense of sanity.

"Robert," Osama said, regaining his composure. "Once again you question my ability, which saddens me. Granted, Turner and his friends are alive so far through sheer luck and the element of surprise. It was bad karma the supply helicopter arrived when it did," he said, picking up the phone receiver. "I have no doubt they are presently heading for the airport in Santa Cruz and my men have been dispatched to intercept them." Pausing mid thought, he spoke into the phone. "Please send in Administrator Fuentes." After hanging up the phone, he said, "Need I remind you, Robert, I have not achieved my status in this organization through lack of good judgment or caution. I have planned for every contingency in the event of trouble, as you soon will see."

The door opened and a short, overweight, balding man with bulging eyes entered the room. He was immediately taken back by the chilling gaze he received from Pencor. Warily, he moved to the center of the room as the guard shut the door behind him. Recognizing Yagato Osama, the portly man nodded politely.

"Good morning, Mr. Osama," he said nervously.

"Good morning, Administrator Fuentes. I trust that you are well" Osama said, knowing the man had done very well financially since the inception of their relationship.

Yagato Osama had been paying Fuentes quite handsomely for his cooperation since Bishamon arrived on Tenerife. He quickly expedited matters that were favorable to Osama, such as getting permits or helping to pad the pockets of many officials on the island. As island administrator, Fuentes had control and unlimited access to all government departments, which made him the logical choice for exploitation by Osama at the onset of his plans.

"Why did you need to see me so urgently?" Fuentes asked. He was still confused as to why Osama's men came to his home so early and whisked him to the complex, without so much as an explanation.

"We have a small problem, Administrator," Osama said, eyeing the man whose suits never seemed to fit right. "You are aware of the Turner archeology project below our complex, are you not?"

"Yes. Unfortunately, my assistant gave them permission as a favor to Professor Santiago from the university, while I was in Spain on business. Of course, I would have denied permission and tied the request up in permits if I had known. It was tragic that he died in that awful accident soon afterward," he said, knowing that it was no accident that his assistant was dead.

"Yes, quite a shame," Osama said, dismissing the topic. "It seems that Turner and his accomplices compromised this facility early this morning, killing many of my associates. They have stolen valuable information from this facility and, in the process, destroyed my private helicopter and stole our supply helicopter. They are a danger to us and need to be dealt with immediately. I want you to use your resources to apprehend them by any means possible, and then bring them to me without any contact or communication with anyone. Do you understand?"

"It will be difficult, but I will try to do what I can."

"You will not try, you will do it!" Osama yelled at the fat man before him, whose forehead now glistened with sweat. "I want them brought to me immediately. If they resist, your police are instructed to shoot to kill." Osama paused for effect and added with a twisted smile, "By the way, how are your beautiful wife and lovely daughter?"

"Uh...they are well," the administrator replied, shaken to his core by the question; the true meaning of this pleasantry driven home with crystal clarity. He was over his head and knew he had no other choice but to comply with Osama's wishes, no matter how terrible. "I will personally contact the Policia Nacional and the Guardia Civil right away and order an island-wide search," he said with a false bravado, knowing failure would mean a violent death not only for him, but for his family as well.

"Your success will be rewarded, Administrator Fuentes," Osama said, waving his hand in dismissal as the guard escorted the administrator out of the office. Upon the door being shut behind them, Osama spoke quietly to Pencor.

"Believe me, Robert; neither Turner nor anyone else will have sufficient time to thwart our plans," he stated confidently. "By this evening, our little present to the United States will be on its way, and we will be on our way to the airport to make our escape. All incriminating evidence will be disposed of prior to that, just as we have planned."

"You have forgotten one loose end," Pencor said, his anger now under control, though still irritated by the costly turn of events of the last few hours. "The scientist who escaped your facility was with the Turners; that is our one vulnerability. He must be silenced before he can implicate us."

"My men are aware of this, Robert. They all have his picture, along with photos of the Turners from the newspaper coverage. If they are discovered by my forces, they have orders to kill them without hesitation," Osama said flatly.

Looking at his watch, Pencor turned to leave the office. "Have my helicopter pilot meet me at the landing pad. I have the reception at the university to attend to assure my alibi for being on Tenerife. I'm making a major contribution to the antiquities department of the college." Stopping and turning to face Osama, he pointed his finger at him and said darkly, "Do not fail me, Yagato. I'll return later to collect my patents." He spun around and walked out the door, wondering what other bad luck could befall him before this was all finished.

Osama reached for the phone and called his security chief, who answered on the first ring. "Have you completed the modification to Pencor's helicopter?" Osama asked.

"Yes, sir, it has been done per your instructions," the security head said proudly. "The pilot has been instructed to await your orders."

"Good," Osama said, smiling at his own cleverness. *It had been bad karma that the Turner team managed to elude him thus far. The arrival of the younger Turner had been unexpected, but not insurmountable,* he thought.

"I have been in constant contact with our people in and around Santa Cruz. They are positioning themselves at all the locations you predicted they might go in the event they fail to reach the airport. We will get them, sir," he said confidently.

"Very good," Osama said. "Contact me the moment they are taken. After that little inconvenience is dealt with, I'll have my welcome surprise for Pencor when he returns."

Hanging up the phone, he opened the desk drawer, picked up a detonator switch, and toyed lightly with the button. *Yes, Mr. Pencor, we will have quite a reception for you. I promise.*

18

The old Tenerife National Guard base was located in a long red brick building on the outskirts of La Laguna, a twenty-minute drive from Santa Cruz. Built in 1907, it served as a military training base until 1982 when total autonomy of the archipelago was achieved from Spain with the fall of the Franco government. Since then, the base had fallen upon disrepair and was converted to the island National Guard base of operations. Only a skeleton crew now staffed the facility during the week. There were even less on this day seeing the Dia de Santiago Apostol festival in Santa Cruz was in full gear.

Sergeant Juan Ortega sat at his desk smoking his pipe, as he did on quiet days. He had just gotten off the telephone with his wife, who was harassing him to leave the base early in order to get to the parade in town later that evening.

"That woman will be the death of me," he bellowed as he slammed the phone's receiver down on its cradle. "Private Carmen, are you married?" He asked the skinny young man filing papers in the file cabinet.

"No, Sergeant, I'm not," he replied curiously.

"For God's sake, don't. It's not worth it," he grumbled as he picked up the roster for next week's mountain rescue training, which had become necessary with the increase of careless tourists getting stranded on the high peaks of Mount Teide.

Ortega looked again at the fax report from the Tenerife Police he received earlier, showing photos and names of people wanted for questioning in a multiple murder, but tossed it back onto the pile of paper work on his desk.

The private smiled at the sergeant's comments as he went about his duties, but stopped suddenly when heard the sound of a chopper coming in from the southwest.

"Do we have an inbound flight scheduled today, Sergeant?" He asked as he went over to the old, rotted wood-framed window and looked out.

"None that I'm aware of, Private," Ortega replied, looking through the papers on his desk.

"It's a Sikorsky transport, Sergeant," he reported as Ortega rose from the comfort of his chair to see for himself. "What is it doing here?"

"Let's go see who may be paying us a visit, Carmen," Ortega said as both men strapped on their side arms. They headed out the door to investigate the strange arrival.

The big CH-53 touched down next to the Guard unit's old Bell Model 205 UH-1H chopper, used for mountain evacuations and local transport. The *Big Iron* shut down its two remaining GE power plants, throwing the surrounding area into silence. Only the wisp--wisp sound of the craft's top rotor blades winding to a halt remained.

The side door opened, and the group of weary refugees from the long night's struggle walked down the steps to the black asphalt of the helipad. They were followed in the rear by its pilot, Captain Saune.

As the two soldiers from the base drew nearer, Captain Saune recognized the sergeant and gave him a wave, moving ahead of the group to intercept him. The confused sergeant gave his commanding officer a salute as he reached him.

"Good morning, Captain," he stated as Saune returned the salute. "I wasn't expecting you here."

"I understand, Sergeant Ortega. We have an urgent matter to attend to, and I will need your help."

"I'm afraid we do have a problem, Sir," he replied nervously, pulling his side arm out of its holster and pointing it at Turner and Samuel as they came towards him. "Stop where you are! You are all to come with me, where you will be held until the police can arrive."

"What are you talking about, Sergeant?" Saune asked, surprised by the actions of his old friend as the private also pulled his gun to cover the group.

"What's this all about?" Turner asked as he walked closer, halting when he saw the gun leveled at his head.

"I'm sorry, sir," Ortega said, "but we have orders from the administrator's office to detain all of you for questioning by the police in regards to possible murders at the Bishamon Satellite Relay Station. This has come from Administrator Fuentes himself. The police report came out a half hour ago stating that an island- wide manhunt has been launched to apprehend Dr. Turner and his associates for the murder of scientists at the facility."

"That's utterly ridiculous, Sergeant," Saune replied in frustration. "There's no truth in that at all."

"That's just great," Samuel said in disgust. "I'm really

starting to get a complex. Everyone keeps pointing guns at us."

"Listen to me, Sergeant. You've known me for fifteen years now, and, in all that time, haven't I always been honest with you?" Saune asked, relaxing his posture and speaking in Spanish to his subordinate.

"Yes, sir, I have the utmost respect for you. That is why I do not enjoy doing this," Ortega replied, lowering his weapon a bit.

"Can we speak in the office?" Saune asked. "The rest can remain here with your private. I promise, they will not cause you any trouble," he said, shooting Samuel a stern look.

"Hey," Samuel said, "I'm the sole of patience, Captain, but if that guy keeps pointing that pop gun at me I'm—"

"See what you can do, Captain Saune," Turner interrupted, "but remember we don't have much time left."

"Shall we, Sergeant?" Saune asked, gesturing at the old red brick office.

"Wait here and watch them, Carmen," Ortega said to his private as the two men walked towards the building and disappeared inside.

"Now what do we do?" Eli asked as they stood waiting on the tarmac.

"It looks as if our friends at Bishamon are using these trumped- up charges to keep us from alerting the authorities. There's no doubt now that Administrator Fuentes is on Osama's payroll, which presents a real problem, seeing he has a lot of power on Tenerife," Maria said in frustration.

"Like I said, miss, Osama's tentacles have far reaches on

this island," Yashiro said tersely. "He'll stop at nothing to gain time now the slide is just hours away, and this little tactic may give him the time he needs."

"He has no control over me," an agitated Alton Burr stated, clenching his fist. "I can go wherever and whenever I please."

"You're up to your eye balls in this little escapade now, Burr," Eli said, really annoyed with the little man's arrogance.

"He's right, Mr. Burr," Turner said. "They will not allow any witnesses to live at this point in the game, including you. You can take to the bank they have most likely run the tags on the jeep you left at the quarry and found it to be a rental. It won't take rocket science to get your name and locate where you're staying. Yes, you could leave, but you wouldn't live to see the sunset," he said as a dejected Burr just huffed and sat down on the warm asphalt.

"Can't we just go to the police and explain the situation?" Maria asked, frustrated that they had come so far and been through so much, only to hit a dead end.

"That's the last thing we should do," Yashiro said. "Osama's men would show up the moment they knew where we had been taken. They are sworn to serve and even die for him, so killing a few local police officers in order to eliminate us is a minor inconvenience to them."

"We need outside help at this point. We must contact the U.S. government somehow," Turner said as he watched Saune and Sergeant Ortega leaving the office and coming their way.

"Secure your weapon, Private Carmen," Ortega ordered.

"But, Sergeant, we must report this to the Island

Administrator."

"We are not reporting anything, Private," the sergeant barked to his subordinate, as the private hastily put his side-arm back into its holster.

"Looks like you were successful in explaining the situation, Captain," Turner said, relieved for the moment.

"I've explained the context of what is happening and we're going to do whatever we can to help you," Saune said with a gleam in his eye. "I can have an assault team armed and ready to go by 1600 hours. Can you be at this address by then?" he asked, handing Turner a slip of paper with an address written down on it. "We can't remain here too long. I'm sure they'll probably have an idea where we have landed by now."

"I had a feeling it was gonna come down to us," Turner said, knowing they could all wind up dead before the day was out. "Samuel and I will meet you then, but first, I want to get Maria, Dad, and the others to a safe place. We'll try to contact the U.S. government somehow, and then get back to you and your men."

"I'm going with you," Yashiro said boldly. "I've helped create this nightmare and I'm going to try to help dismantle it. You will need me to gain access to the complex, and I am the only one who can successfully manipulate the Interferometer frequencies. That is, if we get there in time."

"He's right about that, Josh," Samuel said. "We may have to knock on the front door if all else fails."

"Sergeant, go get the satellite phones in my office, along with my spare side arm and ammo belt," Saune said as Ortega quickly hurried back to the facility. "We can keep in contact that way, Josh. You can also use it to make contact with your government and get the warning out," Saune said, tossing a set of keys to Samuel. "Take my van; it's parked alongside of the building. I'll go with Ortega."

"It's 10:30 now. That should give us time to get to your father's place at the university." Turner said to Maria, looking at his watch as Samuel sprinted off to retrieve the vehicle.

"Don't take any unnecessary risks, Josh. By now you can be sure the Tenerife authorities and Osama's men are looking for you," Saune said. Sergeant Ortega returned, carrying two Global Star satellite phones. He handed one to Turner, along with a military issue 45-automatic and fresh ammo belt.

"Don't worry, Captain, we'll see you in a few hours," Turner responded as Samuel pulled up to the group in an old, white 1992 Ford F-150 van.

"The bus is leaving folks. All aboard," Samuel yelled out the driver's window. The weary entourage climbed in the side sliding door. Saune and Ortega waved, and then headed back to the building to retrieve their weapons from the arms locker.

The short ride to La Laguna and the University of San Fernando was uneventful, with each of the van's occupants suspiciously eyeing the other vehicles on the highway as they wound through the busy streets. At one point, they all slouched down as a police cruiser passed by in the other direction with its sirens blaring loudly.

La Laguna, Tenerife's original capitol, was now a busy university town, with old narrow checkerboard streets crisscrossing through the city. It offered a distinct charm with many historical homes dating back to the 1500s.

Professor Carlos Santiago's home was situated just a short walk from the main campus. Built in 1906, the Casa Del Luga originally served as the university library until 1975 when it was then converted to living quarters for university faculty. The traditional Spanish-Colonial architecture was beautifully accented with lavishly designed entrance portals and rustic wooden balconies off the second floor, which offered a commanding view of the snowy heights of Mt. Teide.

Carlos Santiago nervously paced the floor of the home's vast study, when he noticed the van coming up the tree-shrouded driveway. He had been worried sick about his daughter after learning that morning of the police manhunt for her and the archeology team. Hoping for some news of their well-being, he quickly ran outside to greet the vehicle as it came to a stop near the stone patio. To his relief, he saw Maria emerging from the back of the van, along with the Turners.

"Maria! Thank God you are alright," he cried, as he ran to embrace his daughter.

"I'm fine, Father," she replied as she returned his hug. The rest of the group filed up to them on the patio steps, with Alton Burr slowly exiting the van last.

"We need to get inside, Carlos," Turner said, cautiously eyeing a car that passed by the driveway.

"Yes, by all means, come this way," he said, motioning the group towards the beautiful two hundred year old hand-made oak doors. He led them inside to the copious study that served as a meeting room.

The study was a cornucopia of Spanish décor, with an abundance of island paintings by local artists and tastefully fitted with numerous hand-crafted high-backed chairs. Contiguous to the old stone fireplace were the last remnants of the library, consisting of a vast assortment of books dating back to the 1600s. All of this was accented by the beautiful hard wood floors that creaked as they strolled across the room.

"Please, sit," Santiago said as his housekeeper, Julia, came into the study. I'll have Julia prepare you some nourishment. You must be famished." He then nodded to his housekeeper, who quickly headed off into the kitchen to prepare a meal.

"Thank you, Carlos," Eli said as he sat wearily into the comfortable chair. "I'd almost forgotten how hungry I was. So much has happened in the last twelve hours," he said, rubbing the back of his aching neck. "I take it you have heard the news reports?"

"Yes, Eli. The police arrived earlier this morning, about an hour ago, inquiring if I had heard from any of you. A short time later, I was visited by two men driving a black vehicle, who also wanted to know where you were. They were definitely not the local authorities, and I gathered from their dialogue with each other that they were Japanese," he said.

"It's our new friends from Bishamon, near our excavation site, Carlos. It didn't take them long to figure out where we could find shelter. I'm sure they're visiting the university as well," Turner said.

"You can be assured they will check every place more than once," Yashiro stated as he looked nervously out the window towards the street.

"What in blazes is going on?" Carlos asked, scratching

his goatee as he sat heavily into his thick plush recliner.

"You don't believe the reports, Father, do you?" Maria asked pulling the work boots off her aching feet.

"Of course not, my dear; it must be some sort of misunderstanding. But what kind of trouble have you gotten yourselves into?"

"Misunderstanding is an understatement, Carlos," Turner replied. "We've stumbled upon an organized terrorist group that has been trying to kill us, due to the close proximity of the dig site."

"Terrorists—here on Tenerife? We must contact the authorities at once," Santiago said.

"For the moment, Professor, we can't do that," Turner replied. "We need time to figure out a way to stop them. It's a long story, sir, and I'm afraid all we can ask of you is to trust us."

Julia returned from the kitchen carrying a large tray. It was topped with a steaming pot of rancho canario, a meat stew with noodles and chickpeas, plus a pitcher of fresh papaya juice. They all savored their first sustenance in almost a day, ravenous from the long, weary night and morning.

Turner, with help from Yashiro and Eli, gave Carlos a brief overview of what transpired during their long night, and the challenges that lie ahead.

"Is this possible?" Said Carlos Santiago, stunned at hearing the account of the Scalar weapon and the tsunami.

"Quite possible and imminent, sir," Yashiro replied. "And we don't have much time left, which is why we cannot afford to go to the authorities at this point."

"And Pencor is involved in this plot as well? It doesn't

make sense. I am scheduled to meet with him at a luncheon on campus at noon. He is going to be honored for making a hefty donation to the antiquities department," Santiago said in astonishment.

"He's been behind the whole dirty business from the beginning," Eli said angrily after finishing the last of his papaya. "Do you have any Ron Miel, Carlos? I could use a stiff drink."

"You'll find it in the liquor cabinet. Go through those doors and into the living room," Santiago responded to his friend. Eli got up and began walking into the other room, followed by Yashiro and Burr.

"Here, Dad," Turner said, tossing Eli the Global Star phone. "Try to contact your friends in Washington while you're at it." As the three left the room, Turner shot Samuel a knowing grin.

"Uh oh, here it comes. There's the look that always scares the hell out of me," Samuel said, knowing his friend had a plan in mind.

"I think it's time we went on the offensive, Samuel," Turner said.

"I was afraid of that," Samuel quipped, knowing that he was also tired of being hunted like an animal.

"Professor, how is Pencor arriving at the University?" Josh asked, his mind still sharp even though he was weary from lack of sleep.

"He contacted my staff, saying that he would be coming by helicopter and landing at the helipad behind the antiquities building. He will then arrive at the main hall, driven by two of his own people. Why?" Carlos asked.

"We may have just found a way to get through that

front door you spoke of earlier, Samuel," Turner responded with a sly look. "Carlos, I want to ask that you please hide my father, Maria, and Mr. Burr here at your home until such time that it is safe. I don't want to place them at any further risk."

"By all means, Josh, you have my word. They will be safe here while I am attending the luncheon."

"Samuel and I will be making an appearance as well, Professor," Turner said, smiling as the plan formed in his mind. "I feel the need to rattle Mr. Pencor's cage a little. Here's what we're going to do…."

19

U.S. Department of State, Washington D.C.

Abigail Conger sat at her desk finalizing the statistics report for James Robertson, Under Secretary of State for Arms Control and International Security. Her report highlighted the recent International Atomic Energy Agency's discovery of the restart of North Korea's uranium enrichment program in Yongbyon-Kun.

One more to add to the list of the numerous violations of the Nuclear Non-Proliferation Treaty by its new leader, Kim Jong-un, whose father's actions have plagued the State Department over the last two decades.

As it had done so many times in the past, the United States sent a formal protest to the Security Council of the United Nations. Abby had personally come to regard the U.N. as an organization rife with corruption that exhibited a blatant bias against the United States. She knew it would be a useless gesture, as prior protests by the State Department were basically ignored.

Abby recalled how three years ago, a North Korean merchant vessel bound for Syria was stopped at sea by a U.S. Navy Frigate.

They discovered it to be transporting a cache of Taepodong-II long-range missiles, capable of a nuclear payload.

As assistant to Under Secretary Robertson at the time, she had been privy to the meeting of the National Security Council with newly elected President Clark. The North Koreans, of course, cried foul to the United Nations and gathered enough support from the General Assembly to garner a formal protest, charging blatant piracy on the high seas against the United States.

The political grand-standing by the President's detractors on Capitol Hill, along with the bleating of the media, resulted in the ship being released and allowed to proceed unimpeded to its destination.

At the time, Abby protested vehemently to her superior, who just smiled at her and said, "Abby, you will learn in time that things such as these have a way of resolving themselves."

She did not understand what he meant at the time, but it became all too clear to her when the North Korean merchant ship disappeared somewhere in the Indian Ocean. North Korea protested vehemently again, but without proof, nothing ever came of it. However, the crew of the Los Angeles Class hunter killer sub definitely enjoyed their practice that day.

"I'll take common sense to political correctness any day," she told herself at the time.

This morning, Abby was finishing her report for Under

Secretary Robertson. She had come in early to assure its completion before his meeting with the National Security Council next week.

Abby always enjoyed the early mornings in the District, as she called downtown D.C. She looked out her third story office on C Street, which afforded her a spectacular view of the Lincoln Memorial and the Potomac River. Her mind wandering, she thought of how she loved her job at the State Department, which enabled her to meet many dignitaries over the last eight years, but left her little time for a relationship.

Maybe it's time I should think about settling down? She considered this as she watched the cars heading west on C Street towards Alexandria. *I must admit, I'm quite taken with that lovable ole' archaeologist who's off gallivanting in the Canary Islands, of all places. Eli is such a sweet man. Maybe someday….* Her reverie was cut short when her phone began to ring.

"Under Secretary Robertson's office: Abigail Conger speaking." "Hello, Abby, it's Eli," the voice on the other end of the line replied. "I'm so glad I was able to get through to you."

"Hello, Eli. I was just thinking about you. How goes your search for the Holy Grail?" Abby asked jokingly. "You were all over the news here. I saw you're—"

"Abby," Eli interrupted, "we've got a serious situation here. I must speak to Robertson. I couldn't think of anyone else to call."

"Situation? What are you talking about, Eli?"

"Abby, I'm talking about the possibility of massive destruction and loss of life to millions. We've stumbled onto a terrorist organization here on Tenerife that is planning to trigger a tsunami from the island of La Palma. If it isn't stopped, it will devastate the coastline of the western hemisphere," he said, as a stunned Abby fell silent.

"Abby? Are you still there?" Eli asked.

"Yes—yes I'm here, but my God, Eli, how in the world could anyone accomplish that?"

"I don't have time to explain the whole situation to you right now, Abby. I do have a scientist with me who knows the details of the plot. He can help validate the threat for Robertson. I *can* tell you that we're certain it will happen today. If it does occur, you will only have a 5-6 hour window to mount an evacuation of the east coast. Do you understand?"

"Yes, Eli, I do," she said hesitantly. "I…uh…I'll put you through to him right away. He's in his office."

She placed Eli on hold, shocked by this revelation, but still not believing such a thing could happen. *This all sounds so crazy*, she thought, wondering how her boss would react. "So help me, Dr. Elias Turner, if you get me fired for this," Abby said nervously as she transferred the call to Under Secretary Robertson.

Ten minutes later, James Robertson exited his office and was a picture of doubt to Abby.

"Abby, cancel my morning schedule and set up a conference call with the directors of Homeland Security and FEMA."

"What do you think, Jim?" Abby asked her boss and friend. "Abby, it's the wildest thing I've ever heard of; something out of a crazy fiction novel. Mr. Turner says he knows you, and now I must ask *you*. Do you trust this man's credibility?"

"I know Eli Turner is a lot of things, James, but crazy is not one of them. He wouldn't risk his reputation over something like this unless he was absolutely sure of himself," she answered as she pulled up a phone list on the computer at her desk.

"I sure hope so," he said as he turned to head back to his office. "If not," he sighed, "I may be out of a job real soon. Put them through when you have them on the line, Abby." Robertson went into his office and shut the door behind him.

20

After finishing his conversation with Secretary Robertson, Eli Turner strolled back into the huge library, scratching the back of his head and wearing a troubled look. "Well, Son," he said. "I was able to get the warning out to Washington, but I don't know if they are going to take the threat seriously. Abby's boss, James Robertson at the State Department, listened to what Yashiro and I had to say and promised to pass it up the line to the proper government agencies."

"That's what scares me," Turner replied. "By the time they go through all the red tape and actually take action, it may be too late. Or, they may not act at all."

"He told me that he would give us a reply as soon as possible. I guess that's all we can expect from them for now," Eli said, pouring a hot cup of coffee from a large ceramic pot that Julia served following their meal. "I couldn't find your rum, Carlos, so I guess this will have to do."

"We're not finished on this end. Not by a long shot," Turner said as he finished the last of his coffee. It gave him the boost that he so desperately needed after almost a day without sleep. "Samuel and I have business to attend to at the luncheon with Professor

Santiago, and then we will meet up with Captain Saune later; just in case the cavalry doesn't come to the rescue."

"Here, Son, take the Global Star phone with you in the event the cavalry needs directions," Eli said tossing his son the phone. "I told Robertson at the State Department to expect you when he calls back, and that we were going to try to stop these mad men from here."

"Not we, Dad; you, Maria, and Mr. Burr are out of this, as of now. I want you to promise me that you'll stay clear of any trouble from this point on," he said, rising up and tossing Samuel the holstered 45-automatic.

"Gee, thanks. Just what I've always wanted," said Samuel, rising up after throwing down the last of his hot coffee. "Thank you, lovely lady, for your hospitality," he added in Spanish to Julia as he kissed her hand in a courteous fashion and caused her to blush.

"Oh, man, you're too much," Turner said, teasing his friend. "Come on, Yashiro, you're a major player in this caper too. We have a job for you."

"Be careful, Son," Eli said seriously. "These guys play for keeps."

"That goes for me, too, Josh," Maria added, embracing him tightly. "Remember, we have a date."

"Don't worry. I'll pick you up at seven," Turner replied, smiling as he softly stroked her cheek with his finger.

"Let's go, amigos," Samuel said from the now open front door. "Oh, and by the way, don't worry about me. I'll be fine," he added in mock jealousy, causing everyone in the room to burst out laughing. Maria watched the three men leave the house, head down the walkway, and then disappear from view into the busy streets of La Laguna.

"Well," Eli said with a sigh, "looks like we just lay low until we hear from them."

"I don't know about you, but I feel useless not doing anything," Maria admitted as she came back into the room. "There's got to be something that we can do."

"Sure, you can do something," Alton Burr said sarcastically as he came out from the study room, "if you want to get yourself killed. I say we follow young Turner's advice and keep out of sight, Miss Santiago."

"I have to agree with the gentleman," Carlos Santiago said as he put on his trademark white cotton coat. "You'll all be safe here. I have to leave now for Pencor's presentation at the main hall."

"You're actually going to have lunch with that monster?" Maria asked incredulously.

"If I don't, he'll suspect something is amiss. Don't worry; I'm a sly old goat, my dear. I can take care of myself," he said, giving his daughter a kiss on the forehead then walking out the front door, leaving the remaining three in an awkward silence.

"Damn," Eli finally said wistfully, "I'd give anything to be done with this mess and scrambling atop La Palma looking for Simon's hidden artifacts."

"Simon?" Burr asked curiously. "Oh, yeah, you did mention that you made a discovery in the tomb. What does it have to do with La Palma?"

"It seems as if the artifacts we were searching for may be on La Palma instead of Tenerife. Maria, did you say that you may know where they are located?"

"Yes, Dr. Turner, I believe I do."

"Oh, stop with the doctor stuff. You're making me feel like an old man," Eli said jokingly. "Just call me Eli, okay?"

"Fine, Eli," she replied with a warm smile. "Let me get out my father's map of La Palma." She walked over to the library map case and pulled out a tube containing a detailed topography map of the island. Clearing the coffee table, she unrolled the map showing the highly detailed terrain of La Palma. The three gathered around the table as Maria began to speak. "On the second parchment that Josh translated last night in the cave, Simon specifically mentioned the island of Junonia. Like I said earlier, that was the name given to the island of La Palma back in the first century," she said, pointing to the volcanic ridge line that segmented the island from north to south. She went on saying, "Here is the Cumbre Vieja ridge with its volcanic craters running north to south. The most recent eruptions occurred in 1949 at the Crater del Duraznero and Crater del Hoyo Negro. Just south of the island's midway point below Duraznero is the four-meter fault line from the 1949 eruption," she continued, gliding her finger down the slope drawn on the map. "It's my guess that here is where Pencor's plan comes into play, utilizing this fault line on the ridge. At this location, just north between the two craters, is a rock formation that was once known as the Rock of the Blessed Virgin, named by the conquering Spanish in the late 1300s. Much of it was destroyed in the 1949 eruption, but I'm positive that this is the Hand of God that Simon referred to in the parchment."

"Who was this Simon?" Burr asked, a plan forming in his mind as he spoke.

"Evidently, he was an unknown disciple of Jesus of

Nazareth. According to the scroll, he was charged by Joseph of Arimathea to protect and safeguard not only the Holy Grail, but also the crown of thorns used to mock him at his crucifixion, and, most importantly, a document written by Jesus himself," Maria replied.

"Mr. Burr, I know from your history that you, of all people, have no interest in such a find. You and your group are out to remove all aspects of religion from our society; why now the sudden concern?" Eli asked, troubled by the man's abrupt interest and change of heart.

"We all seek the truth, Dr. Turner," Burr replied, belying his real motives. "Our efforts in the Secular America Movement have been, simply stated, modeled to protect the separation of church and state as provisioned in the U.S. Constitution. We want to assure that religion of any sort is kept in a non-public forum, as it should be," he said, his voice rising in crescendo, knowing that his true plans were far more reaching in scope.

"Well, for your information, Mr. Burr, you and your cronies have been touting that ridiculous ideology for years. Most Americans do not know the truth: that those words, 'separation of church and state' appear nowhere in the Constitution. In the first amendment, it clearly states that Congress shall make no law respecting an establishment of religion or prohibit the free exercise thereof. Any first year high school student with a decent history teacher should see that it meant there would be no established national church for the colonies of the United States at the time. In layman's terms, Mr. Burr," he stated, pointing his finger at him, "no church of the United States period."

"I don't agree with that premise, Turner," Burr said, his

anger now clearly visible.

"The federal government," Eli continued, enjoying his taunting of Burr, "was prohibited from setting up a state religion, such as Britain had at the time, but there was no restriction against the practice of religion. That is where people like you have twisted the truth. Thomas Jefferson's comment concerning the separation between church and state was made in a letter to a group of Baptist clergymen in Danbury, Connecticut around 1802, a group that feared a state-sponsored religion. Jefferson assured the Baptist Association that the first amendment guaranteed there would be no establishment of any one denomination over another. It was never intended, as you and your group continues to suggest, that our governing bodies be divorced from Christianity and its founding principles. Rather, its purpose was to protect the church *from* the state. Your group, and, the likes of it, has twisted the true meaning to a public that doesn't know the real truth, so don't give me that song and dance that you're serving the public interest."

Burr forcibly held back his rage, deciding to let it go for the sake of his plan. *For now*, he seethed in his tormented mind; *I'll be silent for now.*

"Alright, guys, calm down. Your personal feelings aside, Mr. Burr, you must admit that a discovery such as this is intriguing. It's an important part of learning the early history of Middle Eastern culture," Maria said, trying to diffuse the elevated emotions of the two men. "A document written by the historical Jesus would be an incredible find no matter what your views."

"She's right, Burr. Besides, we'll never know if those artifacts are lost forever," Eli said glumly. "If those mad men manage to trigger that landslide on La Palma, Simon's treasures will be lost forever."

"Why not go and find them now?" Burr asked, playing his hand. Eli looked at him incredulously.

"You can't be serious," Eli responded. "With all of Osama's men and the island's police looking for us, we'd be picked up in a heartbeat."

"They won't be looking for us on La Palma. Remember, I have a helicopter at my disposal still sitting at the airport. I can contact my pilot and have him land at a secure location close by," he said, baiting the hook, knowing that Turner would never pass up the chance to make his discovery.

"Eli, Josh told us we should stay out of sight, remember?" Maria said.

Eli stood silently for a minute, intently thinking of the options that lay before him.

The find of a lifetime, he thought, *and it could all be lost by tomorrow. I can't let that happen.* After a long pause, Eli said, "Call your man, Mr. Burr, and tell him that we'll meet behind the square at the Palacio de Nava. The market will be empty today because of the upcoming festival in Santa Cruz. We can be there in fifteen minutes," he said, picking up his hat.

"Right away, Dr. Turner," Burr said as he headed for the phone located in the study, happy that his plans were now coming together.

"Eli, I can't believe you are going to risk this," Maria said in protest. "If you're dead set on going through with this madness, then I'm going with you."

"No, Maria, I—"

"No arguments, mister," she retorted in a tone that told Eli not to dispute the subject anymore.

"Okay, I'm glad to have your help, but I also want you to keep an eye on *him*," he said, motioning to Burr on the phone in the other room. "I don't trust the man."

"Yes, Mr. Burr," the pilot said over the phone. "I can leave right away. The item you asked for will be in the backpack, along with the rope and gear you requested."

"Very good," Burr responded with a self-gratifying smile on his face. "Do you know where the old market place behind the Palacio de Nava in La Laguna is located?"

"Yes, sir. I'll look for you." The pilot responded. "My ETA will be about thirty minutes." Burr hung up the phone and returned to Eli and Maria.

"We're all set," he said smiling. "My pilot is bringing rope and some light equipment in the event that we need them. He'll be at the pick-up point in thirty minutes."

"Good. We should be going then," Eli said as Maria jotted down a note on her father's stationary.

"I'm leaving my father a note, so he'll know our location. I don't want him to worry if he returns and finds us gone. I'll also leave the number for Josh's satellite phone if he needs to reach him."

Finishing the note, she folded it and placed it atop the antique coffee table in the library, then grabbed her windbreaker.

"I'm ready if you are," she announced with a gleam in her eye. "Let's go," Eli said as the three walked out the door and into the streets of La Laguna, never suspecting their ill-conceived trip to La Palma would place them in the heart of the maelstrom.

21

The luncheon at the university dining hall had been elegantly prepared and stood to be an exceedingly profitable event for the university's antiquities department. Robert Pencor's generous contribution of a check for a quarter of a million dollars was graciously accepted by the university president and the head of the antiquities department, Professor Carlos Santiago. In acceptance speeches on behalf of the university, the two administrators praised the benevolence of Pencor and lavished their new benefactor with adulation.

After concluding the luncheon with a rich dessert of sweet rum banana pie topped with a glazed walnut sauce, the faculty and guests indulged in conversation among themselves. Students, dressed as waiters for the event, hurried about clearing tables and serving coffee as the function now wound down to its final moments. Many of the guests began slowly making their way to the lavish garden outside of the main hall. They exited through its huge pinewood doors, cut from the trees that covered the slopes of the island.

Robert Pencor still sat at the head table. Weary of this facade, he feigned interest in a conversation with a large woman adorning big hair. She rambled on about the intricate process of preserving the mummified remains of the Guanche that were discovered on the slopes of Guimar earlier that week.

His mind was happily preoccupied with thoughts of his final retribution against the people who cost him so much. His long sought out vengeance against the United States would be satiated soon, followed by power and fortune achieved from the introduction of his Zero Point Generators.

Pencor was sipping his coffee and smiling insincerely at the annoying woman, when a lone figure approached his table and sat down across from him. Pencor gave the man a disinterested glance, and then froze as he locked onto the stranger's blue eyes. He had seen this look before; a look that his many years of business instincts recognized as dangerous. The unfamiliar eyes held a gaze of pure determination and self-assurance that broke Pencor's calm demeanor, but only for a moment.

"Do I know you?" Pencor asked abruptly, disengaging from the conversation with the big-haired woman. She gathered her pocket book and began saying her goodbyes to the others.

"I would assume that you'd know me by now, Mr. Pencor," the stranger replied in a confident tone. "I'd have thought a smart guy like you would have more security around him. Oh, but I forgot… your henchmen are all over the island looking for a bunch of poor archaeologists."

The words caused Pencor's armor to crack in surprise,

and he now experienced something he had not felt in years: fear.

"Who are you, and what do you want?" Pencor hissed to the man seated opposite him.

"The name is Turner, Mr. Pencor, Josh Turner," he replied. "Did you really think that we would just disappear? No, Pencor, I just wanted to tell you that your little party is going to come to an abrupt end," Turner paused for effect. "The United States government has been warned of your twisted scheme to trigger the tsunami. As we speak, measures are being taken to put you out of business," Turner stated, hoping the man would take the bait.

"You're bluffing, Turner," Pencor said, now smiling and finding his composure again. "Even in the off chance they do know, they'll never be able to stop us in time. Believe me, Turner, it is only a matter of time before you and your friends are caught. Your fortune thus far has been a minor nuisance, but nothing more. I am impressed that you and your little band know far more than I presumed, but it doesn't matter, because you and your associates will be dealt with soon enough. Nothing will stop my retribution against the United States for its lack of foresight," he said confidently.

"What you're doing is wrong. What will be accomplished by killing so many innocent people?" Turner asked, stunned by the man's lack of humanity.

"Be it a hundred people or a million, Mr. Turner, it's of no consequence to me. They will pay for the irreparable damage they wrought on my industrial empire with their contrived witch hunt. Their fates were sealed at that moment as far as I'm concerned, and you coming here has sealed yours as well," he said with a malevolent grin.

"Are you that sure of yourself?" Turner said coldly, staring the man in the eyes and playing the game to its utmost. "I just wanted to let you know who is going to bring you down." He could see the rage building in Pencor's eyes as a waiter came up beside Pencor to serve him more coffee.

"Your being here only makes it easier for me, Turner," he hissed as he began to reach into his jacket for his revolver. "I'll just say that I was defending myself from a madman."

"Don't even think about it, amigo," the waiter said quietly to Pencor, sliding the coffee backward to expose the barrel of the 45- automatic leveled at his head. "Though putting a piece of scum like you out of your misery would make my day," Samuel whispered in dead seriousness as he moved behind him slowly.

Pencor froze, not knowing what to do next, and then slowly lay his hands on the table in front of him. The big-haired woman walked around the end of the table, giving Turner his opportunity to act.

He jumped up and put himself in front of the woman and Samuel followed his lead. The two quickly melted into the throng of guests, making their way outside the main hall and disappearing into the University Hall garden outside.

"I think you rattled his cage quite nicely, Josh," Samuel said as the two men sprinted to the side of the twenty foot statue of a Guanche Chieftain. They stopped and turned to see an enraged Pencor running out of the hall and looking about the garden for his antagonists. Turner saw that he was on a cell phone; no doubt to the Yakuza escorts who had driven him to the luncheon from the helicopter pad on campus.

"Yes, you fool!" Pencor yelled into the phone. "They were just here. Find them, or else," he hissed, shoving the phone back into his coat as the black four-door Mercedes pulled into the parking area in front of the University Hall garden.

The vehicle slowed to a stop when its driver spotted Turner and Samuel beside the Guanche statue. A bulking figure stepped out of the passenger side, smiling a toothless grin at the two as he started walking slowly towards their precarious position.

"We have to go it alone from here, Samuel," Turner said to his friend. "You know what you have to do, right?"

"Yeah, Josh I do, but I don't like the idea of splitting up and leaving you unarmed."

"It's the only way we have a chance at this, Samuel. We must split them up and then meet at the helicopter if all goes well."

"Yeah, but what if it doesn't?" Samuel asked.

"Don't worry about me," Turner said, knowing his Quechuan friend would risk his very life for him. "You just be careful and meet me at the chopper as soon as you can. Carlos said he would buy us at least a half hour. I want you to meet up with Captain Saune if I'm not there when the time comes, okay?"

"Hell, you'll be there Josh; you're like a bad penny," Samuel said, smiling as he took off in a sprint for Laguna Street just outside of the campus square.

The huge Japanese man coming at them saw Samuel take off. He signaled the driver to follow with a wave of his hand, and then set his sights once again on Turner. Seeing his friend was clear and their plan might work, Turner ran in the direction of the many classrooms and lab buildings in the rear of University Hall. He had the fortune of being more agile than his pursuer, but without a weapon it would be a short reprieve in a deadly contest.

The bulking Yakuza mercenary ran at a slower pace, keeping his 9mm Glock out of the public's view. He reached the rear of the garden just as the throngs of guests were dispersing into the parking lot. He wanted a clear shot at Turner without drawing attention, so he took his time. Osama had told them that he wanted them either dead or alive, but to him, dead would be much more amusing.

Back at the campus hall entrance, Pencor had been side-tracked right on cue by Carlos Santiago, buying Turner and Samuel precious minutes.

"Here, my dear friend," Carlos bellowed, offering Pencor a glass of Malvasia. "A toast to our illustrious benefactor," he offered, raising his glass in salute.

"Yes…uh…yes," a distracted Pencor responded. As he took a sip, he scanned the perimeter of the garden in time to see the big Japanese guard disappear behind the building. Finishing off the glass, he handed it back to Santiago saying, "Professor, my apologies, but I must be getting back to the airport right away. An important matter has come up that requires my direct attention. Do you have transportation readily available since my driver has been detained?"

"Of course, Mr. Pencor. I understand completely," Carlos boomed in his normally loud voice. "I'll have Peter take you to the helicopter pad. With all this traffic from the festival, it may take a little longer, but Peter knows La

Laguna quite well and can negotiate these streets very easily," he said as he waved his arms to a small mustached man sitting on the bench along the street.

"Very well, Professor. It will have to suffice," Pencor responded as he saw his black Mercedes disappear around the square pursuing Samuel.

Following Santiago to his transportation, he contemplated calling Osama and castigating him once more for his ineptitude, but decided it would be better served in person when he returned to the weapon complex. *Could it be possible the United States government is aware of our plans?* He considered this as he climbed into the car and Carlos gave the driver instructions. *We must move our plans ahead, and quickly.* He sat back in the seat as the driver hopped in and started the vehicle.

They headed out the drive into the busy street where they were immediately overwhelmed by the heavy traffic bound for Santa Cruz. Pencor nervously tapped his fingers on the console as the traffic moved along at a snail's pace.

This is not good, he thought. *Not good at all.*

While Pencor found himself caught in traffic, Samuel was running down a narrow busy street past the shops and cafes well known to the university town. He glanced back from time to time to make sure the black Mercedes was still in pursuit.

After years of hiking the high Andes in Peru, a light run in such a low altitude did not even cause him to work up a sweat. He passed many shops that were closing early for the festival and people going about their daily routines, until he finally reached his goal; the Teme Internet Cafe.

Built in 2002, the brightly decorated cafe was full of

students and a smattering of tourists, all using the computers for emails and chat. Samuel stopped running for a few moments so that his pursuer could see him, then headed inside the establishment. Seeing Yashiro sitting at a table, he walked over and sat down across from him.

"Are you sure you know what to do, amigo-san?" Samuel asked the Japanese scientist.

"I'm ready, Samuel," Yashiro answered as Samuel slid the 45- automatic across the table. It was still wrapped in a linen towel from the dining hall.

"I want to be sure that no innocent bystanders get hurt from our actions, Yashiro, so make it a good performance," Samuel said as the two stood up and started walking towards the door to the street outside. "I just hope they don't recognize you."

"I'm positive they won't," Yashiro said, following Samuel out the door with his hand on the gun still hidden in the towel. "These are Osama's goons that do his dirty work on the island. They seldom get to the weapon facility."

"I hope, for our sake, you're right. Okay, Yashiro," Samuel said as the black Mercedes came up to them. "The camera's rolling. You're on."

Less than a mile away, at the University, Turner made his way to the antiquities building, one of the original structures of the university still in use today. He entered the large front doors and went inside its main lobby, noting the familiar Spanish decor of high ceilings designed in eloquent mosaic patterns. On the walls, he saw many ancient Guanche artifacts that had been restored to their original beauty and design. He found his way to the old wooden staircase in the center of the lobby and sprinted up to the second floor containing classrooms and laboratories.

Turner was well aware that his pursuer was not far behind, and that he had to formulate a defense quickly. As Turner reached the end of a long hallway, he opened the door to the artifacts preservation lab. He then heard the loud creaking sound of the main door being opened downstairs in the lobby, surprised that the hulking Japanese assailant had gotten there so soon.

The preservation lab was a long rectangular room that, in the dim light, looked like a bizarre mortuary with two rows of metal tables running side by side all the way to the end. Normally a bustling lab with students and archaeologists going over ancient finds, Turner was now alone amidst ancient Guanche mummies that were discovered by his father at the tomb near Guimar. Rows of long, metal rolling tables held many of the ancient remains that were covered with white sheets. This gave the lab the eerie appearance of a mortuary. Turner quietly made his way to the window at the back of the room.

He quickly glanced outside the window and saw Pencor's Raven-44 helicopter sitting on the helipad, with its pilot standing nearby smoking a cigarette. Two large trucks were parked adjacent to the pad, used to transport equipment to and from the dig sites on the island.

Turner knew he only had a few precious moments before the Yakuza mercenary checked each room and ultimately discovered him, so he looked about in an effort to find anything that he could use as a weapon to defend himself. He walked over to a large table at the center of the room where he saw artifacts spread out on its top. He found old leather leggings, a few stone axe heads, and a well-preserved spear still attached to its long shaft.

An axe head against a gun is not much of an even match, he thought, his mind racing feverishly for any advantage. He quickly moved up the center aisle where the faces of two thousand year old Guanche mummies seemed to taunt him with their frozen death masks.

Moving in the room's dim light, he bumped against one of the preparation tables containing etching fluid, used to clean the stone artifacts. He sent it crashing to the floor, and the sound of shattering glass echoed throughout the silent building.

The huge Japanese assailant was coming out of one of the rooms upstairs when he heard the sound. He smiled to himself as he made his way down the hall to the door of the preservation lab. Pausing at the door, he said, "I know that you are in here, Turner. You have no means of escape. By playing this little game, you are making it more difficult for yourself. Come out now, and I promise to make your death a swift one." After a moment, and, with no response from within, he grinned with satisfaction and slowly turned the doorknob. He pushed the old wooden door open with his pistol. "You should have taken that option, Mr. Turner," he hissed as he entered the room, senses attuned to any movement within. "I have acquired many techniques for bringing about a slow and painful death, as you will soon discover."

The giant of a man walked slowly and deliberately down the dark aisle between the rows of tables containing the mummies. He noted that one table held an object larger than its neighbors

that was covered by a white sheet. He silently walked up

to it; leveled the gun at the object and with one swift motion, pulled the sheet off. The absence of the sheet revealed a Guanche wrapped in a thick ancient blanket; its long, dead, hollow eyes staring back at the mercenary. He grinned, threw the sheet back over it, and then continued his search down the dimly-lit aisle. Moving stealth-like to the rear of the room, he smiled as he saw another table covered with a sheet. This time, the bottom of a rubber heel was protruding from the end.

"Welcome to the world of pain, Mr. Turner," the huge man said, sneering as he slowly approached the table.

Back on Laguna Street, the black Mercedes came to a halt in front of the internet cafe. Its darkened, tinted window on the driver's side rolled down to reveal the driver pointing a gun at Samuel. Yashiro quickly went into action, speaking in Japanese to the driver.

"No," Yashiro said forcefully. "Osama wants anyone captured to be delivered alive to the facility. He plans to use them as a hostage to lure his other friends out into the open." The driver, caught off guard, lowered the weapon and asked, "Who are you? I don't recognize you."

"I'm just one of our Oyabun's many operatives. You must know that he doesn't make it a habit of identifying all his people," Yashiro responded abruptly, hoping the ploy would work. "We must get him to the helicopter on campus where we can transport him. I'm sure Osama will greatly reward your diligence."

Falling for the ruse, the driver put the gun down and said, "Very well. Put him in the back seat, but keep him covered."

"You," Yashiro barked, nudging Samuel with the 45 still

wrapped in the towel. "Get into the back—move!"

"Okay, okay. Just don't shoot," Samuel replied, feigning trepidation as he opened the rear door and slid across the seat to the opposite side. Yashiro slid in next to him.

The sedan pulled onto the busy street, slowly making its way back to the university campus. Yashiro discretely slid the gun across the seat to Samuel, who shot Yashiro a sly wink of approval for his command performance.

"Do you have anything to bind him with?" Yashiro asked the driver as the car left Laguna Street and headed up one of the many side streets in town.

"There are plastic tie wraps and duct tape in the trunk that we can use," he replied. Just then, Samuel sprang into action, raising the gun and pointing it directly at the back of the driver's head.

"Thanks for the lift, amigo, but you can pull into that next alley on your right," Samuel said with a smile as the driver's eyes went wide with shock. Doing as he was told, he made the turn and slowly went up the deserted alley.

"Stop here," Samuel ordered as the driver complied and came to a halt. "Now, very slowly, hand me your weapon grip first. No funny stuff."

"You're not going to kill him, are you?" Yashiro asked hesitantly as the driver handed Samuel the pistol.

"Unlike this guy and all of his friends, I'm not a cold-blooded murderer. I'll only kill him if he gives me a good reason" Samuel replied to Yashiro's relief.

"What are we going to do with him?" Yashiro asked as he opened the door.

"You heard the man. There are tie wraps and duct tape in the trunk. We'll just truss him up like a Christmas turkey and let him marinate in the trunk," Samuel responded, motioning the driver to get out of the vehicle.

Minutes later, the driver safely secured in the trunk, his hands and feet bound and his mouth duct-taped. Yashiro put on the driver's jacket, then the two backed the car out of the alley and continued to make their way to the helicopter behind the antiquities building.

"I sure hope Josh is alright. That other guy looked pretty nasty," Samuel said in a concerned tone, not knowing that at that very moment Josh Turner was in a struggle for his life.

At the preservation lab, Turner could feel his heart pounding in his chest. He remained motionless, breathing ever so shallowly as he heard the footsteps come ever closer. He tried to put the ominous threats made by his pursuer out of his mind, and focus on the fight that lay ahead of him. He knew this was to be a struggle with only one victor. Once engaged, there could be no holding back. Adrenaline now coursed through his body as the shadow of the huge killer passed by his fragile table shelter.

The toothless Japanese mercenary grinned as he slowly brought his 9mm Glock to bear on the head of the figure under the sheet. In one swift motion, he yanked the sheet off only to reveal another lifeless mummy; its dead eyes still looking upward as the two shoes at the end of the table fell away to the floor.

That was Turner's cue. He jumped from the table behind the assailant and hit the man square in the back with the ancient four pound stone axe head. Taken by surprise, the huge man fell onto the table in front of him. He and the ancient corpse crashed to the floor, smashing the table to fragments. The big man gasped at the wind being knocked out of him, but still held the gun firmly in his hand. Turner then leaped onto the mercenary's back and jammed his knee into the man's spine, causing the Yakuza mercenary to groan in agony. In that same moment, Turner brought the weight of the stone axe down onto the 9mm gun, crushing the man's trigger finger and snapping the slide bolt mechanism off, rendering the weapon useless.

Furious and wincing in pain, the hulking Japanese managed to swing his body around and smash his huge forearm into Turner's head. The horrendous blow sent Turner reeling against the table behind him, causing him to see stars and drop his only weapon to the floor.

Even with a partial fracture to his spine, the huge, vindictive killer slowly rose up from the debris-strewn floor, his breath rasping in pain and defiance. He lunged toward Turner, unleashing a lethal kick aimed at his head. He scarcely managed to avoid the full force of the kick by rolling to his side at the last moment. However, the killer's boot slammed into his shoulder, causing a blinding flash of pain that ran down his arm.

Turner painfully backed up; keeping his eyes on the man as the hulking figure approached him once again. Pointing his mangled finger, he said, "Once I've killed you, Turner, I intend to find that pretty lady that was with your group. She will die very slowly as well, but not until I've enjoyed her completely," he hissed, spitting blood from his shattered lips.

The mere thought of this monster's intent with Maria produced a rage in Turner that he'd never experienced before. He locked his eyes coldly on his assailant and, with a yell, rushed the killer. He smashed into the man with all the strength that remained. Turner's onslaught sent the two men crashing to the floor amidst the splintered remains of the mummy and debris from the examination table.

The giant Japanese man promptly wrapped his arms around Turner's mid-section, lifted him up off the floor and began to squeeze with a vise-like grip. Feeling the breath forced out of his lungs, Turner looked wildly around for anything that would cease this painful torment. Nearing the point of blacking out, he saw the stone axe head lying on the floor near them. He raised his left leg and kicked the side of the killer's right knee, sending the two crashing to the floor. The killer continued his death grip as Turner struggled to grasp the stone axe.

Darkness was beginning to fill his world as he finally felt his fingers touch the cool stone axe. With his last conscious effort, he picked it up brought it squarely down onto the Yakuza's nose. It shattered the cartilage into oblivion and sprayed blood everywhere. The huge man howled in pain and released his grip on Turner, just long enough for him to pull back and fall free of his tormentor. Rising up and gasping for breath, Turner backed away from the monstrous form lying before him. Turner made his way to the artifact table as the bloody, murderous demon rose up once more. He picked up a sharpened metal leg from the shattered remains of the table. Now exhausted and in excruciating pain, Turner saw the bloody remains of a toothless grin leering at him as the killer again came towards him, the pointed table leg raised over his head.

Turner's sense of compassion and civility was instantly replaced by a pure, unadulterated hatred for this monster of a human being. The Japanese man yelled and rushed at him with his makeshift spear poised to strike. Turner quickly grabbed the ancient spear from the table next to him and thrust it forward. As the huge freight train bore down on him, Turner sent the still-pointed spear head plunging deep into the Yakuza mercenary's chest. The bloody hulk dropped the table leg and leered sickeningly at Turner as a gush of blood seeped from his mouth. Then, with a long rasping sound, he fell to the floor dead.

Shaken and in pain, but thankfully still alive, Turner stood frozen, looking at the gruesome scene before him. All the horrific events of the previous day converged like a raging flood in his mind as he sunk to his knees and wept. With the events of the last day pouring out in despair, he knelt there in the blood and debris for what seemed to him an eternity. Eventually there was nothing left but a powerful resurgence of fortitude and determination to save his father and friends from these monstrous people hell-bent on death and destruction to all who got in their way.

Turner stood up as if reborn. Tired, but with a renewed conviction to see this through to its end, he put his shoes back on and headed for the door. Pausing for a brief moment, he glanced coldly over his shoulder and spoke to the dead mercenary. "You and your friends can all go to hell, and I'm going to help you get there," he stated coldly as he slammed the door behind him and went back down the stairs to the entrance.

Once Turner was outside the building, he took a painful, breath of fresh air and felt the warmth of the mid-afternoon sun on his face. *I'm damn lucky to be alive*, he thought as he picked up the Global Star phone he had hidden in the bushes in front of the building and put it in his back pocket.

He made his way around the right side of the old building to a cluster of large palm trees at the rear, where he stopped behind the largest tree. He saw Samuel, hidden from view behind one of the trucks, and, Yashiro talking animatedly to the helicopter pilot, who was seated inside the Raven. He was powering up the engine of the aircraft in preparation for takeoff.

Samuel made it, he thought, breathing a sigh of relief. *This just might work after all.* He made his way out of the cover of the palm tree and stealthily made it over to the commandeered Mercedes.

Within a few minutes after Turner's arrival at the landing pad, the car transporting Pencor pulled around the side of the antiquities building to the sight of the now vacant helicopter pad.

"Stop the car!" Pencor yelled to the driver as he threw open the door to the vehicle, which came to a sudden stop. Leaping out, he ran towards the helipad, furious at this new development. Looking skyward, he saw his private Raven-44 helicopter heading south in the direction of the desolate slopes of Mount Teide. He then looked around to see his Mercedes sitting at the far end of the lot next to a supply truck, empty and with its passenger door left open. "They've taken my helicopter," he hissed in fury as he turned to see his driver speeding out of the parking area and leaving him alone. "No matter," he said, pulling his cell phone from his jacket pocket and calling Osama at the Bishamon complex.

"Yes, what is it?" Osama's voice said on the other end

of the line.

"It's Pencor. I'm still at the university," he said abruptly. "It seems that once again, the ineptitude of your associates has failed to apprehend Turner and his friends. He still—"

"Robert, what are you talking about?" Osama interrupted, agitated by his continued lack of respect.

"Young Turner and his companion have stolen my helicopter, you fool. They must have forced my pilot at gunpoint and are now heading over the western slopes of Teide," Pencor roared, his blood pressure rising.

"Are you sure they are over Teide?" Osama asked.

"Yes I'm sure. I can see it now from where I stand. They must have somehow managed to subdue your people since my car is here abandoned," he replied impatiently.

"Do not worry, Robert, I have matters well in hand," Osama said casually, smiling as he toyed with the detonator button in his hand. "You must return as soon as possible if you wish to see the execution of the final Electromagnetic Pulse Wave. I was assured it would be safely implemented at around six o'clock."

"Another thing," Pencor said irritably, ignoring Osama's calm demeanor. "The younger Turner confronted me at the luncheon and threatened to stop us somehow. I fear he may have been able to contact the United States government. If that is true, we must move ahead quickly and get rid of all evidence that could tie us to the tsunami."

"Nothing will be found, Robert. Since you left earlier we have been transporting all non-essential equipment and documents by truck to our warehouse at the airport. After the landslide has caused its destruction, I will have the equipment dismantled and sent back to Japan. They will be far too busy tending to the catastrophe to focus on us for long," Osama said confidently.

Looking at his watch, he noted that it was now approaching three o'clock in the afternoon. Slightly reassured by what Osama just told him, he started walking back to his Mercedes.

"Just take care of Turner," he snapped, hanging up on Osama. "A shame," Osama said, hanging up the phone and circling his thumb over the red button on the radio detonator. "I was hoping to be able to use this as a surprise for you, my dear Robert."

He pushed the button and held it for five seconds. "This should take care of the troublesome Mr. Turner and his comrade."

Osama reached again for the phone and dialed his operative on the Moroccan coast. He motioned to a man in overalls to take a file cabinet that was located on the far wall and load it on the transport truck.

"Tanaki, here," the voice on the line rang out.

"This is Osama. It's time for your men to commandeer the two container ships. Do you anticipate any problems?" He asked.

"No, sir, we expect very little. Our men are standing by as we speak. We can be at sea within the hour," he replied with conviction.

"Good," Osama said, beaming. "I want those ships in deep water by eighteen-hundred hours. Do you understand? We predict the tsunami will have a slight effect on the coast of Africa, so you must be in deep water to avoid any complications."

"Understood, Oyabun. We will arrive in Kobe in two

weeks." "Very good, Tanaki. Do not fail me," Osama said as he disconnected the call. "Things are coming together very nicely." He smiled and threw the detonator switch into the trashcan next to his desk.

As Pencor reached his Mercedes, he was startled by the sound of a muffled roar in the distance. He turned to see the flaming remains of what was once his helicopter, falling to the desolate slopes of Teide. Staring in morbid fascination, he was relieved that Turner and his associate were now dead, but was troubled as to how Osama managed it so quickly. *It must have been a hand-held rocket launcher*, he thought as he shut the passenger door of his sedan and walked around to the driver's seat.

Noting the last of the flaming wreckage as it disappeared onto the rugged slopes, he smiled to himself saying, "You weren't that clever after all were you, Turner?"

22

The White House, Washington D.C. 9:30AM

"Damn it, James, we don't have any intelligence to go on. How in hell do you expect me to order the evacuation of the entire eastern seaboard without any proof of a threat? The loss of life alone from the mass panic would be catastrophic," Stephen Boyle, Director of the Federal Emergency Management Agency, decried while slamming his fist down on the desk in the Oval Office. "If this turns out to be a false alarm, we'll be the laughing stock of the country. Hell, we still have a black eye from the hurricane Katrina and B.P oil spill debacles."

"But, what if it's valid, Steve, and we don't act?" Under Secretary of State James Robertson countered. "We'd be partially responsible for the deaths of millions of American citizens because we failed to issue a warning in time. How could we live with that?"

"Even if this so called tsunami were to occur, how can

we be sure the wave would be so destructive?" Tim Byrd, Director of Homeland Security, asked from his seat opposite the President. The President listened silently, but intently, to the ongoing debate with his advisers.

"We are awaiting a response from Jack Pollack, geophysics scientist at the Woods Hole Oceanographic Institute," replied Robert Laird, the President's scientific adviser. "I gave him the scenario and asked for an evaluation of all the facts we have available."

"How in the hell did this get under the radar scope of advanced intel?" Robertson asked in frustration.

"We can't be everywhere, Jim," Tim Byrd responded defensively. "Most of our resources are tied up monitoring the intentions of Al-Qaeda; add to that the resources needed in Iraq, Afghanistan, Iran, Libya and Syria. Oh, did I fail to mention North Korea? It doesn't take a rocket scientist to see that we are—"

"Gentlemen, calm down. This will get us nowhere. I want to stick to the specific threat, and forgo the finger pointing," President Clark said in a calm demeanor, folding his hands as he leaned forward in his high-backed leather chair.

Alan Clark was in his first term as President. He'd won easily as a third party candidate, handily defeating both his republican and democratic opposition. The nation had grown weary of the ongoing, constant grandstanding, division, and unfulfilled promises of both parties. Clark, a man of vision and fortitude, saw the opportunity and struck.

Tactfully using the bully pulpit, he made both parties in the Senate and House accountable for what they did, or did not, accomplish. The public responded positively with a consistent sixty-nine percent approval rating. Unfortunately, he became very much a political target for the extreme left and right wing groups, who were being successfully shut out of power and voice with the American people.

"Before we act, we must have all the information available to us first. Is that clear, gentlemen?" Clark stated, as the men gathered around him nodded in agreement. "We must establish that we—"

The buzzer on the phone interrupted him mid-sentence, and he quickly pushed the speaker button.

"Mr. President, Dr. Jack Pollack from Woods Hole is on line three."

"Thank you, Maggie," he said as he punched the line button. "Hello, Dr. Pollack, are you there?"

"Yes, Mr. President."

"I have you on conference so my staff can hear. Can you shed some light on the scenario Bob Laird put before you earlier?" He asked.

"Yes, sir, I can. We have studied this hypothesis here in the geophysics center at Woods Hole since we learned of the supposition made in the late 90s. There are two basic trains of thought on this matter. The first, made by many geophysicists, is that if the Cumbre Vieja were to erupt on La Palma, the force of the eruption would most likely cause the crater to collapse into itself as opposed to its flank sliding into the sea. The infrastructure of La Palma would be affected adversely, but no landslide would mean no tsunami and very little loss of life," he said as Clark looked at the advisers gathered about him.

"And the second train of thought?" Clark asked the Woods Hole scientist.

"The second train of thought, and, the one I subscribe to, is the immense volume of heat generated by an eruption would super-heat the trapped water in the higher elevations of the Cumbre Vieja. It is similar to a dike of solid rock holding millions of liters of water underneath the flank of the volcano. This expansion could result in the outer rock surface losing its cohesion. The only place it would have to go is down to the sea," he said, pausing for a second to see if there were any questions. Hearing none, he continued. "The Swiss Federal Institute of Technology, using state of the art laboratory equipment, did a model showing the landslide's impact on the ocean. They found that it would be thousands times larger than any slide ever studied in the past."

"Dr. Pollack, Robert Laird here," the President's scientific adviser interrupted. "What would be your personal opinion of this landslide on La Palma if it was ever to occur, and how would it affect the U.S. mainland?"

"My personal opinion," he said, pausing for a few reflective seconds then continuing, "is if it occurred per the models, the initial wave height leaving the island would exceed one thousand feet in height." Clark noted the look of astonishment on his advisers' faces as Pollack continued. "As it reached the deeper oceanic waters of the Atlantic, the wave would be imperceptible on the ocean's surface. This huge volume of moving water, traveling at hundreds of miles per hour, would possibly be hundreds of kilometers in length from front to back. Once the wave hit the shallows off the coast, the front of the wave would begin to slow down, but the rear would continue at its rate of speed, causing the wave to rear up in height," he continued saying as the men in the

Oval Office looked at one another somberly. "The frightening aspect of this wave would not only be the possible height of one to three hundred feet. This monster, instead of just breaking on the shore line, would travel with its powerful momentum far inland, up to fifteen miles or more, devastating everything in its path."

"You're saying the Swiss scientists couldn't be sure of their size accuracy?" Tim Byrd of Homeland Security asked, breaking the stunned silence in the room. "So how can we be sure a wave of this height is possible?"

"We have scientific evidence of a prior collapse in the Canary Islands around one hundred twenty thousand years ago." Pollack countered. "Some scientists believe that evidence can be seen today in the Bahamas. Many of the islands were reshaped in the form of chevrons from the immense force of that wave. There are also many huge boulders that were lifted up off the ocean floor, some weighing over a thousand tons, which were deposited well above sea level. To put this into perspective, Mr. President, imagine the March 2011 tsunami catastrophe in Japan, but six to eight times bigger in size."

"My God," Robertson said in a whisper as silence fell upon the Oval Office at hearing the horrific depiction put before them.

"Thank you, Dr. Pollack," the President said flatly. "You've been very informative and I appreciate your efforts."

"You're quite welcome, Mr. President. May I ask you something? I am not aware of reports of activity on the Cumbre Vieja. Is there a problem?"

"No, Dr. Pollack. We're just planning ahead in case this scenario ever plays out," Clark lied, disliking the fact that he could not be honest with the man, but wanting to keep this situation under wraps for the moment.

"That's good to hear," the scientist chuckled nervously. "My wife and kids are down in Long Island staying at my sister's beach house."

"Thank you again, Dr. Pollack. Good bye," the President said, disconnecting the line and hitting the page button.

"Maggie, get me Admiral Borland." "Right away, sir," she said.

"I think it's high time that we had a chat with this Turner fellow," Clark said, rapping his fingers on the desk. "We need to obtain all the information we can."

"I agree, sir," the Homeland Security head affirmed. "Right now, he's our only source of intelligence in this situation. However, in the last hour or so, we haven't been able to contact him on the number he provided."

"He did say to me earlier this morning the terrorists involved in this plot were out to silence him and his group," Robertson said as the phone buzzed on the President's desk.

"Yes, Maggie."

"Sir, I hate to disturb you but I have a gentleman from the U.S. Geological Survey on the line. He insists that he speak to FEMA Director Boyle. He says it's urgent."

"Put him through, Maggie, I'll have Mr. Boyle pick up," he said, handing the receiver to Boyle.

"Stephen Boyle, here," he said as the others watched pensively. "Mr. Boyle, I'm sorry to disturb you, but my name is Peter

Markson. I'm with the U.S.G.S. here in the D.C. bureau, and I'll come right to the point. We may have a situation developing in the Canary Islands that could have far reaching implications to our country's safety," he stated in a serious tone.

"Yes, go on, Mr. Markson," Boyle replied, giving the President an apprehensive look.

"Well, we have one of our field scientists on the island of La Palma and she has observed volcanic activity, but it contradicts all of our current data reports. I have the utmost confidence in her abilities, so we decided to do further investigation with a series of satellite images. The standard imaging revealed nothing of concern as far as an upwelling of the lava dome so I was about to dismiss it…until I saw the infrared image. The thermal imaging verifies an intense magnification of thermal temperatures on the Crater del Duraznero, which is indicative of a pending eruption," he said, pausing for a moment. "Have you ever heard of the mega-tsunami scenario?"

"Hold on, Mr. Markson, I think the President should hear this," Boyle said, motioning the President to place the call on conference. "I think we just received the verification we need, Mr. President," he said nervously. "The Cumbre Vieja volcano on La Palma is active."

23

La Palma Island, Western Flank

Geologist Rosalie Harris was back on the Cumbre Vieja. She positioned herself carefully on the edge of the Crater del Duraznero, making notes of the newly-formed fumaroles that were opening along the perimeter of the crater.

She noted the vents of the fumaroles were allowing gases from deep within the magma chamber to escape, ranging from mere water vapor to life threatening gases such as sulfur dioxide and carbon dioxide.

Rosalie wisely decided to keep her distance to record ground temperatures and monitor the seismic activity. She felt the first tremors en route to the ridge line towering thousands of feet above the small towns that lay in the shadow of the old volcano.

Apprehensively aware of the seismic activity that was now increasing in strength on a regular basis, she used her infrared digital thermometer to measure ground temperatures as she carefully traversed the crater's ridge. Adding to her confusion, the ground temperatures were becoming too extreme for the absence of any upwelling of the dome in the crater.

"It doesn't add up," she'd told Pete Markson just fifteen minutes prior. "You did the right thing by sending out a broadcast warning. This is not a normal volcanic event, and I can't judge whether it's going to pop or not. We don't have any seismic data from the local survey that jives with what I am seeing here. I don't see any upwelling or indication of a lava dome, but the fumaroles I see don't lie. There's a lot of internal heat pressure building in the magma chamber," she'd said as another slightly larger tremor rumbled beneath her.

"Rosalie, I've spoken to the FEMA director and the President about your mega-slide scenario and they seemed strangely interested in what I gave them. Are you sure something like that could possibly happen?" Markson asked apprehensively.

"Pete, I don't have a measured scientific answer for you, but your satellite infrared imaging shows a vast amount of heat generating on this ridge. Whatever the scenario, we would have been negligent if you had not sent out an advisory. What they do with it is up to them," she said in earnest.

"I hope you're wrong about that slide, Rosalie. Can you imagine the destruction that would be caused by such a tsunami? Rosalie, I want you to get out of there now. It's too dangerous to remain on that ridge line."

"Don't worry, Pete, I don't have a death wish. I'm leaving right now to help the local authorities coordinate an evacuation of the towns beneath the western flank. I'll touch base with you as soon as I get a chance," she said, disconnecting the call before he could respond.

Now, putting her infrared digital thermometer back in her backpack, Rosalie precariously began making her way back down the slope of the crater, slipping on the loose basalt as she proceeded. She continued to follow the old fault that looked as if a giant hoe had scooped out the earth and plowed a deep furrow for miles.

If this flank is going to let loose, it most likely will start along this fault, she thought. She quickened her pace as another tremor, much stronger than the last, shook the ground beneath her. As the tremor subsided, she heard the distinct sound of a helicopter coming closer. She looked up and saw, through the dense smoke- shrouded summit, a blue and white Bell Ranger helicopter flying low above the huge fault. She watched as the agile craft slowed just beyond the next peak and then began its descent downward as if it were going to land.

***

The sleek Bell Ranger's 206-B Rolls Royce gas turbo-shaft engine was beginning to feel the effects of the heavy concentrations of carbon dioxide that it flew through along the Cumbre Vieja's ridge line. The engine whined in protest from the lack of oxygen in its turbine intakes as the RPM warning light began to flicker.

"We can't stay here long," the pilot announced through the flight intercom headset that all four occupants wore. "We've got to get out of this pocket of volcanic gases."

"There," Eli Turner said, pointing to a flat outcrop just ahead of them. "Set us down there. It seems to be away from the heaviest gas emissions. We'll have to hike to the rock formation that Maria pinpointed. It should be just a short hike back along the fault line." "Eli, there's a lot of thermal activity going on along this ridge," she warned, pointing to the vast amount of steam and smoke cascading from the entire length of the ridge. The pilot quickly descended to the relatively safe plateau below the fault line. "Are you sure we should do this?"

"We'll be in and out of there before you know it, Maria," Eli said in an effort to calm her apprehension. "If there is any evidence of Simon's cache of artifacts accessible, we'll know pretty quickly whether it's retrievable or not."

"I hope so," Burr interjected, now wondering if it was such a wise decision to go ahead with his plan as he saw the forces of nature at work beneath him. "If this thing goes off while we're here, we're all dead."

"It's either now, or never folks. Looks like this thing is going to blow no matter what Pencor and his goons do at this point," Eli said as the chopper set down lightly on the flat surface of basalt.

As the turbines whined to a halt, the three exited the Bell Ranger's rear door and stepped onto the barren landscape that looked like an alien world. Burr quickly walked around to the other side to retrieve the backpack and rope from the pilot.

"Wait here until we return," he instructed the pilot, who nodded in understanding. Burr grabbed the pack and threw Eli the coil of nylon rope, which he slung over his arm. The three set off, making their way up a small rise to the twelve foot fault line, its trench running along the ridge that partially slipped in the 1949 eruption. Heading north along the trench line, they saw little vegetation save the small outcrops of rock grass that had precariously taken root over the years.

The trio came to an abrupt halt when a jolting tremor shook the earth beneath them for a moment and then ceased. After looking at each other for a few uneasy moments, they started walking again. Now sweating profusely from the elevated temperatures and heavy mist of steam, they came to a deep gash in the earth that wound around a large formation of rocks. Eli stopped as he saw a lone figure coming out of the mist ahead of them.

"Hello!" A woman's voice called out as the figure from the mist started walking toward to them.

"Howdy," Eli said, coughing as the pungent sting of sulfur permeated his sinuses.

"You people should get out of here now," the woman said, pointing to the caldera she just came from and covering her mouth with a handkerchief. "There are a lot of poisonous gases being released, not to mention the threat of rock slides. You're putting yourselves in a lot of danger if you remain."

"And you are?" Burr asked indignantly.

"I'm a field scientist with the U.S. Geological Survey. I'm warning you that this volcano could erupt any time and if you—"

"We're well aware of the situation," Eli interrupted her. "We are not going to be up here long, but if you are going back down, you must get a warning out to the towns beneath this volcano. They need to be evacuated as soon as possible."

"I'm already on it. I am going to help the local authorities once I get down. They've begun issuing the warning already, so do yourselves a favor and get off this ridge now."

"We'll take it under advisement. Thanks," Eli said as the three started off in the opposite direction.

"Fools!" Rosalie yelled, shaking her head in disbelief as she turned and headed into the shrouded mist.

Ten minutes later, the three came to a breach in the acrid mist, where they saw a large formation of rocks sitting just above the fault line.

"There it is." Maria yelled as she ran toward the rock. Though damaged greatly during the 1949 eruption, the distinct shape of a hand could be clearly made out as the three continued to their goal. Climbing out of the fault line on large step-like rocks, they maneuvered to a point just above the deep trench. Eli looked in wonder at the formation, curious as to what secrets it held.

"What are we looking for?" Burr asked as the three stood at the lower base of the huge stone hand.

"Simon's scroll indicated the relics were beneath the Hand of God," Maria replied, eyeing the rock for anything unnatural while walking slowly along its massive base. "There's been so much erosion and shifting over the centuries," she added. "It may take days of excavation to find any sign of a burial chamber."

"I'll check the high side of the rock, Maria," Eli said, making his way up the side of the monolith, and then disappearing into the mist around its upper corner.

"Search for anything that looks like an opening, or for any unnatural cuts in the rock face." Maria instructed Burr as the two slowly worked their way along the base, scraping the loosened basalt from the base of the rock with their hands.

It began as a slight tremor, running along the depression in the fault line from the Crater del Duraznero and traversing the entire length of the break in the earth. Increasing exponentially in strength, the tremor made its way to the huge rock formation. The tormented earth began to shake beneath them as the fault line fractured under the tremendous forces at work along the Cumbre Vieja ridge. As the new fracture began to widen and a vast column of noxious gasses were released, the three explorers were thrown to the ground like rag dolls.

Maria and Burr lay debilitated under the relentless onslaught of nature, as loose rock and earth beneath them began cascading into the newly created chasm.

"Hold on," Maria yelled at the top of her voice as she and Burr began to slide down towards the gaping crevasse below them. Burr screamed in terror as he found himself sliding uncontrollably toward the newly created ninety-foot gash in the earth, belching its poisonous gases from deep within.

The cataclysm seemed to last for an eternity. Then, suddenly and mercifully, it abated as quickly as it had begun. Maria laid on her back in the sudden silence gasping for breath. Burr opened his eyes and shrieked in terror to see his legs dangling precariously over the edge of the newly formed crevasse, with the loose dirt slowly cascading out from beneath him. Holding onto the small outcrop of rock, he began yelling for help.

"Eli, we need the rope," Maria screamed as she slowly, and, on all fours, started making her way down the still sliding embankment to the helpless Burr, who was frozen in fear.

"Maria—freeze!" Eli yelled as he came around the boulder seeing the situation. "Moving will only make it worse." He slipped the rope from over his shoulder, and then fastened a climber's taut line hitch on the one end. In one fluid motion, he hurled the looped end down towards Burr where it landed just out of reach and to his right. Eli's second attempt found its mark and landed on Burr's right arm. He grabbed at it wildly, sending more loose basalt cascading down into the chasm beneath him. He managed to slip the taut line hitch over his shoulders and slide the knot tight just as his precarious ledge finally gave way. He began careening into the abyss until the line snapped taut, leaving him dangling in midair.

Eli managed to wrap the free end of the line around a small jagged boulder, just in time for it to snap taut as Burr's body weight reached the end of the rope.

"Maria, I want you to slowly make your way to the rope and grab on," he yelled, grasping the rope with both hands and planting his feet firmly on the jagged boulder. Maria slid crab-like on her back and finally reached the safety of the rope. She grabbed on and pulled herself up to Eli's position by the huge boulder.

"Okay," Eli said once she was safe, "start pulling with me." The two began to pull with all their might as the dead weight of Alton Burr slowly began to rise to the edge of the chasm. Burr, now nearing exhaustion, scrambled to get a foothold as he reached the ledge. Finding firm footing, he pushed with his legs and used all his remaining strength to surmount the edge of the precipice and get back onto the steep, rocky slope. Eli and Maria continued to pull, and, after a few more moments, Burr was reunited with the pair. The three of them slouched down in total exhaustion.

"I'm starting—to think—that this wasn't—such a hot idea," Maria said, gasping for breath every few words.

"Thanks for coming after me," Burr said, out of breath. "I thought I was a goner. Maybe we should reconsider this venture, take the lady's advice, and get the hell out of here."

"What, and not see the lovely entrance that was uncovered by that last quake?" Eli said coyly, standing up and brushing off his pants with his hat.

"You found it," Maria yelled in excitement as she stood up.

"All the loose basalt that was extricated by the slide exposed an entrance just above the rock's high side," he said as the three carefully made their way to the elevated side of the huge monolith.

"There it is!" Eli said, pointing to a small opening the size of a manhole cover.

"Hand me a flashlight," Maria told Burr, who reached in his backpack and produced a small spotlight.

"Hope it still works." he said, handing the light to her. Maria was pleased the light snapped on when she slid the switch. She aimed it at the opening and peered down into the darkness below. The light cut through the swirling dust from the recent quake, revealing a smooth, basalt floor. It was about nine feet down a gradual incline to get underneath the huge hand-shaped boulder.

"It's a skylight," Maria said excitedly, still looking into the darkened chamber.

"A what?" Burr asked.

"A skylight is a breakthrough in the ceiling of a lava tube, where lava was once forced to the surface during an eruption," she replied, turning off the light and facing the two men. "In this case, the skylight was covered by a rock that became dislodged during that last tremor. I can see it smashed on the lava tube floor."

"I'll get the rope," Eli said, going back to the front of the huge boulder and retrieving the line. Looking around when he returned, he saw a boulder that would suffice as a tie off for them to repel into the lava tube.

"The wall is sloped gradually so we can easily make a descent and then return without much difficulty," Maria stated, throwing the rope into the cave below, and then looking at Eli.

"What happens if another quake hits while we are in there?" Burr asked apprehensively.

"God hates a coward," Eli replied nervously. "Oh, I forgot, you don't believe in God, do you? You gotta' love the irony in that." He grabbed the line and started his descent into the cave, laughing as he disappeared below.

He may hate a fool even more, Burr thought angrily as he followed Maria down the rope into the unknown.

24

"**M**r. President, you are talking about a preempted military strike on a sovereign country. I strongly advise against any such action, as the repercussions would be dire," said Admiral Thomas Borland, the current Commander in Chief of the Atlantic fleet, designated COMLANTFLT. "We have enough problems at the United Nations to deal with, without adding another situation to the mix. Their current thinking is that we have a proclivity to shoot first and negotiate later. We must first contact the proper authorities on Tenerife."

"Tom, the U.N. be damned. I understand and appreciate your position on this matter but, as President, I have an obligation to protect the people of the United States and I intend to do so. All I am asking is if we have any naval assets in the vicinity of the northwestern coast of Africa?"

"Sir, the nearest carrier group is in the Persian Gulf, but without flyover permission for our aircraft to cross foreign airspace, any military incursion would have to do an in-flight refuel," the admiral said. "Even if we were to launch an air strike now, it would take over five hours to reach the target area."

"That may be too late, based on the information we have gathered pertaining to this situation," President Clark said in frustration. "Do we have anything that is closer?"

"Well, according to the CNO, we do have an Austin class LPD amphibious transport dock that shipped out from Rota, Spain last night with two escort frigates. It's headed back to Norfolk for decommission," Borland stated, looking at the chief naval officer's daily positioning status report.

"Admiral," the President said, slightly annoyed, "in layman's terms please. What is an LPD?"

"My apologies, Mr. President, the LPD is an amphibious assault ship used to transport and land Marines, their equipment, and supplies in combat or rescue assignments. It is supported by its own helicopters or vertical take-off and landing aircraft, if so assigned. They can carry up to nine hundred Marines for specialized missions. The Austin class is being mothballed since they were built in the late sixties."

"Admiral Borland, that will suffice quite nicely," Clark said, his hopes elevated, but only a little. "I want you to divert the…what is the name of the ship?"

"The *Hazleton*, Mr. President."

"Yes, the *Hazleton*. I want you to transmit orders to divert it to the Canaries at all possible speed. Even if we find we don't need the military assets, I have the feeling that La Palma is going to need some evacuation and humanitarian assistance," Clark said. "At best, it will provide

257

us with a valid reason for our presence in the vicinity."

"Very good, Mr. President, I'll have the CNO issue the orders right away," the admiral replied without emotion. "What message would you like to relay to its captain?"

"Once the vessel is en route, I'll contact the captain personally. This is going to be a tough one to explain, so once you've had him alter course, have the personnel at COMLANTFLT put me through to him."

"I'm on it, Mr. President."

"Thank you, Admiral," Clark said, hanging up the phone and turning to Under Secretary of State Robertson.

"Have you been able to reach Turner yet?"

"No, sir, I keep getting a no-service intercept signal. Either it's off or disabled somehow."

"Damn! Without specific data, we are shooting at ducks with a peashooter. I know we can obtain the general information on the location of this Bishamon facility on Tenerife, but we cannot afford to take out an innocent facility or observatory, which are in the general vicinity of the target zone. We need a spotter on-site, and Turner's phone has GPS tracking capabilities. Keep trying to reach him, Jim," he said, looking at FEMA Director Stephen Boyle. "What about the tsunami threat, Mr. President? "Boyle asked.

"Do we issue an alert?"

"Steve," Clark said, pausing for a moment as he took a deep, thoughtful breath. "I want you to issue an alert to the media and to the Emergency Alert System affiliates on the east coast only. Have them explain that an evacuation warning will be in place as of noon today, Eastern Time, for the entire eastern coastline of the United States. At that time

I'll be issuing a statement to the press," he said, knowing there was no turning back now. He had committed himself totally.

"I hope to God we're right about this, Mr. President," Boyle said tersely.

"Mr. Boyle," the President said, looking up from his folded hands. "I hope to God that we're wrong."

"Any follow-up from the U.S. Geological Survey yet, Bob?" Tim Byrd from Homeland Security asked Presidential scientific adviser Robert Laird.

"Yes, they're getting reports from La Palma of increased seismic activity and growing volcanic gas emissions along the Cumbre Vieja ridge," Laird replied, looking at his most recent report. "The island has issued an evacuation order for the towns in the vicinity of the active region. They have—"

"Mr. President," James Robertson interrupted, "Turner's phone—it's finally ringing."

25

The black Mercedes with the Bishamon symbol emblazoned on its side sat in the deserted parking lot behind the university's antiquities building. A jubilant Robert Pencor was sitting behind the wheel.

Relishing in the death of the younger Turner and his associate, Pencor watched, with morbid fascination, the now smoldering remnants of the Raven-44 helicopter high on the barren slopes of Mt. Teide.

"I hope you enjoyed your ride, Turner," he mused as the last of the wreckage's smoke disappeared into the clouds that shrouded the long extinct volcano. *The elder Turner and the woman will be found eventually and silenced as well,* he thought confidently as he checked the ignition for the keys and saw they were not there. He leaned forward to feel under the seat for the keys, becoming irritated at this new annoyance. Suddenly, he was startled by a clinking sound coming from beside him.

"Looking for these, amigo?" an all too familiar voice asked in a mocking tone. Pencor turned his head sharply to the left to see a smiling Samuel Caberra dangling the car keys in one hand and pointing a 45-automatic at him with the other. "Slowly hand me your weapon," Samuel ordered in a deadly serious tone. "Very slowly," he repeated as the passenger side of the Mercedes opened to reveal Turner, who climbed in and smiled at Pencor.

"No, it can't be!" Pencor raged. "You weren't on the helicopter?"

"Sorry to inconvenience you, Pencor, but there was a last minute change of plans. From the looks of things, it was a damn good idea," Turner said to the man, whose face was now turning the color of crimson, much to Turner's pleasure. "Our friend here is definitely a candidate for anger management, Samuel, wouldn't you say?" Turner said, as Yashiro walked up behind Samuel holding the pistol that was taken from the former driver of the Mercedes.

"Out of the car, Pencor," Samuel said, motioning the barrel of the gun at him.

"What do we do with him?" Yashiro asked, nervously holding the gun.

"I think the turkey we placed in the trunk earlier needs some stuffing, eh, amigo-san?" Samuel said, tossing Yashiro a good- humored wink as Yashiro smiled back.

"It'll be my pleasure, Samuel. Toss me the keys."

"Okay," Turner said quizzically. "I give up. What are you talking about?"

"Never mind, Josh, it's an inside joke," his friend answered as the two proceeded to escort Pencor to the rear of the car.

Minutes later, Robert Pencor was neatly gagged and tied up in the trunk. Not requiring the Yakuza driver any longer, he was dragged off and tossed into the nearby dumpster.

The three men then made their way through the busy streets to the outskirts of La Laguna, and the location that Captain Saune had provided them earlier. As they drove, they talked about what they needed to do to ensure that Osama would be stopped.

"Not to change the subject, Josh, but it *is* a good thing we didn't take that helicopter, or we would have all wound up as seagull food," Samuel said, looking at his friend as they turned onto Granada Street.

"I figured it would be easier to gain access to the compound using one of their vehicles; just one big happy Bishamon family," Turner replied. "The way I see it, Osama thinks we're dead, so he won't be expecting us to show up at his front door. We now have Pencor's access card, and I have a feeling Pencor himself will help us get past Osama's bullies at the main gate."

"Speaking of bullies," Samuel said, regarding the ugly bruise growing on Turner's face and a slightly swollen and split lip. "You look like hell. I'm sorry I wasn't there to help you out, amigo. That brute must have given you a bad time of it."

"Yeah, but you should see him. He definitely won't be doing the fox trot for a long while," Turner answered, rubbing his still tender jaw. "We need to end this, Samuel; we need to end this soon."

They continued to drive until in the distance they saw the military transport vehicle in front of a modest, sky blue, single- story home at the end of the street. "I'm tired of running and killing, but most of all, I miss my dad," he said remorsefully. "I had just started to set our relationship straight when this mess started."

"Don't worry, Josh," Samuel replied. "Your father loves you very much. He knew you needed room to find yourself, and was content to wait as long as it took for you to decide what you wanted in life."

"I just want to let him know that, but I'm not sure if I'll ever get the chance, considering what lies ahead of us," Turner said.

"You can tell him when you see him, amigo," Samuel said assuredly, giving his friend a jab in the arm that still throbbed from the earlier life-and-death struggle with the brutish guard.

"I guess you're right, Samuel," Turner admitted. "At least Dad and Maria are out of harm's way at Carlos' house. But before we head out to this madman's compound, I want to call him."

Their black Bishamon sedan finally pulled to a stop in front of the house with the address Saune had given them earlier. Shutting off the engine, they all hopped out of the vehicle and proceeded to walk up the flagstone walkway. The brightly painted Tenerife pinewood door was abruptly thrown open at the very moment they reached it. The three found themselves staring into the business end of an M-16A1 rifle.

"Whoa...it's us!" Turner yelled, freezing mid step and backing up with his companions.

"You might have picked a better mode of transportation," Captain Saune said, lowering his weapon and motioning at the black Mercedes, its ominous emblem on the door. "We thought you were some of Osama's party favors coming for a visit." He threw the door open and quickly ushered the three into the house.

Turner was amazed and impressed to see eight men in Army Combat Uniforms. The ACUs were newly designed uniforms utilizing universal camouflage: ideal for woodland, desert, and urban surroundings. They all carried a late 70s model M-16A1 rifle, which sported a 30-round magazine and a 40mm M203 grenade launcher attached. Each soldier was also wired with a SmartCom SCV08 VHF lapel-attached radio with an earpiece for silent communications. Seeing no threat, the men returned to putting on their face camouflage and checking out their gear.

"These are my best men, Josh," Captain Saune said proudly as he closed the door behind the three newcomers. They followed Saune across the room and into the kitchen. "Here," he said, motioning the trio to a porcelain pot. "I've made some coffee; we're going to need it."

"We've had a bit of luck, Captain, and might have a way to gain access into the compound without too much trouble." Turner said as he poured himself, Samuel, and Yashiro a much needed cup of coffee. "We've managed to capture Pencor, who is resting comfortably in the trunk and patiently awaiting his starring role in getting us past the Bishamon gate guards."

"You've got Pencor?" Saune said, laughing aloud. "I'll bet he's none too happy about that situation."

"That's an understatement, Captain. I've never seen a man turn that shade of red before. I'm personally looking forward to ripping the duct tape off his mouth. He's such an angry individual," Samuel said with a broad smile.

"I take it you and your men are ready to go," Turner said, noting the rugged-looking men in the other room, silently going about their preparations.

"Unless you have anything else to add to the equation; we planned to use the Bell 205 Huey to launch an assault from the lower end of the Bishamon facility where we commandeered the Sikorsky. Since you have the Bishamon vehicle, you can launch an assault from the upper level at the gate. With a few well-placed satchel charges, we can easily access the hatchway underneath the facility, neutralize any resistance, and make our way in. Then, with Yashiro's help, we can set charges to take out that Scalar weapon."

"Captain, you can't just blow up the Interferometer device," Yashiro cautioned. "There is a protocol that must be adhered to in order to shut down the exothermic event. You must—"

"Whoa, Yashiro, can you explain that in plain English, please?" Samuel asked, waving his hands in ignorance.

"Sorry," he said, then continued. "Osama has two transmitters in place beneath the site. Both have been emitting offset electromagnetic-pulsed timed waves for months now. These powerful electromagnetic waves, built up over time, have a seriously high ground potential that has to be released somewhere. When the Bishamon complex was constructed, they built EM drain fields beneath the facility to slowly release the massive G-potential after the desired effect has been reached," he said, pausing as the three men listened intently.

"Okay, I'm with you so far," Turner said. "Go on."

"The buried drain fields are lined with huge storage cells, capable of discharging the massive potential slowly as the emitted standing waves diminish. If the transmitters were to fail suddenly, or if you were to destroy them, the wave potential feedback would be massive and the drain fields would not be able to handle it. No one knows for sure, as it has never been put to the test, but I would assume the resulting feedback would cause an explosion equivalent to a thermonuclear blast; with a super-charged shock wave that could level much of the island's infrastructure." Yashiro said, seeing the stunned look on his comrade's faces.

"Good God, this keeps getting better and better," Samuel said. "I guess we can't just go in and pull the plug on his little toys then?"

"Absolutely not."

"What do you suggest we do, Yashiro?" Turner asked at length. "If I can gain access to the control room computer, I can do two things. First, I can reverse the exothermic mode to become endothermic in nature. That means reversing the EM potential without interrupting the timed pulses. In effect, this would create an ambient vacuum potential in the magma chamber and cause a massive cooling effect. The superheated energy would be extracted from the chamber and dispersed in the drain fields at Bishamon. It could be enough to stop the heat expansion and limit the eruption on La Palma, which will most likely happen now, no matter what we do. It could possibly keep the mega-slide from occurring by reducing or eliminating the source of the massive heat. That's if we able to get there in time."

"And the second thing you can do?" Turner asked, still trying to comprehend the scope of what was being unleashed on the world by these lunatics.

"Well, after a brief cooling period in endothermic mode, I can start backing off the standing waves and hope that I do it at a rate the fields can withstand. If I back it down too quickly...."

"Yeah," Samuel said. "We all go for one big ride."

"I believe it can be done, but we must get there as soon as possible. The longer we wait, the less chance of success," Yashiro said.

"Our odds of gaining access to the facility are a little better now that we have Pencor as our trump card," Turner said. "Better, but it's still going to be tough. We'll have to coordinate our assaults with you, Captain, starting with your landing at the helipad below. Once the fun begins, it should draw most of the opposition away from the main gate. Then we'll make our move with Pencor seated next to me and Samuel covering him from the back. Once inside using Pencor's swipe card, we'll head for the control room where Yashiro can do his neat tricks. Let's just hope we're not too late already."

"I know," Captain Saune said. "We heard on the police band the volcano on Cumbre Vieja is beginning to erupt."

"That's to be expected," Yashiro said. "It must go through its natural pre-eruption phase even with the aid of the Scalar weapon. We're seeing the precursor to the final EM burst programmed at the Bishamon facility."

The Global Star phone in Turner's cargo pants pocket began to ring, startling everyone present. He quickly pulled the phone out and answered it.

"Turner," he said

"Mr. Turner," said a voice on the other end, "we've been trying to get through to you for quite a while. This is Jim Robertson from the U.S. State Department. I'm here with President Clark and the directors of FEMA and Homeland Security."

"Well, Mr. Robertson, we've been a little preoccupied here with people trying to kill us all day," he said sarcastically, rubbing his aching jaw. "I am glad to hear from you at last. So, have you looked into the situation my father explained to you earlier today?"

"Indeed we have, Mr. Turner. I need to tell you that a few of us were a bit skeptical about the scenario laid out by your father, but recent events on La Palma and verification by the U.S. Geological Survey have precluded any doubt as to the threat posed to our country. Let me put you on speaker so we all can hear," he said as Turner heard the faint click and subsequent feedback of the speaker phone.

"Mr. Turner, this is Alan Clark. I was hoping that you could shed a little more light for us on the situation there."

"Well, Mr. President," Turner said, holding back a laugh as Samuel gave him a Queen Anne salute. "As far as we can tell, we've only a few hours at best to prevent this slide from happening." We have been pursued by the island authorities on false charges by this Osama character, which may have bought him the precious time needed to complete his dirty work on La Palma. Fortunately, we've avoided capture thus far and—"

"Mr. Turner, this is Stephen Boyle of FEMA," his voice interrupted. "Who is this Osama?"

"All you need to know is that he one of the leaders of the Japanese Mafia; the Yakuza to be exact. He and his goons have infiltrated the entire island's government in this plot, so we can trust no one at this point. That is why we must act on our own," Turner replied. "We did manage to capture the other conspirator; a guy named Robert Pencor."

"Pencor!" Boyle said incredulously. "How in God's

name is he involved in this affair?"

"Listen, Mr. Boyle, it's all about power, money, and, most importantly for him, vengeance against the U.S. for 'causing the collapse of his industrial empire,' as he so eloquently put it. He wants to cripple the economy of the United States with this massive tsunami, and then he plans to flood the world's markets with his new free energy device called a Zero Point Generator. It will make him the savior of mankind in the eyes of many poorer nations," Turner said, pausing for a second. "He will reap the praise, profits, and power, controlling most of the world's energy supply by rendering oil refinery and production obsolete. Those who resist, in the wealthy oil-driven countries, will find it more and more difficult to procure oil as more and more nations go online with his ZPGs. Eventually, they will have to succumb to his demands as oil suppliers dry up. It will wreak havoc on the world's economy for years."

"I still can't believe that he would threaten the lives of millions with so much profit at stake," Boyle said. "Why wouldn't he just go about it in a legitimate fashion? I'm sure he could be reasoned with and—"

"You're not listening to what I'm saying, Mr. Boyle," Turner interrupted angrily, his patience running thin. "Pencor and his Yakuza associates are mad, cold-blooded killers, hell-bent on power and destruction. His goal is vengeance, pure and simple, and you are not going to be able to reason with him. Any sense of morality within his twisted mind is long gone. So, unless you plan on providing us with some help now, we have got to act before all hell breaks loose on La Palma," Turner said, his head starting to ache from pain and a mounting fatigue.

"But, Turner," the FEMA man persisted, "Pencor has to know that world opinion will turn against him when it is discovered that he is responsible."

"Look, Boyle," a frustrated Turner finally exploded on the phone, "you bureaucrats absolutely astound me with your arrogance. Do you actually believe that most of the world's countries would give a damn about the United States if a catastrophe were to occur on its soil? Don't delude yourself, mister. Whether it be from hatred, envy, or just plain economic posturing, the majority of the world's leaders would wag their fingers at Pencor saying, 'gee, that wasn't a very nice thing to do.' Meanwhile, behind closed doors they fall over themselves as they rejoice in our downfall and welcome Pencor as their energy savior. A person like Pencor doesn't give a damn about world opinion. So, if you are planning to help us stop these lunatics, you need to let us know now because you're wasting valuable time," he concluded, clenching his left hand in a fist as anger welled within him.

"Mr. Turner. Believe me, I want as much as you to put an end to their plans," President Clark interjected in a calm demeanor. "As we speak, a United States Naval vessel is en route to assist in your attempt to thwart Pencor's plans. I will be in contact with its commanding officer within the hour, and will make it absolutely clear to him that all of his resources are completely at your disposal. Mr. Turner, we appreciate the sacrifices you and your friends are making in an effort to defend our country, and we will do everything in our efforts to help you. Once I've spoken to the ship's commander, I'll have him contact you on your satellite phone. Please be sure to keep it with you."

"Thank you, Mr. President. I don't need to tell you that we are all pretty tired here, but we will do the best we can. We have a small combat unit from the Tenerife National Guard who are willing to risk their lives in an effort to help, and we're preparing to move out as soon as we finish speaking with you."

"Mr. Turner, this is Jim Robertson again. If we can manage to get aircraft within striking range, we may be able to take the weapon out with conventional weapons, but we will need a description of the weapon your father spoke of in order to relay a precise target."

"Mr. Robertson, according to our friend Yashiro, a scientist for Bishamon, the Scalar weapon he describes is protected beneath the facility. According to him, the abrupt shutdown of the EM waves would cause a shock wave equivalent to a thermonuclear explosion that would more than likely kill many of the island's inhabitants. I would highly advise against using an air strike until we can gain entry to the target, find out the situation, and hopefully reduce the weapon's output levels."

"Then we are all counting on you, and your team, Mr. Turner. I only hope we can get there in time to be of assistance," President Clark said sincerely. "The captain of the USS *Hazleton* will be contacting you for instructions. God's speed and good hunting," he said, and then the line went dead.

"We need to get going now, Captain," Turner said.

Saune was well ahead of him. He threw Turner a 45-automatic with a full ammo belt, and tossed an ammo belt to Samuel. Then he and his eight men prepared to leave.

"Once both teams have gained access to the facility,

we'll rendezvous at the control room," Turner added as he handed the Captain a crudely-drawn map of the floor plan of the complex, made in haste by Yashiro.

"It should take you about forty-five minutes to reach the facility from here," Captain Saune said, strapping on his side arm and tossing Turner his binoculars. "We'll head back to the base and take off in the Huey, so we can coincide with your arrival at the Bishamon facility."

"I'll call you on your Global Star when we are within ten minutes of the target," Turner said.

He and Samuel stood up and headed for the door. Yashiro was getting ready to follow when the phone rang once more. Turner answered as he paused at the doorway.

"Josh," the familiar voice of Carlos Santiago boomed over the phone. "Thank God I got through to you. We have a serious problem." A sudden fear for the safety of his father and Maria leaped into his weary mind. "Your father, Maria, and that Burr fellow have taken a helicopter to La Palma to search for those damned artifacts. I'm sure you have heard the Cumbre Vieja is erupting," he said in a worried tone.

"Damn it!" Turner yelled, slamming his fist against the door. "When did they leave?"

"According to Maria's note, they left right after I went to the university luncheon," the Professor replied. "I was hoping that you might have heard from them."

"Unfortunately, no, Professor," he replied, closing his eyes in frustration. "I told them to stay put until we gave them the all clear. It's not like my father to do something this risky. I hope when they see the eruption occurring, they'll have the good judgment to get out of harm's way," he said, hoping they were okay. "I'll contact you if I hear from them. Good-bye, Professor."

The weight of this new development added to his anxiety and sense of foreboding as he, and the others, filed out of the house towards their vehicles. Turner knew he had to stay focused on his present task. Any distractions at this point could cause the death of Samuel and the others. He had to remain sharp, at least until this nightmare was over, and worry about his father and Maria later.

If there is a later, he thought as he, Yashiro, and Samuel climbed into the Bishamon sedan.

The two under-manned assault teams drove off towards the heights of Mt Teide and the foreboding Bishamon weapon facility. Each was lost in thought, wondering what the next few hours would bring, and, who would live, or who would die.

26

North Atlantic Ocean,

578 miles southwest of Rota, Spain

The late afternoon sun presented a brilliant light show dancing off the blue-gray waters of the northern Atlantic as the sixteen thousand ton amphibious transport made her way through the gentle swells of the unusually calm seas. The USS *Hazleton* left the naval base in Rota, Spain and was accompanied by her two Knox Class support fast frigates, the *Blakeslee* and the *Milford.* She was on her journey home to Norfolk, Virginia, where she would be decommissioned and mothballed after a long and illustrious career.

An Austin Class LPD-4 amphibious transport, she was the last of her series when Congress decided not to fund their overhaul and modernizing back in 2003. The more modern LPD-17 had been set in motion as her replacement.

Despite her age, the *Hazleton* was still a formidable strike and support vessel. At a length of five hundred sixty-nine feet, her two Foster Wheeler 600 psi boilers powered twin

De Laval GT turbines, providing a hefty twenty-four thousand shaft horsepower.

The *Hazleton*, with a crew of twenty officers and three hundred ninety-six enlisted men, carried three CH-46 Sea Knight helicopters and one deadly AH-1F Cobra Strike helicopter. In addition, it carried a Marine contingent of four hundred men that could easily be deployed from its well deck. Located astern, the well deck could ballast down, flooding the stern and enabling its six LCM-6 landing craft access through its huge drop down gate.

The old LPD-4 served as command and control for numerous amphibious assault missions in its past, and as a civilian disaster relief ship on various occasions when natural catastrophes occurred around the world. She had been assigned to the Eisenhower Carrier Group for the last two years in the Iran Theater, but the constant mechanical problems and outdated hardware forced her to be recalled home.

The captain of the *Hazleton* sat in the bridge command chair sipping his coffee and feeling the familiar gentle vibration of the ship's four electrical power plants, capable of powering a small town.

Captain Jason McKnight was a formidable man of fifty-two. Known as 'Ole Mac' by his crew, he had been in the Navy for over thirty-two years now, and skipper of the *Hazleton* for the last fifteen, making this final voyage a bittersweet one for him. He held a certain fondness for this old ship as he gently stroked his salt- and-pepper beard and stared out across the calm ocean waters.

A sad end to a damn good ship, he thought as he took another sip of coffee. He glanced about the old bridge, taking note of the classic metal wheel box and rust-colored wheel; handles on either side to hang on to in foul weather. *She might be old, but she is a good ship with a fine crew*, he mused as he noticed Lieutenant Commander Jack Ewell entering the bridge house.

Though the *Hazleton* was ending its illustrious career, McKnight was thinking about the stark contrast of the new AEGIS Class guided missile destroyer that he would command after a month's shore leave. He welcomed the challenge, but he would miss the specialized missions that were afforded by the LPD Class ships.

"Duty roster, Captain," Lieutenant Commander Ewell reported, interrupting the captain's reverie as he handed him the clipboard.

"Thank you, Commander," Mac said, perusing the schedule and nodding approval as he handed it back to him for posting. "What's the word from the chart room in regards to weather for our voyage to Norfolk?" Mac asked his first officer.

"Clear sailing until we get within two hundred nautical miles of Norfolk. We'll run into a weak low-pressure system that's projected to move up the coast. They expect waves from four to six feet, but nothing out of the ordinary," he replied, handing the roster to Ensign Swann.

"Might as well be a damned cruise ship for all the excitement we're gonna' see," Mac said sarcastically, finishing the last of his coffee and setting down the cup. "I'm gonna' miss this old ship, Commander Ewell."

He rose from the old captain's chair, walked to the port side of the bridge, and looked at the map on the chart table.

The red phone adjacent to the captain's chair buzzed

loudly and Lt. Commander Ewell answered it.

"Bridge: Lt. Commander Ewell," he answered nonchalantly.

"Radio shack, sir," an excited voice spoke on the other end. "I have a satellite call for the captain. It's the President of the United States."

"You're joking," Ewell replied incredulously.

"No, sir, I'm not. President Clark is on the horn, and he wants to speak with Ole Mac. Sorry, sir, I mean Captain McKnight."

"Standby," Ewell said as he held the phone up and motioned to Mac. "Captain, radio shack says they've got a call for you from the President."

"I'm not in the mood for practical jokes from CVBG today," McKnight said angrily, walking over and grabbing the receiver. "McKnight here," he said coarsely.

"Standby, Captain, I'll patch him through to the bridge," the radioman said. Mac listened to the click of the transfer, and to the new voice that came over the satellite link.

"Good afternoon, Captain McKnight. This is Alan Clark."

"Yes, Mr. President." Mac responded in surprise, recognizing the President's voice immediately and staring wide-eyed at his first officer. "How may I assist you?"

"Captain," President Clark stated. "I wish I were calling under better circumstances, but a matter of National Security has arisen that will necessitate expeditious action by you and your fine crew. I have no doubt that you will respond in the fine tradition of the United States Navy."

"Our ship and crew are at your disposal, sir," Mac replied ingenuously.

"Orders from Admiral Borland at COMLANTFLT are being sent to you as we speak. I wanted to communicate with you directly as to the extreme importance of this mission, and what could happen if we fail," the President said in a dire tone as Mac snapped his fingers at Lt. Commander Ewell and signaled him to retrieve the clipboard hanging from the chart desk. McKnight listened intently to the situation that was presented to him by President Clark as Ewell handed the pen and clipboard to him.

McKnight jotted down specific notes as Clark described to him the threat relayed by the Turners.

Lt. Commander Ewell could see the serious look in his skipper's eyes, growing in intensity as he continued listening. McKnight finished the conversation by saying. "I understand the gravity of the situation, Mr. President, and we will do our utmost to assist you. We'll contact Turner when the time is appropriate," he said, writing down the number on the clipboard. "Yes, Sir. Goodbye." Hanging up the phone, he gave his first officer a look that he had not seen in several years.

"Captain, what's going on?" the mystified officer asked.

"Jack, get on the horn to the chart room and have them plot a course to the Canary Islands. Once plotted, set course immediately and at full speed. Have the chart data relayed to the Combat Information Center. I'll be there later and will explain to everyone, understood?" He barked, picking up the bridge phone and buzzing CIC.

"Yes, Sir," Ewell said dutifully, not questioning his orders as the CIC picked up the Captain's call.

"CIC: Lieutenant Minichino here."

"Lieutenant, this is the Captain. I want you to come to battle ready and I want all chopper pilots and senior officers to the briefing room ASAP," he ordered as Lt. Commander Ewell finished communicating his orders to the chart room.

"Captain," Ewell asked pensively. "What's going on?"

"Jack, you're not going to believe this one," he stated as he headed out of the bridge. "You have the bridge, Commander. Once the new course is set, I'll come to the briefing and explain everything."

He disappeared out the hatchway and headed down into the heart of the ship. The bridge crew just looked at each other in stunned confusion.

Twenty minutes later, the *Hazleton* and her two escorts were plowing through the open waters of the North Atlantic en route to the Canary Islands. The *Hazleton's* two twelve thousand shaft horsepower engines whined in protest as she cut through the gently rolling ocean swells. The ship had been placed on battle alert and stations were manned. McKnight walked into the *Hazleton's* briefing room, located amidships behind the Combat Information Center. Those present rose as he walked in, but Mac waved his hands in protest.

"Remain seated, people," he stated as the men and women sat back down in their seats. "This mission comes directly from the President, the Joint Chiefs, and COMLANTFLT," he announced, wasting no time getting to the crux of the situation. "This may be the most important mission this ship and crew will ever be assigned, so I want everyone on their toes. The lives of millions of Americans depend on our success."As he spoke, Lieutenant JG Minichino handed out the hastily assembled CIC report outlining the threat from the island of Tenerife. Those gathered in the room read the report in stunned disbelief.

After giving his crew a moment to peruse the document, the captain continued. "Our mission is two-fold. First, we must aide the operatives on the scene at Tenerife. Our Marine contingency will provide full air and ground support until the operatives inside the terrorist's facility can render the weapon safe. Second, we need to get our people out of harm's way if the order comes for a Tomahawk strike on the site. The strike is a last-ditch effort and would be carried out by the *Milford*."

After ten more minutes of questions and answers, Captain McKnight dismissed his staff. "That's all, people. Get to your stations. I want Lieutenant Minichino, Colonel Sears, and Major Zibrinski to remain," he said over the rush of excited conversation as the contingent filed out of the briefing room.

Colonel Kyle Sears was a seasoned Marine pilot and had been flying the AH-1F Strike Cobra helicopter since the second Iraq war, and in operations in Afghanistan. This hard as nails, highly decorated Marine took his profession seriously and, in his twenty- five years in the corps, had earned the respect and admiration of his peers. Many times he'd put his own life at risk to help his brothers-in-arms through tough combat situations. He now sat down in the front row as the rest of his peers filed out of the room. "Captain," Sears asked directly, "why the hell can't we just take the damn thing out now?"

"No can do, Colonel," Mac countered. "If we were to take it out too soon, we'd risk heavy collateral damage to civilians on the island. I can't explain the science behind it, but you must go with me on this one."

"Will we encounter resistance?" Sears questioned.

"Colonel, from what the intel on-site has reported, most likely, but to what extent is unknown. That is why you must coordinate with this Turner fellow. He seems to be up to his eyeballs in this mess and is launching an assault with a handful of the island's National Guard. I want you to signal them from the Cobra upon acquisition and get any tactical data that you may need."

"This Turner is a civilian?" CH-46 pilot Major Sid Zibrinski asked in disdain. "We have to rely on a civilian?"

"Until you and your Marines get a foothold on the complex, he's going to have to suffice. You are to secure the facility, take out any combatants, and offer complete aid to Turner. This comes from the President, Major, not me," said Mac. "That's all I have, unless you have any other questions."

"Yeah, I just hope this guy, Turner, has some balls and common sense," she said with concern. "I don't want to drop my people into a firestorm due to bad intel."

"You never give us guys a break, do you, Sid?" Colonel Sears said, jokingly jabbing the twenty-five year veteran female Sea Knight pilot Sidney Zibrinski in the arm.

"Never let up, I say," she replied, smiling as the two Marine pilots stood and exited the briefing room, leaving Lieutenant Minichino alone with the captain.

Lieutenant JG Minichino was watch officer for the Combat Information Center, which was the tactical heart and soul of the vessel's coordinated strike force. A ten year Navy man, he prided himself on precision and total accuracy. He was affectionately known as 'mixer man' by his shipmates, a title bestowed upon him for the astute manner of mixing up a variety of exotic cocktails while on shore leave.

"Captain, the quartermaster in the chart room reports that we're one hundred ninety-five nautical miles from Tenerife," Minichino reported, reading the data off the clipboard he held. "At our present speed of eighteen knots, we're looking at a six hour ETA at best."

"Eighteen knots, huh?" Mac grunted in disdain. "We can launch the Cobra and the three Sea Knights, correct?" he asked his CIC Officer.

"Yes, Captain, we can, but it would be a one way trip until we came within island range to recover," Minichino replied. "We can send in the Cobra now, as it has a range of two hundred seventy- four nautical miles. I'd delay launching the Sea Knights. Fully- loaded with twenty-five Marines each, they would be cutting it close as the combat range is one hundred eighty-four miles, Sir."

"Make it so, Lieutenant," he said. Mac picked up the briefing room phone and buzzed the engine room.

"Engine room," a voice yelled over the din of the steam turbines.

"Chief, this is the captain. I damn well know that this vessel can push twenty-one knots or better. Seeing I ordered top speed, may I inquire as to why we are presently only making eighteen knots?"

"Captain," the young engineer responded nervously, "these engines are getting up in years and I'm worried they might blow under too much stress."

"Then by God, let 'em blow!" Mac roared loud enough for the entire engine room crew to hear over the loud speaker. "I want all you got, Chief, understood?"

"Aye, sir. I'm on it," the rattled chief replied, sweat forming on his forehead as he put down the intercom mic. "You heard the man," he said to his crew in the engine room. "Fire 'em up, and pray we don't have a shit-storm."

Mac made his way back to the bridge, followed by Lt. Commander Ewell. He walked to his chair, his senses attuned and adrenaline flowing, feeling alive for the first time in a very long time.

"I just hope we're in time to help those poor bastards on Tenerife," he said to Ewell, who nodded in agreement. They heard the Claxton sound on the launch deck where Colonel Sears was going through his pre-flight checklist and preparing his AH-1F Strike Cobra for launch.

"God only knows what will happen if we arrive too late."

27

The sun was now making its descent behind the twelve thousand foot peak of Mt. Teide, casting shadows upon the rocky summit road leading to the Bishamon complex. Turner sat behind the wheel of the idling black Bishamon Mercedes, overlooking the sheer drop-off where Paulo met his cruel demise the night before.

Seeing the wreckage of the rover far below only intensified his anger for the man that Samuel and Yashiro were now extricating from the trunk of the vehicle.

He and Osama will be brought to justice for their barbaric actions, he promised himself as he sat silently and steeled his mind for the fight ahead. For him, the last twenty-four hours of death, destruction, and fight for survival culminated into this one final act that would end this ongoing nightmare. He not only had to save his father and Maria from these murderers, but also the countless, nameless individuals that faced certain death if the tsunami actually occurred.

He looked at his watch and saw that it was well past

four o'clock. Though his mind was prepared for the conflict ahead, shades of doubt mixed with a twinge of fear crept into the deepest recesses of his soul. He doubted that they could succeed and wondered if it would have been more expedient to hide out until it was safe. For a brief moment, he wanted to avoid the peril that lie ahead and let the rest of the world deal with Pencor and Osama. He feared that his friend Samuel would somehow die because of his wild roll of the dice. He quickly dismissed the notion, knowing the lives of untold millions depended on their success. *I have to hold on for their sake*, he thought, pushing the demons of fear and anxiety from his mind.

Turner had finished conversing with Under Secretary Robertson on the Global Star phone just before they stopped to remove Pencor from the trunk. The conversation with Robertson troubled him deeply as he watched his demented passenger unceremoniously lifted out of the trunk. Robertson's words still echoed in his ear.

"Mr. Turner, you need to be aware that if you fail to neutralize the Scalar weapon at the facility, the United States Navy frigate *Milford* will be authorized to launch its Tomahawk missiles to eliminate the threat," he had said flatly.

"If you do, sir, you may be causing the deaths of hundreds, perhaps thousands of innocent people here on Tenerife," Turner countered in protest.

"That is understood completely," Robertson retorted, "but the President is getting a lot of pressure from some people in the Senate. They are stating the argument of minimal collateral damage on Tenerife, as opposed to the countless lives lost here at home. Though it is regrettable, this is not negotiable. That weapon, along with the entire facility, *will* be neutralized if you fail to succeed," he said in finality.

"You're not giving us much leeway," Turner argued.

"I'm sorry, Mr. Turner, but we have no other choice at this point. We will give you sufficient warning on your SmartCom VHF radios now that you have given us the frequency. The USS *Hazleton* is en route to La Palma as we speak and will give you ample warning," he said. "If, and when, the order comes to launch, you and your teams will be evacuated by the support choppers that will be launched from the *Hazleton*. You must be clear on this, Mr. Turner. When you get the order, you had better get your asses out of there."

Now, as he sat alone in the Mercedes, he realized that no matter how he looked at this scenario, many innocent people were going to die. He was furious at those responsible, and regarded them now as a cancer that needed to be completely eradicated.

Robert Pencor, with his hands still bound, was hurriedly shoved into the passenger seat by Samuel, who shut the door behind him.

Pencor glared at Turner, but his usual controlling demeanor was quickly unsettled. He saw a fury in the blue eyes of Turner that bore through him with an intensity and hatred he had never seen before.

"I hope the damn facility comes down on your head, Pencor," Turner hissed at him. "Animals like you don't deserve compassion. The scary thing is the rock you crawled out from under probably holds more like you."

"Mr. Turner," Pencor said, feigning control of the

situation. "People like you and your father are weak. It's the powerful that will always control the world, and there is nothing that you or your misguided leaders in Washington can do to alter the fact that the world's economic configuration is about to be completely redrawn. I intend to hold power in that new global structure and my Zero Point Generators will ensure that, Turner. You, or anyone opposing me, will be eliminated like a bug under my shoe," he spat caustically.

"We're going to make sure that you don't get that chance," Turner replied as Samuel and Yashiro climbed in the back seat. "We're headed now to stop your Scalar weapon and put an end to your sick, twisted scheme."

"You mean you're taking me to Osama's facility?" Pencor asked in perverse joy. "Good," he said laughing aloud. "I'm sure my associates will be more than glad to see you, and your friends. You should have made your escape when you had the—" His ranting was cut short as Samuel jammed the barrel of his 45 stiffly into the back of Pencor's head.

"Amigo, if you don't shut your trap, I'm personally going to throw you off the next cliff we come to, understand?"

"Very well," he responded, knowing these were desperate men and that desperate men, in his world, always made fatal errors. *All I have to do is to wait until the time is right*, he mused with a malevolent grin as the Mercedes sped up the access road to the Bishamon compound.

After a few miles, Turner could see the foreboding facility and its rolling gate. He pulled over and came to a stop on the side of the gravel road.

"Cover him. I'm going to have a look-see," he said, as he got out and walked to the rear of the car with the binoculars Captain Saune had given him. He peered through the binoculars at the facility and slowly lowered his gaze to the gate area. He saw a transport truck with at least fifteen armed men, who seemed to be loading the back of the vehicle with supplies. Shifting his view to the gate, he saw four armed guards milling about the guard shack. Without taking his eyes off the compound, he hit the transmitter button on his VHF radio link.

"Captain Saune, do you read me?"

After a few moments his earpiece came to life with the sound of Saune's voice behind the noise of the Bell 205 Huey helicopter.

"Go ahead, Josh. I read you," he replied.

"We're positioned about a quarter mile from the main gate. I'm seeing at least nineteen armed combatants in the compound's front gate area, and have no way to tell how many of Osama's goons are stuffed inside the facility," Turner reported. "What's your ETA?"

"Give us ten minutes, Josh. We're coming in from the western slopes with the sun at our backs." Saune responded. Samuel got out of the car and walked back to his friend, while Yashiro continued to guard Pencor.

"Roger that, Captain. We'll await your signal, and then move out. Good luck to you and your men," Turner said.

"And to you, my friend," Saune responded, with utmost admiration for this steadfast man that he had come to respect. "See you in the control room. Saune—out."

"We have about ten minutes, Samuel," Turner said solemnly, lowering his binoculars and seeing the smile on the face of the tough Peruvian.

"Are you ready, amigo?" Samuel asked in a carefree manner, as if they were merely going to a ball game.

"Ready as I'll ever be," he replied, looking at his friend. "You're a good friend, Samuel; you didn't have to go along with this nutty plan, you know."

"Hey, don't worry. It's a cinch getting in there," he stated, pointing to the Bishamon building in the distance. "Besides, we have Pencor, so we don't need no stinking key," he added, in an exaggerated accent that caused Turner to laugh aloud.

"Samuel," he said after a few silent moments. "If I don't make it out, I want you to tell my dad...."

"Hey, Josh," Samuel softly interrupted. "No more talk like that, okay? You'll see your dad real soon." After many silent minutes, the two heard the classic thumping sound of the Bell 205 coming from the western flank of the mountain.

Pulling the 45 from the holster, Turner looked at his friend and smiled a wide grin. "Lock and load, my friend; it's Miller time."

"If it's all the same to you, Josh, I'd rather have a Corona," Samuel responded. The two jumped back into the car and started up the road toward the gate as the Bell 205 Huey came into view above the landing plateau at the lower access of the compound.

"'Cry havoc, and let slip the dogs of war.'" Samuel whispered from the back seat, quoting Shakespeare's Julius Caesar and poking the back of a confused Pencor's head with his pistol.

"You didn't finish the quote, pal," Turner said as they

neared the gate, his mind now steeled for the conflict that lie ahead.

"'...That this foul deed shall smell above the earth with carrion men, groaning for burial.'"

28

Unbeknownst to Captain Saune, the Bishamon guards had been doubled at the lava tube's entrance as a result of the brazen escape that morning by he and Turner in the Sikorsky. The Bell 205, flown by he and his men, quickly dropped into the compound's landing platform.

The unexpected arrival of the Huey managed to catch the Yakuza soldiers off guard, allowing the crucial seconds needed for them to touch down on the makeshift landing pad and stir a dust cloud into the air. Those precious seconds gave Captain Saune and his men time to leap from the side door of the Huey and make a run for an outcropping of boulders some fifteen feet distant.

The precious moments ended abruptly, however, as the Yakuza soldiers quickly recovered and gunfire erupted from the lava tube entrance high above them. The Tenerife National Guardsmen dove for cover behind the boulders, but Saune and his men quickly returned a deadly barrage of weapons fire from their M16A1 rifles. The six mercenaries quickly scattered for cover under the onslaught.

Saune knew in seconds they were in a strategically precarious position. He didn't expect the entrance to be this heavily guarded, but rather hoped that minor resistance would have made it easier for them to summit the rise to the cave entrance. With a loud alarm blaring from the facility above them, the six combatants at the lava tube entrance were soon re-enforced from within the facility. They unleashed a fierce volley against Saune and his men, trapped in their exposed position far below.

"We're sitting ducks here, Captain," Sergeant Juan Ortega yelled as he let loose another flurry of shots at the cave entrance. "We have to get to higher ground."

"I'm aware of that, Sergeant," Saune yelled back, scanning the area for a possible means of gaining a better tactical position. "There!" he yelled, pointing to the loading platform that served them during their wild escape earlier that day. "We'll split and start a flanking maneuver at the loading platform where the conveyer belt is. "You four," he yelled, pointing to the four soldiers at the far end of the boulder. "I want you to lay down staggered left-to-right grenade fire every five seconds. That should give time for the rest of us to make it to that metal platform."

Understanding the captain's plan, the four men at the end readied the 40mm M203 grenade launchers that were attached to their M16s.

"On my mark—" Saune yelled, counting to three under his breath. "Now!" he yelled as the last man in his skirmish line jumped up and fired the rifle-propelled grenade. The subsequent explosion sent the surprised Yakuza men scrambling for cover. The bloody remains of one of Osama's men showered the lava tube's entrance. Captain

Saune and the other four men jumped into action and scrambled towards the metal platform. Ten meters seemed like a mile as the next of Saune's men unleashed another grenade. The Yakuza guards eventually realized the potential flanking maneuver and responded with a murderous spray of gunfire, killing the last man of Saune's group just before he reached the cover of the platform. The four remaining at the platform returned fire and eliminated another of Osama's men.

Though in a better position, Saune had a sickening feeling in his gut that his chances were becoming slim at best. Although his two teams were helplessly outnumbered, they continued firing upon the men at the lava tube entrance high above them. Hoping for a miracle, he punched the lever on the conveyor belt to no avail. *The Bishamon personnel must have disconnected the power to the unit after this morning. I hope Josh is having better luck up above than we are down here,* Saune thought as he let loose a grenade from his rifle at the cave entrance.

As the desperate battle raged on the landing plateau below the Bishamon facility, the black Mercedes approached the main gate above the facility. Slowing the vehicle, Turner could make out the distinct sound of an alarm resonating throughout the perimeter of the complex. He saw, to his relief, the large contingent of Yakuza soldiers deserting their loading duties at the transport truck and scrambling back into the building through its main doors.

"They're going down to access the tunnel from the supply room on the lower level." Yashiro said. The four remaining gate guards saw the Bishamon vehicle approaching and dutifully opened the long, rolling gate.

"Not a word, Pencor," Samuel threatened from behind him in the back seat, "or your retirement comes early. Do you understand?" Pencor nodded and smiled as Turner used his controls to open the electric window on Pencor's side. He lowered it halfway as the car rolled to a stop at the gate. A wide-eyed guard, excited by the sound of gunfire below, saw Pencor in the passenger side and waved them through without fanfare. He then returned to the guardhouse after closing the gate.

"So far so good," Turner said as he pulled the car up close to the double steel doors that led into the bowels of the facility. "Do you have the access card, Yashiro?" he asked, shutting the engine off, and putting the 45 back in its holster.

"I've got it right here, Josh," the little Japanese scientist replied as he held up the magnetic swipe card used to unlock the main doors in the facility. "It should get us into the control room as well."

"Let's do this," Turner said, climbing out of the car, followed by Samuel and Yashiro. Pencor slowly opened his door and, as he got out, looked around him for any possible opportunity to make his escape. Samuel watched as Yashiro ran the magnetic card through the door lock slot. Pencor quickly bolted into a run towards Osama's guards just as the buzzer sounded and the door unlocked. In the split second that Turner pulled the door open, Pencor began yelling and pointing to the three intruders at the door. Samuel started to react as Pencor ducked behind the loading truck.

"Never mind him, Samuel. He's useless to us now. Get inside quickly," he yelled as the three ducked inside the ominous building. Gunfire from the gate guards peppered the door as it closed behind them. Turner saw a steel rod lying next to the door that was most likely used to prop the door open, and shoved it through the handles of the double doors, effectively locking it from within.

"That will buy us some time, guys," he said pulling out his weapon and hearing the reverberation of grenade explosions from deep within the building's structure. As Turner surveyed their surroundings, he saw the main entrance atrium filled with wooden and steel crates labeled in Japanese. Stark in appearance, the room tapered to a long center corridor that seemed to traverse the entire length of the facility. He saw stairwells on the right side descending to the lower level and stairs on the opposite end rising to the upper level.

His survey was interrupted by the sounds of men coming down the stairs, yelling excitedly in Japanese. Turner and his companions ducked behind one of the large steel crates, hoping the men would not see the steel rod locking the front door. Luckily, the men were intent on joining the firefight below the facility, and failed to notice it as they ran past the door and proceeded down the stairwell.

"Okay, Yashiro, give us the layout again," Samuel said as the three stepped out from their cover.

"Those men were coming from the upper level. It houses the security office and Osama's suites. This is the main level," the Japanese scientist said, pointing down the corridor. "All of those doors along the corridor are the sleeping quarters and bathrooms. At the end of the corridor is the control room, which is usually guarded from the inside."

"What is down those stairs?" Turner asked, pointing to

the stairs on the right corner of the atrium.

"If you go down those steps, it turns to the left and you'll come to another corridor that mirrors this one. If you take a left at the end of the corridor, it leads to the supply room directly above the lava tube. Just across from that is Osama's lab, where he most likely killed my friend Wari and the other scientists we saw in the tunnel when we were escaping this morning."

"And the Scalar weapon..." Turner asked. "Where is that located?"

"Go right at the corridor and down the hall to the left. On the right side are the dining rooms. At the end of the corridor is the ZPG room, which is directly below the control room on this level." "You're not thinking of doing what I think you are..." Samuel said to his friend.

"I'm sure they know that we've crashed their little party, now that Pencor is loose," Turner said as he started walking towards the right stairwell. "I want you and Yashiro to get into that control room and stop that weapon. I'm going to go below and see what mischief I can get into."

"I'm not comfortable with us splitting up again, amigo," Samuel said apprehensively.

"We have to do this quickly, Samuel. Radio me on the VHF link when you have secured the control room. Captain Saune and I will join up with you later." Turner quickly disappeared down the stairs. Just then, the buzzer on the main door locking mechanism sounded, and despite it being violently pushed from the outside, the steel rod held firm.

"I hate it when he does this crap," Samuel said indifferently, as he and Yashiro sprinted down the long dimly-lit corridor. A red strobe light was flashing in alarm above the two large steel doors that led into the complex's control room. Peering through the small rectangular glass panes on the doors, Samuel saw two armed guards standing adjacent to the doors with their backs to them. Beyond them were three men in lab coats he assumed to be the remaining scientists loyal to Osama.

"Okay, Yashiro, get ready," Samuel whispered, ducking down below the glass panes. "After I swipe the lock open, I'm going to rush the guy on the right. You take care of the guard on the left. Got it, amigo-san?"

"Got it." Yashiro replied nervously, gripping his pistol.

"On three…" Samuel whispered. On the count of "one", he swiped the access card through the slot, unlocking the door with a buzz. Samuel launched his full weight against the opening door, sending one of the unsuspecting guards sprawling to the floor. Samuel's sudden entrance shocked the three scientists at the control panel across the room. He was followed by Yashiro, who nervously pointed his pistol at the other standing Yakuza guard. The mercenary could see the fear in Yashiro's eyes. Reacting swiftly, he raised his weapon at the tiny Japanese man, who stood frozen in terror.

Samuel, seeing Yashiro's plight, deftly fired two rounds into the guard. The dying man fired wildly as he fell, striking Yashiro in the same shoulder that was hit the night before. Wincing in pain, he fell back against the wall, and slid down to the floor. The other guard, recovering from his initial shock, scrambled to retrieve his weapon that was knocked from his hands by the opening door.

He rose up quickly and rushed Samuel, hitting him square in the mid-section. Samuel fell to his knees and his

45 went sprawling across the floor. The hardened mercenary lashed out a bone shattering roundhouse kick to Samuel's head, which narrowly missed. Samuel's instincts took over as he launched himself inside the man's killing zone. The agile Quechuan's vise-like arm encircled the Japanese man's neck as the guard's eyes went wide with surprise at the quickness of his opponent. In one swift upward and turning motion, he snapped the Yakuza guard's neck, killing him instantly. The force of Samuel's forward momentum made them both fall to the floor.

Adrenaline now coursing through his body, Samuel saw one of the scientists reaching for the dead guard's weapon. In one fluid motion, he drew his hunting knife from its sheath and flung it with an accuracy developed from the many years hunting in the Amazon Rain Forest. The Japanese man wearing the lab coat shrieked in pain as the knife found its mark and plunged deep into the man's left thigh. As the scientist fell to the floor in pain, Samuel rolled to his right to recover his 45-automatic. Springing to his feet, he pointed it at the remaining two scientists, who appeared to be in shock at the bloodshed they had just witnessed.

Samuel made his way over to Yashiro, who lay with his back against the wall. He was moaning in pain from the bullet wound in his now bleeding shoulder.

"I'm sorry," Yashiro sobbed weakly as he nursed his shoulder with his good hand and looked up at Samuel. "I couldn't shoot...I just couldn't do it."

"Don't worry, amigo, it's alright. Are you still able to do your work?" he asked, pointing to the control room's computers.

"Yes, help me up," he said as Samuel grabbed him around the waist and hoisted him up to his feet, all the while keeping an eye on the other two scientists. Yashiro, in pain from his wound, walked over to the computer terminals set up at the control room's semicircular work station. Samuel motioned with his weapon for the other two scientists to come with them.

"You're too late, Fuiruchirudo," Osama's lead scientist, Fuyuki Seijun, hissed defiantly at Yashiro as he painfully pulled the hunting knife from his leg. "We reached optimum output twenty minutes ago. There is no way to stop the eruption and landslide on La Palma now."

"If I'm right, there may be a way to neutralize it," Yashiro replied as the lead scientist glared at him skeptically. "If I can reverse the electromagnetic wave patterns to endothermic mode, it might reduce the heat from the magma chamber on La Palma enough to halt the process."

"That is total madness, Fuiruchirudo," Seijun yelled in obstinacy as he threw the blood stained knife across the floor. "If you were to do that, you'd cause a reflective shock wave. The field drains below the facility could never manage to dissipate that amount of endothermic feedback. The shock wave would level most of the island."

"We shall see," Yashiro responded with self-assurance. "Why don't you stop this madness, and help us put an end to this?"

"I will never help you," he hissed.

At that point, Samuel decided this had gone on long enough. "You two," he said, pointing the gun at the scientists. "If you won't help then I'm going to lock you up." He motioned them to help Seijun to a closet on the left side of the control room. With the three men now safely in the closet, Samuel braced the door by sliding a large cabinet in front of it.

Seijun pounded his fist on the door from the inside yelling, "He's going to kill us all, you fool!"

"Well, amigo, at least you'll have a front row seat." Samuel walked back over to Yashiro, who was intently going over the data on the computer.

"He's right about the levels," he said to Samuel as he stood behind him. "They are at maximum. I hope I can reverse the process in time, if at all."

"If anyone can do it, you can, amigo-san" Samuel said as he patted him on the back. "Josh and I have faith in you. If we didn't, we wouldn't be here now."

"Thank you, Samuel," the small Japanese scientist responded as he began typing commands into the system. "I won't let you down."

"The way I figure it. If it doesn't work, we won't have much time to complain about it to the management, will we?" Samuel said as he turned and started towards the doors. "I'm going to see what trouble my partner is getting himself into. Will you be okay here?" he asked when he reached the door.

"Yes, I'll be fine," he replied, "but smash the access card unit on the outside so no one else can enter. Just bang on the door if you need to get in."

"I'll take care of it, Yashiro. Good luck my friend, and thanks." Samuel said, leaving the stalwart Japanese scientist alone with his dangerous task. Samuel shut the doors to the control room and, with a resounding blow from the butt of the 45-automatic, disabled the card access unit.

Samuel knew he needed to check with Turner on the lower level, but before he got a chance, he heard a large number of men descending the stairs at the other end of the corridor in the atrium. He quickly ducked into one of the adjacent rooms that served as sleeping quarters. Once inside, he could hear muffled conversation far down the hall and decided to wait there until it was safe to proceed.

***

Following Yashiro's directions, Turner had descended to the bottom of the stairwell and made a left into the short hallway that intersected the main corridor on the lower level. The sound of weapons fire increased in volume as he cautiously peered around the corner, looking first to his left where the supply room was located and then to his right. The corridor was a mirror of the one on the upper level, but with fewer doors along its length. In addition to the sound of the battle outside, he could feel a strong vibration beneath his feet; one similar to the feel of an electrical generating station.

Hearing the sound of men running through the corridor, he slipped back into the dimly-lit stairwell. With his back to the wall, he saw two Yakuza guards run into the supply room to join the battle raging against Captain Saune and his men.

Seeing it was clear, he sprinted away from the supply room and down the corridor in search of the source of the mysterious vibrations. He found his way to the locked double doors at the end of the hallway and peered into the reinforced rectangular windows.

These must be the Zero Point Generators, he thought, staring in amazement at the two huge free-energy generators surrounded by thick panes of polymer glass. One entire unit was approximately thirty feet in diameter and nine feet in height. In the center of each, mounted on insulating plates, were what looked to be rows of four huge magnetic tubes. There were large connecting cables projecting outward from the side along the base to a set of polymer-encased coils at the unit's apex. On the generator's outer sides were large capacitor banks with power cables feeding into a panel in the room's center. *Incredible that these devices supply this facility with free energy,* he thought in amazement, while looking quickly over his shoulder to make sure it was still clear. *In the hands of people of integrity, this device could solve the world's energy dependency as well as clean our environment.*

Turner forced himself to stop wasting time, turned and ran up the corridor where he stopped at a large door on his right. On the door was displayed a red sign in Japanese, which looked to him like a warning placard. Turning the handle, he found it unlocked, and, quickly slipped inside the large room, quietly shutting the door behind him.

The room was fifteen feet deep and thirty feet in length, but it was what he saw that sent shivers down his spine.

So, this is Osama's Scalar weapon, he thought, looking at the two menacing nine foot diameter parabolic dishes located at the center of the room. It's the source of the two EM waves bombarding the magma core deep beneath La Palma.

He studied the huge parabolic dishes bolted securely to the reinforced concrete floor. Attached were huge snake-like cables projecting from the back of each. One cable wound its way upward through the ceiling, while the others went down into the floor. *Probably the storage drain cells beneath the ground that Yashiro spoke of.*

Looking to Turner like something out of a sick sci-fi movie, he moved carefully towards the array. He avoided walking in front of it, though Yashiro had assured him the EM waves were traveling through the vacuum of space-time.

Realizing that he was wasting valuable moments, he quickly clicked on the transmitter on his VHF radio.

"Captain Saune, this is Turner. Do you read me?" he asked. After a few moments of silence, the earpiece crackled to life with the sound of Saune's voice almost completely drowned out by gunfire.

"Josh," Saune yelled over the din of rifle fire. "It's not going well here. We're pinned down at the loading platform and barely holding our own. I didn't anticipate this much resistance. We're facing at least twenty or more combatants up at the lava tube entrance. I may not be able to meet you in the control room."

"Samuel and Yashiro should have made it to the control room by now, and I'm on the lower level," Turner replied. "Is there anything I can do to help you from this end?"

"Unless you have a squad of armed men with you, I'm afraid not. You wouldn't last a minute if you came down to the tunnel. Just take out that Scalar weapon. We'll keep them occupied here as long as we can. Saune, out—" he said as the earpiece fell silent.

Turner felt a sickening feeling of despair rising in his chest as he continued to stare at the two horrid weapons before him. *How could they possibly hope to succeed with the odds so against them, and where in hell was their help?*

His earpiece came to life once more with the familiar voice of his friend. "Josh, can you read me?"

"Yeah, Samuel, how are you two faring?"

"We had a bit of trouble at first and Yashiro was wounded, however, we managed to secure the control room. No one can gain access unless Yashiro lets them in from the inside. He's now trying the reversal process."

"Do you think he can pull it off, Samuel?"

"It's going to be a tough road, Josh. He said the EM levels were already at maximum after we busted in, so I just don't know."

Turner, still staring at the ominous looking Scalar weapons, clicked his transmitter button to reply to his friend. However, he was cut short when a familiar voice from behind said, "Drop the gun, Turner." Releasing the transmitter button, he slowly raised his hand, and then dropped the 45 to the floor. "Now, slowly kick the gun away from you," the voice said. He complied, kicking the weapon away from him, and then turned to see Robert Pencor and a pale looking Japanese man with a patch over his eye. The two were flanked by two armed guards who were leveling their AK-47s at him.

"A valiant effort, Turner," Pencor said flatly, "but a useless and costly one as you will soon find out. Oh, excuse my bad manners, Mr. Turner. May I present to you my associate, Yagato Osama," he said, gesturing to the pasty looking man that stood beside him.

"Another one of your slimy friends," Turner said in contempt, desperately looking for a way out of this predicament.

"Mr. Turner, you disappoint me. I would have hoped for more respect than that," Osama responded. "But be assured, I plan to teach you proper respect."

Turner had to stall for time. He knew he was a dead man if he failed, so he went for the man's vanity, hoping that it would work.

"I'm quite impressed with your set up, Osama," he said. "Your Zero Point Generators are really quite amazing devices—"

"They are my devices, Mr. Turner," Pencor interrupted angrily. "The ones here are merely small prototypes in comparison to the larger industrial applications that I've developed. They are ready for deployment after the tsunami has wreaked havoc in the west."

"Somehow, I find it hard to believe that you developed them, Pencor," Turner said, his mind racing for any advantage.

"Very astute of you, Turner," Pencor said with a laugh. "I found it quite effortless to procure the device designs due to the stupidity and lack of foresight of many scientists in the United States. The original designers can cry foul all they want, but in the end, it won't matter. I will be untouchable."

"So, basically, you stole the designs from the efforts of others and plan to gain from their hard work and sacrifice." Turner said.

"Stealing is such a harsh word, Turner. I prefer procure. It has a more professional sound to it, wouldn't you say?"

"And what about the Scalar weapon..." Turner asked, continuing the tactic. "Did you procure them as well?"

"No!" Osama snapped back. "They are mine; the end

result of decades of research and testing by my organization, Mr. Turner. Behold, the weapons of the future," he said arrogantly, giving Pencor a disdaining look. "With the Scalar technology, we can strike any place in the world at any time; create earthquakes, eruptions, and tsunamis.

"I witnessed some of your handiwork in 2008, off the coast of New Guinea. A lot of good people died because of you," Turner said angrily.

"That was only the test run, Turner," he said with a laugh. "You should have considered yourself lucky it was such a small event. One of our proposed ideas was to use the exothermic weapon to cause the eruption of what is called a super volcano in the caldera that exists beneath your Yellowstone National Park. Our scientist considered the venture far too risky. The entire earth's climate could have been affected as a result, so we have put that plan on the shelf for the time being. Imagine, Mr. Turner, meters of ash covering most of the cities and agricultural heartland of America. Most would have died of lung related illnesses from breathing in the ash-laden air. Farm animals would have perished and eventually most people would have died from starvation."

"Only a diseased mind would ever think of doing something that terrible," Turner said, wanting to put this maniac out of his misery.

"Speaking of minds, you bring up a good point, Mr. Turner. I failed to mention that we can even affect the mind with a little device I have in the next room. You will have the pleasure of seeing it demonstrated first hand," Osama said, motioning the guards to take him.

"You cannot hope to stop the mega-slide now, Mr.

Turner," Osama said, as Turner was dragged forcefully into the corridor and toward the adjacent room. "It's over, Turner. You and your rag-tag group of soldiers below are hopelessly outnumbered by my men and shall all die in vain." He laughed loudly as Turner, hearing the sounds of the firefight below the complex, was dragged into the room.

"Where are your two friends, Mr. Turner? Telling us may save you a great deal of suffering," Pencor said as they entered the room with a warning placard similar to the one where the Scalar weapons were deployed.

"They went down through the supply room entrance to the lava tube to help our friends below," he lied, still hoping to buy Yashiro and Samuel precious moments. He looked around the large, sparsely-furnished room and saw it looked part laboratory, part medieval dungeon. On one wall, where he was now led, was a series of leather straps mounted head and chest level, with more along the floor. Turner was callously strapped to the leather bindings. He struggled to free himself to no avail.

"I'm sure that you are lying about the location of your friends, Mr. Turner," Osama said smiling. "We will no doubt find them, and soon they can join our little party."

He walked over to the other side of the room, to a long bank of control panels with cabling similar to the ones Turner had seen in the Scalar weapon room. He saw the familiar, snake-like power cables descending from the ceiling into a large metal box affixed with built-in dials connected to what looked like an oscilloscope. Another smaller cable, similar to a black coax cable, fed into the back of what looked like a ray gun bolted onto a metal table. The gun was about three feet in length and looked like a conventional weapon, except for a conical barrel the size of a pocket mirror at its end.

"This is one of my favorite Scalar toys, Mr. Turner," Osama said proudly as he toggled the power switch on at the control box and caused the gun to pulsate with a loud hum.

"Electromagnetic weaponry has a multitude of applications, Mr. Turner. One of them is this device, which uses the science of longitudinal waves to affect the mind," he said, gently stroking the top of the barrel with his hand. "This is my psycho-energetic stimulator or, what I prefer to call, the Mind Snapper gun. That has a nicer ring, doesn't it?"

"Your twisted mind snapped long ago, Osama," Turner said, angry that Osama continued toying with him. "You, and that other piece of shit," he said, shooting a glaring look at Pencor, who smiled with growing anticipation.

"I've become quite adept at its many uses, Mr. Turner," Osama continued, ignoring the insult and aiming its laser targeting system at Turner. He was helpless to resist, as the red targeting tracer cast its glow on Turner's forehead. Osama continued his emotionless rant. "I discovered that when the offsetting EM wave patterns are used at the lower levels, it renders a victim's mind open to any suggestion. I can persuade even the most stalwart mind to kill a friend, or their entire family. I can even induce you to believe that you are on fire, Mr. Turner. In your mind you are burning alive, though in reality, you are quite safe and comfortable," he said with a shrill laugh. "You'll experience the pain and horror associated with literally being on fire for as long as I see fit to indulge myself." Pencor, with his back facing

Osama, watched in rapt fascination and smiled at Turner's torment. He had not seen the Mind Snapper gun at work, and looked forward to the demonstration.

"You two," Osama yelled in Japanese to the guards standing by the door. "Find the other two intruders that were with him and bring them to me. If they resist, kill them." The two men quickly obeyed, exiting the laboratory in search of Samuel and Yashiro. Only the three of them remained. "I must say, Robert, it was fortunate that I came down when I did and discovered the main doors barred shut from the inside," Osama said to Pencor, who merely grunted in agreement as the red tracer laser disappeared from Turner's forehead. Osama quickly swiveled the gun's tracer onto the back of Pencor's head, and simultaneously powered up the longitudinal wave generator. Turner saw, to his horror, Pencor's face go expressionless. It was like staring into the face of a department store mannequin. Osama began to laugh loudly.

"Before I have my fun with you, Mr. Turner, I wanted to let you see the full capabilities of my beautiful device. At half power, the mind begins to lose all concepts of memory, feelings, or desires," he said as he inched up the power on the wave generator. Turner watched in revulsion as Pencor's eyes began to bulge horrifically from their sockets, followed by uncontrollable drooling from the corner of his mouth.

"Pencor has outlived his usefulness to me, Mr. Turner," Osama stated, gently toying with the EM wave's power dial. "I tolerated his insolence long enough to gain my power from his financial backing. The fool doesn't realize that while he was in Morocco, I had the original patents to his ZPGs transferred to my name and my operatives there took over his production facility. Robert was graciously going to let me have a percentage of the profit, but I prefer to have it all." He smiled, staring at his motionless one-time benefactor. "Once the completed industrial ZPGs now loaded on container ships in Morocco are commandeered by my men, they will be safely transferred to my production facility in Japan. I will have complete control the world's newest and most profitable power supply."

"You'll never get away with it, Osama!" Turner yelled in protest, struggling frantically at his bindings.

Ignoring the outburst, he said, "At full power, Mr. Turner, the cells of the mind are completely and utterly destroyed." He slowly turned the dial on his instrument of death to its optimum power.

Pencor's sickly, bulging eyes went dull and lifeless. In an instant, the rich, maniacal corporate leader fell to the floor like a rag doll. Osama slowly backed the longitudinal wave generator down to its lower level, laughing as he did so.

"Why don't you just get it over with?" Turner yelled in defiance, knowing that he would never see his father, Samuel, or Maria again. He now resigned himself to his fate, and was saddened that he had dragged Samuel into this nightmare. However, he was relieved that Maria was still with his father somewhere on La Palma. *Anywhere was better than here*, he thought, as once again Osama leveled the tracer laser onto Turner's forehead.

"A most effective device wouldn't you say?" Osama said, tormenting Turner even more. "Unfortunately, it has limitations in preciseness at a distance. I would have loved tormenting Robert longer but, sadly, I must leave. You, however, will be able to enjoy my little toy much longer than Robert did. I'm sure someone will find you eventually, but by then I'm afraid you will most assuredly be insane," he said as he powered up the EM wave to a lower output level.

Turner instantly felt his mind disconnect from reality. He felt nothing; no pain, fear, joy, or malice. He just stared, sightlessly and thoughtlessly, at his tormentor across the room.

"Mr. Turner," a voice boomed in his mind. "The room that you are in is ablaze. The flames are getting closer and closer to you. You cannot move." The echoing voice screamed in his mind as he suddenly felt the heat and saw flames about him. He wanted to scream, but found he could not as the inferno engulfed him. "You are burning alive, Mr. Turner." The echoing words roared in his mind and it seemed as though blinding, agonizing pain erupted through Turner's body. Nevertheless, his body was perfectly still in its bindings. There was no escaping this horrid torment. This was indeed hell and he was right in the heart of it. His mind tried to scream in agony, but it did nothing to relieve his distress.

Osama walked to the door and looked at Turner one more time saying, "I leave you to your karma, Mr. Turner. I have a plane to catch." He then left the lab and headed back up the stairwell to his office. Osama casually gathered his papers and prepared to vacate, while his expendable mercenaries took care of the intruders below.

***

Upstairs on the main level, Samuel had heard the voice

on Turner's VHF telling him to drop his weapon, but after that all had gone silent. He knew his friend was in serious trouble, but he could do nothing to help as long as the guards still occupied the atrium. Peeking out the door and down the corridor, Samuel saw at least ten armed men milling about in the atrium. They were talking excitedly among themselves, and it appeared as if they were waiting for orders.

After what seemed an eternity, he heard the sound of someone in authority yelling orders in Japanese, which sent the Yakuza soldiers quickly down the staircase. He could see, through the slight crack in the open door, two guards heading his way and readied his weapon. As they got closer, he gently closed the door. The two shadowy figures passed by his darkened hideaway and went directly to the doors of the control room. Samuel heard the men begin to shout when they saw the shattered access card unit dangling uselessly against the doors.

Bursting out of the door, Samuel fired at the two mercenaries just as they began turning their weapons on him. With the guards now dead, Samuel quickly grabbed an AK-47 from the floor and then ran down the corridor to the stairwell that led to the lower level.

As he bounded down the stairs, he prayed he wasn't too late to help Josh. He was going to find his friend, and God help anyone who got in his way.

Samuel assumed the guards that preceded him went down the access hatch in the supply room to aid in repelling Captain Saune and his men. He quickly looked into the room as he heard the firefight raging below. Seeing no one, he moved across the hall to the next room. Looking into the room through the small glass pane, he saw a strange looking weapon with a red tracer laser that emitted a reddish glow from the barrel. He slowly opened the door, 45-automatic at the ready and the AK-47 strapped over his shoulder. Slowly stepping inside, he was stunned to see Turner strapped to the far wall by leather restraints. He hung suspended and motionless; his eyes staring wide as though he was in pain and afraid. The laser tracer centered on his forehead.

Samuel quickly ran up to the weapon and, using the full force of his powerful arm, ripped the entire unit off its mounts. The force of the blow sent the gun and its equipment crashing to the floor with a loud hissing sound. He ran back to Turner who now, with his eyes shut, slumped lifelessly in his leather confines. Samuel feverishly removed the bindings and carefully lowered Turner's limp body to the floor. As he did, he heard the excited voice of Yashiro shouting over the VHF radio.

"It's working! It's working!"

29

As Yashiro celebrated his successful attempt at reversing the effects of the exothermic waves from the Scalar weapon, Eli Turner, Maria Santiago, and Alton Burr were on La Palma moving deep within the bowels of an ancient lava tube under the monolithic, hand-shaped rock formation.

Using the rope, the trio managed to descend into the tube through the skylight that opened as a result of the earlier seismic tremor. Once inside, they discovered the lava tube had collapsed centuries ago in the direction leading up to the caldera. The solid basalt barrier had effectively sealed the chamber, allowing them only to proceed on a downward trek. They now traversed the slope with the aid of a single flashlight.

Eli felt the seismic shocks increasing in frequency and in strength, but after traveling over one hundred fifty feet inside the lava tube, the heat was much worse than the tremors. It was becoming unbearable as the three, drenched in sweat and eyes burning, continued slowly forward in the darkness.

Eli grabbed on to Maria as another violent tremor shook the earth beneath their feet for the duration of ten seconds. This caused Burr to lose his footing and crash headlong onto the floor of the chamber.

"This is a fool's errand, Turner," Burr yelled in painful anger after his knee smashed into the tunnel's floor. "We need to get out of here before we're all killed."

"As I recall, this was your idea, Burr. There's nothing stopping you from going back and waiting for us," Eli yelled in response, steadying himself now the tremor had subsided.

"He may be right, Eli," Maria said, agreeing with the lawyer. "This is becoming too dangerous. The tremors are getting worse by the minute, and I'm worried about poisonous gases in here."

Pausing in thought for a moment, Eli finally said, "You may be right, Maria. I don't have the right to endanger your lives looking for something that may not even exist. It's a shame that we have come so close to discovering something amazing, but now it may be lost forever because of this damned volcanic activity. Let's get the hell out of here," he said in frustration as he turned and started retracing his steps toward the opening.

Burr, now elated and relieved that nature was about to do his dirty work for him, led the way back through the tunnel. He was thrilled that any religious artifacts, if here, would be entombed for all time. His future plans could go on unimpeded.

The three had covered the first thirty feet back when a bone- jarring seismic quake hit them without warning. It sent them cascading to the floor as ancient fissures in the walls on either side of them began fracturing. The black basalt crumbled away from the wall, allowing jets of super-heated steam to escape through newly- formed fissures.

Eli looked nervously at the others. He noticed the path ahead of them had partially collapsed, threatening to seal them all in a permanent tomb. All that remained was a narrow opening just large enough for one person at a time to squeeze through. The scattered basalt dust settled all around them as Eli heard the ominous hissing sound of steam being released in the dark recesses of the lava tube behind them. He projected the beam from the flashlight around the tunnel to survey the damage, but stopped when the light reflected off something glimmering on the wall.

"Maria! Look!" he yelled in excitement, pointing the beam at a large section of basalt that had fallen away from the side of the tube. A natural ledge was revealed, and sitting on the ledge was a small rectangular box.

"Oh my God, do you think we've found it?" Maria asked as the two made their way over to the narrow, waist-high ledge.

"It must have been buried by past eruptions, sealing the ledge with loose basalt rock and protecting it," Eli said as he gently grasped the object. He pulled it free from the crumbling rock that entombed it for almost twenty centuries.

The ancient wooden box was encased in copper sheathing. Oval shaped handles, forged from bronze, were what reflected the light from Eli's flashlight. It measured approximately eight inches high by fourteen inches long. One of the wooden knobs at its base had broken off.

Eli brushed the dust off the top of the small chest. The

structure of the chest was still intact, but its copper exterior was dulled by the centuries of dirt and debris lying atop of it.

"Leave it," Burr protested from the narrow opening that led to the entrance. "We have to get out now, before it's too late."

"Let's take a look," Eli said, in childlike amazement, oblivious to their present danger. He ignored Burr, who had moved to the other side of the tunnel.

"I just wish Josh were here to see this," Eli whispered, smiling at Maria, who was now soaked with perspiration from the intensifying heat in the lava tube. He slowly lifted the lid to the small ancient chest and placed it at the side of the box.

Shining the light inside, the two saw an ancient woven fabric covering something. Maria, ever so carefully, lifted the woven material off its contents and gasped in awe. They looked at each other for a moment and Eli could see tears mixed with sweat running down Maria's face.

There, on the left side of the chest lying on its side was a wooden cup made of olive wood. The cup was simple in design and measured barely five inches high, with a deeply carved bowl that had no stem; its base was the same diameter as its top. Delicately hand painted designs inscribed on its side were still discernible after almost two thousand years. In the center of the chest was a roll of copper sheathing, which Eli identified immediately as a copper scroll. "Look, Maria," he said excitedly. "It's just like the ones found in 1952 in the cave at Khirbet Qumran on the shore of the Dead Sea. The copper scrolls found there were scribed to preserve religious text."

"Look at this," Maria said, pointing to the opposite end of the box. "That's the remains of euphorbia milli, a thick, thorny brush plant that grows throughout the Dead Sea region, and was common to the vicinity of Jerusalem."

Eli marveled at the remains of the thorn brush. Although fragmented through the centuries, the interweaving of the thorny brush could be clearly discerned.

"We found them," Eli said joyfully. "After two thousand years of speculation, stories, and myths, we have factual proof."

"Imagine what could be written on that copper scroll," Maria said as the two archaeologists stood, mesmerized by the treasures that lay before them.

They gazed in amazement for a few moments until the silence was broken by Alton Burr.

"I'll take those now, Turner, if you don't mind," he said. Eli and Maria looked at Burr to see him brandishing a gun.

"What in God's name do you think you're doing, Burr?" Eli said. They were suddenly stunned back to reality by Burr's action.

"What I originally came here to do; make sure that free-thinking people are not subjugated back into the stone ages from the likes of these superstitious relics."

"But what if they are real?" Maria cried out in frustration. "These are part of history, and you have no right to keep them from the rest of the world."

"You said earlier that you wanted to find the truth, Burr," Eli said. "Well here it is, looking you square in the eye. We were meant to find this chest. Think about it,

Burr, do you really contend that everything that has transpired up to now has been merely by chance? Discovering Simon's parchment, our escape from those madmen on Tenerife, the quake that revealed the opening to this lava tube, and the one in a million chance that we would be at the precise spot where the chest was located when a tremor occurs, revealing it to us after two thousand years; these can't be mere coincidences."

Burr's eyes softened for a moment as he reflected on the elder Turner's reasoning, but the fires of his deeply-rooted passions regained control once again.

"I don't care about what you consider to be the truth, Turner. My truth, and, the truth of those I speak for, won't be silenced by a hand full of ancient trinkets," he spat, as he waved the gun back and forth. "You were a fool to believe I wanted to help you, Turner. I plan to make sure these relics never see the light of day. I will never stop in my task of ridding our society of ideology that is based on myth and superstition."

"Yeah I know, you keep using that concept of moral ideology as an excuse for your hatred," Eli said. "What happened to you to make you hate religions so much?"

"I was hoping nature would have resolved this little problem without the need for violence. If I had realized that this volcano was going to erupt, I would have never suggested us coming here. I knew that you would not be able to let it rest," Burr said, ignoring the question that burned into his tortured soul.

"You didn't answer my question, Burr. Why do you hate religions so much?" Eli asked again softly, hoping to gain the intellectual upper hand as the heat in the tunnel became more oppressive. "A person of any faith strives to live an upright life based on their core beliefs. How does that hurt, what you call, a free- thinking person? A free-thinking person, as you describe, has a right to choose based on facts along with all the evidence presented. By doing this, you are being a hypocrite of the very ideology you purport to stand for. Why don't you—"

"Shut up!" Burr yelled as he waved the gun wildly at them, not wanting to hear any more as his tortured mind screamed at him. "Stand away from the chest, both of you."

Eli and Maria slowly backed away from the ledge where the copper chest sat. As the two backed up to the opposite wall of the lava tube, Burr slowly walked over to the ledge. Looking quickly at its contents and then back at the two archaeologists, he swung his backpack off his shoulder and opened it. Burr proceeded to pick up the woven thorn bush, which pricked his finger and drew blood, and then forced it into the backpack along with the olive wood chalice.

At that moment, Eli felt a sudden sense of serenity and peace that he had never felt before; expunging any feeling of fear, or trepidation of their predicament. As in a slow motion world, images of his dead wife and his son permeated his mind. Those were followed by visions of a good and fruitful life doing what he loved. He felt young and reborn, as if he were a brash, youthful student back at Texas A&M. He looked at Maria and smiled at her.

"It's okay, Maria," he said gently as he grabbed her hand, holding it for a moment. "I think I understand now. Please tell Josh that I love him." He released her hand then started walking towards Burr, who now held the copper scroll in his hand.

"Stay back, Turner," he spat with malice in his voice. He pointed the pistol at Eli, who just smiled and continued to approach.

"You were part of this plan also, Burr," Eli said, coming closer as he raised his hands and outstretched his open palms towards the copper scroll.

"Eli, no!" Maria screamed as the single shot rang out, reverberating throughout the lava tube over the racket of the escaping steam from the newly formed fissures. Eli slowly fell to his knees as blood began to issue from the wound in his chest, streaking red crimson on his shirt. He continued to hold his hands upward at the copper scroll that Burr held tightly. Just then, the scroll began to glow and Burr stared incredulously at it.

"This is my truth," Eli said softly as the copper scroll began to illuminate the cave with a blinding light. Terrified at the sight, Burr threw down the radiating scroll, which rolled in front of Eli as Maria stared in astonishment.

"What kind of trick is this?" Burr yelled as Eli, illuminated by the brilliant glowing scroll, smiled at Burr.

"No trick, Burr. Like I said, this is my truth," Eli responded serenely, as if he were disconnected from his now bleeding body. "Nothing is impossible. If I have the faith to say to this mountain 'move', then it will move." Now feeling the pain of his wound, he slowly slumped to the floor.

Maria ran over to him, knelt down, and cradled him in her arms. "Eli," she cried softly. "Why?"

At that moment, forces beneath the Cumbre Vieja

were going through turbulent changes. The Scalar weapon had abruptly changed from dispersing momentous heat within the magma core to one of absolute cold from the weapons conversion to an endothermic wave form by Yashiro. It was as if someone had dispensed a titanic iceberg into a sea of boiling water with the same catastrophic reaction.

The heat began to quell instantly within the magma chamber kilometers below the island, resulting in a tremendous shock wave from the instant cooling. The pressure wave radiated toward the surface, causing a thunderous sonic boom heard hundreds of miles away from its epicenter. Windows were shattered all over the island of La Palma and people were shaken to the ground from the devastating shock wave that now moved across the waters at super- sonic speeds. This final chaotic insult was far too much for the already weakened western flank of the Cumbre Vieja to endure. Ever so imperceptibly, a half-trillion ton of rock began to lose its friction force under the superheated caldera and slide toward the sea far below the ancient volcano.

Back in the lava tube, the tremendous sonic boom and subsequent shock wave stunned Maria and Burr. Its thunderous report deafened them and left a ringing in their ears. Maria threw herself on top of Eli, who lay motionless on the floor bleeding from his chest wound. Burr was forcefully thrown backward against the basalt wall, striking his head and falling unconscious.

The fault line traversing the Cumbre Vieja's ridge ruptured violently along its entire length with an agonizing crack that sounded like a gigantic thunderclap. Maria, her ears still ringing loudly, saw the ground beneath Burr suddenly split apart as she desperately tried to drag Eli away from the ever-widening fissure.

After dragging Eli to the high side of the lava tube, she saw a light emanating from the ceiling of the dust-laden tunnel and realized it was actually the light of day. Astonishingly, the ground above them was being peeled back, rumbling downward like a colossal sliding roof.

Alton Burr, who now began to regain consciousness, felt himself being dragged helplessly by the momentum of the widening crack into the deep chasm that was forming beneath him. He screamed in terror as he clawed desperately at the loose basalt, not able to gain a firm hold. Sliding further and further downward, he soon found himself wedged at the bottom of the forty-foot deep fissure.

The earth trembled violently around Maria as she felt a hand touch her shoulder. Eli said something, but with the ringing in her ears from the shock wave, she could not hear his voice. She made a gesture to her ears, signifying her lack of ability to hear him.

"Get the backpack," Eli mouthed, pointing weakly to the bag lying dangerously close to the chasm. Beside the backpack sat the copper scroll that now ceased its luminance. He looked at her pleadingly, and then shut his eyes in pain. Maria started to crawl along the still trembling rocky floor toward the gigantic fissure, which was still slowly moving. She gazed at the scroll, wondering what made it emit such a radiant light. Maria then carefully picked up the scroll and put it in the backpack with the other items.

The ringing in her ears finally began to subside, and she was able to discern the sound of Burr screaming somewhere below. She carefully crawled to the edge of the newly-formed precipice, where she looked down to see Burr lying helpless at the bottom and howling in agony. His right leg was mangled and crushed under the huge sliding landmass, which slowly pulled his body inward like a gigantic paper shredder.

"You've got to help me!" Burr cried out in blinding agony as another sliding jolt pulled him in further. His hip joint was ripped out of its socket as he let out a blood-curdling scream. Maria looked at Eli, who lay silently with his eyes closed coughing up bits of blood. *He has done nothing to deserve this fate*, she thought angrily. *He has been my mentor and friend and almost a father to me*. She gazed at him with affection then looked back down at Alton Burr, who held out his bloody outstretched hand.

"Go to Hell, Mr. Burr," she yelled down to him in anger, leaving Alton Burr to his fate.

Maria clutched the backpack and crawled back to Eli Turner. With her eyes now closed, she held on tightly to Eli as the momentous trembling of the slide slowly progressed. Burr's tortured screams mercifully ended after the first few minutes. Then suddenly, the trembling began to cease. Miraculously, the tremendous island-sized landmass stopped its progression to the sea. In the unexpected silence, she opened her eyes and smiled to see Eli looking up at her.

"Don't forget my hat," he said weakly. Eli smiled back at her and coughed as the stain on his blood soaked shirt began to spread further.

"God forbid, you'd lose your hat," she said tearfully, reaching behind him and picking up the elder Turner's outback hat and placing it gently on his head. "Do you think you can manage walking?" Maria asked as she opened his shirt and stuffed her bandana onto the wound. This caused him to wince in pain.

"Not if you keep doing that," he managed to reply in protest. "I've got to stop the bleeding, Eli. I'm sorry," she said as she got up to look around at what was left of the lava tube. The dust was starting to settle and she could now see the magnitude of what had just occurred. Immediately, she realized just how precarious their position was.

The ancient lava tube was now part of a ledge that ran the entire length of the Cumbre Vieja. It was the demarcation point where the western flank separated and began its slide to the sea, then astonishingly ceased its downward trek. They were now on a ledge that overlooked a gaping three-hundred foot drop, with no way up or down. She saw the huge hand-shaped monolith where the rope was once tied had tumbled down the side of the caldera. It shattered into a million pieces, taking with it their only way off the ledge.

Maria hesitated for a moment when she heard a sound coming from overhead. She finally saw the blue and white Bell Ranger that transported them to La Palma coming up the rise. She began yelling and waving frantically at it. The pilot just barely escaped from the plateau when the shock wave had begun. He assumed that his party had been killed by the massive quake but came up the ridge line to look for survivors. He could not see Maria and Eli on the ledge, so he continued flying east to the safety of Tenerife.

"There goes our ride, Maria," Eli said weakly, looking at the sleek Ranger as it headed out of sight. "What now?"

Maria fumbled through the backpack searching for anything that could help them. Pulling Burr's cell phone out of the backpack, she smiled. "We'll have to call for a cab."

After dialing the number, she looked up at the sky. As the late day sun began its slow descent to the west over the Atlantic Ocean, the horizon turned a crimson red. Tons of ash still belched skyward from the Cumbre Vieja caldera as its magma core slowly began to cool; receding back into the Earth.

30

Behind the loading platform outside of the Bishamon facility, Captain Saune and his remaining men continued their desperate firefight with Yagato Osama's Yakuza soldiers. They had not made any progress since their helicopter drop-off earlier. The situation was dire and without a miracle, Saune knew in his heart they were all going to die.

Saune stood and fired the last 40mm grenade from his rifle launcher, but with no luck. Osama's men were well-entrenched high above in the cave entrance. Two more of Saune's men lie dead as the soldiers fired unmercifully down upon the bullet-ridden metal platform. He and his sergeant huddled with their backs to the platform as another barrage of bullets whizzed over them. Both were down to their last ammo clips.

"Captain," Sergeant Ortega yelled above the rain of bullets spraying overhead. "I don't think we're gonna' get out of this one alive. Do you think we should surrender?"

"These guys don't take prisoners, Ortega," Captain Saune yelled back, resolving that this was to be their last stand. He only hoped that Turner and Samuel would succeed in their mission inside the complex.

"Captain Saune," a voice came through on his earpiece, which he knew to be one of the men over by the boulder. "We're running low on ammo here. Two of the men are already out," he reported anxiously. Saune hit the transmitter of his radio VHF replying, "Conserve your ammo and make every shot count."

He then slumped back, low against the platform, knowing that it was a hopeless situation and he was to blame for the deaths of these good men. Hitting the transmitter again, he spoke. "Gentlemen, whatever happens, I want you all to know that you fought with valor and it has been a privilege to serve with all of you." He closed his eyes, feeling death's grasp coming closer with each moment.

Suddenly, from the earpieces they wore came a crackling sound.

A new voice boomed over each man's VHF link.

"To the combatants on the ground, this is Colonel Kyle Sears of the United States Marine Corps. What is your present situation, and can I be of assistance? Over...."

All the embattled Tenerife National Guardsmen cheered with elated hearts at hearing those words. Captain Saune wiped a tear of relief from his eye, smiled at the sergeant, and hit him joyfully on the back.

"Colonel Sears, we've got some men down here that are real glad to hear your voice," Saune said. "I am Captain Rafael Saune of the Tenerife National Guard. We are in a desperate situation here, Colonel. We're pinned down below the Bishamon facility on its western flank. Our opponents control the high ground above us in a cave opening beneath the facility. We cannot advance and our ammo is low. Over...."

"Roger that, Captain," Sears responded. "I have an ETA of three minutes coming from your northeast. We have your VHF signal pinpointed and on our screen. Just keep your heads down, gentlemen, 'cause when I get there, I promise all hell's gonna break loose. Over...."

"Roger that, Colonel, but please be advised, the combatants in the tunnel entrance have ground to air missiles. Over...."

"Not a problem, Captain. Thanks for the heads up. Sears, out...."

The AH-1F Cobra, armed to the teeth with its front-mounted, three-barreled, 20mm Gatling cannon and side-mounted 70 mm rockets, roared up the western slope of Mt. Teide in the direction of the melee. Its GPS guidance was up-linked to the USS. *Hazleton*, which was now a mere twenty-five nautical miles off the northwest coast of La Palma and approaching at full speed.

At that moment, the USS *Milford* was already preparing its deadly Tomahawk Block III TLAM missile for launch. It now awaited the final inertial guidance programming that would maneuver the 1440kg missile over water. Once the five and a half meter rocket, loaded with 450kg payload of explosives, made landfall, the Terrain Contour Matching (TERCOM) system would engage and direct the weapon over ground contours to its target.

"I'm going hot on the master arm switch, Ward," Sears said to his co-pilot gunner. He then toggled the weapons control switch, giving Ward the rocket and gun control. Pressing the zone arm switch, the rocket management system display unit came to life and armed the Cobra's complement of side-mounted missiles.

"Roger, Colonel. I set the PEN-M dial to SQ and have green on the board," he reported, setting the penetration and detonation of the rockets to *super-quick* mode on the rocket management system display unit. "Heads up display is powered and set in normal mode, Colonel."

"Okay, Lieutenant, here we go," Sears said as he brought his Cobra down from the summit of Mt. Teide and followed its ridge toward the lower slopes.

Cruising at an altitude of one thousand feet above the desolate landscape, Sears could clearly make out the domes of the astronomical observatory on the higher ridge. He could see, farther south, a lone building sitting on the ridge of an old caldera. He scanned the surrounds of the complex and saw the thick black smoke from the weapons' fire. He knew, without a doubt, he'd found his target.

"Get ready, Lieutenant Ward," he ordered to his CPG. "I'm going to stand off just to the northwest and let you acquire."

"Roger, Colonel," Ward replied as the sleek Cobra pitched upward and came to a standstill, hovering within view of the Bishamon facility. "Colonel, I see the cave entrance, but can't make out where the friendlies are."

"Hang on, Lieutenant; let me give you some altitude," Sears replied, lifting the craft higher above the ridge.

"Got 'em, Colonel," Ward said in a calm tone. "They're about one hundred fifty feet below the cave. A little close for my likings, but they should be alright."

"Let's do it," Sears said with finality, banking the attack Cobra in toward the plateau like a bird of prey.

Captain Saune was the first of his men to see and hear the Cobra coming in over the ridge as bullets whizzed past their precarious position behind the platform. Sergeant Ortega had taken a wound to the left arm from shrapnel as one of the many rockets launched against them exploded just to their left.

"Heads down, men," Saune yelled over the VHF transmitter as he and his fellow guardsmen dove to the rocky, dirt-strewn ground. The Cobra deftly swung into a direct line of sight with the lava tube entrance, hovering above Saune and his men as dust and debris from the rotor wash swirled about them. As the aircraft hovered above them, Saune managed to gaze upward at the deadly aircraft emblazoned with the U.S. Marine Corps insignia on the side of the fuselage.

The Yakuza soldiers in the lava tube were equally surprised to see their new antagonist, but were not deterred in their mission to repel all intruders. They subsequently poured out weapons' fire at the Cobra as it hovered just three hundred feet distant, while two other mercenaries leveled their ground-to-air rocket launchers at Sears' aircraft. That was the last thing they ever did.

Lieutenant Ward unleashed the devastating fire power of the 40mm Gatling guns, disintegrating the occupants of the outer part of the lava tube with blood and gore spraying everywhere. Ward unleashed two 70mm side-mount rockets that slammed into the recess of the lava tube and caused a fearsome explosion. The cave belched a fiery blast outward, leaving a trail of thick black smoke as the flames subsided.

The carnage was absolute. The long and weary firefight, which had almost cost the lives of Captain Saune and all of his men, ended abruptly in a matter of seconds. Saune slowly rose from the protection of the metal loading platform and looked up at the cave entrance that was still expelling thick, black smoke.

"Captain Saune, you are clear for incursion." Colonel Sears' voice reported over the VHF, "We'll provide air cover from here. Over...."

"Nicely done, Colonel. I owe you a drink," Saune responded as he and his men approached the bullet-ridden conveyor belt.

"Once this is over, Captain, I'll take you up on that drink," Sears replied. "Be advised, Captain, that a contingency of Marines are en route, and will disembark on the compound within the half hour. Over...."

"I'll be glad to have the company, Colonel," Saune stated as he and his men sprinted up the side of the conveyor belt toward the cave entrance. Saune shot Ortega a smile as he followed him up the rise with his wounded arm.

"I'll be damned if I'm going to be left out after all we've been through," Ortega said defiantly, as the remaining Guardsmen ascended to the summit of the cave entrance within minutes.

With Saune in the lead, they slowly entered the tunnel as the thick acrid smoke from the Cobra's rocket blasts began to subside. The scene of slaughter in the tunnel made even a tough, seasoned soldier like Saune shudder. Of the roughly twenty-five Yakuza soldiers defending the complex, only a few body parts grotesquely strewn about the lava tube floor remained. Large sections of the cave's basalt sides had collapsed, but the tunnel was still negotiable. They hastened their pace as fast as the slippery, blood-soaked tunnel floor would allow until they reached the metal ladder.

Looking upward, they saw the mechanized hatchway to the complex was still open. However, the upper torso of one of the Yakuza soldiers who attempted to retreat back into the facility was blocking their way. The ghastly remains of his upper body still held the ladder rungs in a death grip.

Fighting the urge to retch from the grisly sight, Saune quickly ascended the ladder. He pried the dead hands free and allowed the torso to fall to the cave floor with a sickening thud. Saune looked down at his remaining men from the ladder. He paused for a moment and then continued into the facility, not knowing what awaited them inside.

31

Samuel heard the arrival of Colonel Sears' Cobra over his VHF as he tried to revive Turner, who now lay on the laboratory floor shaking violently "Josh, can you hear me?" Samuel said to his friend, as the trembling subsided and his eyes slowly opened.

"Sss...Samuel," his weary voice said. "Wh...what happened?" "It's okay, pal. You're alright now." Samuel replied as Turner forced himself up on one elbow, rubbing his forehead in an attempt to relieve his pounding headache. "Hey, the cavalry has arrived, Josh. There's a Marine chopper outside that should be able to take care of Osama's henchmen."

Turner realized the VHF earpiece had fallen out of his ear. Putting it back in, he told his friend, "I hope to God I never go through anything like that again."

"You big baby," Samuel quipped, causing Turner to burst out in laughter and his head to hurt even more. "By the way," Samuel added, "Yashiro has managed to reverse the process of the whatchamacallit."

"That's good news, Samuel." Turner said slowly rising

to his feet, almost passing out from the dizziness that ensued as the room spun around him.

"Easy, Josh...go slow. You've taken a pretty good beating in the last few hours. You need to sit out the rest of this," he said.

"We're not finished yet, Samuel, not by a long shot. Pencor is dead," he said, pointing to the body lying across the room, "but Osama is still on the loose. Unless he's managed to make a run in one of the vehicles, he's still gotta' be here somewhere. I'm going after him because I have a little score to settle," Turner stated, taking a deep breath and trying to shake off the intense weariness that now crept into the very essence of his being.

"Fine," Samuel started to say, "I'll go with you, and we can—" "No, Samuel," he interrupted, "I need you to stay with Yashiro

until Saune and his men can get access. I have to do this alone. Here..." he said, reaching into his pant's cargo pocket. He pulled out the Global Star phone and turned it on. "Go back to the control room with Yashiro and get a hold of Robertson in Washington. He'll be expecting our report. If he doesn't hear from us, he'll signal one of the ships to take out the facility with a Tomahawk missile. He needs to know the plan to reverse the Scalar weapon is working and to hold off on *that* launch. I'll meet up with you later." He tossed the phone to his Quechuan friend, and then bounded out the door.

Samuel knew better than to argue with him, knowing his resolve and stubborn determination. He had seen this look many times in the past so he simply smiled and shook his head.

"Go get 'em, amigo!" he offered, shaking his head as he tossed his 45-automatic to Turner who then disappeared out the doorway. Turner filed up the staircase hunting for his tormentor. His head still throbbing, he no longer held any sense of compassion for this monster. To him, it was beyond all reason that a man could subject so much suffering on a person and derive a twisted pleasure from it. How he could relish the thought of killing millions of innocent people with his wave of death? It was insanity. He felt no pity or sense of civility at this point. Osama had to be stopped.

Turner reached the atrium where they had entered earlier. He heard the momentous rumbling of explosions coming from deep below the facility, not knowing that Colonel Sears had just laid waste to all living things in the lava tube beneath the complex. Moments later, he heard through his earpiece the Marine pilot giving Captain Saune the all-clear to advance and that U.S. Marines were a half hour away. Needing to concentrate, he yanked out the earpiece and started ascending the stairs leading from the atrium to Osama's offices. An eerie silence took hold of the complex as the incessant gunfire and explosions from below ceased. He reached the top step to find the corridor not as lengthy as the one below and with only two sets of doors on either side of the hall.

Brandishing his 45 in the dim light, he stealthily made his way down the hall. He looked into one room and found it devoid of guards. Just as he approached the next door, it opened without warning. Two armed Yakuza guards ran out into the hallway, almost crashing headlong into Turner. He didn't hesitate as he unleashed his weapon on the pair. He kept firing, feeling no empathy for them, and they both swiftly fell dead at his feet.

If Osama is hiding on this level, he knows I'm here now, he thought, continuing down the hallway. *I must move quickly.*

He heard a small noise in the last room on the left and made his way to the door. Taking a deep breath, he kicked the door open to find Osama standing in the middle of the room. He had a cell phone in one hand, a briefcase in the other, and looked shocked to see Turner standing before him.

"Going somewhere?" Turner hissed as he walked into the room with his gun leveled at Osama, who just smiled back at him.

***

As Turner was facing his nemesis on the upper level of the complex, Samuel rejoined Yashiro in the control room. He was let in by the tiny scientist, who had been peering nervously out from behind the Plexiglas window pane on the door.

"I'm glad you're back," Yashiro said in relief as the two walked back over to the computer console. "With all of the gunfire and explosions stopping, I was getting quite nervous as to what had happened."

"You mentioned that your idea was working. Does that mean we're out of the woods?" Samuel asked as the Japanese scientist continued typing, unimpeded by the conversation.

"Well, yes and no," he stated, indecisively, fingers flailing away on the keyboard. "I was able to successfully convert the Scalar weapon from exothermic mode to endothermic and—"

"Hold on," Samuel interrupted, waving his hands in frustration. "Give it to me in dumb person lingo, alright?"

"I was able to halt the Scalar weapon's heating process in the magma chamber beneath La Palma and begin the endothermic cool down by reversing the EM flow. This is what is termed as a cold explosion in the Scalar weapon mode. When applied at full power, it literally draws all heat out of the target zone. Since this facility was designed for exothermic mode, it doesn't have the required EM drain field to draw off the massive energy channeled from the magma chamber." He paused, making sure he had not lost Samuel yet. "The chamber is cooling slowly, but I must increase the drain slowly, or it will cause the feedback explosion I warned you of. I must do this process in increments to dissipate the energy to a safe level. It's going to take a little time to complete this; probably an hour or more," he said as he ceased his typing and looked expectantly at Samuel.

"Looks like you'll have all the time you need, amigo-san. I guess you didn't hear, huh?" Samuel said, noticing the earpiece of Yashiro's VHF was unplugged from his ear. "Never mind," he said, shaking his head as he pulled out the Global Star to call Under Secretary of State Robertson. Before he could dial, though, it began to ring.

Samuel answered and was surprised to hear Maria's voice on the other end. He listened in stunned silence as Maria recounted the flight to La Palma, the discovery of the relics, and their conflict with Burr, who now was dead. Samuel shut his eyes as he heard Maria report the Western

Flank of La Palma had started to shift seaward, and that Eli had been shot and needed medical attention.

"Stay where you are, Maria," Samuel said emphatically, "we'll get to you somehow, I promise. Things are almost under control here, so we can send out a rescue chopper to your location."

"We have no place to go, Samuel," she replied. "We're stuck on a ledge, and the ash fall from the eruption is getting worse by the minute. It's getting hard to breathe, so please hurry," she pleaded as suddenly the connection went dead. Samuel got on the VHF and tried to call Turner. He wasn't answering.

"Damn," he yelled, startling the scientist. "Stay with it, Yashiro, and keep that damned earpiece in." He ran for the door, and then headed down the corridor to the atrium. Regrettably, his heightened sense of urgency caused him to forget to call Robertson in Washington D. C.

32

The gigantic, cold-blast shock wave that emanated kilometers beneath the island of La Palma wreaked havoc on the tiny island. Fortunately, injuries in the immediate vicinity of the shock zone had been few, thanks to the evacuation process by the local authorities of the small towns and villages adjacent to the Cumbre Vieja.

United States Geological Survey field scientist Rosalie Harris had been knocked to the ground as a result of the momentous shock wave on a small rocky peninsula just below the Sol La Palma Hotel.

Now deserted, the once beautiful lodging took on the appearance of a battle zone since all of its windows were blasted out by the percussion wave. Tables and chairs were toppled over, with debris strewn everywhere. The elegant terra cotta roof atop the grand structure was now covered in ash from the erupting volcano. The once five-star rated hotel now had a grayish, ghostly appearance.

Rosalie had been on the rocky point when the shock wave hit, which afforded her a good view of the Cumbre Vieja. She watched in horror as the entire western flank of the ridge line suddenly began to slide downward, after a riotous crack that sounded similar to a sonic boom. The huge island-sized slab of earth, only moments later, completely stopped its movement. She stood transfixed for the next five minutes, awed by the enormity of the vision she'd just witnessed.

Rosalie's hands trembled violently as she placed the call to Peter Markson at the Geological Survey office in Washington D.C. to report the calamity.

"Pete, the whole damned flank of the Cumbre Vieja shifted at least sixty to eighty meters," she yelled excitedly over the still trembling cell phone in her hand. "Our worst fears could be happening here. If that flank lets go, we may be looking at the mega-tsunami scenario."

"Rosalie, calm down," Markson replied as he shuffled his data reports on his desk. "Are you absolutely sure about this? I need to know the facts."

"Are you shitting me? I just witnessed the facts, Pete. I've never experienced anything like that in all my years climbing craters. The shock wave I just felt was like nothing I've read in the textbooks. It just doesn't happen, and I have no clue as to what's going on in the magma core. All bets are off as to the normality of this eruption, but the fault fracture and slippage from the loss of friction beneath the land mass are real enough," she said, watching the billowing ash plume belch from the crater high above the island.

"Okay, Rosalie, I've got to report this to the President. He talked about ordering an evacuation alert for the east coast earlier. This will probably set things in motion, so you have to be sure."

"Pete, the damned thing slid and then stopped. That's

all I can report at this point," she said in finality.

"Got it, Rosalie. I'm going to advise the White House on your report," he said as he rummaged through his papers to obtain the direct line. "Rosalie, I want your ass out of harm's way now, you understand?"

"Don't worry, Pete. I'm leaving now," she replied as she started up the gradual incline toward the now empty hotel. "I'm headed to the southern end of La Palma and I will contact you if there is any change."

Hanging up, she sprinted to her vehicle as more ash, like black snow, began to drift down onto the asphalt lot of the Sol La Palma. Taking one last look at the newly formed gigantic fissure high above the Cumbre Vieja's western flank, Rosalie thought for a moment of the people she had run into earlier at the fault line. After a moment's reflection, she concluded there was no way they could have survived. She sped off, heading south on the Calle Del Remo highway, toward the relative safety of the island's southern tip. As she drove through a small village and noticed its abandoned shops and homes, she had no idea that two of the people on the fault line were in a desperate struggle to survive.

"God help us if that flank lets go," she said to herself. "God help us all."

33

Turner pushed the door shut behind him as he slowly approached Yagato Osama, while keeping his eyes fixed on his adversary. Contempt and an intense rage welled up within him as he confronted the author of this hellish nightmare. "It's over, you bastard. You're beaten," he declared, aiming the gun directly at Osama.

"Far from it, Mr. Turner. You and your friends have been a nuisance, but nothing more. Even if my plans don't play out as I had hoped, my organization will continue to thrive and I will never be implicated," he said with a smug grin. "Money is power, Mr. Turner. With it, comes the ability to influence opinion and action. I've made sure that Pencor will be held totally responsible for his plans, with no evidence to connect me. I will return to my country a free and rich man," he said smiling, seeing a flicker of doubt on Turner's face.

"We'll provide the collaboration necessary to put you away for a long time," Turner shot back, becoming weary of the exchange.

"We shall see, Mr. Turner," Osama said laughing aloud. "We shall see."

"Slime like you shouldn't be allowed to prey on the lives of innocent people," Turner said, raising the gun and pointing it at Osama's head. The Yakuza leader continued to laugh.

"You can't kill me, Turner. You don't have that predator instinct," Osama said calmly.

Turner considered his words, which were in part true. He wasn't a cold-blooded murderer, but his mind screamed at him the reality that this man would somehow beat the system and live to threaten the world, again and again.

"You are weak, as are your countrymen, Mr. Turner," he continued, knowing now he had gained an advantage. "You and your—" *Click*.

To Osama's shock, Turner pulled the trigger, but the gun had been emptied on the guards in the corridor. The Yakuza leader quickly hurled the briefcase containing the ZPG patents at Turner's head, barely missing him. He then ran to the room adjacent to his office, threw the door shut, and locked it from within. Turner dashed after him and slammed into the locked metal door. It took three attempts of Turner smashing his full weight against the door in order to break the lock. The splintered locking mechanism finally failed under the assault and the door flew open to reveal an empty room. He looked around, desperately hoping to see where Osama had gone.

There must be a false panel somewhere in here, he thought, and started banging on the walls of the room to find it. At that moment, Samuel burst through the front door brandishing an AK-47 taken from one of the dead guards in the corridor.

"Josh! Where are you?" the Quechuan yelled as he ran to the room's center.

"I'm in here, Samuel," Turner replied coming out of the empty room next to Osama's office.

"I take it that you didn't find him."

"I had him, but he gave me the slip." Turner replied angrily. "This place must be honeycombed with passageways for a quick getaway. He ducked into here and then disappeared. He must be—" Turner stopped mid thought as he saw the grave look on his friend's face. "What is it, Samuel?"

"We've got another problem, Josh. Maria and your dad are trapped on the Cumbre Vieja on La Palma. Maria called and said the land slide had begun and they were stuck on a ledge above it. And that's not the worst of it, Josh."

"What Samuel?" he asked, fear rising in him.

"Your dad's been shot by Burr. Maria says it's serious and that he needs medical attention soon."

"Let's go," Turner said as he, followed by Samuel, ran out of Osama's office and down the corridor to the stairs.

"What about Osama?" Samuel asked as they bounded down the stairwell.

"To hell with him!" he replied forcefully. "We've done enough. Let the authorities deal with him." As they hurried into the atrium, they ran into Saune and his men, who had just finished checking the rooms in the lower level.

"It's good to see that you two are alright." Captain Saune said relieved to see them in one piece. "The lower level is clear of resistance and so is the tunnel. The Marine Cobra took out almost all of Osama's men and is hovering outside to provide support."

"The upper level is clear, except for Osama. He's still somewhere in the facility. He must have hidden passageways in the building." Turner said as the group made their way to the door of the control room. "We need to get to La Palma now, Captain. Maria and my father are in trouble. Can you take us there in the helicopter?" he asked as Samuel pounded on the door for Yashiro to let them in.

"No way, Josh. Osama's henchmen made short work of the old Huey with a few rockets from their hand-held launchers. It's completely scrapped," he said as the Japanese scientist opened the door to the control room.

"Damn!" Turner yelled in frustration as they walked over to where Yashiro had been working to disable the Scalar weapon. "There's got to be a way to get to them."

"I've done all I can at this point," said Yashiro, who had fashioned a bandage for his wounded arm out of his lab coat.

"I've succeeded in converting the weapon's EM waves to an endothermic cold mode and have taken it as high as I dare go. Any higher and the field drains below won't be able to handle the immense EM feedback. I've programmed the system to start a gradual reduction of the output levels until it shuts down. Barring any unforeseen circumstances, it should be completed in an hour or so," he reported, pleased with the fact that he was finally able to contribute somehow.

"Nice work, Yashiro. It was a good thing we ran into

you in the lava tube," Turner said, his attention still focused on the plight of his father and Maria.

"Don't worry about Osama, Josh," Saune said, seeing the anguish in Turner's eyes. "He's not going anywhere and before long this place will be swarming with your Marines. We'll flush him out soon enough."

The VHF radio then crackled in their ears. "Captain, this is Sears. What is your situation? Over...."

"Colonel Sears, the facility is clear of active resistance and is secure. There is one combatant still hidden somewhere in the facility, but poses no threat at the moment. Over...." Saune reported.

Samuel whispered, "Don't forget the three scientists I locked up in there," he said, pointing to the chair still propped up against the supply room door.

"That's good to hear, Captain." Sears responded. "Major Zibrinski will be landing a squad of Marines within a few minutes. They are at your disposal."

Pressing the transmit button, Turner cut in. "Colonel, this is Josh Turner. Could you have them land at the facility's main gate area out front? We'll meet them there. Over...."

"Affirmative, I will advise the Major to expect you. By the way, Mr. Turner, you and your associates did a nice job today. You have saved the lives of a lot of people with your efforts," the Colonel said respectfully. "Sears, out...."

"I have an idea," Turner said, his eyes brightening. "Let's go, Samuel."

"Uh-oh," Samuel replied in usual fashion as they filed out of the control room's doors and back down the corridor to the atrium. The team then exited the Bishamon facility, grateful to be leaving the place where so much death and destruction took place. Most importantly, they were grateful to still be alive.

The sun was descending over the Atlantic Ocean to the west as the CH-46 Sea Knight helicopter that was launched from the *Hazleton* loomed into view. Coming overhead, the big transport chopper descended gracefully. As it touched down on the rocky grounds of the main gate, it threw debris everywhere.

Turner and the other men waved in acknowledgment as the rear door to the aircraft opened. Fifteen fully-armed Marines hit the ground, quickly securing the perimeter and the now vacant guard shack.

A tough looking lieutenant made his way over to them, and Saune greeted the lieutenant with a handshake. The Marine lieutenant could see the weariness in Turner's eyes along with the cuts and bruises adorning his face and head.

"Lieutenant, Captain Saune here can give you and your men a heads-up on what's inside," Turner yelled over the din of the Sea Knight's twin rotor blades and roaring GE T58 turbo-shaft engines. "I need to speak to the pilot."

"That will be Major Zibrinski, sir," he yelled back.

Turner slapped him on the back, and then ran for the open rear door of the Sea Knight. He was still guarded by a Marine, who allowed him and Samuel access.

"We have visitors, Major," the Marine medic standing at the rear of the CH-46 Sea Knight's flight deck announced. He motioned to the two ragged looking men approaching from the rear of the craft.

"I'm expecting them, Lieutenant," she replied, releasing her seat restraints and rising up from the pilot's seat. She squeezed past the medic and entered the transport bay of the big chopper, greeting Turner with an extended hand. "Mr. Turner, I presume?" she asked as Turner shook her hand. "I'm Major Sidney Zibrinski. Colonel Sears told me to expect you."

"Pleased to meet you, Major. This is Samuel Caberra," he said, motioning to his Peruvian comrade who waved from the seat he had plopped into.

"If you don't mind me saying, Mr. Turner, you look like hell. Would you like our medic to give you a go-over?" She asked, seeing the battle scars on Turner's face from the last twenty-four hours of constant abuse.

"There's no time for that, Major. I need a huge favor from you. Two of our people are trapped on the volcanic ridge on La Palma. One of them is my father and he's been shot. Can you help me?" he asked. He knew it was a long shot, but he had to try.

"Sorry, but no can do, Mr. Turner. I've got a group of Marines here that I'm responsible for," she replied as the second CH-46 came into view from the cockpit window. It touched down ninety feet away from them.

The anxiety and turmoil that had accrued over the last day finally reached its zenith. Turner was weary, aching, and now distraught over his father and Maria. They held on precariously to life with only one chance for survival. Turner erupted in uncontrolled anger.

"Damn it, Major! We've been through hell the last twenty-four hours, putting our lives at risk in an effort to stop these madmen from washing out the entire east coast of the United States. Hell, we're not even sure if we've stopped it in time. A lot of people are dead and more may die before this thing is over. My father is at risk of dying from a gunshot wound on that God-forsaken island just twenty minutes away, and you tell me, 'no can do'?" He turned away and sat down next to Samuel, totally frustrated and feeling utterly helpless.

As tough as Sid Zibrinski was, she couldn't help but feel empathy for this man and what he had been through. She liked his attitude and figured she would have probably reacted the same way, so she decided he was gutsy enough to go out on a limb for.

"Let me run it past Colonel Sears, Mr. Turner," she conceded, climbing back into the pilot's seat. She put on the ANR flight intercom set and contacted her superior on the Cobra. She related Turner's request to the colonel, who still hovered over the west flank of the Bishamon facility. Turner looked on in hopeful anticipation. He saw Zibrinski nodding in affirmation a few times, followed by her saying, "Yes, sir, will do, stand-by." She motioned for Turner to put on her flight intercom set and said, "The colonel wants to speak with you."

Putting on the headset and adjusting the boom mic, the Major gave him the thumbs-up.

"Go ahead, Colonel Sears; this is Turner," he said, preparing for the disappointing response and the argument that would ensue.

"Mr. Turner, I've ordered Sid to comply with your request. There's plenty of space on the other two Sea Knights for her

Marines. I think that is the least we can do for all you and your companions have been through," he responded. Turner's heart jumped for joy at hearing the news. "I know there will be hell to pay for allowing this, but I'm willing to risk it. Tell Major Zibrinski I'll radio the *Hazleton* and tell them you have engine problems and are heading back. That will give you ample time to do what you have to do on La Palma. Our hospital on the *Hazleton* can treat your father's wounds." He paused for a moment. "Mr. Turner, I have instructed the Major to abort the mission if the situation becomes too risky. Understood?"

"Yes, Colonel, and thank you," Turner replied, adding, "I owe you a drink!"

"That's the second offer I've had today," he said, laughing as he spoke. "Go on, Turner, tell Sid to get going. The third Sea Knight is coming in now so we're covered here. Sears, out...."

"Let's go get your father and his friend, Mr. Turner." Zibrinski said with a wink as she powered up the transport chopper's GE turbines and hit the stow lever for the aft ramp. Turner smiled back gratefully as he stood up and made his way to the rear of the craft where Samuel still sat, sprawled over two chairs with his eyes shut.

"We're on our way to La Palma to get Dad and Maria," he announced happily, slapping his friend on the shoulder.

"It's about time we got some amenities on this all-inclusive Canary Island vacation," Samuel replied lazily. His eyes were closed, but he was still smiling.

The CH-46 Sea Knight rose skyward and banked to the west, leaving behind the Bishamon facility and its aura of death and mayhem behind. As they headed out over the Atlantic Ocean,

Zibrinski could make out the tiny island of La Palma in the distance. She noted the ominous plume of ash rising from the high peaks. It was being carried off to the southwest by the wind currents.

The sun was almost below the horizon as they sped across the open expanse of water. No one on board could ever envision, in their wildest nightmares, the horrific act of nature they would soon experience.

***

Inside of the Bishamon control room, a large wall panel was pushed out from within. It fell to the floor as Yagato Osama stepped out from the hidden stairwell. It was one of many throughout the complex used for extreme situations such as this. Ruffled by his unexpected encounter with Turner, he had now regained his composure. While behind the wall, he overheard the conversation minutes earlier.

"Fuyuki, where are you?" he yelled abruptly. Looking around the dim, empty control room, he heard muffled voices and banging on the supply room door. He kicked the chair that was bracing the door and it opened to release three disheveled scientists, grateful to finally be set free.

"It's over, Oyabun," Fuyuki Seijun said in defeat. "They have managed to reverse the effects of the Scalar waves on La Palma. We must escape. Soon this place will be swarming with American soldiers," he stated, his voice rising in panic.

"It is not over, Fuyuki. Begin the corrections on their meddling and continue with the process," he roared. The three scientists quickly sat at the terminals and began to key new data into the program Yashiro had recently reversed.

"I was able to contact my helicopter at the airport, and have instructed him to arrive here in a few hours when it gets dark. We have a secure place to hide until then. Don't worry," he said calmly, pointing to the false wall. "We are not finished yet, Fuyuki. They will soon pay for their interference."

34

Aboard the USS Hazleton, Captain Jason McKnight stood on the foredeck of his vessel smoking his pipe. As his ship sped through the calm waters of the Atlantic on its mission, in his mind he was going over all contingencies. As he studied the strange mushroom-shaped, black cloud in the distance, Lt. Commander Ewell came rushing down the steps to join him on the foredeck.

"Captain, the radio shack has Admiral Borland at COMLANTFLT on the horn again, and he wants to speak with you." Mac calmly tapped his pipe on the deck railing and emptied its contents into the sea. He followed Ewell back up the steps and onto the bridge.

"What's our distance to the Canaries?" he asked picking up the bridge's red phone and covering the mouthpiece.

"The closest landfall is La Palma at eighteen nautical miles to the southwest, sir," his first officer responded.

"McKnight here," he barked into the phone. He knew that it was an admiral, but he didn't care.

"Captain, this is Admiral Borland at COMLANTFLT.

Have you anything new to report on the situation on Tenerife?" he asked gruffly.

"The CIC reported that Colonel Sears met with some weapons fire at the target zone, but the facility's perimeter has been secured. The Sea Knights are touching down at this moment with Marine backup for the clean-up OPS," Mac reported, drumming his fingers on the armrest of his chair.

"Has there been any report from the civilians on-site as to the status of the terrorist weapon?" Borland asked in a tone that bordered on frustration.

"No, Admiral. Nothing definitive since the report from Sears that said they were having some success. The civilians were supposed to give us the go, or no-go. As of now, we haven't gotten an all-clear," he replied.

"In the absence of any confirmation, Captain, I've got orders from the President to proceed with the Tomahawk strike. The guidance data has been satellite down-linked to the *Milford* for execution," he stated. "The U.S. Geological has reported to the President the La Palma volcano is erupting, and a partial slide on the western flank has occurred. Without any confirmation from the teams on-site as to the condition of the terrorist weapon, he has no other option than to eliminate the source of the weapon."

"But Admiral, what about the—"

"Mac, I don't like it either. But with the threat of that landslide possibly becoming a reality, the President has to act, and act now. You have your orders, Captain," Borland snapped back at him. "Recall the teams at once and commence with the Tomahawk launch. The President wants that device neutralized ASAP."

"Yes, sir," Mac said in frustrated compliance, hanging up and then ringing the Combat Information Center.

"CIC: Lieutenant Minichino," the voice said on the other end. "Lieutenant, this is the Captain. I want you to recall the away teams and EVAC the civilians at once, then get me the Captain of the *Milford*. We have our orders to launch," Mac barked over the phone, not happy about this turn of events.

"Aye, Captain," the CIC Officer responded as the line went silent.

"Damned politicians," he barked aloud to no one in particular as the bridge crew averted his gaze. He paused, staring out at the plume of smoke in the distance, assuming it was the ash cloud from the eruption on La Palma.

"I'm sure that it will work out fine, Captain," Ewell said in an attempt to defuse his commanding officer.

"I hope to God they're right about this," he said to Ewell, who looked at him apprehensively. "Firing that Tomahawk now that we have almost secured that facility is like putting perfume on a pig, Commander. It's still gonna wind up being ugly and smelly when it's done," he said, letting out a deep breath.

"Okay! Let's get this show on the road," he said in finality. "Commander, have the launch deck special detail stand-by to receive the away teams."

"Yes Sir, Captain," Ewell said, alerting the aft deck by way of its ship-wide intercom.

Mac walked back out of the wheelhouse and onto the open deck as the cool evening breeze blew across his weathered face. Looking at the ominous dark plume in the distance, he felt that something just wasn't right. Something in the back of his mind was troubling him, but he couldn't put his finger on it. With that in his mind, he went back onto the bridge where Ewell awaited his orders.

"Commander Ewell, what is our current depth?" he asked his first officer, still gazing at the cloud to the southwest with a growing dread.

"We're at only thirty-two fathoms, Captain," he stated as Mac shot him a troubled look. "Chart room advised that we are crossing a volcanic undersea ridge that will give way to deeper water in about an hour," he said quickly to put his skipper at ease. "We still have plenty of maneuvering room. Is there a problem, Captain?"

"I don't know, Commander; there could be. I'm just covering my ass for all contingencies," he answered slowly. Then it finally hit him; the reason for his growing anxiety. A sudden rush of learned experience and old seaman's tales rushed through his mind as Ewell stared at his focused eyes.

"Captain, are you alright?"

"Commander," he shot back with a forceful conviction, "I want all water-tight doors shut. Secure the launch well for heavy seas, and aweigh the special sea and anchor detail. Advise the *Milford* and *Blakeslee* to do so as well. Now," he ordered.

"Aweigh anchor detail, sir?" Ewell asked in confusion. "Do you have a problem with my order, Commander?"

"No, sir! I'm on it," he replied in compliance as he sounded the claxon, and issued the orders ship-wide.

"Just covering my ass," Mac whispered to no one. He stared with growing apprehension at the foreboding plume of smoke in the distance.

35

As Turner and Samuel neared the island of La Palma to aid Eli and Maria, Captain Saune stood at the door of the Bishamon facility. He was accompanied by the brawny Marine lieutenant and Yashiro. The lieutenant established three teams to do a methodical sweep of the entire facility, to flush out any remaining resistance and hopefully find Osama. The thirty Marines and what was left of Saune's men stood ready to proceed, when from deep within the building, they heard the distinct crack of three gunshots. The soldiers all came to alert at the sound, while Saune and the lieutenant moved aside the door.

"I thought you said this place was secure, Captain," the Marine lieutenant remarked.

"Secure as we could make it with five men, Lieutenant." Saune shot back, rebuking the off-handed remark. "The rest of my men are lying dead on the lower side of this damned rock!"

"My apologies to you, Captain," the lieutenant said in embarrassment. "I didn't mean any disrespect."

"None taken, Lieutenant."

At that very moment, the ground beneath them began to rumble, building in magnitude for at least thirty seconds before subsiding as quickly as it had begun.

"Something is wrong!" Yashiro yelled in a panicked voice. "That should not have occurred after my final corrections were made. We need to get back into the control room now."

"Okay, team leaders, move out," the lieutenant yelled. The three squads entered the now dark atrium, and then split off to their assigned levels to begin their search. The Marines and the remaining National Guardsmen began to search each of the living quarters along the center corridor, while Saune and Yashiro made a sprint towards the control room door. The access box, smashed earlier by Samuel, dangled uselessly against the door as they reached it.

"You're going to have to shoot the door open, Captain." Yashiro said, peering into the room through the Plexiglas pane. "Something is terribly wrong," he whispered as he looked about the room. One of the Marines came running up to report that the living quarters along the hall were all clear.

"I need you to open this door, Corporal," Saune stated, motioning to the lance corporal's rifle.

"Stand back, sir," he said as he raised his weapon and let loose its fire power against the lock, splintering it along with much of the frame. Saune entered the room first and made sure that it was clear, followed by Yashiro and the rest of the detachment.

Yashiro walked over to the computer console station and froze at what he saw lying on the floor in front of it.

There lay the bodies of the three Japanese scientists they encountered earlier, all executed with a bullet to the head. He fought the urge to be sick and averted his eyes from the grisly scene before him as he turned his focus to the computer display.

"Looks like Osama's handy work," Saune said, rolling the bodies over with his boot. "That must have been the shots we heard outside."

"Oh my God, no!" Yashiro said incredulously. "They've reestablished the exothermic EM waves in the magma chamber beneath La Palma. I'll have to repeat the entire process again."

"You do that while we look for Osama. There has to be a false wall in here someplace," Saune said as he and his men fanned out along the perimeter of the room. "Look for any gaps or openings in the panels."

Their search was interrupted when the Marine lieutenant burst into the control room yelling. "We've got to clear out of here now, Captain. They've ordered the Tomahawk strike on this facility. We've got just ten minutes to be airborne."

"No!" Yashiro yelled, panic in his eyes. "They can't do it until I have reduced the EM wave levels. There's no predicting the shock wave levels that may result from the sudden shut down of the Scalar weapon."

"Here on Tenerife?" Saune asked the scared Japanese scientist. "Here and on La Palma as well. I can't be sure of the after-effects. You've got to stop the strike," he pleaded.

"There's no time to argue, sir," the lieutenant ordered, motioning his men to vacate the control room.

Frustrated and defeated, Yashiro hesitantly left the

console. He followed the fleeing soldiers out of the control room and down the corridor, and then exited the doomed complex. Outside, the two remaining Sea Knights were powering up in preparation for lift-off as the men filed into the rear access ramps. With everyone accounted for, the two CH-46 helicopters lifted off from the compound's main entrance area and headed to safety.

At that same moment, fifteen miles from La Palma, a turbulent flash and roar emitted from the fore deck of the USS *Milford* as its deadly TLAM Block III lifted off. The TERCOM GPS guidance system of the weapon locked in on its target as it cruised four hundred feet over the calm, turquoise waters of the Atlantic Ocean.

***

Deep in the bowels of the Bishamon facility, a winded Yagato Osama reached the lowest level of the complex that he had designed specifically for an emergency evacuation. He now stood at the base of a thirty-foot steel ladder that descended vertically from the false wall in the control room to a small concrete room that led to a large steel door. He spun the circular latch on the steel door, unlocking the oval shaped entryway. He then pulled it open to reveal the entrance to a lava tube.

His engineers discovered this tube during the facility's construction, and had reported to Osama that it made a gradual decent to an opening in the mountain about three quarters of a mile distant. The mountain opening was not accessible from the exterior due to a steep drop off, but a helicopter could airlift a person out if necessary. In the opposite direction of the tunnel, coming from the caldera, the ceiling had collapsed centuries ago. To Osama, this was the perfect means of an escape in the event of an emergency. He had his construction crews secretly build the concrete room and then break through to the lava tube. As a finishing touch, he had ceiling light fixtures suspended along its entire route.

Regaining his breath, he entered the cool, dimly-lit lava tube and slammed the large reinforced steel door behind him with a loud, muffled clunk. Then he drove the one-inch diameter steel slide bolts into the sides, locking the door from the inside.

Osama sat down against the cool basalt rock to rest, pleased with himself at his ingenuity and resourcefulness. Once Fuyuki and his assistants had re-established the Scalar weapon's exothermic mode, they were expendable to him. Retrieving the side arm from the dead guard that Turner's people killed, he terminated the three men as effortlessly as a person killing a fly.

I will not be beaten by that fool, Turner, or the United States. When I alone have the wealth and power from the ZPGs that Pencor so graciously provided me, I'll be untouchable, he thought vainly.

Minutes later, a grinning Osama began to slowly make his way down the lava tube to the tunnel entrance, and to freedom. At that precise moment, the Tomahawk missile struck the Bishamon complex.

The missile penetrated into the heart of the complex, detonating as it reached the core. The resulting explosion sent a monstrous fireball into the early evening sky that was seen from all over the island. People everywhere on Tenerife stopped to look at the curious aberration coming from the old dormant volcano. Osama felt the tremor of the explosion, but paid little mind since he was safely away from the complex at that point.

The ZPGs in the facility were completely destroyed in seconds, terminating the power to the Scalar weapon's two parabolic dishes and huge electromagnetic oscillators. The EM waves that were directed towards La Palma reacted just as Yashiro had feared. The immense power carried in the EM waves over the vacuum of space-time now had no origin, nor termination point. With no direction, the powerful EM waves exited to the nearest reference points. The first was the Bishamon facility, and the other was at the convergence point deep within the magma chamber on La Palma.

Osama halted his progression as he felt a new tremor. He listened to the growing reverberation in the ground increase in veracity as the earth began to shake beneath him. What followed next was a shock wave of tumultuous force that shook the entire lava tube and sent Osama reeling to the rocky floor. The last thing he saw before the overhead lights went black was the ceiling of the lava tube cascading to the floor in a thunderous roar, effectively sealing his only exit route.

The complete and utter darkness consumed him to his very core. He cursed himself for not bringing a flashlight, since he now found himself confined to the darkness like a blind man. Slowly getting up, he shuffled his way toward the direction of the cave, only to find a huge pile of debris blocking his route.

I'll have to go back the other way, he thought, growing uncertain and for the first time in his life, afraid.

Osama slowly stumbled his way back to the entrance of the facility. With relief, he found the door by groping in the dark for the cool steel. He tried to slide the steel bolts on the lock, but was unable to budge them. With ensuing panic, he desperately began screaming and pulling on the slide bolts. To his dismay, the collapse of the facility and tons of falling rock had jammed the steel door on the outside and twisted the frame.

Winded and terrified, he sat down and tried to figure a way out. There was none. He was trapped, all alone in the darkness, with no way out. His muffled screams went unheard for three hours as he lay on the floor cowering in panic. Total madness set upon him after four days. While immersed in darkness, he could see into his own mind, the hundreds of people he'd murdered in his long, violent reign, all looking at him from the blackness of the sealed lava tube. They were condemning him, laughing at him, and taunting him.

Yagato Osama, the powerful Japanese Yakuza Oyabun who controlled the life and death of many; the man who would be rich and powerful, died a very slow and lonely death.

36

For Eli Turner and Maria Santiago, still trapped on their precarious perch on La Palma, the situation was becoming dire. Though the massive landslide had ceased its progression, the tremors became numerous once again as a result of Osama's reactivation of the exothermic Scalar weapon. Their brief respite on the narrow ledge of basalt high above the deserted town of Puerto Naos was now shattered by a series of violent shock waves from deep within the fiery magma chamber beneath the Cumbre Vieja.

The volcanic ash presented their most immediate danger, as tons of toxic, airborne ash emanated from the eruption and rained down upon them. Likened to dirt-laden snow, the suspended particles of crystalline silica irritated their eyes and throat, causing uncontrolled coughing and burning in their eyes.

Maria now cradled the elder Turner in her arms. She had fashioned makeshift face masks by ripping her parka into small pieces and tying them around their faces. Using the remainder of the material, she applied direct pressure to his chest wound in an effort to stem the blood flow. Doing so had also somewhat helped his breathing. She knew that if he didn't get required medical attention soon, he would not survive.

"I'm not able to get through on the cell phone," she yelled to Eli as another tremor shook the fragile ledge beneath them.

"It must be atmospheric interference due to the eruption," Turner said weakly. "We're lucky that you got through the first time."

As another massive tremor hit, Maria closed her eyes and held on to Eli. She covered his face as pieces of basalt rock and dust fell from the outcropping rock above them. The fierce trembling precipitated another fissure just to the right of Maria. As it began to fracture, the crack traveled towards the edge of what used to be the floor of the lava tube. She opened her eyes to find herself looking at an increasingly widening fissure and she scrambled to drag Eli away from its edge. With a resounding crack, the tiny ledge they had just been laying on tumbled downward into the void beneath them. What remained was a balcony-sized section of floor that was now the only thing keeping them from falling to certain death far below.

"I'm so sorry for getting you into this mess, Maria," Eli managed weakly as the tremor subsided. "Please forgive me."

"No one twisted my arm to come here, Eli. This is not your fault," she replied. She picked up his hat that had fallen off during their frantic repositioning and placed it into the back pack. "Besides, it was worth the risk to actually find these relics and to know they're real. It'll be sad if they are lost again."

"Maria, I don't think I'm going to make it," he said weakly as he looked into her eyes and had another coughing fit. "I want you to tell Josh that I met my end doing what I loved the most, and that—"

"Don't talk like that!" she yelled, tears of despair beginning to flow from her eyes. She knew they were both doomed if help didn't arrive soon. "Just hang on. We'll get out of this somehow. I know Josh and Samuel will find a way," she added optimistically, even though she knew that it probably wasn't to be.

More ash and debris began to swirl about them, accompanied by a sound that she thought was another tremor. Realizing that this was most likely the end, she held on tightly to Eli and laid back in silent resignation. As she gazed above her, Maria realized that this wasn't a new series of shock waves, but a much more familiar sound.

The huge CH-46 Sea Knight appeared out of nowhere and hovered above her like the vision of an angel. Maria jumped up on the ledge and started shouting.

"Eli! They're here! We're gonna' make it!" she yelled, looking at the elder Turner, but seeing that he was no longer conscious. Her sudden joy was transformed to despair as the Sea Knight drifted away from them and moved upward along the ridge. "No!" she screamed. Waving her arms wildly, she saw Turner leaning out of the emergency door of the chopper as it moved slowly away from them. "Please, don't leave us," she cried again as the Sea Knight moved further and further away.

With the access door behind the cockpit of the Sea Knight open, Turner and the Marine medic peered through the swirling debris of dust and ash. They searched for any sign of life on the now devastated rocky slope, while Samuel rooted through the box seat behind them for the rescue harness assembly. Major Zibrinski kept a close eye on the pilot caution panel indicators for any sign of engine trouble as she hovered along the partially collapsed fault line.

"If the map coordinates for the rock formation you spoke of are correct, we should be in their vicinity," Zibrinski said over the aircraft intercom sets that all of them now wore. "Be advised, we won't be able to stay here too long with the amount of ash in the air. The particles in the ash will basically sand-blast these engines until they seize," she stated as the big Sea Knight pivoted around to give the men behind her a better view of the rocky edge of the slope.

"Any luck, Mr. Turner?" the major queried as she held the CH- 46 on a steady track.

"Nothing yet, Major," he replied tersely, seeing the devastation caused by the eruption and separation of the fault line. "Most of the ridge is obscured by ash. It's going to be difficult to see anyone down there."

"This is impossible. We'll never find them in this," the medic said nervously as he surveyed the disaster below them.

"We'll find them, amigo," Samuel said optimistically, but beginning to have some doubt as to their success. *This is like trying to find a needle in a burning haystack.*

Just then, the CH-46 intercoms came to life with the familiar voice of Colonel Kyle Sears. "Sid, swing around and fly south along the ridge. I've got two targets on my thermal imagery; one standing and one down. Over...."

Sears, after receiving the recall from the *Hazleton,* made

a side trip en route to see if he could lend support. He now stood five hundred feet from the top of the newly-formed rock slide that menaced the small towns and sea far below.

"Roger that, Colonel," Zibrinski responded in acknowledgment as she deftly swung the big chopper around and headed south towards the small ledge holding Eli and Maria. "Okay, I have a visual on them," she said as she swung toward the tiny outcropping of basalt and came to a halt over the two besieged archaeologists. "Alright, gentlemen, get that winch going and be damned quick about it."

"Major," the co-pilot said anxiously, "I'm getting a caution light on the number two turbine gearbox. It's the ash intake into the compressor."

"Awe, crap," Zibrinski said, and then advised the rescue team behind her. "We have got to do this now, guys. We're flirting with engine trouble, but I'll hold for as long as I can."

"Got it, Major," Turner replied as he grabbed the Blue Water rescue harness from Samuel and began climbing into it like a pair of trousers.

"What do you think you're doing?" the medic yelled in protest as Turner began suiting up. "You're not trained in rescue recovery."

"Are you?" Turner asked as he grabbed the aluminum locking d-ring karabiners and snapped them on the end of the Kern mantle nylon rope.

"No, but—"

"Just get your medical supplies ready to receive my father when I come back up. He can't wait for you to finish bringing both of them in," he said in decisiveness as he swung himself out of the hatchway and into the swirling wind of the rotor wash. Samuel manned the winch controls and proceeded to let out the line, lowering Turner down to the miniscule ledge below.

He reached the rocky ledge in moments. Maria's strong grip pulled him close to the wall and away from the steep ledge. He was stunned to see the amount of blood his father lost and was heartsick to see him so lifeless and pale as he knelt beside him.

"Dad, can you hear me?" he yelled over the roar of the Sea Knight's rotors.

"Go! Take him first, Josh." Maria yelled, looking at the anguish in his eyes. "I'll be alright."

"Okay, Maria," Turner said, brushing her cheek with his hand, "I'll be back in a minute. I promise."

He grabbed his father around the mid-section, and wrapped his arms and legs around his limp body. Giving Samuel the thumbs-up sign, the line went taut as the two started to rise upward.

"What's your engine situation, Sid?" Colonel Sears asked over the radio.

"Number two turbine is giving me trouble and…" she paused for a long moment. "Shit! There goes the CHIP alarm on number one," she said, signifying metal fragments in the 90-degree gear box.

"Sid, you've got to abort right now," Sears said in an alarming tone.

"No problem, Colonel, I've got plenty of time. The first survivor is coming aboard now."

"Major, that's an order! You can't risk your aircraft trying to save them both. Abort now!"

"Sorry, Colonel, he's already on his way down for the second survivor now," she lied, hoping to gain a precious few moments.

Turner reached the entrance to the Sea Knight carrying his father, while Samuel and the Marine medic grabbed his unconscious body and pulled him inside. They laid him on the stretcher and the medic went to work immediately. Samuel hit the electric winch motor, sending Turner back down to recover Maria.

"Major, these turbines are going to flame out soon if we don't get the hell out of here," the co-pilot warned with trepidation, even though he was willing to follow the Major's orders to the very end.

"We just need a few more minutes. Don't worry, kid, this is a tough old bird. *He'll* hold together," she said to the co-pilot, and then whispered softly, "I hope...."

Maria watched expectantly as Turner was lowered back down on the electric winch line. She grabbed his outstretched hand as he came within reach and pulled him in away from the edge of the precipice, while Samuel let out more slack on the Kern mantle rope.

"I told you I'd pick you up at seven," Turner said smiling, referring to his promise to her in the lava tube the night before.

"I never had any doubt," Maria answered, her eyes revealing a longing that over-shadowed their weariness from the long ordeal. They both took one last glance at the destructive forces at work around them and prepared to ascend to the Sea Knight, when all at once the devastating process unleashed by Osama struck without warning.

At the precise moment of the Tomahawk's annihilation of the Scalar weapon on Tenerife, the catastrophic chain reaction predicted by Yashiro came to a frightful realization. The EM discharge that resulted from the sudden cessation lashed out violently, venting its massive power at the interferometer zone within the magma chamber kilometers beneath the Cumbre Vieja.

Like a monstrous snap at the end of a whip, the massive discharge erupted into a huge plasma orb within the confines of the molten rock beneath La Palma causing a titanic explosion in the convergence zone. The immense pressure generated was the final catalyst in the sequence of events that would ultimately culminate in the Cumbre Vieja's final death throes. The gigantic conflagration of molten rock and heat in the magma core burst outward, taking on a life of its own as the entire caldera began to cave in on itself. The collapsing cooler sediments near the surface reacted violently with the extreme heat within, precipitating a second explosion of apocalyptic proportions that sent a colossal shock wave in all directions.

Turner, with only seconds to react, instinctively grabbed Maria by the hand as the precarious perch that held them quickly disappeared into the chasm. The force of the motion sent him slamming into the hard basalt ledge and Turner felt something snap in his left arm. In pain and near the point of blacking out, he held onto Maria's hand with all his might as the two dangled in mid-air, whirling about like toys on a string. His mind screamed at him in pain to let go and just sink into the blackness, but he fought it with every inch of his being.

In seconds, the Sea Knight was swept away by the

convulsive force of the pressure wave. Zibrinski called upon all of her skills as a pilot in an effort to counter the now wildly pitching CH-46. It yawed to and fro like a drunkard, falling down and away from the slopes.

The huge pressure wave tossed Samuel effortlessly against the opposite wall of the aircraft's cabin. He feverishly tried to regain his footing as the Marine medic could do nothing but hold Eli Turner down.

Although his arm was aching and going numb, Turner held tight and refused to let go. He glanced up to see the enormous mushroom cloud of the erupting volcano as it billowed skyward. He saw flashes of lightning within the dark, broiling tempest as it expelled into the atmosphere. Turner looked down at Maria and saw her transfixed on what was transpiring beneath them. Zibrinski finally managed to regain control of the Sea Knight, and she leveled it out above the black sand beaches just below the city of Puerto Naos, a city that had only seconds to exist.

The landslide predicted by Pencor and Osama had been successfully averted earlier, but the unbridled eruption caused by the destruction of the Scalar weapon changed the course of events. The ridge line along the Cumbre Vieja evaporated as it imploded into the massive caldera and interacted with the fiery magma.

The lower elevations well below the fault line were being held by the friction force of gravity alone. Now, suddenly free of the massive slab of land above, it released its tenuous grip on the surface and slid downward like a monstrous earthen avalanche, gaining strength and momentum as it swept through the city of Puerto Naos.

The city vanished in seconds under the onslaught of the

rushing mass of earth and rock, leaving nothing left to indicate that it ever existed. The few looters who foolishly remained met with a sudden and violent death, being entombed for all time.

Turner stared in rapt horror as the massive, on-rushing thick slab of earth hit the ocean. The burst of energy moving at one hundred fifty miles per hour resulted in a gigantic splash of earth and sea. The tremendous displacement of seawater by the non- yielding mass of descending land created a huge upwelling of ocean, the likes few in recorded history have ever witnessed. As if a giant wave machine had been switched on, a towering wall of water over five hundred feet high was ejected out towards the open Atlantic Ocean, its height relative to the generally shallow waters of the Canary archipelagos.

Turner was suddenly jolted back to reality by the jarring motion of the electric winch being activated by Samuel, who had finally regained control. The two dangling archeologists slowly made their way to the doorway of the Sea Knight. Samuel, seeing the situation, raised Turner above the entryway and gave him the opportunity to take hold of Maria. He reached out, grabbed Maria by her belt and backpack, and pulled her swiftly into the safety of the CH-46's cabin. He then lowered Turner and retrieved him inside the cabin as well. He fell onto the metal deck, in pain and exhausted beyond all comprehension.

"We've got them on board, Major," Samuel said over the headset intercom. Let's get the hell out of here!"

"I'm one step ahead of you. We're on our way." Zibrinski replied, happy to still be in one piece after the wildest ride of her entire career.

After catching his breath, Turner crawled over to his father's side as the medic had just finished placing an intravenous line in his arm.

"I've done all I can for him here, sir," the medic yelled over the racket of the rotors. "We'll contact the *Hazleton* and have the hospital prepared for him when we touch down."

"Thank you," Turner yelled, nodding in understanding as he slid his arm under his father and raised him up so he was cradled in his arms. The Marine medic had stopped the blood flow from the wound, but the damage was done as Turner looked upon his father and saw him open his eyes.

Eli had regained consciousness and saw his son looking at him.

This caused the elder Turner to smile.

"I knew you would come for us, Son," he said weakly as Turner leaned closer to hear him. "Forgive a foolish old man and his wild eyed schemes. I—"

"Dad, save your strength. We'll talk when you're safely on the ship."

"No Josh," he said, coughing up blood as he spoke. "There's no time. I want you to know that I've lived a full life and..." he paused, tears welling up in his fiery blue eyes, "I want you to know how proud I am of you, and that I love you very much."

"I love you, too, Dad." Turner responded softly.

"Follow your heart, Son," he said, coughing again in spasms as Maria and Samuel drew near to their stricken friend. "And once you find what you want, never let it go," he said, looking at Samuel and Maria, who also had tears in their eyes. "That is all I can give to you; all a father can give to his son." He said, coughing a bit more as Turner, with tears in his eyes, smiled at him.

"You've given me everything I could ever ask for, Dad."

"Never forget, Son, I will always be a part of you," he said in a faint whisper as Eli Turner let out his final breath. The fiery light in his eyes was gone as they shut for the final time.

"Dad, no…." Turner said silently as he gently cradled his deceased father in his arms and silently wept.

"I'm sorry, Josh." Samuel said as he placed his hand on his friends back and fought off his own tears.

The three sat silently for the remainder of the flight as the CH- 46 Sea Knight headed seaward for the *Hazleton*. Physically and emotionally, they had nothing left. After twenty-four hours of fighting to survive, overcoming violence and death, and endeavoring to save the lives of millions of people, they were exhausted. As each of them shut their eyes, they reminisced of old times and good times with Eli.

After a long silence, Major Zibrinski finally contacted Colonel Sears in the attack Cobra. He had also been struck by the violent shock wave but, through sheer nerve and piloting skills, had averted the aircraft from certain destruction.

"Are you okay, Sid?" he asked over the radio, happy to hear her voice.

"Yes, sir, we're fine here. It could have been a lot worse," she replied as the two aircrafts flew over the frothing ocean, which was blackened with debris from landslide. "Our number one turbine is still running a little hot, but number two has settled down. We'll make it back okay."

"I'll fly as your wing, Major, until we reach the *Hazleton.* That is if they're still afloat," he said hesitantly. "I was able to get out a warning on the tidal wave to the *Hazleton.* I sure hope that she was in deep water."

"Have you received any transmission from them since?" Zibrinski asked.

"They said they would contact us when it had passed, Sid. All we can do is wait."

"I hope to God that I never see anything like that again, Colonel," Sid confessed, shaken by the violent display of nature's fury.

"I hate to think what's going to happen when it reaches the U.S. coastline," he said wistfully. Forcing himself back into the reality of the current situation, he switched on his comm- system.

"USS *Hazleton,* this is Cobra Alpha three, two-niner. Do you copy? Over...." Nothing but an eerie silence permeated the headset as the two pilots began fearing the worst.

"USS *Hazleton,* do you copy? Over...." And still, there was silence.

37

Aboard the USS Hazleton, Captain Jason McKnight had mere moments to react to the hurried warning given to him by Colonel Sears in the Cobra. He had felt uneasy for the last hour because of one of his gut feelings; feelings that he learned to pay attention to during his long career. In this instance, it would serve to save his ship and crew.

Picking up the ship's intercom, he announced as calmly as he could, "This is the Captain speaking to all hands: clear all decks and man for heavy seas. A tsunami of substantial proportions is heading in our direction and will be bearing down on us in moments. I repeat, clear all decks and verify activation of all water tight doors."

Throwing down the mic, he grabbed the watch binoculars and looked to the east. He saw immediately what looked to be a shrouded fog bank on the horizon. The fog bank that he knew to be a colossal wall of water now approached them at the speed of a jet aircraft.

"Aweigh anchors," Mac yelled in stunned horror as the wave's monstrous crest loomed closer and could now be seen clearly. "Do it now!" He bellowed as Commander Ewell grabbed the mic and gave the order to the anchor detail.

Mac recalled an earlier story of how one of the ships that survived the Lituya Bay mega-tsunami in Alaska back in the 1950s had been at anchor. The weight of the anchors maintained the ship's forward direction into the huge column of water and had prevented its destruction. He didn't know if it would work for them, but he was running on raw instinct now as the terrifying apparition rose ahead of them like a demon unfolding its blackened wings.

The vast wall of seawater had subsided in height as it moved into deeper waters, but at one hundred eighty feet in height, it was still a blood-curdling sight to behold.

Mac surveyed his bridge crew and saw the abstract horror in their eyes as they stood transfixed upon the unfurling monstrosity. He knew he had to shake them back into action.

"Helmsmen, bring her bow into the wave first and do it now!" he barked as the young helmsmen nervously spun the wheel and brought the vessel straight into the rapidly approaching wall of water. As he did, Mac picked up the intercom mic and yelled, "Engine room: I need full speed, now!"

The wave was upon them now. It reared up and blocked out the portal's view of the evening sky like a giant, tormented, greenish-black mountain the old ship had to surmount. As the ship began its ascent over the massive wave, Mac hoped with all his being that the weight of both six ton anchors would keep her bow down, rather than flipped backward like a piece of flotsam in a storm.

The speed of the awesome wave made it almost impossible for the old ship to reach its pinnacle. As the angle of the *Hazleton* increased, the ship was slowly taken backward, spilling charts and anything not bolted down to the deck.

"Hang on, everyone!" Mac yelled above the deafening roar of the frightening apparition from hell that carried the *Hazleton* and her two escort ships higher and higher. Captain McKnight's last minute decision to release anchors paid off for the ship and her crew, as the anchors' massive weight dragged over the ocean floor at a frightening speed. The gears of the motorized friction-brake winches controlling the anchors sheared off in seconds, sending the twenty-five pound steel links hurtling outward at a frenzied speed. Smoke from the burned-out winches soon filled the ship's bow section. Though useless against this massive onslaught, the two anchors were enough to keep the bow of the *Hazleton* straight into the wave.

"C'mon, baby, you can do it," Mac grumbled under his breath. All of a sudden he heard the massive snap of the anchor links as each were torn from the ship's capstans. In one horrific surge, the bow of the *Hazleton* buried itself into the hellish blackened water.

The immense pressure smashed the two windows on the port side of the bridge, sending a torrent of seawater cascading inward. Two of the bridge's crewmen were hurled backward against the bulkhead. Total chaos ruled as the lights on the bridge went out, momentarily thrusting them into total darkness.

Mac closed his eyes, expecting this to be the end. He steeled himself amidst the panicked shouts of the bridge crew as total blackness engulfed them. He was suddenly snapped back to reality by the shout of Commander Ewell.

"We're through! We're gonna make it!" Mac opened his eyes to see light of day again as the bow of the *Hazleton* surged through the other side of the wave and down the back side of the roguish beast. The water behind the wave was a torrent of foam-laden white caps for as far as the eye could see. The once calm, aqua-blue ocean was awash with a sickening dark green and brown hue from all the debris.

It was a miracle they made it. The bridge crew let out a cheer as Mac exhaled slowly in relief. Ewell was tending to the two crewmen who were slightly injured from the force of the impact with the bulkhead, while the excess water drained off of the bridge. "What's their condition, Commander?" McKnight calmly asked his first officer, who was helping the two crewmen up.

"Porter here will need a few stitches in the back of his head, but they're okay," he replied, amazed and elated to still be alive. The crewmen returned to their stations as Mac picked up the ship's intercom mic.

"To all hands: the wave seems to have passed. However, I want everyone to remain at stations until I'm sure we are no longer in danger. I want all departments to provide damage reports as soon as possible, and make sure all hands are accounted for. Take all injured to the infirmary for immediate treatment." He paused for a moment, and then said, "We've just encountered something that no one in our lifetime will hopefully ever see or experience again. You performed your duties well, people. I'll keep you informed; that is all."

"Nicely done, skipper," Ewell stated happily, relieved to

have survived the hellish ordeal. "It was a brilliant move dropping anchor. It probably saved us."

"Knowing the brass as I do, they'll probably dock my damned wages for losing two perfectly good anchors," he said gruffly, but glad to get the compliment.

Just then, one of the crewmen burst onto the bridge, wide-eyed and yelling in excitement.

"Captain! You have got to see this. The sides of the ship have been stripped clean."

"What are you talking about, Seaman?" Mac responded. He went to the hatchway and stepped out onto the open bridge walk. "My God!" he exclaimed as he gazed upon what used to be a fully- rigged ship. Everything that wasn't part of the ship's superstructure had been ripped away from its mountings by the force of the giant wave. Derricks, booms, vents, and life boats were torn off the structure from the massive assault. One grotesquely twisted life boat boom stood as silent testimony to the awesome destructive power of what just transpired.

Mac turned and headed back to the bridge. He picked up the red bridge phone and rang the flight deck.

"Flight deck, this is the Captain. What is the condition of the landing platform? We've got choppers incoming."

"The deck is clear, Captain. We're standing by to receive."

"Very well, stand by for an ETA from the CIC," he said disconnecting the line and redialing.

"CIC: Minichino," the voice on the other end replied nervously.

"Lieutenant, what's the status of our away teams?" he asked as he groped for his pipe in his pocket.

"Captain, we lost power to the comm links and tracking systems when we were hit by the wave. They have switched over to back up, and we are reacquiring their position now," he stated. "Captain, the chartroom says that monster wave carried us over six miles. Also, the *Blakeslee* reports no serious damage, but the *Milford* is listing badly to port after sustaining heavy damage. Luckily, both ships have reported only minor injuries, no fatalities."

"That is good news, Lieutenant. Have the away team's communications link patched through to me on the bridge. I need to speak to Colonel Sears."

"Yes, sir, right away."

"Alpha three two-niner, this is the *Hazleton*. Do you copy?" he said. After a long moment, a response finally came.

"*Hazleton*, this is Alpha three two-niner, it's good to hear you Captain," Sears' voice boomed over the bridge loud speaker.

"Colonel, it's good to still be here. You are clear for landing on the platform."

"Roger, Captain; be advised that we have visitors on the Sea Knights."

"It wouldn't happen to be Turner, would it?" he asked. "That's affirmative, Captain. It's Turner and his team."

"I'm looking forward to shaking his hand, Colonel. *Hazleton*, out...." He picked up the phone again and called the radio room. "Radio shack, get me Admiral Borland at COMLANTFLT." After a few minutes, the admiral's voice came over the other end.

"Go ahead, Mac. What have you got?"

"Be advised, Admiral, there's a tsunami headed your

way. We just barely survived the front end of it here off the coast of La Palma."

"Can you give me a height estimate, Captain?"

"I'd say between one hundred fifty and two hundred feet, sir." There was silence from the other end of the line. "Admiral...are you there?"

"I got that, Captain. I'll report this to the President," he said. "You are to continue your mission of offering aid and assistance to La Palma. They're most likely going to need it. The State Department will be contacting the local government there, and I'm sure they will be grateful for the help."

"What about the east coast of the United States, Admiral?" Mac asked, somewhat apprehensively. "They're gonna get the full brunt of this tsunami."

"Evacuation and relief efforts have already been implemented back home, Mac," Borland said. "All we can do is wait and see what transpires."

"God help them," Mac said. "I've seen tsunamis in my life, but nothing the likes of this."

"My people will keep you posted, Mac. Just do what you can there for now." Borland finished, ending the conversation.

"Commander Ewell," McKnight said to his first officer as he hung up the phone. "Once we've retrieved the away teams, set course for the western coast of La Palma. Have the well stand by to dispatch the LCM-8s with relief supplies," he ordered as he looked out at the crimson sky that announced the coming night. "It's been one hell of a day," he said to no one in particular, "one hell of a day."

***

The massive surface wave generated by the La Palma landslide quickly subsided from its original height as it moved into the deeper waters of the Atlantic Ocean. Fortunately, the *Hazleton* and her escort ships were spared the initial wave coming off shore towered at almost four hundred feet. Its height rapidly diminished to nothing more significant than a one meter hump as it traversed the vast, deeper regions of the Atlantic Ocean. It was almost imperceptible to the many ocean-going vessels and container ships traveling its surface.

The tsunami pressed onward, relentlessly reaching out for anything in its path as it moved closer and closer to the shoreline of the eastern seaboard. Ultimately, the massive pressure wave traveled up the continental rise to the shallower waters of the mainland, unstoppable in its quest for landfall. It seemed to sense the cities lying in its path and, with relentless fury, bore down on their hapless inhabitants.

38

At noon that day, President Alan Clark announced the initial threat of the tsunami to the nation. He spoke of the impending danger and issued a coastal evacuation warning for the entire eastern seaboard. Though not mandatory at that time, the warning served to place the populace on standby alert. The announcement coincided with the emergency broadcast system interruption of all media outlets, such as television and radio.

To handle the immense traffic flow expected, state and local emergency management bureaus were dispatched to coordinate evacuation routes from the coast in conjunction with police and National Guard units.

Many citizens decided not to wait for the mandatory evacuation. They fled well beyond the fifteen-mile safety zone prescribed in the warning broadcasts by the U.S. Geological Survey and FEMA.

Massive traffic jams ensued along the coastline as people packed the few belongings they could carry and fled to points inland. Some found respite with friends and family. Others, not knowing where to go, crowded the streets in panic and confusion, which worsened the situation for law enforcement.

The Federal Emergency Management Agency, under the direction of Stephen Boyle, had been mobilized well in advance. In his mindset, the confusion and lack of planning that transpired after Hurricane Katrina would not happen on his watch. Relief teams with supplies, mobile emergency rooms, and medical units were deployed all along the coast.

By 1:45 Eastern Standard Time, the FEMA mobilization began to fan out just as the partial landslide on La Palma occurred. It was then that the President issued a mandatory evacuation and also reluctantly ordered the Tomahawk strike on Bishamon complex.

President Clark sat pensively, having just received word of the approaching tsunami from Admiral Borland. He closed his eyes and endeavored to imagine the devastation that was about to befall his country. His mind whirled as he tried to contemplate all that would transpire in the aftermath of this catastrophe.

Clark had been hesitant at first in using the Tomahawk missile. He received the report that progress of the initial landslide had been halted, but had no confirmation from the Turners of their success in halting the Scalar weapon. He had been advised by the Senate Majority Leader, Speaker of the House, and others on Capitol Hill that failing to take action would be irresponsible to the American people.

The conference call debating the issue was heated at times. When the fiendish plot was linked to Robert Pencor, Senate Majority Leader Dobson suddenly became quite agitated, and insisted that swift action be taken.

A senator for twenty-five years, Leader Dobson had

served in the Senate hearings during the investigations into Pencor and held little compassion for the former oil tycoon.

Clark was second-guessing himself. He wondered if the natural course of events, or his actions with the release of the Tomahawk, had unleashed the hideous nightmare presently headed for the east coast. Turner warned him of the risks of taking such measures, even though his scientific adviser could not confirm nor dismiss the results.

"Mr. President," FEMA Director Stephen Boyle said, interrupting his reverie, "all disaster teams have been mobilized, and are standing by. Our evacuation teams report the process is going as well as can be expected. Major coastal cities are reporting total gridlock. All exits out of New York City are at a standstill, even with all access roads and tunnels designated one way out. The smaller coastal cities and towns are proceeding in an orderly fashion, but law enforcement officers making last minute checks are finding bands of armed looters all along the coast. In some coastal cities, total anarchy has erupted and law enforcement is being fired upon."

"It's like the roaming gangs in New Orleans after Katrina, but on a much grander scale," Homeland Security Director Tim Byrd said in disgust.

"Furthermore," Boyle continued, "many people have decided to remain and ride it out despite our recommendations to evacuate."

"Those fools don't know what they are up against," Under Secretary Robertson added to the conversation.

"Stephen, I want all of our people out of harm's way by 5:30," President Clark said. "If there are those who insist on risking their lives foolishly, then it's their decision. I won't risk the lives of the good men and women under our authority for the sake of fools and looters."

"I'll make sure all departments get that directive, Mr. President," FEMA Director Boyle stated.

"Mr. President, I think we have basically covered all contingencies on this crisis," Robertson said optimistically. "By our actions today, many American lives will have been spared a tragic death."

"No, James," the President countered. "We owe most of this to Turner and his associates on Tenerife. If it wasn't for them, we would have been blindsided by this act of terrorism. They're the real heroes on this day."

The Oval Office became strangely quiet as each reflected on the massive undertaking that lie before them. Alan Clark's mind couldn't stop thinking about Senator Dobson. *Why was he so insistent on the missile strike? My gut tells me he's hiding something,* he thought in a troubled manner. The buzzing phone interrupted his silent respite.

"Yes, Maggie."

"Mr. President, I have Peter Markson from the U.S. Geological Survey on the line."

"Put him through, Maggie," he replied as Markson's voice came on the other end of the line.

"Mr. President, I thought you should be aware that according to our calculations, the wave will be somewhat less in size than predicted. Our field scientist on La Palma reported that approximately one half of the predicted land mass slid into the sea. This should have a negating effect on its size when it reaches the mainland of the United States."

"That's the best news I've heard all day," Clark responded, relieved to hear any positive news under these circumstances. "What can we expect as far as wave height?"

"It's difficult to be precise, but our people feel we may see a tsunami run-up of thirty to fifty feet, possibly more. Seeing we have no tsunami buoys in the Atlantic Ocean, it's a best guess scenario. We are pretty sure the worst of the wave will impact the Mid-Atlantic States.

"Rest assured, Mr. President, there will still be tremendous damage from the momentum of this tsunami. Structural damage will be significant, but its run-up inland should be greatly reduced. Although it is still bad, we think it is likely to affect two to three miles inland from the coast line rather than the original ten to fifteen we predicted," he said.

"Thank you, Mr. Clarkson. Let us know if you discover anything new. Good-bye," Clark said, hanging up the phone.

"All we can do now is wait, gentlemen," President Clark said, folding his hands together. "We wait, and hope for the best."

39

Atlantic City, New Jersey

It was a typical warm summer evening in the posh New Jersey resort town of Atlantic City. The setting sun shimmered off the Towering hotel casinos' glass facades. Interspersed among the glamorous casinos on the strip were a multitude of high-rise condominiums and apartment complexes, home to many long-time residents who lived and worked in the thriving resorts.

This evening was markedly different. The normally bustling city streets were strikingly devoid of activity, casting the resort area into an eerie silence never before witnessed. The countless tour buses that inundated the town on a daily basis were nowhere to be found. Most had been commandeered by the New Jersey State Emergency Management Team for the evacuation of the city's countless visitors and residents who had no means of escape from the danger zone.

The Atlantic City Medical Center transported its

patients to the outlying community hospitals, where they received the care that was needed. Critical patients were being airlifted to specialized facilities in Camden and Philadelphia.

The only people remaining were those who opted to stay, in total disregard of the evacuation order issued earlier in the day.

Many residents felt a false sense of security in the numerous casino towers and residential high-rises that lined the beachfront of Pacific Avenue.

There were others that remained in defiance of the evacuation order. Lawless, anarchistic mobs now roamed the silent streets, plundering and looting the vacant shops, stores, and hotels that lined the streets and boardwalk.

These bands of armed gangs were kept at bay by the authorities earlier in the day. However, the emergency management's mandated retreat from the danger zone at 5:30 allowed the hordes of looters and criminal elements to make their presence known.

Numerous, bloody firefights erupted throughout the city. The most violent were the attempted assaults on the casinos, where outnumbered security personnel did their best to halt the onslaught. The few casinos that completely evacuated were totally ransacked by multitudes of fortune seekers. Overturning and smashing thousands of slot machines on the casino floors, they carried their ill-gotten booty of coins out using table cloths from the many restaurants within.

Hundreds of armed people now wreaked havoc in the streets, committing murders, robbery, and rape on a grand scale. These were the worst of mankind; the debased, cruel, and anarchistic ones. They held no fear of justice and rejected any sense of remorse. They killed for the sheer joy of it, and shot at the occasional state police helicopter that came within range.

Law and justice ceased to exist at this dark moment in time, but a justice more cruel and swift than anyone's worst nightmare was moments away. Indiscriminate in its fury toward the innocent or the guilty, its unseeing and uncaring malevolence moved in like a veil of death.

At 7:03 PM eastern time, more than a thousand people reveled on the vacant boardwalk and beach. They enjoyed their bounty of stolen money, beer, and liquor, courtesy of many businesses throughout the city. Many violent encounters erupted, most ending in gunfire as bodies lie scattered all along the town's beaches. It was a massive celebration of lawlessness, with most in attendance intoxicated beyond any semblance of sound reason and oblivious to the fate that was about to consume them.

The New Jersey State Police helicopter approached from the downtown area, flying north towards the midtown section by the beachfront. Under command of the emergency management team stationed off shore in nearby Galloway Township, Trooper Tom Putney was making one final pass in a last ditch effort to warn those who might be foolish enough to remain on ground level.

To his utter amazement, he saw the throngs of people milling on the beach and boardwalk, with many actually swimming in the ocean.

"Command, this is Zulu-Victor-two-six-three. I'm coming up on the mid-town sector now. Be advised, hundreds of people are on the beach and many are in the water. I'm going to try to warn them. Over…." he said, reducing his speed and coming to a hover high above the boardwalk.

"Roger, Zulu-Victor-two-six-three; be alert for weapons fire. Other patrols report being shot at from the ground. Over…." the dispatcher responded.

"Copy that, command, will advise. Out…." Putney replied. He picked up the external PA microphone and switched it on, then began descending toward the boardwalk. "To you people on the beach: you must get to higher ground immediately. Failure to do so will put you at extreme risk of losing your lives," he shouted into the microphone, above the disturbance of the helicopters rotors.

He saw the flashes of gunfire immediately erupt from below him. One bullet smashed through the fuselage just above his head and exited the other side of the aircraft.

"Damned fools," he yelled, quickly pitching the helicopter away from the boardwalk and passing over the beach in the direction of open water. He checked the gauges for any sign of engine trouble from the barrage, but could see none. Reaching a distance off the beach that was safe from gunfire, he saw a forty-six foot Cigarette speed boat cruising slowly below him.

My God! They're having a party, Putney thought in stunned disbelief. He realized there was nothing he, nor anyone else, could do for these people. Putney prepared to swing his craft around to leave, but stopped when he saw a sight that he would carry to his grave.

The water's edge began to draw back from the beach, further and further, as if a gigantic blue-green carpet was being rolled up. The velocity of the outflow turned the Cigarette boat completely around and carried it with the rushing current until it finally bottomed out on the sand. The sleek, bright red craft was left sitting high and dry, more than three thousand feet away from what used to be the shore line.

Putney could do nothing but stare at the horror-stricken faces of the boaters as they abandoned the speed boat and began running wildly toward the beach. Most of them became bogged down immediately in the loose muddy bottom, stuck like flies in a spider's web. Putney could see their silent screaming and desperate waves to him for help.

He glanced at the beachfront to see a mass of people strolling down to the now exposed ocean bottom, seeking a closer look at the phenomenon.

Putney, not able to endure the sight anymore, decided to leave. As he spun the craft around, he witnessed a sight that would haunt him for years. His eyes locked on a rapidly approaching, monstrous wall of white foaming water. Higher and higher, the boiling maelstrom rose from the depths. The sixty-foot high wall of death and destruction bore down on the unfortunate individuals on shore, their fates now sealed.

He saw the boaters once stuck in the mire beneath him vanish under the crushing force of the huge wave. He averted his gaze as those on the beach desperately trying to flee the onslaught were swallowed up by the rushing torrent mere seconds later.

The huge wave, driven by tremendous pressure, hit the famous Atlantic City boardwalk with a thunderous crash. It splintered the planking into millions of lethal shards as it continued to rush into the city streets. Cars, trucks, and people were washed away by the white foaming death. The front of the massive wave smashed into the plate glass window fronts of the casinos, causing a roaring deluge of debris-laden water to flow through their lower floors. It leveled everything and drowned anyone in its path.

Putney rose in altitude as he surveyed the specter of death and destruction. His mouth had gone dry and his hands trembled from the magnitude of the upheaval he was witnessing below. From his higher vantage point, he watched as the wall of water swept across the entire city landscape, exiting at the bay front and continuing toward the mainland. He could hear the excited reports coming across the radio from the many helicopter pilots in the area. They vividly described the catastrophe they were witness to. Putney remained silent, however, numbed by the awesome power of nature he just observed.

He looked down upon the ghastly sight of floating cars, debris, and bodies. The waters flowing through the city streets were blackened by dirt and debris stirred up as the wave continued its destructive march inland. After what seemed an eternity for Putney, the waters begin to flow back out to sea. Like a giant vacuum, it carried a mass of refuse and ravaged bodies with it; back to the abyss from where it came. Putney saw many survivors on the rooftops of the hotels and high rise condos. They stood huddled together, beholding the devastating spectacle below them. He finally found the inner strength to contact his superiors.

Still shaking as he watched a multitude of bodies flowing back into the dark ocean, he said with a breaking voice, "Command…they're all dead. Those on the ground never had a chance."

"Roger, Zulu-Victor-two-six-three," the dispatcher said solemnly. "You did all that you could. We have to concentrate on the survivors now. Do you want to return to base for relief?"

"No," he replied after a moment's reflection, "I'll start plotting survivor locations for Coast Guard rescue teams. There are many stranded on the rooftops that are going to have to be evacuated. We've got a lot of work ahead of us, Command," he said gravely, "a lot of work."

40

The aftermath of the great tsunami was a daunting effort to recover from. Fortunately, the wave held to the expectations of U.S. Geological Survey scientist Peter Markson, and limited its devastation to less than three miles inland. It was a reprieve for the communities that populated the eastern seaboard and the lives of millions were spared. The wave height was even less in the far northern and southern states, limiting the amount of destruction in some of the most highly populated areas.

The sad testimony of the looters and criminals played out relentlessly in the world media, but in reality, a vast majority of unsung American heroes stepped forward in the tsunami's aftermath. Good and caring Americans rose to the occasion, flooding the east coast with an outpouring of money, supplies, and volunteers from all over the country. Relief workers in the thousands flocked to the stricken shores to respond to the disaster. The ultimate death toll from the tsunami, though never actually confirmed, was around nineteen thousand. Most of the drowning victims were never recovered, claimed by the sea for all eternity.

The loss of infrastructure amounted to trillions of dollars, and all national resources were directed to the cleanup and reconstruction effort. When the waters finally receded, very few countries initially came forward to offer any form of assistance. As the true scope of the tragedy unfolded, however, countries such as England, Germany, Canada, and Japan were among the first of many to respond. An outpouring of aid from China also came in the form of materials, funds, and workers.

As events unfolded in the aftermath of the La Palma incident, it became clear the United States acted prudently and within reason in their attempt to avert the disaster. The *Hazleton* and her crew were instrumental in providing relief in the form of food, water, and medicine to the stricken people of the island of La Palma.

As promised by Yagato Osama, a trail of incriminating evidence linked Robert Pencor to the dastardly act of terrorism. His lifelong obsession with fame finally became a reality. Robert Pencor's name would be vilified forever as the mastermind of the East Coast Tsunami, and the one responsible for the death of thousands.

The Yakuza connection in the matter never came to fruition. The powerful organization quickly and expediently destroyed all evidence and eradicated all persons linked to the project. Rumors and conspiracy theorists had a field day on the internet and in publications with their conjecture, but the organization managed to slip beneath the radar. Their terrible Scalar weapons were hidden away for another time and another place.

The artifacts recovered by Eli Turner, and, ultimately saved by Maria Santiago during her escape from the catastrophe on La Palma, caused a worldwide fervor. The cup and thorn brush were placed on display at the San Fernando University Museum on Tenerife by Carlos Santiago after rigorous examination and carbon dating by experts in the field of archeology and anthropology. The rolled copper scroll, attributed to be the actual writings of Jesus, was sent to Switzerland for the careful process of unrolling.

A press conference was held to announce the verification of the carbon dating of the items back to the first century. Millions of the faithful now flocked to the Canary Islands to view the purported cup of the Last Supper and remnants of the crown of thorns.

Heated discussions among theologians had already begun and would rage on for years as to the validity of the finds.

As for Alton Burr, A formal statement from the hierarchy dismissed Burr as a "lone fringe element," thereby distancing themselves from his actions.

The Zero Point Generators that would have made Pencor and Osama the most powerful men in the world, once again faded into obscurity, no doubt aided by those who had the most to lose.

Three days out of the Safi seaport in Morocco, the two container ships bearing the huge industrial ZPGs that were seized by Osama's minions exploded in a fireball that lit up the night sky over the Indian Ocean. The two ships mysteriously disappeared beneath the waves and all hands were lost. That same day, Pencor's production factory in Morocco erupted into flames from incendiary explosive devices that were strategically placed. Both incidents had been carried out by Kasim and his operatives under contract with a group of wealthy businessmen located in the United States.

***

That evening, in an office on Capitol Hill, the phone rang in a room occupied by a lone individual smoking a cigarette.

"Is this line secure?" the voice on the other end of the line asked in his southern drawl.

"Yes it is, my friend," the man in the dimly lit room in Washington replied, flicking the ash from his cigarette into the ash tray. "I trust you have good news?"

"You betcha'," the voice said amiably. "I've just received confirmation from our contact we've had working in Morocco. Pencor's ZPG production facilities and his ships have been eliminated completely. Your efforts in persuading the President to launch the missile strike against Pencor's facility in Tenerife assured the disposal of the ZPG patents and their designs. I guarantee that no documents will ever reach the public regarding this affair," the southern man said.

"You *are* certain that no links can ever be made to my office?" "No links at all. My associates are quite thorough and cautious, especially when it comes to our continued profits," the oil company executive stated boastfully. "Don't worry, Senator Dobson, your secret is safe with us. A most handsome campaign contribution will be made to you for your efforts in this matter.

Senator, the Zero Point Generator may someday become a viable energy source," he said in a cold tone, "but not today."

EPILOGUE

Two weeks after their harrowing brush with death at the Bishamon facility and on the island of La Palma, a healing Josh Turner and Maria Santiago sat silently at a table in the Cofradia de Pescadores restaurant in Santa Cruz. The coolness of the Tenerife evening was a welcome respite from the unseasonably warm weather the Canaries were experiencing over the last week.

With all the festivals now over, a quiet hush permeated the island, especially in the wake of the events on La Palma. Thanks to the quick actions of the La Palma authorities, very few deaths were reported in the wake of the horrendous landslide that buried the city of Puerto Naos and a few other unfortunate towns. Geological teams from around the world descended upon the island in the aftermath to study the effects of the slide and the Cumbre Vieja eruption.

When the news of the terrorist plot came to light, many in the island administration came under close scrutiny. Most officials resigned to avoid the formal inquiry that was scheduled to commence later that month.

Administrator Fuentes, who had been instrumental in setting up the Yakuza element on Tenerife, was found executed in his car three days after the La Palma event. His pinky finger had been cut off and placed in an envelope. A calling card from his former employers, the envelope was stapled to his forehead. Found in his coat pocket was forged documentation that implicated him to the terrorist plot, in the company of a now demonized Robert Pencor.

The heroic action on Captain Saune's part to stop the terrorists catapulted him into the limelight. He was unanimously offered the unexpired term of administrator by the island's governing body, which he gratefully accepted. He was handily reelected at the next election and became a force for good throughout the island of Tenerife.

Turner sat reflectively, staring at his Jose Cuervo Black on the rocks as Maria watched him in silence, allowing him his quiet reverie. The dislocation and fracture of his left arm during the rescue of Maria was still tender, but the treatment on the USS *Hazleton* allowed it to heal quite nicely.

Sitting in silence, Turner's mind drifted back to a week ago. His father had been interred at a special place of honor on the island of Tenerife. His final resting place was on the western slopes of Mt. Teide, overlooking the Atlantic Ocean. It was a small, simple ceremony commemorating the life and achievements of the prominent archaeologist, recognizing his extensive contributions to the field.

Turner recalled with fondness the eulogies shared by Maria and Carlos Santiago, along with a special and surprising testimony by Samuel Caberra. Samuel brought tears and laughter to all present with his eloquent and hilarious memories of his adventures with Eli Turner over the years. Even Yashiro Fuiruchirudo, who risked everything to stop Osama and his gang, attended the ceremony to pay his respects.

The solemn assemblage was joined by Colonel Kyle Sears and Major Sidney Zibrinski, along with a complete honor guard unit of the United States Marine Corps. The twenty-one gun salute at the conclusion of the ceremony echoed throughout the high, snowcapped peaks of the ancient volcano as Turner's father was finally laid to rest. Eli Turner would always be remembered by those fortunate enough to have been a part of his life.

"Oh, I'm sorry, Maria." Turner said, coming back to the present. "I was just thinking about Dad. Do you think that he would have changed things if he could have?" he asked pensively.

"Not a chance, Josh. He knew the danger involved," Maria replied. "Even at the end, knowing the risks involved, he did what he had to do for the sake of preserving the past. It was very much a part of him."

"I still don't understand why he chose to confront Burr in the lava tube on La Palma," Turner said. "He had to know that it would end badly."

"Josh, all I can say," Maria said sincerely, "is that something came over him; something I can't explain. It's as if he knew his sacrifice would not be in vain. It all began when the copper scroll started to glow."

"That's the strangest part of the story, Maria. You don't really believe it was some mystical event, do you?"

"Well, Samuel insists the luminance of the scroll was probably due to the Scalar weapon's EM wave somehow affecting it, but Yashiro told me later that at that precise time the weapon was not transmitting its waves towards the island."

"I guess we'll never know for sure," Turner said in resignation, taking a sip of his drink.

"Josh, your dad knew that you love the archeology field as much as he did," Maria stated, grabbing his hand across the table. "His real hope was for you to be happy in whatever you choose to do with your life."

"I discovered too late that he was a good and wise man," Turner said as the waiter brought over a basket of fresh baked bread. "I owe it to him to continue his work and the ICAP organization," he added as the musicians in the lounge began playing a song called Twilight's Love.

Maria stared momentarily into the bright blue eyes passed down to him by his father. As the music played softly she said, "I love this song."

"Would you care to dance?" Turner asked softly, finally letting go of his preoccupied thoughts.

"I thought you'd never ask," Maria replied, smiling brightly as the two walked slowly over to the small wooden dance floor. They embraced in a rhythmic motion that soon caught the attention of the diners surrounding them. Those in attendance at the restaurant that evening recognized the couple from the media coverage that ensued over the last few weeks.

A hush fell upon the room as the patrons watched the two gracefully move across the dance floor like two lovers brought together for the first time.

Maria's sweet perfume permeated Turner's senses like a warm summer's breeze. For him, the room became devoid of all people; only Maria existed in his world right now. He savored the feeling of her warm body against his and her tight embrace. He listened to the song's lyrics and closed his eyes.

"*And now I long for twilight's love, which fills the loss within my heart.*

God's gift to me I never knew, till now as we do part."

Turner felt at peace as they continued to hold each other in tight embrace long after the music had ended. As they tenderly kissed each other, the restaurant's patrons applauded the two young lovers. Slightly embarrassed, they walked back to their table.

As they sat down, the two were greeted by Samuel. He had come to the restaurant looking for them.

"Hey, amigos," Samuel said with his usual flair, joining the two at the table. "How are you doing?"

"I'm doing okay, Samuel. I'm going to be alright," he responded as Maria greeted Samuel with a kiss on the cheek. "Would you care to join us for dinner?" he asked his friend. Samuel grabbed Turner's glass of water.

"Sorry, Josh, but I have a hot date with Major Zibrinski," he replied with a knowing grin that caused the three to break out in laughter.

"You dog!" Turner said jokingly. "Have you no respect for military protocol?"

"Hey amigo, a man's gotta' do what a man's gotta' do," Samuel said, adjusting his only tie. "I'm picking her up at the hotel in thirty minutes, but I came by to tell you about the copper scroll that Maria and your dad found. They were finally able to safely unroll it and make a translation of Aramaic text. The sad part is that most of the etching on the scroll was worn away and undecipherable."

"Did they find any clues that might authenticate who wrote it?" Turner asked inquisitively.

"No, but what they were able to decipher was short and somewhat vague, but I think for you it will be very profound," Samuel said as he pulled a piece of paper from his suit coat pocket and began reading the translation:

"'I must leave you soon, my beloved. Where I go, you cannot follow. The Son becomes the Father, and the Father becomes the Son. Be steadfast in the days to come as I am no longer with you, for trying times will come unto thee.'"

"Wow," Maria said, looking at Turner in amazement. "You would think it was a message for you."

"Sounds like it, huh?" Turner said reflectively.

Turner looked into Maria's eyes. He longed to stay with her, but he knew in his heart the reality they were not destined to be together; at least not at this present time.

"Maria, I, uh, I don't know how to say this, but...."

"You don't need to say anything, Josh," she said gently. "It's written all over your face. You'd make a lousy poker player. Just be with me tonight and don't worry, I'll be here waiting if you ever get tired of digging in the dirt."

"It's something I have to do, Maria. I have to do it for Dad."

"I understand, Josh, but remember I'll be here if you need me. Wait, I almost forgot...I have something for you," she said, reaching down for a cloth bag she brought with her. "I forgot to give it to you at your dad's funeral."

Turner let out a breath as she pulled his father's tattered outback hat from the cloth bag and handed it to him. "You'll need this, Mr. Josh Turner," she said tenderly.

"I don't know what to say," he replied with welling eyes as Samuel looked on with a wide grin.

"Just do as good a job as your father did and make him proud," she said with tears welling up in her eyes. "And don't forget to call from time to time, alright?"

Turner slowly placed the hat on his head. He looked at Samuel and said, "What do you think, pal?"

"It looks good on you, amigo. Besides, you'll need it where we're going. We've been assigned by ICAP to assist in a field study on a new Cretaceous mass extinction theory in Nepal. It looks as if they were impressed with our finesse here on Tenerife. Are you up for another adventure?" Samuel said, winking at Maria as she laughed.

"As long as there are no more volcanoes!" Turner said firmly, putting his father's hat gently on the table. "I've had my fill of them, thank you."

Turner picked up his glass, reflected for a moment, smiled at his friends, and made a toast. "Here's to my friends, to ICAP, to history, and to my father, Eli Turner."

"Here! Here!" they all said, glasses clinking together.

As Samuel and Maria chatted, Turner mused over the words written on the ancient scroll. Was it purely a coincidence, or was this somehow a message from his father? Turner would never know for sure, but somehow he did know that he would no doubt have more adventures ahead of him…many more.

About the Author

Tim Fairchild was born and raised in Southern New Jersey where he grew up in a small town named Pleasantville.

Upon graduation from High School, and attending St. Petersburg College in Florida, he went to work for New Jersey Bell Telephone and made a thirty-two year career with them; retiring as a Central Office Switchman from Verizon Communications in 2003. Fairchild is married to his wonderful wife, Beverley for thirty-four years now and has two daughters, Melissa and Kristen.

During the years between 2000 and 2003, Fairchild discover a taste for travel and discovering new cultures with four mission trips. Two were to Honduras and one to Belize to help with hurricane relief. The final one in 2003 was to Chosica, Peru.

In 2011, Fairchild and his wife moved to their current home in the beautiful state of Maine where he now writes full time.

Strongly influenced by such authors as Clive Cussler and Tom Clancy, plus having a strong interest in adventure in exotic locales, history, and science, it was only natural that Fairchild chose the genre of adventure. Fairchild has successfully completed two courses in writing fiction, and with his new-found knowledge, applied it to his writing style.

Fairchild's first action adventure novel, ZERO POINT, was finally completed and released in 2011 and was a Grand Master Finalist in the Clive Cussler Collectors Society's 2012 Adventure Writers Competition.

Coming Soon "Blood Rain"

From the vast expanse of the towering Himalayas, to a mysterious stone monolith in the foothills of Georgia; Josh Turner must stop a doomsday cult before they can unleash a terror on mankind hidden in the darkness for over 70,000 years.

The Adventure Continues...

About the Adventure Writer's Competition

The Adventure Writer's Competition, sponsored by the Clive Cussler Collector's Society, is dedicated to the discovery and promotion of unknown authors in the adventure genre. The organization conducts a biennial competition where "unpublished authors" vie for a $1,000 prize and the coveted Grandmaster Award.

To date, three Grandmaster prizes have been awarded at the Society's annual convention: 2008 to Jeff Edwards for The Seventh Angel, 2010 to Ian Kharitonov for The Russian Renaissance, and 2012 to Peter Greene for The Adventures of Jonathan Moore: Skull Eye Island.

For further information about the competition, please refer to the following links:

http://facewbook.com/AdventureWritersCompetition

or email the director of the Competition Kerry Frey directly at: adventurewriterscompetition@gmail.com

www.ingramcontent.com/pod-product-compliance
Lightning Source LLC
Chambersburg PA
CBHW051544250626
47157CB00001B/173